CLOSER TO HOME

JILL HANNAH ANDERSON

Closer to Home

Red Adept Publishing, LLC

104 Bugenfield Court

Garner, NC 27529

https://RedAdeptPublishing.com/

Copyright © 2024 by Jill Hannah Anderson. All rights reserved.

Cover Art by Streetlight Graphics[1]

No part of this book may be reproduced, scanned, or distributed in any print-ed or electronic form without permission. Please do not participate in or encour-age piracy of copyrighted materials in violation of the author's rights. Thank you for respecting the hard work of this author.

This is a work of fiction. Names, characters, places, and incidents either are the product of the author's imagination or are used fictitiously, and any resemblance to locales, events, business establishments, or actual persons—living or dead—is en-tirely coincidental.

In honor of Vietnam Veteran Ken Moe and all who served in Vietnam

Chapter One
May 7, 1977

Joleigh Moore lay under a scratchy blanket that reeked of mothballs, her skin clammy with sweat. No air was moving in the far back of old Mr. Hoover's station wagon, where she'd hidden herself. And when Mr. H belted out a falsetto "Dancing Queen" along with ABBA on the radio, Joleigh used the wool blanket to stifle her giggles, surprised to find she could laugh after everything that had happened.

It must be nerves. And panic. Grief too. But now was not the time to dissect her roller coaster of emotions. She pulled the blanket back to check the time on her beloved watch, a high school graduation gift from Unity eight years ago. It was 9:07 a.m. They'd been on the road over three hours, so Mr. H would need a bathroom break soon. Joleigh planned to wait until he crossed the border into Minnesota before she bailed out. She needed more miles between her and trouble, between her and Woodland, Missouri.

Mr. Hoover was on his way to pick up his grandson and the grandson's belongings from a college in St. Cloud, Minnesota. According to the road map Joleigh had studied before smuggling herself inside his vehicle, it was about a seven-hour drive, not including stops. She would have some explaining to do if Mr. H noticed the lumps underneath the pile of blankets he'd tossed in the back for wrapping his grandson's things.

Not that Mr. H wouldn't understand. He would. But telling him would put him in jeopardy. The fewer people who knew, the safer they'd all be.

Especially Joleigh.

When Mr. H finally stopped to fill up with gas and use the restroom, Joleigh lay as flat as she could so the gas station attendant wouldn't spot her. If only she could shrink herself. It was something she used to wish every day after a classmate gave her the nickname "Much Moore" in grade school. She'd inherited her father's robust Irish frame instead of her Korean mother's petite one. Except for her mom's skin coloring and dark almond-shaped eyes, Joleigh took after her dad—strong and sturdy.

Joleigh guessed her biracial heritage would stand out in Minnesota, much as it did in her small Missouri town, unless she ended up in a large city. But skyscrapers and concrete weren't for her, even if they promised a better chance of acceptance.

It didn't matter. Wherever she ended up would be temporary. Once things blew over, she could return to Woodland. Back to living alone—again.

First, she'd lost her parents. Then Unity. Then Mack.

Throughout Joleigh's twenty-seven years, people often described her as solid and reliable. But Joleigh had a better description.

She was a jinx.

Two days earlier

Mack drank beer, not margaritas, yet he used Cinco de Mayo as an excuse to tip back several more than usual that night. As if that important day in Mexico's history was cause for celebration in small-town Missouri. As if Joleigh gave a flying fig about celebrating anything. She was exhausted and behind schedule.

She'd begun the day by trimming her goats' hooves. Joplin, in her usual sassy style, gave her plenty of attitude compared to docile Groovy. After feeding the goats and chickens, she'd planted several rows of vegetables in the garden and worked on fence repairs for the chicken coop.

Joleigh should have set her leech traps hours before. Instead, she'd caved to Mack's request of beef stroganoff and homemade breadsticks for supper. With his truck in for repairs again at the garage, he'd been using Joleigh's pickup, which meant she was cut off from her few weekly interactions with people. She enjoyed her trips to town to drop off eggs to sell at the corner grocery and leeches to sell at the bait shop, but for the past week, Mack had dropped them off on his way to work.

No wonder I talk to the animals.

Mack should have fixed his truck before it completely fell apart, but it was one of a long list of things Mack should have done.

Quit complaining, Joleigh scolded herself as she gathered two five-gallon pails and leech traps from the shed. At least him needing her truck meant he'd stayed with her the past several days. Mack tended to bounce back and forth between her home and his parents', although he'd spent more time at Joleigh's after her adoptive mother, Unity, passed away in February.

Right before Unity died, in a moment of clarity, she'd whispered to Joleigh, "Promise me you won't bury your life along with mine." Yet three months later, Joleigh still had no plan for her future. Leaving home meant change, and she'd already experienced enough change to last a lifetime.

"I guess that's what I like about Mack," Joleigh told Joplin as she stopped by the pasture fence. The goat's nose nudged Joleigh's palm as she petted Joplin.

She'd known Mack since she was eleven, the year Unity adopted her. Unity taught Joleigh so much more than how to live off the land. She'd taught her how to embrace life, and she'd pushed Joleigh to pursue her dreams, right through her first year at college. When Joleigh came home that first summer, Unity sang every lyric to "Bridge Over Troubled Water," a Simon and Garfunkel song that came out that year, emphasizing that it was Joleigh's time to shine.

Only it wasn't. Instead, after her sophomore year at college, Joleigh came back for the summer and spent a fair amount of time helping Unity locate misplaced items and answering questions she'd already answered minutes before. It was then that Joleigh grasped how Unity's self-reliant, cheerful personality was slowly changing to that of someone who was easily confused and agitated.

Joleigh quit college then, moving back home to care for Unity as Alzheimer's slowly took over her mind.

Joleigh cared for Unity for nearly six years until Unity passed away back in February. In the months since, she swore that she sometimes heard Unity's voice, especially through music. Music and singing had been something that Unity held on to right until the end—one of the hundred things Joleigh missed about her.

At least Joleigh had Mack. Yes, he drank too much. He hadn't been the same since he came back from Vietnam. Easygoing Mack had been one of her best friends since high school and the only long-term boyfriend she'd ever had. She dated a few guys during her two years of college but nothing serious. Serious or not, things with Mack were familiar, comfortable. If he fed that feel-good craving of his with recreational drugs, it was his business, not hers.

That night, once Joleigh gathered her leech-trapping equipment, she watched Mack as he gathered brush for a campfire in the rock ring next to her home, wondering how he would categorize their relationship.

"I'll get this started," Mack said as she walked past him. "You'll be back in an hour?"

She knew he would have several empty Busch beer cans lined up on the ground next to his lawn chair by the time she finished setting the leech traps.

"Yep." Joleigh headed toward the setting sun at the edge of the vast acreage of farmland she'd inherited from Unity. She took a left at the bend in the driveway and walked deep into the woods, where two swamps had blessed Unity and Joleigh with leeches every year to sell to the local bait shop until the supply dried up when the water temperature rose in late June.

Mack had made it clear years ago that he would never help her trap leeches. "Go wade through the water in 'Nam, and you'll change your mind about wanting anything to do with those damn slimy things."

In the last few years, Unity's mind had been unable to focus on anything, so Joleigh became used to setting the traps on her own. It was one of many signs that Joleigh had done the right thing by quitting college, although she'd gone against Unity's wishes for the first time. Joleigh could no more leave Unity alone with her faltering memory than she could have cut out her own heart. And in those final months, Joleigh found herself missing Unity even while she was alive.

Joleigh sensed Unity's presence as she set the last leech trap before she turned on her flashlight to guide her through the dense woods back toward home. *Her* home, thanks to the paperwork completed the winter Unity caught pneumonia and her decline in health had snowballed.

Dying at age eighty was a crime for someone as full of life and spunk as Unity had been.

As she walked, Joleigh debated her options. *I should go back to college, finish my degree in biology.* But after Unity's death, Joleigh had struggled to concentrate on anything other than caring for the animals and upkeep on the hobby farm. *Maybe I'll go back to waitressing this summer.* When she moved home from college to help Unity, Joleigh had enjoyed the lifestyle balance waitressing gave her—a slice of human interaction to offset Unity's quietness and the solitude of the hobby farm.

Shouting from the distance interrupted Joleigh's thoughts. She heard several male voices, more than just Mack's. It had to be close to ten o'clock. She crept up the incline from the swamp, leaving her five-gallon buckets by the shore. Turning off the flashlight, she inched her way toward the house more than a hundred yards away.

Truck headlights illuminated the driveway, shining toward the campfire where she'd left Mack with his cooler of beer an hour ago. Shadows and shouting replaced the peaceful setting. She edged closer until she was a mere twenty yards from the clearing.

Four men stood by the campfire, arguing with Mack. Two of them held baseball bats. Joleigh covered her mouth to keep from making a noise.

"Where the hell is it?" one man shouted, raising his baseball bat above his shoulder.

"I don't have it. I swear!" Mack's voice cracked.

Joleigh fought the urge to demand to know what they wanted.

After a lot of yelling, most of it jumbled, Joleigh caught her name.

"I told you. Joleigh's not here. She went to visit a relative!" Mack shouted.

"Her truck's here," one of the men pointed out.

"She took the bus to visit a sick relative in Arkansas. I'm using her truck while she's gone."

At least part of what he said was true. *What do these men want with Mack?*

Joleigh's nerves prickled as if a porcupine danced inside her. She retreated to hide near the swamp. It had rained over an inch the night before, leaving the foliage on the ground damp enough to soften her footsteps. She hated to leave Mack. Yes, he was well over six feet tall with plenty of bulk, but four men against one meant trouble.

Joleigh was searching for a sturdy branch to defend herself when a loud *crack,* followed by a bloodcurdling scream, made her freeze. *The baseball bats.*

She whipped around. The campfire flames highlighted blood dripping down the side of Mack's face.

A second later, one of the men hit Mack again with his bat.

Mack stumbled to the ground, bright sparks from the campfire illuminating his bloody face. *Oh my God, they're going to kill him!* Reason cemented Joleigh to her hiding spot behind a giant pine tree as she silently pleaded with Mack to get up, holding herself back from charging in to defend him.

Between Groovy and Joplin's loud bleats and the incessant clucking of the chickens—the utter chaos disrupting the animals' calm world—Joleigh feared the men would include her animals in their rage attack.

It wasn't until one man said, "Holy shit, Darrell, I think you killed him," that Joleigh let out a gut-wrenching wail. She choked back the bitter taste of bile, wiping her eyes and nose with her sleeve.

The men were so busy yelling at each other that nobody looked her way. The man referred to as Darrell had appeared taller than Mack when he threatened him with the bat. They ran into her house and turned every light on. Sounds of arguing and banging things around filtered through the open windows. Joleigh imagined they were looking for whatever it was they'd wanted from Mack.

Joleigh had taken a step forward, hoping to check on Mack, when loud popping noises filtered through the trees. It was her young neighbor's truck backfiring as he made his way home, just as he did every night after he ended his ten o'clock work shift. He had spoken with Mack at the garage recently about getting the truck's timing fixed, but he obviously hadn't done it yet.

The noise, sounding eerily like gunshots, pulled the men running from her house.

"Wh-what the hell was th-that?" one of them yelled, looking around the yard.

"We need to get out of here. What're we gonna do with him?" another man shouted.

Someone knelt next to Mack and put a hand against his neck. Joleigh had moved as close as she dared, still hidden in the trees.

On the nights Mack stayed at her house, he would flinch and cover his ears at the sound when the truck backfired, sometimes running into the bathroom and shutting the door. Along with a hundred other things—like the leeches—it could throw Mack back to his time in Vietnam. He'd survived his time in the war. Now he lay motionless, no longer bothered by the noise.

"You killed him, Darrell. You stupid idiot," the kneeling man said. "Now what?"

Joleigh used her dirty sleeve to cover her sobs, inhaling swamp muck. Maybe the man was wrong. Another backfire echoed as her neighbor's truck turned past her driveway.

"J-Jesus, let's g-get out of here!" The stuttering man climbed into the truck they'd left running. Two others bent over, took Mack by the arms, and pulled his limp body up. Joleigh worried they would load Mack into their pickup's bed. Instead, they dragged his body to the bonfire as the third man stoked the fire and added more kindling. Another backfire rang in the air as they dragged the top half of Mack's body into the fire.

Joleigh let out an animalistic cry.

And the men turned their heads toward the woods.

Chapter Two

Lying on her back, Joleigh spotted the green Welcome to Minnesota sign through the back window of Mr. Hoover's station wagon. Hours earlier, she had caught the aroma of hard-boiled eggs but hadn't smelled any food since then. Surely, he would stop again before he arrived in St. Cloud. According to the map, it was about three hours from the Minnesota-Iowa border.

Joleigh snuck a handful of raisins from her canvas bag. She couldn't eat anything with a scent or anything that made her thirsty, like the nuts and jerky in her bag. If she drank anything, she would need a bathroom—which Mr. H should require again soon. It was something she had observed during her years waiting tables. Old people used the bathroom a lot.

Midday sunshine beat through the windows, the breeze from his rolled-down window barely causing a stir in the far back. Joleigh needed a shower, food, water, sleep... and a family. Everyone she loved was gone. All she had left were her goats and chickens, but she'd had to leave them behind. The water and feeding system set up for them would last a few days.

The tick, tick, tick of Mr. H's turn signal cut into the song on the radio. The station wagon slowed, and Joleigh watched the scenery along I-35N out the window as he exited the interstate.

Joleigh stayed flat under the blankets, peeking out as the vehicle came to a complete stop. She spotted storefronts, and a sign above their parking spot read Ruby's Restaurant. Several windows lined the building. If that was Mr. H's destination, she would need to get out before they seated him near the windows overlooking the sidewalk.

She pulled the blanket back over her when the vehicle jostled as Mr. Hoover swung open the car door. "Yes, in-deedy, home cookin'. Says so on the sign." He enunciated his words with a grunt. As he stepped out of the vehicle, the car's suspension rose.

Joleigh waited a bit before peering through the car window again. With no sign of Mr. H, she grabbed her hidden canvas bag and backpack then opened the back door of the station wagon. She stepped out, closed the door, surveyed the area, and hurried down the sidewalk before turning at the first corner.

Heat radiated off the sidewalk as Joleigh headed toward a gas station. She used the restroom, then wiped her face, neck, and armpits with a damp paper towel and pulled her long dark hair into a ponytail. She changed from jeans and into jean shorts and shoved her hair up under a St. Louis Cardinals baseball cap.

After she left the gas station, Joleigh headed down an alley, away from downtown and Mr. H—away from her old life, at least for a while.

She came upon a wooded park and settled on a bench under a maple tree. After pulling the canteen from her backpack, she guzzled some water then unpacked two sticks of venison jerky and an apple. Children played in a playground on the edge of the park, and their screams and giggles carried in the light breeze. After Joleigh finished her snack, she pulled on her backpack again and slung the well-worn canvas bag over her shoulder.

A walk through the park helped stretch the kinks out of her body. She followed the sidewalk as it continued past the park and toward a lake in the distance. As tempting as it was to take a dip, she had more important things to do.

Joleigh made her way back to town, blending in with the small crowd. Downtown was made up of businesses such as Grandfield

Grocery and Grandfield Bakery lining Main Street. Her mouth watered as she passed the bakery, the aroma of fresh cinnamon rolls enticing her. But she needed to save every penny she had.

A bell above the Ben Franklin store door announced her entrance. A middle-aged woman behind the counter smiled at Joleigh, her store smock matching her rosy cheeks.

Joleigh approached the counter. "Hello. I'm new in town and looking for a place to stay tonight. Is there a cheap motel nearby?"

"Welcome to Grandfield." The woman gestured with her arm as if she were presenting the town to a potential buyer. "The Snuggle Inn is a few miles north along the interstate exit. Or there's Nielson's Nest Motel down the road here."

"Thank you. Is Nielson's Nest inexpensive?"

"Oh yes, and they keep the place clean. Follow Main Street toward the interstate and take a right. You'll see it tucked behind the frontage road before you reach the woods."

"Thanks again." Joleigh left the store and kept to that side of the street until she neared Ruby's Restaurant. Mr. Hoover's station wagon was gone. She spotted a pay phone on the corner, which she could use when it was time to call Mrs. Hoover and ask her to check on the animals.

Joleigh had come up with a cover story while she had hidden out in the woods the past two days. Nobody had seen her in Woodland for a week, since Mack had been using her truck. When she spoke with Mrs. Hoover, she would tell her Mack had dropped her off at the bus depot earlier that week so she could visit a sick cousin in Arkansas—the story Mack had told his killers.

Joleigh hoped someone from Mack's work would call around looking for him when he didn't show up for work on Friday. And she hoped it wouldn't be his parents who found him. When she'd crept into the house later that night to pack her belongings, she'd left the mess the men had made as they searched her house, and she avoided where Mack lay. If she so much as doused the fire or moved him, they would know she had been there.

Yes, the men appeared to have heard her scream, but with all the commotion and noise, she hoped they'd assumed it was an animal.

It had pained her to leave Mack's body, to not clean him up, cradle him in her arms, call his parents. If there had been a way for her to report Mack's murder without being accused herself, she would have done it. But she had no proof the men had been at her house, and there was no way to identify them.

Joleigh shook the image of Mack's dead body away and fanned her face.

She had spent that night huddled down by the swamp, pulling out her leech traps, since she was supposed to be out of town. She'd expected the men back the next day and had stuck around to see if they showed up, or Mack's friends from work, or his parents.

But nobody came looking for Mack. So, late Friday night, Joleigh filled the feeders and water for the goats and chickens then walked a quarter mile to the Hoovers' house—a home she'd visited often over the years—at four o'clock on Saturday morning.

The Hoovers' youngest child, Paula, had been Joleigh's best friend. Two weeks earlier, Joleigh had visited with Mr. H at the grocery store. They talked about Paula's pregnancy with her second child, the new home she and her husband purchased in St. Louis, and Mr. H's eldest grandson attending college in Minnesota. Then he'd mentioned his upcoming trip north to move said grandson back to live with them for the summer. The details of that trip had come in handy when Joleigh planned her escape.

Sweat formed rings under Joleigh's armpits as she trudged the last few blocks to Nielson's Nest. In the parking lot, three vehicles were parked in front of rooms. The beige-stucco building's windows were trimmed in dark-brown paint that matched the sloped roof.

Joleigh opened the office door, a bell above it announcing her entrance similar to the bell at Ben Franklin and other small businesses.

An elderly man with slicked-back silver hair, wearing a short-sleeved white dress shirt and brown polyester slacks, greeted her with a smile. "Good afternoon, young lady. How may I help you today?"

"Good afternoon. How much is a room for one person for the night?"

"That'll be six dollars, local calls and local TV channels included. Just one night?" He studied her over his bifocals. Joleigh no doubt reeked, and she fought the urge to sniff her armpits. The freshening up she'd done in the gas station bathroom was a poor substitute for a shower.

She thought for a moment. "Is it cheaper by the week?"

"Yes, the weekly rate is thirty dollars. Would you rather do that? I would need a partial payment up front." He bowed his head, as if apologizing for asking for money.

"Of course, I understand." A week would give her time to check out the area in case she needed to stay for a while. "I'll pay for the week today. Thank you."

The office was clean, and the man's clothing was clean. As long as her room had a bed, a shower, and no rats, she would be fine.

"Just one week, then?" His eyebrows rose. "Fishing opener is next weekend, and from that point on, most of our rooms are reserved. Once Memorial Day weekend hits, we are booked solid until Labor Day."

Joleigh's brain struggled to think past the next few hours, much less the next week. She forced a smile. "Yes, one week. It's nice that you're so busy."

"The steady business is great, but after hunting season, our winters are slow." He extended his hand to shake Joleigh's. "I'm Mr. Nielson, and the missus and I are here most of the time." He gestured to the door from where he'd entered. "We live in the back."

"Nice to meet you. I'm Joleigh Moore." Her shoulders relaxed at his warm, firm handshake. He appeared to be near eighty, and his calm and kind demeanor gave Joleigh a feeling of safety—for the week, at least.

"There is a drawing of the motel layout on the back of your room door," Mr. Nielson said. "The motel makes an L shape. At the opposite end of the parking lot, where the rooms turn and face the woods, there is a snack area. That is where the ice machine and vending machines are located. If you have questions at all, please don't hesitate to ask."

Five minutes later and thirty dollars poorer, Joleigh opened the motel-room door to a tidy room featuring a double bed, dresser, small table, and bathroom. She set her backpack and bag on the table and flopped back onto the bed, not daring to close her eyes.

Nothing seemed real anymore. Not the staying in a motel in Minnesota—her first time out of the state of Missouri. Not the hiding out in the back of Mr. Hoover's station wagon. Not the deserting her home and animals. Not the sifting through her belongings to pack only what was necessary. And not Mack's horrific murder.

Joleigh thumbed away tears, then she pushed herself off the bed and headed to the shower. The hot water sprayed like liquid heaven. Minutes later, she stepped out of the bathroom with a renewed purpose. She dug in her canvas bag for the square Tupperware container that held two PB and J sandwiches and inhaled one before taking the ice bucket down the sidewalk in front of the room and filling it from the ice machine in the snack area.

It was not yet four o'clock, but Joleigh could have easily gone to sleep for the night. Instead, she unpacked her bags, laying everything she had with her out on the bed.

She'd wrapped her treasured leather-bound plant journal in a pair of jeans. Other items included clothing, a map, a Swiss Army knife, a folding hatchet, a fire starter, a waterproof poncho, and a few hand tools.

Joleigh didn't have the money to stay anywhere for an extended period, but she could live in the woods for some time, if it came to that. Or maybe the police would find evidence pointing to Mack's killers and arrest them, and she could be home within the week.

She eyed the contents of her bags. She had chosen carefully, making sure to not take anything that the men may notice missing, because she knew Mack's killers would return. Whatever "it" was they'd wanted, they hadn't found it that night. So she had left the dishes in the sink, left Mack's empty beer cans, left the radio on, and after packing, left the home she'd lived in for sixteen years.

She'd also dug up the emergency cash Unity had saved over the years and kept under a stall in the barn where their cow used to live. The money wasn't much, but it would buy her time. In the coming week, she would get a good feel for the area and decide whether to stay for a bit or move on.

Joleigh leaned against the headboard and opened the leather plant journal Unity had started soon after Joleigh's adoption. They had added to it over the years, and Unity had included plant and herb information from several states she'd lived in before settling in Missouri. The knowledge would be helpful if Joleigh needed to stay in the area for a while.

As she opened the heavy journal, she felt something thick slide around in the back of it. When she flipped through the pages to the back, she gasped. There, clipped inside an herb folder, was a wad of hundred-dollar bills.

Thousands of dollars. And they weren't hers.

Chapter Three

Anxiety fueled Joleigh's heart, sending it racing like a cheetah. The money was likely the "it" those thugs were looking for. Mack had to have been involved in something illegal. He'd returned from Vietnam with a bum shoulder and back and with a taste for drugs more potent than the pot he'd smoked in high school. She'd ignored that drug use, along with his cash ebb and flow.

But why hide the money at my house and why in my plant journal?

As tempting as it was to use the cash, Joleigh wanted nothing to do with tainted money. Unity had taught her to live within her means, no matter how minimal those means might be. If Joleigh was careful with her own stash, she could live in or around Grandfield for a month, but she hoped it wouldn't come to that. The next few days would tell her if the coast was clear to go back home via bus.

First things first, though. Her stomach growled so loudly it echoed in the motel room. She placed the money—all seven grand of it—back inside the journal, stashed the journal between the mattress and box spring, tucked some of *her* cash in her shorts pocket, and set out on foot to Ruby's Restaurant. A warm breeze tickled her neck as she walked, offsetting the sun's heat in the cloudless sky. Downtown Grandfield resembled downtown Woodland enough that Joleigh could almost pretend she was back home, heading to the diner where she used to work instead of Ruby's.

She stepped inside. Several ceiling fans whirled overhead, and booths lined the walls with a few dozen red Formica tables in the center. Sunshine from the windows overlooking Main Street illuminated the chrome edging on the tables and chairs.

It was too early for the dinner rush, so only a few tables were occupied. Joleigh didn't like crowds and didn't want questions. All she wanted was a hot-beef sandwich with mashed potatoes and gravy, the hot-plate special of the day.

A young waitress set a menu and glass of water in front of Joleigh. "Welcome to Ruby's. I'll be back in a minute." She headed to another table, leaving a hint of Love's Baby Soft perfume behind.

The waitress was back soon to take Joleigh's order.

"I'll have the special, please, and a glass of milk," Joleigh said.

Her next stop would be the grocery store to stock up on things like milk, along with a Styrofoam cooler to keep things cold. Eating in her room would save money. After a good night's sleep, she planned to check out the rest of the town and locate other nearby woods besides the ones next to the motel.

If Joleigh needed to stay longer, she would need more cash. If she found nearby woods, she would also check for ponds and swamps. If she found leeches, surely the town had a bait-and-tackle shop. Maybe she could sell to them. Joleigh knew little of the leech supply outside of Woodland, where it had been a lucrative cash business, but she had a few hours of daylight left, enough time to walk around town and locate a bait shop.

Leech season was short in Missouri, typically done by late June. Being farther north in cooler temperatures, she might have another few weeks—if she had to stay that long. She closed her eyes and whispered a silent plea that she would be home before then.

There were too many ifs square dancing with whys in Joleigh's head, swinging one another round and round until she expected her thoughts to fly out her ears.

The waitress interrupted Joleigh's thoughts when she placed before Joleigh a plate mounded with a thick hot-beef sandwich, a generous scoop of mashed potatoes with a gravy pool, and a heaping serving of corn.

As she dug into the hearty meal, two men in bib overalls, sitting a few tables away, were conversing about hunting season. Their words caught Joleigh's attention, since hunting season was months away.

"Yep, I guess old man Grady's ticker gave up last year after laying him flat for months," the younger of the two said. "That's why nobody's been at their cabin for almost two years."

"Well, most of the Grady kin have moved too far away to make it worth the trip. They may be ready to sell. I got a feelin' they'll want to divide the acreage up amongst their crew. Guess I'll find out if they come up this fall."

"Don't you have enough hunting land already, Ken? You think they'll sell you a forty?"

"They might. I want the back forty that butts up against my eighty."

The older man, Ken, lives near an abandoned hunting cabin? Joleigh absorbed this information as she finished off her meal. If the cabin wasn't too far from town, she could walk out there to check it out. She needed to keep her options open... if she could bring herself to break into a place that wasn't hers.

Add more ifs to your list, Joleigh.

The men shuffled out of Ruby's as Joleigh took her last swig of milk.

When the waitress appeared with the bill, Joleigh said, "I have a question about the two men that were sitting over there. I think one of them is Ken, an old friend of my parents'. Do you know where he lives?"

The waitress scrunched up her nose and wrinkled her brow. "I think the Blaze place is out west on County Road Twelve. Can't be five miles from town. He's got that huge rusty tractor parked next to his driveway."

"Yes, I bet that's their friend." Joleigh cleared her throat, the lie dry as topsoil. "Blaze, you said, right?"

"Yep, Ken Blaze," the waitress confirmed.

Joleigh thanked the young woman and followed her to the cash register to pay her bill.

Outside Ruby's, Joleigh took a right. She found a bait shop one block south of the gas station down the service drive, a convenient location for people driving north on I-35 and close enough to downtown.

When Joleigh entered Grand Bait & Tackle, she was greeted by the sound of gurgling water running through the minnow tanks. She approached a tall teenage boy stocking shelves with fishing lures.

"Hello, can I please speak with the owner?"

"That's my parents," he said. "My dad's not here, but Mom is in the back, doing inventory. I'll get her."

Minutes later, a middle-aged woman Joleigh assumed to be his mother followed the boy—who, upon closer inspection, appeared closer to her age—over to Joleigh.

"Hello. I'm Joleigh Moore, and I'm new to Grandfield." She stepped forward to shake the woman's hand.

Instead of accepting Joleigh's outstretched hand, the woman's glare followed Joleigh's bare arm—an arm with a skin tone darker than hers—up to Joleigh's face—a face with different-shaped eyes from anyone Joleigh had seen so far in this small town.

The woman gave Joleigh a brief nod. "Yes?"

Joleigh swallowed her frustration and the sting of racism. The tragedy of losing her parents at age nine had led her to stumble through her early years, eating her way through grief to cushion herself from the boomeranging from one foster home to the next. During those years, she endured not only nicknames like "slant-eyes" and "chink" but also, thanks to her added weight, "Much Moore."

Unity had taken her in, dusted her off, loved her, taught her, and adopted her. And with each step, Joleigh's self-confidence had grown.

She coated her voice with butter. "I'm wondering if you have a leech supplier. I assume you sell leeches?"

The woman crossed her arms over her chest. "Yes, and we're happy with our supplier."

No surprise there. Joleigh thanked the woman for her time and left, still unsure of the leech supply in the area. She walked six blocks to Grandfield Grocery, thankful the temperature had dropped a handful of degrees.

Joleigh bought milk, cereal, bread, and a few other staples, plus a cooler. The grocery bill came to seven dollars and thirty-six cents, and Joleigh made note of the expense on the small tablet tucked inside her pocket. She would need to count every penny. Back in her motel room, Joleigh showered, stocked her cooler with ice from the motel machine, and fell into bed, exhausted.

Tears escaped down her cheeks and onto the pillow, an overwhelming sense of loss pinning her down. Mack was too young to die. He had his faults like everyone else, but he had always been there for her. *Not anymore.* And although grief cut like metal shards through her, she knew it would be much worse for his parents.

Joleigh forced herself to think of something else, sending her mind drifting back to her first years with Unity. It was a habit she'd started once Unity's memory deteriorated and their lively conversations waned. The one thing Unity had held on to right until the end was her love of music, especially songs with silly lyrics. They hadn't owned a TV, instead listening to music or reading each night. When they worked in the gardens, they entertained each other with goofy songs, the nine-transistor radio playing by their side.

As Joleigh lay in unfamiliar surroundings, she quietly sang one of the first songs Unity taught her, "Who Put the Bomp" by Barry Mann, popular around the time Unity adopted Joleigh. At random times, Unity would ask the silly questions from the song, grinning as if waiting for Joleigh's answer.

Joleigh sang a few lines and swore Unity's raspy voice sang along. She imagined Unity's presence, almost feeling the brush of Unity's gentle kiss on her forehead and hearing her reassurance that all would be fine in the morning, just as she'd done when Joleigh was young. And as Joleigh nestled in the clean, comfortable bed, she almost believed those words.

Chapter Four

Sunshine filtered through the dark-orange curtains, illuminating the harvest-gold walls and waking Joleigh from a restful sleep. She'd slept very little on Thursday and Friday night while hiding out in the woods.

The red letters on the alarm clock read seven ten. Joleigh had never been a late sleeper, even when her parents were alive. They spent so much time on the road, going to activist and political rallies, that she was often up early to travel with them or to be dropped off at a neighbor's apartment to be taken care of.

For the first time in what seemed like forever, Joleigh didn't hop out of bed as soon as she opened her eyes. There were no animals to feed, no chores to do. There was nothing to clean or repair. No Unity to care for. No Mack to make breakfast for. *Nothing.*

The guilt of not stepping in to help Mack bit at her conscience like a rabid dog. But reason told her she would be lying right next to Mack in the campfire if she'd charged in to try to save him.

Instead, she'd written a note to Mack, part of her cover story, after she packed that night. She slipped it between the flour and sugar canisters and crumpled it up as if Mack had read it days earlier, hoping the men wouldn't notice that it hadn't been there when they'd gone into her house.

Thanks for taking care of the animals while I'm gone. I'll call you when I can from my cousin's house. Don't know when I'll be back, depends on her recovery. xx Joleigh

Mack and Joleigh had never spoken of love, but they cared enough about each other that if he had asked her to marry him, she would have said yes. No matter that Unity had told her a hundred times not to settle for anything in life—Joleigh would have settled for him. She could have stayed where everything was familiar, married someone she was comfortable with. Not her ideal family, but Joleigh wouldn't have that, no matter where she lived or who she married.

It was one of the few conversations she remembered having with her mother, taking place shortly before that November day in 1959 when the Volkswagen van her parents were riding in with friends lost control on a trip to hear John F. Kennedy speak at a political rally in Wichita. A day that forever changed Joleigh's life.

Her mother, Yeona, who'd changed her Korean name to Ellen after arriving in the States with her husband and a young Joleigh, had taken the time that day to put a stop to Joleigh's incessant requests for a sibling or two.

They were sitting at the small kitchen table in their tiny apartment as Joleigh ate macaroni and butter, a meal she'd made herself. "But why, Momma?" she asked. "Everyone else in my class has a sister or brother. Some of them have a bunch and told me I could have one of theirs."

Her mother had sighed. "Ah, my little Joleigh Ellen." Joleigh knew that when her mom used Joleigh's middle name, a serious conversation would follow. "I guess you are old enough to understand." She glanced at her husband sitting in their living room, working on something Joleigh figured had to do with their upcoming trip.

Young Joleigh didn't like the Kennedy man. He was one of the reasons her parents were rarely home.

"We have tried to have more children." Joleigh's mother took her hand, her mother's skin a shade darker than her own. "Many of my relatives back in Korea are childless, so we are lucky to be blessed with you. Some people can have children. Others can't."

She'd given Joleigh's hand a gentle squeeze before Joleigh yanked her hand away.

"I thought the stork brought babies," Joleigh said. "Can't you ask the stork to bring me a sister? I can stay home from school in case it shows up." She blamed her parents for never being home. The stork might have stopped by their apartment already, but nobody was there.

At her words, Joleigh's father had come to stand by the table, placing his enormous hands on Joleigh's shoulders. "Ah, sweet girl of mine, how I wish it were so easy." He crouched in front of her, his dark wavy hair and bright blue eyes illuminated by the bare bulb hanging from the ceiling. "Babies come from a man and woman loving each other, and sometimes, no matter how much you love each other, babies don't show up. Some families don't get as many babies. And I'm an only child, unusual for an Irish family. It's not so bad."

He'd hugged Joleigh, who welcomed his solid comfort. But she didn't believe him. She'd seen the sad, puppy-dog-eyes look on her father's face a lot when he thought she wasn't looking. Mom had blamed it on the Korean War. Joleigh had blamed it on him not having enough children to make him want to stay home.

Joleigh lay in bed, her chest aching as she remembered the day she came home from school, expecting her parents to be back, only to find an empty apartment. When the neighbor lady explained to Joleigh about her parents' deaths, the agony of knowing she would never see them again came along with the sorrow of knowing any chance of getting a sibling was gone.

She pushed herself out of the motel bed and opened the curtains to sunshine then slid open the window to let the cool morning breeze filter in. Not only would she never marry Mack, she would never have children with him, although that likely wouldn't have happened anyway. Even after several years of occasional sex with no protection, she'd never gotten pregnant.

Dwelling on the past didn't help Joleigh with her future. She turned on the radio. The news projected a high of seventy-five for the day. She had six days to decide what to do, all of it hinging on Mack's killers getting arrested.

After a breakfast of milk and two PB and Js, Joleigh packed her backpack and headed out the door, making her way toward County Road Twelve and hoping the waitress had overestimated the distance to Ken Blaze's property. Few cars drove by.

She took a deep breath of the heavy, pungent odor of manure spread across the rolling farm hills. Dew sat atop the plowed fields, sparkling in the early-morning sunshine. Joleigh's fingers itched to hold the rich, dark soil reminiscent of the fields at home. As she walked alongside the open fields, she sang "Out in the Country" by Three Dog Night. The song, a favorite of hers, encompassed how Joleigh felt about embracing nature.

Fifty minutes into her walk, she came upon a rusty tractor in the front yard of a farmhouse with the name Blaze on the mailbox. She continued past the tractor and spotted a driveway that led into the woods.

Joleigh made her way down the narrow, overgrown dirt driveway and encountered a handmade wood sign nailed to a massive tree trunk. It read Lonesome Lads, which sounded like a sappy romance song instead of a name for a hunting cabin. There were no recent tire tracks flattening the knee-high weeds in the driveway.

The woods shaded her from the sun, a welcome reprieve. The cabin was larger than Joleigh had pictured, with gray cedar-shake siding. Moss covered several shingles on the roof, and a stovepipe stuck out of the peak. Two windows faced the driveway, and cement steps led to the side door where the driveway ended.

Joleigh stopped about fifty feet away and stared at the cabin as if it might come alive. Tall grass tickled her bare legs, and she swatted at a mosquito. She took a long drink of water from the thermos she'd packed. *This is as far as you go, Joleigh.*

A dirt road ran parallel with the driveway on the other side of the cabin. She walked through the woods toward the road to her right, toward the sound of running water. A nearby creek gurgled over boulders as it meandered through the property. It appeared to come from the direction of the Blaze property and continued under the dirt road.

Joleigh spent an hour walking through the woods, following trails trampled down by wildlife, identifying plants she could use and shooing away mosquitos that buzzed around her head. She would need to make a paste from her dried lemongrass leaves to keep the bugs at bay. Dandelions bloomed, and she was tempted to pick some. Their stems were more nutritious than spinach, and they also made a good salve. As Joleigh continued, she spotted moss she could use as an antibiotic and several morel mushrooms that would be a tasty addition to a meal. Until she knew where she would be in a week, however, there was no use in harvesting anything.

She stood with her eyes closed, hearing the gentle breeze whisper through the tree branches, pretending she was back home. All Joleigh wanted was a place to call home, and she'd had it, thanks to Unity. As she listened to water trickle through the creek, she wondered if the home she'd known for years would ever feel like home again. Between watching the life slowly seep from Unity and witnessing Mack's grisly murder, Joleigh's happy memories felt buried in tragedy.

According to what Mr. Hoover had told Joleigh, he and his grandson would be back in Woodland by Sunday night—tonight. Joleigh would wait and call the Hoovers in the morning. Certainly, by then, someone would have found Mack.

JOLEIGH STEPPED INSIDE the phone booth on Main Street shortly after seven the following morning and pumped in the required coins for the first three minutes. She would need to find another way to make phone calls in the future, or she would be broke within a week.

After several rings, Mrs. Hoover answered. "Hello?"

"Hi, Mrs. Hoover, it's Joleigh. I'm in Arkansas taking care of a sick cousin and haven't heard from Mack. He's been caring for my animals, and I'm concerned that he hasn't called me." She closed her eyes, concentrating on organizing her lies. "I'm calling from a pay phone, so I don't bother my cousin while she's sleeping."

"Oh dear, Joleigh! We have been wondering where you've been." Mrs. Hoover's voice rose a few octaves.

Joleigh rubbed her fingers over her closed eyes, an emotional headache brewing. *Remember, you know nothing.* "Is something wrong?" Joleigh kept her voice calm.

"Yes! When will you be home? I think it's best if we discuss this in person."

"I'm not sure. My cousin is very sick and doesn't have anyone else to care for her."

Mrs. Hoover gulped several times, as if fighting off tears. "Well, I hate to tell you this over the phone, but there's been an accident." Joleigh pictured Mrs. H. pacing her kitchen with its yellow Holly Hobbie wallpaper. "Mack's dead, Joleigh. I don't know how else to say it, but there it is. I am so sorry, sweetie, to have to tell you this horrible news over the phone. They found his body next to your campfire yesterday morning. It appears he may have drunk too much and fallen into the fire." Her voice cracked on her last words.

Joleigh gasped into the phone. "What?" She didn't need to feign shock. People coming to the conclusion that Mack had an accident was an outcome she hadn't considered. But the fire had burned his head and torso. *Had it camouflaged his head wounds?*

Joleigh was curious what conclusion the police would draw. Maybe she could go home safely. But it wasn't the police she was afraid of. Those men would be back, looking for the money. Looking for her.

"Wh-Wh-When did it happen?" Joleigh fought back panic as she relieved the horror.

"We don't know. I'm sorry I don't have more information for you. It sounds like Mack didn't show up for work on Friday. When he didn't show up again Saturday morning, his boss called Mack's parents. They called your house several times, and after getting no answer, they drove to your home and found him."

Joleigh teared up as she imagined his parents driving up to the scene. She covered her mouth as huffing sobs escaped. "How awful for his parents! I wish I was there, but I don't dare leave my cousin. I'll call Mack's parents later." She paused. "Is Mr. Hoover home to check on my animals? I hate to ask him to do that, but they need to be fed."

"He's in the barn right now. He arrived home last night from picking up our eldest grandson at college in Minnesota. Don't fret about your animals. We'll take care of them. Lord knows you've got enough going on right now."

"Thank you so much. Also, I'm guessing my house is unlocked. Would you mind locking it? You remember where the hidden key is?" When Joleigh and Unity had been out of town for Unity's hospital stays in St. Louis, the Hoovers had served as caretakers.

"I remember, yes. Of course, I'll check your home, make sure the lights are off, and lock it when I leave. You take care of yourself now. Don't worry about things here."

"Thank you. I appreciate your help." She gulped, swallowing the grief of Mack's murder, a murder that might pass as an accident.

"Anytime, Joleigh. I'm so sorry about Mack. He was a nice young man."

Joleigh fumbled in her canvas bag for a tissue. "Yes, he was. Thanks again. I'll call you tonight after five to see if you hear more news about what happened to Mack and to make sure everything was okay with my animals and house."

She hung up and blew her nose before opening the phone booth door, releasing the heat from inside along with her lies and heartache to dissipate in the air.

Joleigh felt as if she'd been buried in a silo and couldn't breathe. *Crying doesn't fix anything, Joleigh. You, of all people, know that.* She ducked into an alley, leaned against a brick building, and took several slow, deep breaths.

Downtown was quiet, since most businesses hadn't opened yet. The drop in temperature overnight had resulted in a thin sheen of frost on the grass and the cold bricks against her back, leaving the back of her sweatshirt damp.

After her parents had died, Joleigh had naively thought she would never feel so emotionally wounded again. Less than two decades later, she was experiencing a similar gulf of emptiness. One that weighed her down as she trudged the three blocks back to the motel.

Chapter Five

It was after ten o'clock by the time Joleigh showered, refilled her cooler with ice from the ice machine, and ate two bowls of cereal.

She walked into the office, where Mr. Nielson appeared when the bell above the door jingled. "Good morning, Joleigh. I hope you are enjoying your stay here in Grandfield."

"Yes, I am. The room is nice and quiet."

"Enjoy the quiet while you can. The fishermen start arriving Thursday for the fishing opener this weekend." His liver-spotted hands circled like tornados, mimicking the coming chaos.

Joleigh tensed. "Do I need to check out early?"

"No, ma'am. You paid through Friday night. We have a few rooms open until Sunday. Some guests like to wait until the crowd thins before they arrive to fish. They'll stay the week." He folded his hands on the counter. "What can I help you with this fine morning?"

"I'd like to check out the area over the next few days. Is there a place to rent a bike?"

Mr. Nielson's brow furrowed. "Hmm... my wife's old bicycle is in our garage. She's not used it for several years due to her arthritis. It's nothing fancy, no three-speed or anything, but it will get you around town, if that's what you're looking for."

"Thank you. Yes, I'd like to check the outskirts of town, specifically any swamps and ponds in the area. May I rent the bike from you?"

"Heavens no, we don't want any money for it. I'll retrieve it this morning, and it is yours to use as you wish. You have me curious, though, about searching for ponds and swamps." His eyes widened.

"Leeches," Joleigh said. "I'm looking for leeches to trap and sell. If I end up staying in town for a while, I need an income. I trapped leeches in Missouri. I checked with the bait shop, and they have a supplier already, but if I find leeches, I'll ask nearby resorts if they'd like to sell them." She didn't want to bad-mouth the bait-shop owner to Mr. Nielson. For all she knew, they were friends.

"That's a unique business. I'm not aware of anyone who traps leeches around here, but I can direct you toward a few swamps and ponds. You don't want to try any lakes?"

"Any place with fish means there won't be leeches. The fish eat them."

"I see." Mr. Nielson glanced at a glass-door Coca-Cola cooler against the wall. "You know, with all the fishermen coming here, if you find leeches, perhaps we could sell some." He went to the cooler, where cans of soda pop and small cartons of milk lined the first few shelves. "Keep them in the cooler. There's plenty of room on the bottom shelves."

"You would do that?" Joleigh hadn't expected such kindness from a stranger. "If I'm able to find leeches to trap, I'd give you a percentage of the profits."

He waved his hand. "We can worry about that later. I'm happy to help in any way I can. To be honest, most of our guests are old fishermen. You're a breath of fresh air, and I am impressed by your tenacity."

Joleigh blushed. "You don't have families stay here?"

"We do, but not as often as they used to. Mom-and-pop motels are being cast aside for hotels with pools, especially for families."

They chatted about the area as Joleigh followed Mr. Nielson to the garage behind the motel. The Nielson home, attached to the back of the office, boasted a fenced-in yard next to the garage.

"I appreciate the use of the bike. I'll have it back this afternoon before five," Joleigh said. "I have phone calls back home to make after five."

Mr. Nielson brushed off the bike seat for Joleigh. "I know the pay phone long-distance rates are steep. You are welcome to use the phone in the office if you'd like." He smiled. "I'd have to charge you the long-distance rate, but I believe it is much cheaper than using the pay phone. And as long as I'm not checking in guests, you'd have privacy."

"That's so nice of you." She wanted to hug him. "I've stocked up on coins for the pay phone, but direct dialing from your phone would be less expensive."

He tipped his head to the side. "I believe our telephone book has a directory of pricing for different areas. Otherwise, we can call the telephone company, and if you give them the area code you're calling, they should be able to tell you the per-minute rate."

After they put air in the bike tires, they walked back to the motel office alongside each other, Joleigh wheeling the bicycle. Inside the office, Mr. Nielson looked up the per-minute long-distance rates from Minnesota to Missouri. Using the office phone would save Joleigh several dollars over the coming week.

"Now, to address your question about the ponds and swamps. There are several you can access within biking distance." Mr. Nielson took a sheet of paper from the counter and drew a rough map of the area, indicating ponds and swamps within a ten-mile radius.

"West of town on County Road Twelve, out by Lonesome Creek, there's a decent-size pothole, but it is a fair walk into the woods. You may enjoy looking around that area, as Lonesome Road will lead you to Lonesome Lake, in case you are interested in fishing."

"Is Lonesome Creek the one that runs through Ken Blaze's property?"

"Yes, that's the one. It's the only creek in that area, hence the name." He looked at her. "I didn't realize you knew Ken."

The name of the creek explained the Lonesome Lads sign in the hunting cabin's driveway. "I just know who Ken is but don't know him personally. Do you know the Gradys who own a hunting cabin next to Ken?" His answer would determine which lie Joleigh would spit out.

Mr. Nielson scrunched his forehead. "I don't believe so. The last name sounds familiar, but if they are seasonal people and have a cabin, our paths have likely never crossed."

Joleigh nodded. "If I decide to stay past this week, I might stay at the family cabin for a while." She avoided meeting Mr. Nielson's eyes. "Nobody's stayed there for over a year, and I didn't want to open it up for just a week."

Her excuse sounded feeble, even to herself. If only she could tell him the truth. But the more people who knew, the more vulnerable she would be.

"Well, then, you must be familiar with the ponds in that area already." Mr. Nielson drew a more detailed map of the area west on County Road Twelve, including ponds past Lonesome Road.

Joleigh folded the map and put it in the pocket of her jean shorts. "I'll see you later this afternoon. Thanks again, Mr. Nielson."

"The missus will be happy her old bicycle is of use. Enjoy the beautiful day."

Joleigh steered the bike back to park it outside her motel room. She stocked her backpack, made sure Mack's cash was safe in her plant journal under the mattress, and headed west on County Road Twelve to explore her options.

As she pedaled out of the parking lot, Joleigh decided she better start writing down what lies she'd told and to whom. Unity would not be proud of her, but she would understand. After all, Unity had been the one who taught Joleigh about self-preservation.

JOLEIGH BIKED BACK into the motel parking lot several hours later, as sweaty and sticky as if she were wrapped in cotton candy but energized after locating three swamps near the hunting cabin.

She stopped at her motel room to shower off the sweat and grime before bringing Mrs. Nielson's bike back to the office. "I have two phone calls I need to make if that's still okay with you," she said. "I'll keep it short and write down the minutes of each call."

"That is fine with me, Joleigh. Here you go." He set out a small tablet with the motel logo on top and a pencil. "I will put the bicycle back in the garage and will be out in our backyard, helping the missus water the plants."

"Thank you."

Mr. Nielson left the office as Joleigh fiddled with the telephone cord, cradling the receiver against her neck.

Her first call was to the Hoovers. Mr. H answered, and Joleigh hesitated. It had been fewer than three days since she'd hidden in the back of his station wagon, yet it felt like three months.

"Hi, Mr. Hoover. I'm calling to see if you have updated information about Mack's death." She cleared her throat to make way for the lies. "I assume Mrs. Hoover told you about my unexpected trip to care for my cousin."

The screech of a chair preceded a grunt from him, and Joleigh imagined Mr. H sitting at his kitchen table. "Oh, Joleigh, Mrs. Hoover filled me in about your phone call this morning, and I'm afraid I have more distressing news for you. First off, to put your mind at ease, Joplin and Groovy are doing well. Same with your chickens. It's your home that is a mess. Do you think Mack would have left it like that?" He drew out his last words, as if it were a sin to accuse the dead of creating a mess.

"Like what, for example? Dirty dishes in the sink?" There had been a few, and other than giving them a rinse, Joleigh left them, knowing if Mack had stayed there alone, he would have left dishes in the sink. She'd also left the kitchen cupboards and the dresser drawers open—left everything as it was after the men searched for the money.

"Yes, dirty dishes in the sink, but also, it appeared he was looking for something, which is odd. Someone pulled your clothing out of the dresser, and the bookshelves had books and papers scattered about. Your sofa cushions were on the floor." He sighed. "It's quite a mess, if I can be honest. I wasn't sure if I should clean everything up or contact the police."

Joleigh wondered if things would be better if the Hoovers contacted law enforcement. Then she could tell them what she'd witnessed. She would have to admit she had lied about being out of town, though, and she had no distinct information about the men, which might shine the limelight on her. She'd learned over the years to not draw attention to herself.

"Um, I'm not sure. Can you wait until I speak with Mack's parents? They may know something, since they were the first ones at the scene." *Listen to me*, Joleigh thought. *I sound like a cop on* The Rookies. It was one of the few TV programs she caught more than once during Unity's stays in the hospital.

"Yes, I'll wait," Mr. Hoover said. "That sounds like a good plan."

After a brief conversation, they agreed Joleigh would call again in the next day or two.

She dialed Mack's parents' number next. Mack's father answered with a gruffness in his voice she hadn't expected. But she'd never spoken to him knee-deep in grief before.

After she expressed her condolences at Mack's death, they spoke of his upcoming funeral.

"I wish I could be there, but I can't leave my sick cousin alone," Joleigh said. "Do you know what happened? I heard he must have tripped and fallen into the bonfire."

Mack's father gulped several times. "No, I don't think so. He had bruises on his body, way more than if he just fell. We've asked around to see if he had friends there with him. It didn't look like he had a party at your house, since there were just a handful of empty Busch cans near the campfire. No more than Mack would drink."

He paused so long that Joleigh expected to hear a dial tone. Instead, she heard papers ruffling. "Law enforcement wants to talk to you. They're calling Mack's death 'suspicious.' Do you have paper and pen to write down their number?"

She rubbed her throbbing temples. *Suspicious? Hell yes, it was suspicious.* And there were four suspects, four men she couldn't pick out of a line-up. Four men looking for Mack's drug money, dirty money that Mack's parents would never want to believe their son would have. Money the men might kill for. Had killed for.

Mack's father rattled off the telephone number of the sheriff's department, and Joleigh's hand shook as she wrote it down. "I'll call them tomorrow. Again, I'm so sorry about Mack." Joleigh's chin quivered. *Sorry* was a bland word to describe the depth of her emotions. *Devastated* and *horrified* were more like it.

After they hung up, Joleigh jotted down the minutes of her calls, adding a minute to each one. She didn't want to shortchange Mr. Nielson. It was bad enough she had to lie to him.

Joleigh left the office, her jaw set as she walked around back to thank the Nielsons for the use of their phone before making a bee-line to her motel room. She flung her body back on the bed covers and stared at the ceiling.

They had trashed her home—apparently much more so than the small mess they'd made while she hid in the woods. At least one man must have come back looking for the money. And they wouldn't stop until they found it.

She shuddered at the idea that everything she'd left behind had been scattered, possibly destroyed. She'd never felt so invaded, so vulnerable. No, going home wasn't in her near future.

Joleigh thought of the vague information she would have to give law enforcement. *Some men showed up at the house and beat my boyfriend to death then dragged him onto the campfire.*

She played devil's advocate, asking herself, *And where were you? What did the men look like? What were they after? Why didn't you help Mack?*

How could she explain? The men had been mostly shadows, illuminated by the campfire. Certainly not recognizable. They could have been from Hannibal or Macon... anywhere. About all she knew was that one man had a stutter, and the tallest one's name was Darrell.

It might sound like *she* killed Mack and was trying to blame someone else, especially since she had the drug money. Joleigh thought back to an argument she and Mack had in town the last time they were at the hardware store together. Mack had wanted to charge tools to her account. Joleigh didn't want to pay for them because he never paid her back for things, which was ironic, since his seven grand—although she questioned if it was *his* money—sat hidden in her motel room. Joleigh didn't enjoy airing their dirty laundry in public, but Mack was in a foul mood that day and wouldn't let it go.

If law enforcement found out about their heated argument and interviewed the owner of the hardware store, it could sound like Joleigh had been angry with Mack. And she had the strength to beat him with a baseball bat and to drag his body into the fire.

The more Joleigh dissected it all, the more she worried she would never be able to prove what really happened.

Chapter Six

Franklin Grady stared out his office window at the bright May sunshine dancing through the trees that never quite shaded the bank. The sun was fine with him. Too many dark days peppered his past. He would never take sunshine, or life, for granted again.

It was the reason he was more than ready to be done with work for the day. Yes, he enjoyed and appreciated his position as vice president of lending, but when spring came to Mason City, so did his itch to be outdoors.

Baseball practice had started the week before, one of the things Franklin relied on to keep his social life social. All but one of his teammates were married, many with kids, and most of them had been his friends since high school, when they played together on the school's baseball team.

It was after five o'clock, and only a few employees remained. Franklin stood, stretched his six-foot-two frame, undid the top button of his dress shirt, and loosened his tie. It was time to get out of the monkey suit and into shorts and a T-shirt for ball practice at six.

Franklin waved goodbye to the women at the drive-up teller window before popping his head into the office next to his and saying goodnight to the bank president. Then he jogged down the steps and out the door to the parking lot, where his 1973 Ford F-350 pickup sat parked under a maple tree. The used truck had been a splurge for him last year.

In the six years since he'd graduated from college and the ten years since he'd left 'Nam, Franklin felt he had gained control of things. He lived where he wanted, ate what he wanted, and worked where he wanted. It was a steady, good-paying job, despite lacking the challenges he craved—a job that enabled him to have money and time to enjoy life.

Yet his was a life too often too quiet, after living in a crowded home as the eldest of nine children then the shit show of the war and four years of partying at college. Baseball was one way Franklin dodged the silence, which meant too much time to think. Nobody who served during a war wanted that.

Franklin's short commute from work to home passed close enough to his family's house that he often stopped by, especially during the past few months. He glanced at his watch and decided there was time for a quick hello before going home to grab something to eat and change clothes.

His younger—and only—brother, David, met him in the driveway.

"Hey, just the guy I wanted to see," Franklin said. A dozen years Franklin's junior, David had almost caught up to Franklin in height over the past year, and soon, David would head off to college.

"You and everyone else," David quipped. He grinned and wiped sweat from his face with the bottom of his T-shirt.

Franklin eyed David's grimy jeans and stained shirt, plus the grease smeared on his left cheek. "What's Dad got you working on now?" With seven sisters all grown and married, David and Franklin were their father's right-hand men, doing the bulk of the fixing and repairing while their dad worked long shifts at the meat-processing plant.

"I'm cleaning out the shed. I swear, there's grease on everything." David shook his head, his dark hair in need of a cut.

Franklin ran a hand over his own bald head. Over the years, his hair had begun to thin on top, and his remaining dark brown hair had taken on a red tint like his mother's. When he started losing his hair in 'Nam, he'd resorted to shaving his head. After arriving back in Iowa in '67, Franklin continued the process, deciding he would rather be bald than look like a clown.

He followed David down the driveway to the back of the house, where the shed sat next to a single-car garage. The aroma of roast beef wafted through the open kitchen window several feet away.

"I don't have baseball tomorrow," Franklin said, taking in the stacks of paint, stain, and motor oil, plus a dozen other cans that were likely as old as him. "I can finish this up." He had nothing planned for Saturday other than dinner with some friends, but David had only three more weeks of high school and deserved time to have fun.

"Thanks. I've got to work tomorrow, but there's a party afterward that I wanted to go to." David wiggled his eyebrows.

"Go to the party. Be a teenager while you still can. You'll be off to college in a few months, studying hard..." Franklin dodged the playful punch David aimed at his shoulder. "I'll be here in the morning."

"Thanks."

"Speaking of your work, any chance you can get a weekend off?" Franklin asked. "I'd like to make a trip to Grandfield, open up the hunting shack, and clean things up before fall. We could bring our rods and reels and do a little fishing on Lonesome Lake."

"I can ask. But I'm the low man on the ladder at George's Grill." David cleaned off his hands with a rag. "Fishing sounds great, though. And I miss the cabin."

"So do I." Franklin checked his watch. "I've got to go. I'll pop in and say hi to Mom first. I need to find out when they want me to start on the paint job." His parents' home needed a fresh coat of exterior paint—another job for Franklin, another reason why he rarely left town for long. But, man, he missed the cabin's peace and quiet—a different quiet than the too-alone-in-the-middle-of-the night quiet. It was a one-with-nature quiet. One he'd missed for nearly two years because of his grandpa Shady's slow and painful passing.

Franklin had heard nothing from his cousins about opening up the cabin. Nobody had dared use it while Shady's health declined. Grandpa Shady had liked to be in control of things, liked to think he called the shots for his children and many grandchildren. It was where Franklin's father got his strict, dominating personality.

It was the reason he hoped like hell that the trip to Grandfield wouldn't include his dad.

Chapter Seven

The motel office opened at seven, and Joleigh showed up a few minutes later to call the sheriff's department's number Mack's father had given her.

Mr. Nielson opened the door between the Nielson home and the office. "Good morning, Joleigh. Need to use the telephone?" The aroma of bacon and eggs wafted through the open door.

"Yes, thank you." Joleigh picked up the call list tucked behind the counter as Mr. Nielson headed back to their kitchen and closed the door to give her privacy. She dialed slowly, reminding herself she'd done nothing wrong.

A Sergeant Williams answered the phone. Joleigh identified herself, and he got right to the point. "Miss Moore, we don't believe Mack's death was an accident. I understand you've been out of town for a while?"

"Yes, I left Wednesday, took the bus to Arkansas to care for a sick relative." Joleigh's fabricated cousin would have to be from her father's side, since her mother's relatives all lived in Korea. Her father was an only child, but this alleged sick woman could be her father's cousin.

"So you know nothing of Mack's actions after you left? And he stayed there to care for your animals? His parents weren't aware of that arrangement."

"My trip was a last-minute thing, so I don't know what Mack told his parents. He planned to go back and forth between my house and his parents' house. I just needed him to feed my animals every couple of days and make sure they were okay."

There was a long pause on the other end. "Miss Moore, I need the truth. I don't have time to horse around here, and the sooner you tell me what happened and where you are, the quicker we can resolve Mack's suspicious death."

Panic clenched her heart. Lying to the Hoovers, Mack's parents, and Mr. Nielson was one thing, but lying to law enforcement was another. She had never mastered the art. "What makes you think I'm not telling the truth?" There was no guarantee he'd believe her even if she told him the truth.

"Because your neighbor down the road said you waved to him Thursday around noon as he drove by on his way to work. You were at the end of your driveway, getting your mail."

Joleigh paced the office, the short telephone cord restricting her movements. Of course, the young neighbor down the road with the truck that backfired. He drove past every weekday on his way to his one o'clock shift at the factory. He may have saved her life when he came home that night in his noisy truck, but he'd unknowingly ratted on her now.

"Miss Moore?" The sergeant broke into her silent cursing of her neighbor. "Care to tell me where you really were Thursday and Friday?"

She crouched under the counter to make sure her voice didn't carry back to the Nielsons' home on the other side of the counter. "Only if you promise not to tell anyone. The more people who know, the more danger I'll be in." Especially the Hoovers. She loved that family. They'd been nothing but kind to her from the time Joleigh and Paula had become friends in sixth grade. But keeping secrets wasn't their strength. Paula's pregnancy was a good example—Mrs. Hoover had called Joleigh and broke the news before Paula had a chance to share it.

"Miss Moore, we don't blab our information to the public. I need the truth from you so that we can enter it in our MULES system, feeding the information to a nationwide APB." His voice sounded like gravel through a cement mixer.

"Can you talk English to me? What are MULES and APB?" Joleigh refused to cough up information until she understood what they would do with it.

"MULES stands for Missouri Uniform Law Enforcement System. It provides and shares rapid access of files to other states through our teletype machines. APB is an all-points bulletin. Whatever you tell me will only be shared with other law enforcement agencies."

Joleigh took in his reassuring words then sat on the floor, her back against the counter, and spilled the atrocities she'd witnessed from the woods, her throat raw from the jagged memories slicing their way back up.

"There were four guys, one of them named Darrell. He was taller than Mack, and Mack was six foot three. He's the one who hit Mack with the baseball bat. One of the other men stuttered, but I don't know if that's because he was nervous. They thought my neighbor's truck backfiring was someone shooting."

The constriction in her chest lessened a bit. "I swear I did nothing wrong." She closed her eyes and rubbed the lids with the back of her hand. "Except that I didn't save Mack. I should have charged after the guys with a heavy branch or something... I should have..." She choked on her *should-haves*.

"No, no, you shouldn't have, Miss Moore." A pen clicking on and off reverberated through the phone line. "I have an idea who a couple of these men are based on your description. It explains the mess Mrs. Hoover said she found in your home on Sunday. It sounds like they came back to your home after we were there on Saturday. Any idea what they were looking for?"

Joleigh sensed he knew the answer and weighed whether to tell him she had "it" with her. If word got out that she'd witnessed the crime, she would rather have those men think "it" was still at her home. Or somewhere else. Anywhere but with her.

"No," she said, "but they wanted it bad enough to kill for it."

"They're known drug dealers, so I have a pretty good guess what they're looking for. Where are you now?"

Joleigh's eyes welled up. "I'm not telling you because I think the men are looking for me. They heard me gasp when I watched them drag Mack onto the campfire, but they couldn't see where I was hiding." She wiped away tears.

"Thank you for the information," the sergeant said. "We didn't suspect you were involved, but it was clear this wasn't an accident. If you won't give me a contact phone number, then you'll need to call here for updates at least once a week. I'd like to say we'll have the men arrested soon, but we've been looking for Darrell for quite some time. It may be best if you can stay out of town for a while."

Joleigh cleared her throat. "Yes, I can. I'll call you next week."

After they hung up, Joleigh took a minute to compose herself. Those men were dangerous enough to be on the sheriff's department's radar, dangerous enough that Sergeant Williams thought Joleigh should stay away. Still, telling the sergeant the truth and him believing her was a tremendous relief.

She wrote "six minutes" on the phone-record sheet and the time of day before she left the office, the door's overhead bell alerting Mr. Nielson of her departure. She hurried out to avoid the chance of him witnessing the tears streaming down her cheeks.

Hoping to clear her mind, Joleigh took a walk down the trail that meandered through the woods by the motel. She had four days to decide her next move, and taking a bus back to Woodland was now off the list. Not knowing how long it would be until she could go home made it hard to plan ahead, but one thing was certain—she would have to move out of the motel in four days.

An hour passed before she walked into the office again. Like an ever-present butler, Mr. Nielson appeared from the door to their house. "Ah, Joleigh. What are your plans for today?" A breeze floated through the kitchen windows, which were opened wide into the backyard.

"I'd like to explore more of the area. Do you think Mrs. Nielson would sell me her bike?" Once she left Grandfield, she would give the bike back to the Nielsons.

He frowned. "I doubt she'll ever use it again, but I will let her make that decision. She's in the backyard and has wanted to meet you. I'll get her."

Mr. Nielson walked back to the house. A few minutes later, he returned, followed by a woman shorter than him but twice as wide, leaning on a metal walker.

"Ah, there you are, Joleigh," Mrs. Nielson wheezed between breaths. "I'm so happy to meet you." Her smile was as welcoming as a sunny day.

"It's nice to meet you, Mrs. Nielson. Your husband has been so kind. I appreciate everything you've both done for me." Joleigh stepped to the side of the counter's end, unsure how far Mrs. Nielson could make it in. No wonder they hadn't met yet—the poor woman struggled to move.

Mrs. Nielson nodded, her neck jiggling and her eyes twinkling. "He's a keeper, that's for sure. Now, what is this nonsense about you wanting to purchase my old bicycle? You're doing us a favor, Joleigh, to take it off our hands. One less thing packed in our garage."

"I need transportation to check out the town, since I plan to stay awhile. Please, I'd like to pay you."

Mrs. Nielson glanced at her husband. "One dollar?"

"Three," Joleigh countered.

Mrs. Nielson threw her head back and howled with laughter. "Well, I've never haggled over a price and ended up with a better counteroffer."

"I appreciate it. The bike will come in handy." Joleigh fished in her shorts pocket and pulled out three dollar bills. "Is it okay if I take it today?"

"Yes, I'll get it out for you." Mr. Nielson gestured toward the garage, and Joleigh followed him after thanking Mrs. Nielson for the bike once again.

After retrieving the bike, Joleigh headed to town. An hour later, her options had been whittled down. The resorts were booked for the summer—the same resorts she hoped would sell her leeches.

Remembering the hotel outside of town that the clerk at Ben Franklin had mentioned, Joleigh biked the few miles north to the new hotel. She about choked when the man at the front desk quoted its nightly rates. "Do you have weekly or monthly discounts?" she asked.

He pursed his lips before placing a call to management then said, "I'm sorry, ma'am, just weekend rates." At the price he'd quoted, Joleigh would never be able to afford to stay there.

As she pedaled back to town, she swallowed her frustration along with the haunting reminder of how she'd ended up in Minnesota. Yes, she could live in the woods, but she didn't know how long she would need to stay. The woods held little long-term appeal.

Thoughts of the hunting cabin drummed in her head. And her plan to trap leeches for income. Joleigh pedaled to Ruby's. Trapping leeches meant she would need coffee cans, and the rumble of her stomach meant she needed food. As a waitress in Woodland, Joleigh was aware of how many cans of coffee a café blew through each week. They would be larger than she needed, but she would take what she could get.

Once she moved out of the motel—possibly to the cabin—she would be farther from town, farther from Ruby's.

Joleigh walked into Ruby's, ready for an early lunch. After the waitress took her order of lasagna, Joleigh asked, "Do you know if there are any extra coffee cans in the kitchen?"

"Let me check. Ruby keeps a few around for storing things." The waitress left and was back a few minutes later, holding two three-pound coffee cans. "Will these work?"

Joleigh grinned. "Yes! Can I have them, or do they need them in the kitchen?"

"Ruby said you can have these." The middle-aged woman raised her penciled-in eyebrows. "I'm curious. What are you going to do with them?"

"Trap leeches." Joleigh chuckled at the horrified look on the woman's face. "At least, I'm going to try."

"Well, if you find them, let me know where, and I'll make sure never to swim in that lake." The waitress put her hand over her heart as if she'd taken an oath.

"Don't worry—they're rarely in lakes. I'm going to try a few swamps around here."

After the waitress left to wait on another table, Joleigh pulled out her small pad of paper and pencil. *Bike?* Check. *Coffee cans?* Check. *Soldering gun?* Check, thanks to Mr. Nielson. When she had been in Mr. Nielson's garage earlier to retrieve the bike, she'd spotted a Weller soldering gun on his workbench and had asked if she could use it if she found coffee cans.

"Of course," Mr. Nielson had said. "I'm intrigued by this process."

Galvanized screening from the hardware store was next on the list.

After lunch, Joleigh stopped to purchase the screen and headed back to the motel, where she used the Nielsons' garage to make a leech trap with the bottoms removed from the coffee cans. She soldered the cans end-to-end then soldered the screen on one end and capped the other with the original plastic cover to make it easy to extract the leeches.

Mr. Nielson stood next to her, observing, as she explained the process. "There are easier traps to make, but they need to be pulled before daylight or the leeches will crawl out. In this type, they can't get out."

Joleigh poked a hole in the galvanized screen and bent the surrounding prongs inward to trap the leeches once they crawled inside.

"Now, I just need bait. Most meat will work as long as it isn't bloody. I've used fish guts, steak bones, even bacon grease rubbed on the inside of the can. I'll check with resorts in the area and see if they have fish guts left over from guests cleaning fish."

Mr. Nielson stepped back and studied Joleigh. "My goodness. I'm eighty-one, and I've learned something new."

"I'll tie a string to the coffee can and put a piece of Styrofoam or cork on the end. The trap sinks to the bottom of the swamp, but the string floats, and that way I can locate it tomorrow."

Back home, she'd worn waders to set the trap farther out from the shore. In Grandfield, she would wade in as far as possible. The bicycle had a wicker basket on the front, and Joleigh planned to bring dry clothing so she could change in the woods.

Mr. Nielson pulled down one of three Styrofoam buckets hanging on a pegboard. "This one is ready for the trash. How much Styrofoam do you need?" He pulled out a Swiss Army knife from his pants pocket.

"A few inches should be good. Thank you."

After biking to the closest resort and gathering enough fish guts for bait, Joleigh pedaled out to the swamp nearest to the Grady hunting cabin later that afternoon, waded in up to her waist, and set the trap. Then she stepped into the woods, toweled off, and changed into the dry clothing before pedaling down the long driveway to the hunting shack. No tire tracks, no sign that anyone had been there since she'd stopped by a few days ago.

Joleigh walked around the cabin then took a deep breath and headed up the cement steps. She opened the screen door, the screen itself flapping from the frame, and tried the door handle. Locked. She didn't really expect it to be unlocked, but people tended to be trusting in rural areas.

There was a window to the left of the door, too far away for Joleigh to look through from the steps. Her five-foot-nine frame came in handy as she stood on her tiptoes and peered into the window. Inside were a small living area, a wood stove, a couch, a floor lamp, and, over to the right, a wooden kitchen table with four chairs.

She continued around the outside of the cabin, peering in each window. Next to the living room was a bedroom with a double bed and dresser. The next window was higher, and Joleigh looked around until she found a large log. She rolled it over to the window, set it upright, and stood on it. The window overlooked a tiny bathroom containing a toilet and sink. No shower or tub, but that was okay. It would be better than living in a tent.

The next window gave a view of a small kitchen that connected with the table she'd spotted. It contained a refrigerator, gas stove, and sink.

Joleigh considered the location's privacy. *But is it worth breaking the law if you can go back home soon?* She shook her head at that idea. "Soon" hadn't been in Sergeant Williams's vocabulary when he spoke of them finding Mack's killers.

Joleigh peered back through the window. The month displayed on the wall calendar was November 1975, reaffirming what she'd overheard about nobody being at the cabin for almost two years.

She tried opening each window. All locked. She wasn't a bobby-pin-wearing type of girl, but she had a feeling that would be all it took to finagle the lock on the front door.

As she surveyed the area, she spotted a woodshed about thirty feet away, next to a line of trees. She walked over to it, seeing a small stack of firewood, and made a mental note that if she had to stay in Grandfield for a while and ended up at the cabin, she would cut and split more wood for them. There was a ledge to the right of the shed door, high enough that she barely noticed it, a ledge that blended in with the wall. On that shelf was a rusty old Bic lighter, and hanging from a nail above it was a key ring with a key on it.

Joleigh mentally pleaded for forgiveness as she turned the key in the cabin door's lock. She'd never in her life broken the law. She reasoned that she wasn't hurting anyone, just checking out her options.

She stepped inside. The couch in the living room she'd spotted through the window turned out to be a hide-a-bed, matching another one along the opposite wall. It made sense. If several families used the cabin for hunting, they needed plenty of sleeping space.

A heavy floor-to-ceiling curtain ran along a high bar, separating the living room and kitchen. Joleigh pulled it closed, revealing a pinecone pattern on the deep green material. "I suppose if people are at the kitchen table, this shuts out noise and light for the people sleeping," Joleigh said aloud.

The faded chenille bedspread, nicks on the dresser, and tears on the sofa-bed fabric gave the cabin a lived-in feeling. It was a place where Joleigh wouldn't have to worry about wrecking things. She opened the knotty-pine cupboards, which contained glasses, coffee cups, and place settings of Melmac in gold, orange, and turquoise.

One drawer contained mismatched silverware. Another held crocheted potholders and musty-smelling dish towels. There was a two-slice toaster on the counter where the toast came out the bottom. An aluminum drip coffee maker sat on the counter. A paint stir stick propped open the door on a Norge refrigerator, and several mouse turds dotted the countertop. It would need a good cleaning if she stayed.

Joleigh had more research to do before she moved in and broke the law—technically *again*, since she'd already done it by going inside a locked cabin she didn't own. Still, after she locked the door and hung the key back where she'd found it, she biked back to the motel with hope in her heart.

Chapter Eight

The following morning, Joleigh rode out to the swamp to retrieve her leech trap and let out a whoop of victory. She estimated there were a couple of pounds of ribbon leeches in the trap. Unity had always taught her to look for signs, and she took the leeches as a sign that staying in Grandfield, at least for a while, was the right decision.

Back in Missouri, she'd sold her leeches in bulk to the local bait shop. With no distributor in Grandfield, she would need to package them herself, which meant she would need dozens of small Styrofoam containers.

Joleigh parked the bike outside her motel room before unloading the leech trap in her room's bathtub. She filled it with cool water and placed the trap filled with leeches in the tub. After changing out of her muddy clothes, Joleigh biked back to town in search of leech containers.

After checking the hardware store first, with no luck, Joleigh stopped at Ruby's. *Bingo.* Ruby's used that type of container for their to-go soup orders. She purchased two dozen containers with lids from the café then biked back to her motel room to separate the leeches based on their size. She packaged a dozen per container.

As she walked into the motel office with the containers, Joleigh grinned like a child opening Christmas presents.

Mr. Nielson's enthusiasm topped hers. "Look at those! I'm impressed." He clapped.

She'd separated the leeches into small, medium, and large and marked the top of each container with an *S*, *M*, or *L* before setting them on the two bottom shelves of the Coca-Cola cooler. "We have anglers checking in tomorrow. Many like to scout out the lakes ahead of Saturday," Mr. Nielson said. "I will let them know we have leeches for sale."

They agreed that thirty percent of the proceeds would go to Mr. Nielson.

Joleigh biked out late in the afternoon to a different swamp west of town, trying out a new spot to set the trap. Thursday morning was a repeat performance but with fewer leeches in the trap than the day before. "Still plenty to sell," Joleigh said aloud as she changed clothes in the thick of the woods before biking back to the motel.

The lines began to blur between Woodland and Grandfield. By late afternoon, Joleigh had learned a lot about the area and found a way to make money. But she missed her goats and her past-their-egg-laying-prime chickens, and she missed Mack. She pinched the bridge of her nose to stop the headache of tears threatening to erupt. Mack's death still seemed like a nightmare too horrific to be true.

It took several minutes before Joleigh felt composed enough to leave her room. After blowing her nose and drying her tears, she shoved cash into her shorts pocket and strolled the few blocks to Ruby's for an early supper.

Downtown was busier than it had been all week. When she entered Ruby's, the place was almost full. As busy as the restaurant was, Joleigh spotted only Ruby and one other woman waiting tables.

It took several minutes before Ruby stopped to drop off water and a menu for Joleigh. Ruby's dark hair was pulled back in several barrettes, and her skin—a shade darker than Joleigh's—held a light sheen of perspiration. Joleigh guessed the café owner to be in her sixties, and although Ruby smiled as she took Joleigh's order for the taco-plate special, her shoulders slumped.

"Is it just the two of you waiting tables?" Joleigh hadn't seen Ruby wait tables when she'd been in before. Ruby typically ran the cash register or was in her office in the back.

"This is what I get for hiring teenagers," Ruby said. "Two called in 'sick,' and I'm guessing they'll be 'sick' the next few days so they can hit the beach this weekend." She rolled her dark eyes.

Joleigh sympathized. She had worked short-handed more than once during her waitressing days back home. It was unfair to both the workers covering the shift and the patrons, who ended up with slow service.

After Joleigh watched two groups of people leave before being served, she couldn't stand it anymore. She eyed the tables of people sitting with no menus or water and got up. Stacks of menus sat on a shelf by the cash register. Joleigh grabbed several and walked over to hand a menu to each person at three different tables before making her way to the end of the kitchen counter, where empty plastic water glasses sat upside down on a square dish rack. The soda fountain and ice machine were next to the counter alongside pitchers of water.

Joleigh picked up a round serving tray, loaded it with several glasses of ice water, and was turning to head back to the tables when Ruby walked through the swinging kitchen doors, carrying a large tray of food. Her eyes widened as they locked with Joleigh's.

"Hold off on my order, Ruby, and I'll help you for a bit. I used to waitress." After Joleigh received a nod from Ruby, she made her way back to the tables.

Over the next two hours, Joleigh set up and cleaned off each table so Ruby and the other waitress could take orders and deliver food. It was after six before Joleigh sat down to her taco plate, with extra tacos and Spanish rice heaped on the side.

Ruby joined Joleigh after she finished her meal, taking a seat across from her. "So, you're new to town, right?" Ruby took a long drink from a water glass.

"Yes, I check out of Nielson's Nest on Saturday."

"Aren't you the one who wanted coffee cans to trap leeches? Are you leaving town?" Ruby furrowed her brows.

"That's me. And no, I'm going to stay here for a while, just not at the motel." Joleigh hoped Ruby wouldn't ask where she was going to stay.

"I'm impressed by how you stepped in and helped tonight. And anyone who traps leeches is a worker. I grew up north of here around Mille Lacs Lake, and my grandpa trapped leeches. They're more plentiful farther north than here, but it tells me a lot about your work ethic." Ruby leaned forward, elbows on the table, and sighed. "As you can see, I'm short of reliable help. You were a godsend today. If you can promise to work through at least Labor Day, I'll hire you right now. Minimum wage, but the tips are good. We will share ours with you from tonight."

Joleigh's mouth dropped open at the offer, and she was certain Unity whispered, *Here's another sign.*

But before she got her hopes up, Joleigh needed to address something. "Are you sure you want to hire me?" She pointed at her eyes. "I already received the wrinkled-nose-go-away look from the woman at the bait shop. I don't want to cause you to lose customers." It was different back home when she'd worked at the diner. The customers knew her there.

Ruby scoffed. "I'm Native American, our most popular teacher at the high school is from Nigeria, and yes, most everyone else in Grandfield—including the tourists—is Caucasian." She shrugged. "Not everyone will like you, but who cares? They know where the door is."

Joleigh envied Ruby's take-no-shit attitude.

"Can I let you know tomorrow? I need to call someone tomorrow morning. If they can take care of my goats and chickens for the summer, then yes, I'd be happy to work here."

"Sounds like a plan." Joleigh followed Ruby to the cash register, where Ruby tucked Joleigh's ticket in the cash drawer as a no-sale. "I'll have an envelope with tips for you in the morning."

As Joleigh walked to the motel, the sun beginning its decline in the distance, she hoped the Hoovers would be willing to care for her animals. And she hoped the owners of the hunting cabin would forgive her for using their place. If she was going to work at Ruby's for the summer—a job she desperately needed—she didn't want to live in a tent for three months.

But as Joleigh was well aware, people didn't always get what they wanted.

Chapter Nine

On Friday morning, after Mr. Nielson opened the office, Joleigh dialed the Hoovers' number. Mr. H answered.

"Good morning," she said. "This is Joleigh."

"Good morning. I hope you're doing well this fine morning. It's a rainy one here today, but we need the moisture," Mr. H said in his usual jovial manner. "If you're calling about your animals, they're doing fine. I popped over to your place early this morning. They're fed and happy, and they send their regards."

His words reassured Joleigh. "Thank you. I appreciate Mrs. Hoover and you taking care of them." She cleared her throat, twirling the phone cord around her finger. "That's why I'm calling. I need to stay here for a while, and I've had an offer to waitress. Since my cousin sleeps a lot and I could use the cash, I'd like to take the job. The problem is that they want me to commit to working through the summer." The lie barely moved her guilt meter, since most of what she said was true. "I know it's a lot to ask, but if you're willing to care for my animals, I'll wire you money for feed expenses and things."

The phone line was silent for a minute as Mr. Hoover processed Joleigh's dilemma. "It won't be a problem for us. Our grandson is staying here for the summer, and he can help too when he's not working. I'm more concerned about Groovy and Joplin missing you."

Joleigh smiled into the phone receiver. He knew her animals well. "I know. I feel awful leaving them. As you and Mrs. Hoover will notice, the chickens are getting to the end of their laying cycle. With Unity so ill, I didn't buy more chicks the last few years, figuring I'd eventually be back to work or college and not have time for the animals."

It pained Joleigh to force out her next words. "If needed, someone could butcher them for stew hens, although I hate to do that, since you should be able to get a few dozen eggs a week out of them." Summer production was higher than in winter. After the devastating loss of Doris, her first pet chicken from when she moved in with Unity, Joleigh had steeled her heart against getting attached to the chickens.

"Let's not even think about that right now," Mr. H said. "Your animals are fine. You concentrate on taking care of your cousin. We have that extra pasture on our property from when we had goats, and if we notice Joplin and Groovy failing, we will bring them over here. Of course, we can't do the same with your chickens."

Disease could spread if they commingled her chickens with theirs. "I understand. Thank you for everything. I'll try to call once a week, before eight in the morning, if that works for you, and I hope to take the bus there sometime soon so I can get my pickup. It would be nice to have a vehicle here for the summer."

"You calling once a week is plenty. Don't spend that hard-earned cash on long-distance phone calls," Mr. H said. "And if you travel back to Woodland, let me know ahead of time and I'll pick you up at the bus station."

"Thank you. I sure appreciate you."

They said their goodbyes. She hung up, wrote the minutes on the phone call sheet, and walked into Ruby's five minutes later, the breakfast rush in full swing and the restaurant well-staffed.

Ruby spotted Joleigh and met her at the cash-register counter. "Good morning, Joleigh. I've got your tips from last night." She opened the register and pulled out an envelope with Joleigh's name on it. "Have you called your neighbor yet?"

Joleigh took the envelope Ruby handed her, coins sliding around inside between several bills. "Yes, and they'll take care of my animals through the summer, so I'll take the job if you still need me."

Ruby came around the counter. "I sure do. Any chance you can work on Sunday morning? It's short notice, but I can't rely on the two who called in sick yesterday, and they're both scheduled for Sunday, which will be busy because of the fishing opener."

Joleigh hesitated, fighting back panic at the suddenness of it all. She'd have to check out of the motel Saturday... and check herself in at the hunting shack. *You criminal!*

She kicked the awful truth aside. "Yes. What time?"

"Ruby's is open seven to seven, seven days a week. Sunday's shift is seven to two. If you have time, I'll go through things with you now so it's not overwhelming on Sunday, and I'll have you fill out the paperwork I need for payroll."

"That works for me."

After Joleigh filled out the paperwork, Ruby went over the menu, the layout of the kitchen, and the sections of tables and booths, and she introduced Joleigh to the other employees.

"I'll be here Sunday to help you out, but everyone is good about answering questions." Ruby patted Joleigh's back. "It's like riding a bike. No matter where you ride, you know to just keep pedaling. You'll feel you're at your old job in no time."

"I hope so." Joleigh smiled at the comfort of Ruby's encouraging touch. "Do you have more empty coffee cans? I picked up two here the other day, and I'll pay you for more if you've got extra. Also, I purchased small Styrofoam containers and lids from here, and I need more for the leeches. Can I order them through you?"

Ruby pointed toward the storage room. "Follow me. I order the coffee in bulk, but the decaf comes in the three-pound cans like what you picked up the other day, and I have extra of those." She opened the door to the storage room. "Is four enough? I like to keep a few extra on hand for the cooks."

"Four is great. Thank you." Joleigh could make two more traps.

Ruby opened a box with stacked Styrofoam containers and lids. "I've got several dozen I'll sell you. I order on Mondays and will order another box, which should keep both of us well-stocked for a while."

"Perfect. I'm biking to the two closest resorts today and will ask if they're interested in selling for me." Joleigh paid for the Styrofoam containers. "I'll see you Sunday morning."

Ruby gave Joleigh a wave before returning to her work.

Joleigh went back to the motel for a quick breakfast before heading out to check the leech trap in the swamp located nearest to the hunting cabin. It was heavy with several dozen leeches, and she repeated the process of packaging them in her bathroom at the motel.

BY LATE AFTERNOON, Joleigh had made a deal with the two resorts she'd checked with for vacancy over the summer. Although she'd been unable to rent a cabin at either resort, both were more than happy to sell leeches for her. They would receive a percentage of the profit, and both owners agreed to let Joleigh take whatever fish guts and bones she needed from their fish-cleaning huts at the edge of the resorts to use as bait.

Feeling a sense of accomplishment, Joleigh made her way back to the motel office. Mr. Nielson was checking in a group of middle-aged men, and while Joleigh waited, she noticed the cooler shelves were empty of not only her leeches but also the beverages. He'd been busy.

While Mr. Nielson waited on the men, Joleigh went to the side closet, where he kept the cases of beverages, and restocked the cooler for him. He mouthed a thank-you to her. After the men left, he gave Joleigh a weary smile.

She returned it. "Wow, you sold all the leeches?"

"I sure did. The men like the convenience of one less stop to make tomorrow morning, unless they're fishing with minnows. Still, they liked that these are leeches right from this area. I don't suppose you trapped more this morning?"

"Yes, the leeches are packaged and sitting in cool water in the bathtub. I'll stock them in your cooler. I got more coffee cans from Ruby's. Do you mind if I use your garage to solder them to make two more traps?"

"Be my guest. You know where everything is." He took off his glasses and rubbed his eyes. "Thanks for restocking the cooler. The day seems to have gotten away from me."

"I'm happy to help any way I can," Joleigh said. "I'd tell you that you work too hard, but I'm sure you already know that. Plus, you've done so much for me, and I'm going to miss seeing you after tomorrow."

"Keep bringing me leeches, so we can still see each other." He said it as if she would be doing him a favor instead of the other way around.

Joleigh looked at the wall clock. It was after four o'clock, yet she smelled nothing cooking like she usually did. "Is Mrs. Nielson feeling okay?"

"Not so good today, I'm afraid. She's been resting most of the day." He dabbed at his brow with a handkerchief, looking as if he could lie down on the counter and take a nap himself.

"Perfect. Well, not perfect that she isn't feeling well, but it's a chance for me to do something for you. I'd like to order you and Mrs. Nielson dinner. I'll pick it up and bring it back here for you tonight."

"You don't have to do that for us. And to be honest, the missus will have toast for dinner. She has a migraine and is feeling a bit queasy."

"Then I'll order dinner for you and me. I'm getting sick of sandwiches." Sandwiches had been her go-to meals over the past week. "What would you like? I can pretty much recite the menu for you, which is a good thing, since Ruby hired me as a waitress." Joleigh bounced on the balls of her feet, realizing she hadn't shared her good news with him.

"Well, that's splendid that you've decided to stay in Grandfield. Good for you."

"I promised Ruby I'd work through Labor Day weekend. We will see after that. That's what my call to my neighbor was about this morning, to be sure they can take care of my animals. They said yes. Now, what should I order us for dinner?"

"It's been a while since I've had the pleasure of a meal from Ruby's. Does she still have stroganoff on the menu? That's one thing me and the missus don't make for ourselves."

A pickup pulled up in the parking lot. Four men stepped out and headed for the office.

"Yes, they have stroganoff. I'll call in the order from my room and pick it up when it's ready. See you soon." Joleigh left as the men entered the office.

It was after six by the time Joleigh made it back to the motel office with two containers of beef stroganoff.

"I just checked in the last group of the day," Mr. Nielson said. "I believe we can eat in peace. Let's sit at the kitchen table. I'll leave the door to the office open." He led the way to their kitchen.

"How is Mrs. Nielson doing?" Joleigh would gladly share her meal with the older woman.

"I brought her tea and toast a while ago. She's resting again. Gets awful headaches, and although I told her you'd be back, she said she wouldn't be enjoyable company tonight." He took plates and silverware out for them. He winced when he sat down at the table, and

Joleigh wondered if he'd be able to get back up if a customer needed anything.

"Mr. Nielson, have you both considered selling?" It wasn't like Joleigh to butt into other people's business, but exhaustion seemed to be pushing him down like a bully. With his wife incapable of helping much, it appeared like an awful lot of work for a man of his age.

"We have, and we've tried. Places like ours are becoming a thing of the past. Newer, bigger, flashier hotels now entice overnight guests or families on a weekend getaway." He shrugged. "'*Que sera, sera,*' as Doris Day would say."

Joleigh stopped spooning stroganoff onto her plate. "My adoptive mother, Unity, loved that song." She'd often said how true the words were, that the future wasn't theirs to see. Unity would have been around Mr. Nielson's age. She had never seemed old to Joleigh until those last years as Unity's memory and body failed her. She'd been old enough to be Joleigh's grandmother, and although Joleigh never called her Mom—which was fine with Unity—she considered Unity to be the mother who raised her.

They enjoyed their meal without interruption, sharing slices of their personal lives. The Nielsons had met through a church function in Minneapolis and never had children. Once they neared fifty, they purchased the motel and moved from Minneapolis. "We had a good business for a quarter century," Mr. Nielson said.

Joleigh tried to keep her story factual up to the night of Mack's murder. Mr. Nielson listened but didn't pry into what made her leave her home and animals, another thing she liked about him. Before she left for her room, Joleigh settled up her phone charges with Mr. Nielson. Her percentage from the sale of leeches more than covered her telephone expense.

"Do they have telephone service at the cabin where you'll stay?"

"No." She hadn't noticed a telephone, and even if they had one, which would be unusual, Joleigh guessed they'd have disconnected their service, since nobody used the cabin.

"If you need to call home during the summer, you can still use our telephone."

"Thank you. I appreciate the offer. I may do that, since it's cheaper than the pay phone."

Joleigh remembered few hugs from her parents but never doubted their love. Out of the several foster homes she lived in, only one family ever showed her affection. Unity had always hugged and kissed her, but that was Unity. She'd only known Mr. Nielson a week, yet Joleigh couldn't help herself. She leaned in and gave him a gentle hug, breathing in the citrus scent of his Brylcream.

"I'll stop in and visit, whether I need to use the phone or not," Joleigh promised. "Plus, I'll keep bringing leeches as long as you need them, or until the season ends—usually late June or early July. Thanks again for everything."

"It has been my pleasure, Joleigh. The missus and I have enjoyed having you here." He patted her back.

"I'll stop in tomorrow morning with more leeches before I check out. I'm sure you'll be busy with anglers tomorrow, and I don't work at Ruby's until Sunday, so if you need help with anything, I'll be glad to do whatever I can. I hope Mrs. Nielson's headache goes away."

"Me too. And I appreciate your offer of help."

"When I'm not working at Ruby's, I'd be glad to help you. You deserve a break." Yes, she would have to cut wood for the hunting cabin and do what repairs there she could in her spare time, but on Mondays and Tuesdays, when she was off from Ruby's, she would schedule time to help the Nielsons.

Without their kindness, her first week in Grandfield would've been much bumpier.

THE NEXT MORNING, JOLEIGH biked west of town as the sun rose above a lake in the distance. With three leech traps to check now, she had needed extra storage on the bike. The bike had a flat rack over the back tire, and Mr. Nielson had a couple of old milk crates. She'd purchased one from him and bought two bungee cords at the hardware store to secure the milk crate on the rack.

It was after eight when Joleigh pedaled into the motel parking lot with her basket weighed down with leeches. She packaged the leeches and ran half of the containers down to the office. Joleigh dropped off the other packaged leeches at the resorts before heading back to the motel to shower and pack. She tidied up the room and loaded up her bike well before check-out time at ten.

She stopped in the office to tell Mr. Nielson goodbye. "I work at seven tomorrow morning. I'll be back here later this afternoon to see if you need more leeches for tomorrow. If so, I'll drop them off on my way to work."

"That sounds splendid. On busy weekends such as this, I open the office at six. We will see you later this afternoon." Weariness tugged at Mr. Nielson's eyes.

Joleigh hoped to find a way to help him.

Anxiety pulsated through Joleigh as she biked toward the Gradys' hunting cabin. The worst thing she'd ever done before this was cut off a girl's pigtails in fourth grade after the girl made fun of Joleigh's weight one too many times. But breaking, entering, and staying at someone else's cabin was so much worse.

Yet living in a tent for three months left her vulnerable to unpredictable weather, and depending on where she could find public land, she would have to make sure it had a lake or river nearby for bathing. There was a campground outside of town, but they allowed only campers, not tents.

Joleigh had done her research on the area's climate in the first two days after she'd arrived in Grandfield and learned their summer nights could dip into the forties. In general, temperatures averaged about ten degrees cooler than Woodland.

If they didn't catch Darrell and the other men by Labor Day, Joleigh worried they never would—which meant she would never feel safe enough to go home.

Chapter Ten

The mid-morning temperature climbed steadily, but a cool breeze offset the humidity as Joleigh parked her bike in the tall grass next to the cabin's steps. She wished Groovy and Joplin were there. She missed their company, and they would keep the long grass mowed. But the overgrown driveway's neglected appearance was a plus for her cover.

She took the key to the cabin door from the small shed. Her hand shook as it turned the key inside the lock. *Is it breaking and entering if you have a key? You're splitting hairs, Joleigh. Unity taught you to not take what isn't yours.*

That didn't stop her from unloading her backpack and canvas bag onto the cabin's kitchen table as if she owned it.

Joleigh found a box of matches on a shelf above the gas stove then turned the knob to ignite the stove. No gas. She turned it back off and pulled the stove away from the wall to turn on the gas valve before pushing it back. When she tried again, there was the whoosh of gas. She lit a burner then turned it down and let it run for a minute before turning off the burner.

Joleigh walked outside to the back of the cabin, where the hundred-pound propane cylinder stood. She tipped it back and forth, the liquid sloshed around, and she guessed it to be around half-full. She would call the gas company and order more sometime in the summer so they would have a full tank by the time she left. She had plenty to use in the meantime for cooking and heating water for bathing and washing clothes and dishes.

Back inside, Joleigh located the breaker panel on a bedroom wall and flipped the few breakers to On. She plugged in the fridge, and it came to life. After wetting a washcloth she'd purchased at the hardware store, she wiped the fridge and top freezer out before closing the door so it would begin cooling.

Joleigh would need to call the power company and find out if she could pay ahead on the electric bill so the owner didn't receive one. She took out the notebook she carried in her backpack and made a list of things to do: call the gas company and power company, open an account at the local bank, and rent a safe-deposit box for Mack's money. She couldn't continue to hide it under a mattress, and she knew she would eventually have to tell law enforcement about it. She also added "check out area garage sales for clothing and other necessary items."

She walked through the woods behind the cabin, checking for fallen trees that weren't rotten, wishing she had her chainsaw. Maybe she could pick up an axe at a garage sale, although items like that were rarely sold, since they tended to last for years.

A wheelbarrow would be helpful, but she hadn't spotted one on the property and couldn't afford one. But she could make a sled from large cardboard boxes and twine to pull the fallen branches and trees back to the cabin. As she walked, she searched for morel mushrooms under oak trees. It had rained Thursday night, and mushrooms loved moisture.

By the time she arrived back at the cabin, she had eight morel mushrooms cushioned in a pouch made by gathering the bottom of her shirt. She picked a few wood ticks off her neck and legs, the pests finding their way in even though she'd tucked her jeans inside her socks. The mosquitos left her alone, thanks to the lemongrass-and-lavender rub she'd made from the dried leaves tucked inside her plant-journal packets.

Once the fridge was cold enough, she placed the fish guts, double-wrapped in ice, inside it. She set her few belongings in the bathroom and her clothing in the dresser drawers and then stood by the bed she would sleep in that night. Joleigh felt like Alice stepping through the looking glass.

Through the bedroom window, Joleigh spotted a long rope strung between two trees. She found a set of sheets in the bottom dresser drawer, filled a pot with water, and heated it on the stove. She had a bar of Fels-Naptha laundry soap she'd brought from home—the soap also worked well on poison ivy and bug bites.

Joleigh found a coffee can containing clothespins under the kitchen sink. She went outside, walked past the clothesline, and through the woods toward Lonesome Road to make sure the laundry wouldn't be visible to traffic on the road. There was a heavily wooded buffer of fifty feet or more, and Joleigh figured she would move out long before the leaves fell in the fall.

She washed and rinsed the sheets and hung them out to dry on the clothesline. With very few groceries left, her lunch consisted of an apple, crackers, and jerky. She would stock up on supplies later in the afternoon. There'd been no room in her bike basket when she moved out of the motel room.

After lunch, Joleigh used the fish guts to bait the leech traps and biked down the gravel road to the path she'd already formed during her several trips back and forth to the swamps. She walked into the water, missing her Seal-Dri waders back in Missouri. They were too expensive to buy another pair for only six more weeks of leeching season. The hardware store had knee-high rubber boots for sale, and if she sold enough leeches, she could afford them.

Lonesome Creek's cool water invigorated Joleigh—too cold to strip down and bathe in but tepid enough that it didn't take her breath away. The stream ran a few hundred yards from the cabin toward where the best leech swamps were located.

Once Joleigh washed off the grime and changed her clothes, she biked into town. She'd put more miles on this bike in a week than she had in years on her bike at home. Her first stops were to check on the leech sales. Between the two resorts and the motel, only seven containers of leeches remained. She promised to return to all three in the morning with more leeches. Although plenty of fishermen would head home on Sunday, many retired anglers would stay the week to fish.

Joleigh collected her percentage of the profits and stopped at the grocery store for staple items, surprised to find she had enough money left to purchase the knee-high rubber boots. Before she went back to the cabin, she stopped back at the motel and snuck a Zagnut candy bar—Mr. Nielson's favorite—under the counter. His back straightened, and he smiled as he continued checking out customers, giving Joleigh a nod before she left. She biked back to the hunting cabin, wearing a smile of her own.

Fresh-smelling sheets and a day packed with exercise softened the edges as Joleigh settled in the unfamiliar bed that night. She remembered one of Unity's last moments of clarity when she had pushed—again—for Joleigh to get out and experience life.

Joleigh had responded, "Look who's talking. You've barely left this property in the past fifteen years." She'd always wondered if she'd stifled Unity's life. The few times Unity had ventured off the property were for things like Joleigh's basketball and softball games.

"You forget I was sixty-four when I adopted you, Miss Lippy." Unity's frail hand had patted Joleigh's calloused one. "I did my traveling and exploring long before you became my daughter. Glad I did too. Now you need to do the same. Don't spend the rest of your life talking to chickens and goats."

Unity had whispered some of her last words to Joleigh as if the weight of their wisdom was too heavy to speak. "Find your own life.

Don't settle for mine. Don't settle for Ma..." A hacking cough had cut the last word. But Joleigh had known what it was. Mack.

JOLEIGH WOKE LONG BEFORE the sun rose on Sunday morning.

Leech work prefaced her first official day at Ruby's. Armed with a high-power flashlight she'd brought from home, Joleigh biked down Lonesome Road to retrieve the leech traps. Using the cabin's kitchen sink made packaging them much easier than kneeling next to the motel's bathtub.

She'd washed her hair the night before, so she only took a sponge bath before packing up her bike, shivering in the damp coolness of the cabin. She put her new red-and-white waitress uniform in the backpack and headed to town as crickets and frogs serenaded her in the early dawn. After dropping off containers of leeches at the motel and resorts, Joleigh arrived at the back door of Ruby's fifteen minutes early, giving her enough time to change into her uniform and go over the menu again.

"It's going to be busy later in the day, since many anglers are fishing this morning before heading home," Ruby told her. "I'm giving you two tables this morning so you can get a feel for things. When you aren't busy, I'll have you fill water glasses and coffee cups, set the tables, things like that." She patted Joleigh's back. "I don't want to scare you off on the first day, although with your experience, you'll be up to speed in no time."

Ruby introduced Joleigh to the employees she hadn't met the other day. Not long after Ruby unlocked the front door, customers filtered in. Ruby worked the cash register and played hostess, seating people at Joleigh's tables on a monitored basis. Between trips to wait on her tables, Joleigh filled two hundred water glasses before the lunch crowd filtered in. She bussed tables and helped the other waitresses bring out orders, and by the time the restaurant filled, Ruby added two more tables to Joleigh's section.

All the people, noise, and frenzy overstimulated Joleigh, as if she stood in the center of a three-ring circus after having spent the past year in near-solitude. But waiting on customers tamped down her anxiety as she concentrated on getting the orders right.

Most people barely gave her a second glance but not all. When the lunch rush was winding down, a booth of lively teenage boys smelling of fish and sweat caught Joleigh's attention. She'd walked past their booth several times when one too many "sneezes" from one teen caught her attention.

Every time she walked by, the boy nearest the end of the booth fake-sneezed, "Ah-chink! Ah-chink!" His friends' laughter followed her as she continued past them, and Joleigh wondered how many times she would have to ignore him. It was her first day. She didn't want it to be her last. Ruby's words of intolerance for such situations guided Joleigh's decision.

She'd seen a box of tissues in the hallway to the kitchen and walked back to retrieve it before approaching the teenager. Joleigh tapped his shoulder. "Need some tissues? You keep sneezing." She smiled and batted her eyes. Joleigh learned years ago to rely on humor to defuse confrontation. It wasn't the way she wanted to handle things, but it was easier than attempting to change someone's mind.

His jaw dropped as he stared up at Joleigh, while his friends howled with laughter.

She pulled out a few tissues and set them on the table in front of him then leaned down and whispered, "Oh, and *bla-ass* you."

The teenager blushed as his friend next to him slapped the table, guffawing. Joleigh heard no more "sneezes" after that.

After Joleigh's shift ended at two, she sat with one of the other waitresses for a late lunch. Ruby's employees received a free meal with each shift, which was a bonus for her.

"This is my favorite part of the day," Bernadette said. Joleigh guessed Bernadette to be in her mid-thirties. "A free meal with no interruptions from children or parents."

"You have children, and your parents live with you?" It didn't surprise Joleigh about the children, but she noticed Bernadette didn't wear a wedding ring.

"Yes, a twelve-year-old daughter and ten-year-old son, and we live with my parents, not the other way around." She jammed a straw into her Tab. "I went through a divorce last year. Living with my parents was supposed to be temporary, but there isn't much for rent around here, and I can't afford to buy a house." Bernadette took a sip of her Tab and grimaced.

"Why do you drink that stuff?" Joleigh had tried the diet soda once. That was enough for her.

Bernadette pointed at the plate set to the side and grinned. "To make me feel better about this sour cream-raisin pie I'm going to devour soon."

Over chicken chow mein, the two shared their backstories, Joleigh keeping to the near truth she'd fed the Nielsons and Ruby. It began raining, and by the time they finished eating, the rain had turned into a downpour. Joleigh had a rain poncho back at the cabin. She would need to keep it in her backpack from now on.

After Bernadette left for home, Joleigh changed out of her waitress uniform in the bathroom. As she stepped into the hallway, Ruby walked out of her office. "I could use a break. I'll give you a ride home. We can toss your bike in the back of my pickup."

"Thank you. I hadn't thought about the weather changing like this." Joleigh thought of her old pickup back home, wishing she had it with her. There was so much at home that she could use in Grandfield, but she reminded herself that this was all temporary. The police would capture Darrell and the others, and once her commitment to Ruby was complete, she could go home.

Joleigh loaded her bike beneath the topper in the back of Ruby's truck before they climbed inside.

"You're west on County Road Twelve, right?" Ruby asked.

"Yes, a few miles out. Do you know where Ken Blaze lives? His place has the old tractor out front. I'm the next place past his."

Ruby glanced at Joleigh, one eyebrow raised. "You're related to Shady Grady?"

Joleigh tucked the name into her memory. She knew that the cabin belonged to the Gradys and several families shared ownership. "Yes." Better to say too little than too much.

"Huh. I know they have a lot of relatives who own the cabin." Ruby pursed her lips together as if in thought.

Joleigh braced herself to get called out on her lie.

Instead, their talk turned to the town's upcoming busy summer tourist season and Joleigh's work schedule of Mondays and Tuesdays off. Her late shift of noon to seven on the weekends was one most younger waitresses didn't want. For Joleigh, it would work well so she could collect and deliver leeches early for the weekend fishermen, as opposed to today's hectic early morning. Her Wednesday and Thursday morning shifts were days she didn't need to trap leeches.

"Waitresses often trade shifts," Ruby told her. "Don't be afraid to tell someone no if you'd rather not. You did great today." The drive took less than five minutes, and as Ruby pulled into the long driveway, she added, "Enjoy your days off. The next couple of weeks will be slower until we hit Memorial Day weekend. See you Wednesday morning."

"Thanks again for the ride."

Joleigh hopped out, unloaded the bike, and hurried through puddles to the cabin. Using the key made her feel less like a criminal, although Joleigh swore she could feel Ruby's questioning eyes on her back as she opened the cabin door.

Chapter Eleven

Franklin would've kicked the wooden bench in front of him if his left foot weren't in a cast already. Kicking it with his good right foot would be a sign of carelessness, and although he had plenty of faults, carelessness wasn't one of them. It wasn't even Memorial Day weekend yet, and his summer already looked bleak.

Sweat trickled down the middle of his back as he sat on the bench, keeping stats for his baseball team instead of covering center field. Frustration ticked inside him like a grenade ready to explode. If he hadn't agreed to paint the outside of his parent's house, if he hadn't listened to his dad's insistence that his ancient, rickety wooden ladder was safe, Franklin wouldn't have fallen and broken his foot when the sixth rung busted in half.

It could've been worse. Franklin knew that. Hell, he'd bathed in the hellhole of worse—chewed it, drank it, monitored it, driven tanks through it. A broken foot was nothing compared to what he carried inside, tucked away like a cyanide pill waiting to be swallowed.

It had been two weeks since his fall. Two weeks with no baseball, no golf, no trip to Grandfield... nothing. He'd tried golfing once, but the cast put him off-balance, which threw his swing off, which tweaked his back, which made him want to throw the club into a tree.

Yes, he maneuvered the handful of steps at work, and he had painted as much of the exterior of his parents' house that he could reach, but none of it was enough to exhaust him so he could sleep at night. For years, he had spent nights on high alert, pacing his home as he stared out the windows into the darkness.

Franklin had spent his first years home from war self-medicating his way through college. But the year before he bought his house, he had been digging in his bedroom closet for something and came across a shoebox of keepsakes from his youth. In the musty contents, between his Boy Scout badges and baseball cards, there was a note scribbled in his childish print: *I hate when Dad screams at us and Mom. I hate when he falls. He does it a lot.*

The day he found the shoebox, Franklin's memories of his youth kicked in. He'd been around eight when he wrote the note. Finding it at age twenty-five was a wake-up call, and Franklin vowed he wouldn't follow in his father's footsteps. His dad had served in World War II, brought his own duffel bag of demons home with him, and eventually wrestled them by the time David, the youngest of nine, was born.

Franklin's job in the loan department of the bank had taught him every penny spent was one less penny saved. Over the following year, while he lived at home, he had saved like hell. The next year, he was a proud homeowner.

But sometimes, like the past several days since his foot injury, Franklin longed for more than just the drink or two he allowed himself in the evening. Sometimes an arsenal of drugs would have been a welcome reprieve.

FRANKLIN STOPPED IN at George's Grill after the ballgame, deciding his sour mood would dampen his team's winning high if he went to the bar with them.

David hovered over the kitchen's grill as Franklin stepped inside the busy café, filled mostly with noisy teens. Thanks to the location being two blocks from the high school, it was a favorite hangout.

Franklin hobbled down the hall to the kitchen and swung the door open. "Hey, when you have a second, come find me."

After placing an order for a double cheeseburger, Franklin found an empty table in the corner. He was halfway through his burger when David joined him.

"What's up?" He used his forearm to push back the hairnet holding back his thick hair.

"I was thinking of taking a drive to the hunting shack this weekend, even if I can't do much." He gestured to his left leg, stretched out in the open alongside the booth's table.

"You're gonna go without me?" David's brow furrowed as if he couldn't imagine that happening.

"Maybe. I won't be able to walk the property—too uneven—or check the roof for leaks, but I can clean up the cabin, get rid of the mouse turds and who knows what else has accumulated." Franklin drummed his fingers on the Formica table. "I called Uncle Russ last week to check if anyone in his family has been there. They haven't, and he's not sure anyone will make it for deer hunting this year."

Their dad had several siblings, but most of them had scattered to different states. Other than Uncle Russ's family, who lived a hundred miles southeast of Franklin, most of Shady's family lived too far away from the hunting cabin, had lost interest in hunting, or were too busy. Franklin had two uncles who lived in northern Minnesota, but he doubted they'd been there.

"I've got to get back to work." David stood. "I'll ask for a weekend off soon so we can go together. That way, I can drive and do the stuff you can't do."

Franklin rubbed his chin. "Five bucks says you won't get a weekend off until at least after the Fourth of July." Summers were too short, too busy. "I hope I lose the bet." He gave David a wink before he turned and headed back to the kitchen.

Hope kept Franklin going. Hope would get him through the summer until his damn foot healed.

Chapter Twelve

B y Memorial Day weekend, Joleigh had spoken with Sergeant Williams twice. He had told her about a detective from their department who'd met with the Hoovers and others who lived near Joleigh, alerting them of Darrell's description in case they noticed anything or anyone suspicious in the area. He admitted he didn't know who the men with Darrell were and could only speculate on the stutterer, which reaffirmed her decision to keep quiet about the seven grand in drug money. Law enforcement didn't know who they were looking for, which meant they couldn't protect her from anyone.

Joleigh called the Hoovers twice. Mr. Hoover reassured her they'd be on the outlook for Mack's killer and was horrified that someone would do that to him "for no reason." She didn't correct him, didn't tell him she'd witnessed the murder, didn't tell him she knew four men were involved, not just Darrell—the only man law enforcement had on record for previous crimes.

Instead, she focused on a more pleasant topic. Mr. H reassured her that her animals were fine. Joplin had apparently taken a shine to their grandson, who checked on the goats and chickens every day, and the chickens were back to laying eggs after a short dry spell.

She'd had no negative pushback from customers since her first day at Ruby's. Joleigh had wanted to correct the teenager that day, tell him that "chink" was a slur referring to people of Chinese descent, and she was Korean. But Asian was Asian to most people, and Joleigh wouldn't waste her breath trying to educate an ignoramus.

Joleigh found one of her favorite regular lunch customers in Moe, a man in a wheelchair who looked to be not much older than Joleigh. Moe worked at the local insurance agency and came in weekdays for lunch. His dark-blond hair touched the collar of his dress shirt, and he sported a mustache. His dark eyes danced with humor every day as he greeted Joleigh with a corny joke.

"It's about time Ruby jazzed things up in here. I was tiring of Madge's sass and Bernadette's exaggerated eye-rolling," Moe said with a devilish grin after Joleigh had been at Ruby's for two weeks.

"Why do I feel like I'm your next sacrificial lamb?" Joleigh folded her arms across the menu he didn't need.

"So, the word is out about me, eh?" Moe wiggled his eyebrows.

"Yes. And they told me if you get out of hand, all I need to do is call you Moses and you'll clam right up." Joleigh playfully tapped his shoulder with the edge of the menu. Moe and a few of his coworkers were regulars, and she had been told to save the corner table by the front windows for them every weekday at noon, if possible. It was the easiest access for Moe's wheelchair.

"Right to the heart, Joleigh. They aim right for my heart." He clutched his chest and closed his eyes, muttering his food choice as if it would be his last meal.

Joleigh wrote his order and chuckled on her way to the kitchen.

AFTER THE BUSY MEMORIAL Day weekend, Joleigh had a windfall of cash between her tips from Ruby's and cash from the leech sales. On the Tuesday after Memorial Day, she stood in line in the bank lobby, flush with cash to deposit in her new checking account, when someone tapped her shoulder.

She turned around and recognized the young man from Grand's Bait & Tackle.

"Hi, remember me? Peter from the bait shop?" His dark-green eyes stood out against his tanned skin.

"Sure I do. How's it going?"

"I'm good, but Mom is pissed about your leech sales cutting into her bait business." His grin took the sting out of his words.

"I gave her a chance. Anyway, if the season here is anything like back in Missouri, it will be over by early July. I imagine your supplier's leeches come from farther north. She'll get over her anger toward me soon enough."

"Hah, I wish." He looked around the bank lobby. Nobody was within earshot. "Mom's brother died fighting in the Korean War. She blames every Korean—hell, every Asian—for his death. Don't take it personally. It's not you. It's her. And she will not like you, leeches or no leeches." He waved his hand as if he could push his mother's ignorance away.

After Joleigh made her deposit and waved goodbye to Peter, she hopped on her bike and pedaled back to the cabin. Nobody won in a war. Her dad had been stationed in Korea and met her mother before the Korean War began, and Joleigh was born two months after the war started. When her class talked about casualties of war in high school, Joleigh considered herself one. Her parents' biracial love had thrown her into a world where she stood out, forcing her to fight a unique battle. She wondered if the world would ever become color-blind.

She was out of high school by the time Cher's song "Half-Breed" became popular. She mentally hugged Cher every time she heard the song.

JOLEIGH HAD MISSED the best garage sale deals on Memorial weekend, but more popped up the first Friday in June. She hit a few, picking up a couple of pairs of jeans, T-shirts, and flannel shirts. On the outskirts of town, an elderly couple held a sale in their pole barn. Joleigh about danced when she came across an axe, a heavy rain poncho, and a small tent there.

She used bungee cords to hold everything together as she biked back, and what didn't fit in her two baskets, she wrapped and tied to the front of her handlebars. If anyone showed up at the cabin, she would need to make a quick escape—another reason she needed her truck.

As she unpacked her purchases and boiled water on the stove to wash her new-to-her clothes, she could almost imagine the cabin as home. But if she stayed past Labor Day weekend, it wouldn't be for long. Anyone from the Grady family could show up by the end of September for bowhunting or duck hunting.

The cabin wasn't a permanent solution, and Joleigh craved permanence. Going home was the best way to get it.

Spending the summer surrounded by lakes was a novel experience for Joleigh. Before her shift Saturday afternoon, she biked to town early enough to enjoy some lake time. School let out for the summer the weekend before. The beach and park were packed with people playing Frisbee, families having picnics, teenagers sunning themselves, and children building sandcastles.

Joleigh parked her bike in the bike corral and waded in the tepid lake, wearing shorts and a tank top, her waitress uniform tucked in her backpack. She walked out until the water hovered below the fringe of her shorts, and she itched to dive in. There was a decent beach near home in Missouri, but she'd rarely spent time there. The thought of showing her body off to anyone bothered her.

In high school, the girls wanted to look like Twiggy. Joleigh was as far removed from Twiggy as anyone could be. The only person who'd ever seen her naked was Mack. Next to him, Joleigh hadn't felt so big and muscular. He called her Wonder Woman because of her strength.

Joleigh watched the sunshine glisten on the gentle waves created by boats passing by, pulling a water-skier or fishing. One passed pulling a bikini-clad young woman slalom-skiing, igniting a Unity memory. "Itsy Bitsy Teenie Weenie Yellow Polka Dot Bikini" played in Joleigh's brain, resurrecting an image of the first time Unity took her to the local beach, the first summer she lived with Unity.

Joleigh, at eleven, wanted to hide her body after years of teasing about the layers of grief and loneliness that covered her. Unity sang the song, popular before their first summer together, and pointed out that Joleigh was wrecking her fun by sitting on the beach, wrapped up in a blanket, instead of splashing in the lake.

"Remember this, Joleigh. You can let the words of others keep you from enjoying life and allow them to control your happiness, or *you* can control your happiness by enjoying what you love."

Joleigh remembered perspiring with the blanket wrapped around her, the air so thick with humidity she could chew it. When she had finally run into the water and Unity taught her how to swim, Joleigh's self-consciousness washed away with the waves. If anyone laughed at her that day, she hadn't heard them over her splashing.

Joleigh's reminiscing was cut off by a man's gruff voice shouting something behind her. She turned around to see a scruffy-looking, bone-thin man drag a young girl from the edge of the water as she pleaded with him to let her go. *Is the man trying to kidnap her?*

Adrenaline shot through Joleigh as she ran to the shore. "Leave her alone!" she screamed, drawing attention to the scuffle. The girl appeared to be around seven or eight, and as she stumbled to her feet, Joleigh yelled again. The child was no longer fighting, and Joleigh couldn't let him get away with her.

She reached them just as the man pulled the girl toward a rusty old truck that looked like it wouldn't run more than a block.

"Let her go!" Joleigh shouted.

The man turned to look at her as if finally realizing others were nearby. "Stay out of our business, slant-eyes." Spit flew with his words.

The girl blinked at Joleigh. Her long white-blond hair was in tangles and her pale-blue eyes had purple bags under them. "It's okay, lady. He's my papa."

Joleigh flinched. "This is how you treat your daughter?" *If he treats her like this in public, what does he do in private?*

He opened the truck door and pushed the girl inside before turning back to Joleigh, fists on his narrow hips. "Listen, missy. You keep your nose out of my business, or you'll be sorry. Go back to where you came from." His emaciated body emitted a combination of body odor and grease as offensive as his words.

Joleigh didn't give him the benefit of acknowledging his threat, but she couldn't shake the helplessness she felt as he fired up the old jalopy and drove away, noxious fumes trailing behind.

The calm feeling she'd experienced minutes ago dissipated, replaced with a reminder of how unfair life was. As she pedaled to work minutes later, her heart ached as she wondered what the poor girl's life was like.

THE FOLLOWING WEEK, Joleigh spotted the girl from the beach sneaking in between a group of people entering Ruby's. She made her way to an empty table, stashed a ketchup bottle under her stained T-shirt, and ran out the door. *What does she want with ketchup?*

It wasn't until after the lunch rush that Joleigh had a minute to ask Ruby about the girl. She described her, but before she began ranting about the no-good dad, Ruby said, "It's Bits. Elizabeth, but everyone calls her Bits."

Joleigh raised an eyebrow. "You know her?"

"Well, I wouldn't say *know*. I know of her and her family life, or lack thereof."

"Did you see her sneak in here earlier and take a ketchup bottle?"

"No, but I'm not surprised. Sometimes it's ketchup, sometimes sugar packets." Ruby shrugged. "I look the other way. I've tried helping, but Howie, her dad, is not only an asshole but also a stubborn man." She shook her head. Ruby's hair was pulled back in a headband, exposing the gray overtaking her black hair.

"Why does she want ketchup?"

"To mix with water and make tomato soup. That's what I heard, anyway. It's frustrating as hell."

"Where do they live? I'd like to help her." In Bits, Joleigh had caught a glimpse of what her life could have been like if not for Unity or foster care.

"Good luck with that. Her dad will chase you off the property with a gun staring you in the face. They live a few miles past your cabin down County Road Twelve. Got a couple of acres and a rundown shack they call home."

"Where's her mom?"

"She left them when Bits was a toddler and then passed away living on the streets a few years later. Hard to believe a mother would leave her child, but I'm not sure if she left Bits as much as she left her husband. I'll say one good thing about Howie, and it's the only thing I've got positive to say. He didn't abandon Bits."

"But he's hurting his daughter by not accepting any help."

Ruby nodded. "Wouldn't it be a perfect world if we could help every child who needed it? For Bits, I do what I can. Several of us do." The two women understood what it was like to struggle as a child. "But it's never enough, you know?"

Joleigh needed to do something. "What do people do? How can I help?"

"I'm in a group of business owners who pay for Bits's school lunches. Another group pays for her school supplies and winter coat and boots each year," Ruby said. "Any money given to Howie gets used on booze, so we have to be careful to get it to Bits through school, where he can't touch it. Summer is when needy children fall through the cracks. We do the same for other area children. Unfortunately, Bits isn't alone in her need for help."

Joleigh finished her shift thinking of little else but Bits. Something in the girl and her situation tugged at Joleigh's heartstrings, a tether she couldn't explain or ignore.

After she biked back to the cabin and changed her clothes, Joleigh headed farther west on County Road Twelve to find Bits's home. It was easy to spot based on Ruby's description. The mobile home resembled a pigpen, with a tar roof, knee-high weeds surrounded by rickety wood steps, and junk scattered throughout the yard.

Joleigh slowed her bike but didn't stop in case Howie was outside, or looking out the window. She didn't care to be shot at. Their pickup sat in the dirt driveway. The scene fueled Joleigh back to the cabin, where she gathered her backpack and some cash and biked to the garage sales in town. She guessed at Bits's size, leaning toward larger rather than smaller.

Two days later, on her day off, Joleigh snuck onto their property and hid by the row of trees between their yard and the road. She ran to their steps with two grocery bags of used-but-clean clothes and shoes for Bits.

It was not yet eight o'clock, and Joleigh hoped the man was a late sleeper. The place was quiet, with no nearby neighbors, no cars whizzing by on the road.

Joleigh placed the bags on the ground close enough so that they'd see them before she hurried back toward the trees where she'd parked her bike. Twenty feet from her bicycle, she heard a loud click and Bits's dad behind her. "Get the hell outta here! You ever step on my property again, and I'll shoot you!"

Joleigh didn't turn around. She didn't want him to see her face and didn't want to pause and give him a standing target. She hustled to her bike and pedaled past their house where the woods protected her. If she'd headed back toward the cabin, he would have had a clear view of her, a clear shot. Instead, she biked several more miles, hunkering down in the woods until her knees quit knocking and it was safe to head home.

His threats and the sound of the trigger click had scared Joleigh, but Bits needed help. Almost as much as Joleigh needed to help her.

A few days later, Joleigh was cleaning a table by the front windows at Ruby's when Bits walked by. Joleigh ran to the door. "Hi, Bits. Can you come here, please?"

Bits's eyes widened as they connected with Joleigh's, and she took off running.

Joleigh followed her down the sidewalks that brimmed with summer tourists. "No, wait, Bits! I'm not angry. I want to help you!"

Bits slowed down and turned back toward Joleigh. "What do you want, lady? You'll get in trouble, you know." She eyed Joleigh before taking a step closer.

Joleigh grinned. "It won't be the first time I've been in trouble. Did you get in trouble when I dropped off those clothes the other day?" Joleigh noted Bits wore a T-shirt and shorts that had been in one of the bags she'd left.

Bits's pale eyes widened. "Those were from you?"

"Yes." Joleigh turned back to Ruby's. "Can you come in here with me for a minute? I've got to get back to work, but I wanted to talk to you about getting you lunch."

"Lunch?" Bits rubbed her stomach.

Joleigh could have fit her hands around the girl's waist. "Yes, lunch. How did you get to town?" They lived over five miles out of town. Bits was too young to be biking—if she even owned one—into town alone.

"I ride Mama's old bike. I come in to pick up our groceries, and I like to walk around and people-watch. It's free, and I'm not hurting anybody." Bits regarded Joleigh with suspicion, as if she would scold her.

Joleigh headed back to Ruby's with Bits trailing behind. She had run this idea by Ruby the other day, and Ruby had given her approval. She led Bits to an empty corner booth. "Here's the thing. We end up with food that we have to throw away. Things like rolls that get a little too hard to serve. If you stop in once or twice a week, we can pack it up for you to take home for you and your dad."

"You mean you'd give us food for free?" Bits squinted.

"You'd be doing us a favor. You know it's a sin to waste things, right? Throwing food away is a waste. Are you heading home soon? I could put together a bag for you now if you have a minute." Joleigh wanted to ask if they owned a refrigerator but didn't want to offend Bits.

Joleigh packed a bag with leftover dinner rolls, scooped peanut butter into a to-go container, and filled a sandwich bag with carrots and apple slices. She'd purchased everything except the dinner rolls yesterday in hopes she would see Bits again.

She handed the bag to Bits. "I don't work Mondays and Tuesdays, but if you're here on a Wednesday or Thursday, I get off work at two o'clock. Stop in and I'll treat you to a late lunch."

Bits's eyes bugged out. "You mean like a real hamburger or something? And potato chips?" She bounced on her bare feet.

Joleigh guided her back to the restaurant's front door. A lump formed in her throat as she remembered when she was young. Her most comforting friend had been a bag of potato chips until Unity adopted her. "Yes. Or french fries."

On Joleigh's way to the cabin after work, clouds covered the sky, the cooling air heavy with the promise of rain. Joleigh took advantage of the clouds, changed into a long-sleeved shirt and jeans, and headed into the woods behind the cabin. As she cut and split firewood, she thought of how fun it would be to take Bits out to the swamps and show her how to trap leeches. To walk with her through the woods and look for mushrooms and edible plants. To show Bits all that the woods and water provided for free.

It's not your place, Joleigh, and Minnesota isn't your home. She focused all her frustrated energy into splitting a chunk of wood.

But that night, as she lay in bed, reflecting on the past five weeks in Grandfield, she contemplated adding one word to her earlier verbal reprimand: *yet.*

Chapter Thirteen

By early July, the population of Grandfield had multiplied. With the Fourth landing on a Monday, the town held its annual parade, fireworks, and water-skiing show on Saturday. Ruby's closed at noon so the employees could enjoy the parade and activities that began at one. Joleigh had splurged on a one-piece red swimsuit through the JC Penney's catalog—nowhere near as revealing as the one made popular by Farrah Fawcett—and had it mailed to Ruby's Restaurant. After the parade, Joleigh and Bernadette, who was childless for the day, planned to hit the lake to swim and watch the water ski show.

Several of Ruby's employees gathered on the sidewalk to watch the parade. One of the first vehicles in the parade was a convertible that held the governor of Minnesota, a man running for reelection in 1978. Politicians made Joleigh's stomach churn. She groaned.

"What?" Ruby stood next to Joleigh. "You don't like the governor?"

"I'm not a fan of politicians."

Ruby raised an eyebrow but said nothing, returning her attention to the parade.

Joleigh didn't want to explain how she blamed President Kennedy for her parents' deaths. If they hadn't been so enamored with JFK, following him all over while he campaigned for the presidency, they wouldn't have been in the overstuffed Volkswagen van that slippery November day in 1959. They would still be alive.

And she wouldn't be standing in Grandfield now, having to swallow the truth and spit out more lies. Ruby thought Joleigh's dad was a relative of that Shady Grady man who died. She could never confess that her parents had died almost twenty years ago.

So instead, Joleigh concentrated on the majorettes and their glitter batons as they tossed them high in the air. The marching band followed behind, playing "Tequila" by the Champs, one of the many silly songs she and Unity had liked to dance to while working.

She would never have met Unity if her parents had lived. Joleigh had loved her parents, but she barely remembered them. Her memories were of smart, busy parents who were so focused on the civil rights movement and politics that they sometimes forgot they had a child.

It wasn't until Unity took her in that Joleigh understood a family could be made from people unrelated. As Unity liked to say, quoting the title of the Beatles song, "All You Need Is Love." It was all Joleigh wanted—love. Well, family and stability too.

Joleigh wondered if she would ever find it again, whether in Grandfield, Woodland, or anywhere. She looked at the crowd lining Main Street and the handful of Ruby's employees alongside her and tried to think beyond Labor Day.

After the parade, Joleigh and Bernadette walked to the crowded beach to watch water-skiers create human pyramids and perform flips from ramps placed in the lake. They enjoyed sloppy joes and ice-cold beer from concession stands in the park.

"What time will your children be home?" Joleigh asked as they headed back to the beach.

"Their dad is bringing them back at seven. My parents' house is a few blocks from the beach, so we walk down and watch the fireworks along the shore," Bernadette said. "Thanks again for taking my shift tomorrow morning. It's often midnight by the time we get home from the fireworks and my children unwind." She smiled. "After them being gone for a week with my ex-husband, I'm looking forward to catching up with them."

"No problem. I've got two days off after that, so I don't mind working a double tomorrow. Plus, Ruby said business will be slow Sunday afternoon because the tourists all head home after the busy weekend."

It was six o'clock when they parted ways and Joleigh biked back to the cabin. Feeling tired yet rejuvenated from the fun afternoon, she didn't mind that the day before had been her last day for trapping leeches. With the swamps and ponds warming up, the supply had dwindled to the point that it was no longer worth her time, but it had been a profitable run.

Joleigh was glad that the leeches had also been extra income for the Nielsons. Ever since Memorial Day, she had made a habit of stopping at the motel and stripping sheets, emptying trash cans, and vacuuming for them. Mr. Nielson had told her they'd employed a cleaning lady until the past few years, when their income could no longer justify the expense. Joleigh always refused to accept payment, so Mrs. Nielson sent home-baked goods and serving-sized portions of meals she'd made, from hot dishes to pasta salads.

After the sun set that night, Joleigh sat in the living room, working on a braided rug for the cabin. In the distance, loons called out to their mates on Lonesome Lake, and crickets chirped in the nearby swamp. She didn't miss the boom of the fireworks—instead, she enjoyed the peace that reminded her of home.

Joleigh worked with strips from various old shirts she'd purchased at a garage sale, the colors resembling the reds, blues, and white of fireworks. Braiding rugs was another thing she'd learned from Unity, one of many hobbies they had shared at night after they completed their chores.

Joleigh stopped working the fabric when the thought hit her. It had been eight weeks since she'd hidden in the back of Mr. H's vehicle. Eight weeks in Grandfield, a town that slowly pulled her in and made her question her future.

Bernadette had offered to cover a shift for her in exchange for Joleigh working a double shift. By the time Joleigh crawled into bed, she had a plan. If Bernadette took her Wednesday shift, she would have three days off, enough time to retrieve her truck and other items in Woodland. The thought of going back made her pulse race. But it was time.

THE MONDAY MORNING after the Fourth of July, Joleigh walked to the bus station with her backpack and settled in for the two-hour-plus ride to Mason City, Iowa. From there, she would transfer buses to take one to Hannibal, the closest drop-off to Woodland. It would be after eight by the time she arrived.

The sun dipped below the horizon when Mr. Hoover picked Joleigh up at the bus depot. She dreaded sleeping at her house, but arriving so late meant she would have to drive through the night, and she didn't trust her old truck enough to risk it.

Joleigh climbed into the passenger seat of Mr. H's station wagon, tossed her backpack on the back seat, and fought the truth clawing its way up her throat, pushing to come clean about stowing away in the same vehicle back in May.

"I appreciate this, Mr. Hoover." She turned to look at his profile as he drove out of the bus-depot parking lot. She'd missed the reassurance of living next door to them.

"It is no problem. It's good to have you back. Who is caring for your cousin while you're here?"

"A friend of hers is staying with her. I'll leave tomorrow by noon to drive back. It'll be nice to have my truck there."

Dusk settled in by the time he pulled into her driveway, the area near her campfire ring sending her heart into palpitations. After law enforcement combed through her home and yard for clues, the Hoovers had picked up the mess Mack's killers had made. Surely those men had stayed away since that first weekend and would have no way of knowing Joleigh was back for a brief visit.

She took her backpack from the back seat. "I'll stop by to settle up with you in the morning." She'd wired money to them for feed and extra for their grandson's help, but it wasn't enough. She would need to discuss with them her animals' future if she didn't come back after Labor Day weekend.

"I'll see you in the morning," Mr. H said.

Joleigh thanked him again as she stepped out and shut the car door. He waited until she unlocked the door and turned on the kitchen light before driving away.

Being back in the house sent a chill up Joleigh's spine. There were too many memories within those walls... and in the yard.

After locking the front door behind her, Joleigh walked slowly through each room, flipping on all the lights. She'd never been afraid of the dark before, never worried about being alone in the house. As a stress headache formed, Joleigh wished for her plant herbs so she could brew tea.

The home needed a good cleaning and airing out—more so of painful memories than stale air. She longed to open the windows, to listen to the breeze whisper through the trees and breathe in the familiar scents of animals and woods, but opening windows would make her feel more vulnerable.

Joleigh settled in the living room, where she pushed a chair into the corner so her back was against the wall. Exhaustion weighed her down, yet it was impossible to turn off her brain. The place had changed. So had she. Eventually, she closed her eyes and slept on and off in semi-darkness.

JOLEIGH WOKE EARLY to the clucking of her chickens and the bellowing of the goats. She jumped out of the chair and ran out to her animals. Joplin, in her spirited style, ignored Joleigh to let Joleigh know she could live without her if Joleigh was going to desert her like that. Meanwhile, Groovy nuzzled Joleigh with her damp nose, ever forgiving, ever pleasant.

The chickens, most past contributing, managed a measly seven eggs among them. Joleigh chuckled. She had a henhouse filled with stew hens.

Dressed in long pants and long sleeves, Joleigh walked her property. She checked the fencing she'd yet to fix and the roof on the chicken coop that wouldn't last another winter but skirted the traumatic campfire area.

It was all too much—the repairs, the loss, the lack of direction with her future. The idea of crawling under the covers and sleeping until the men were behind bars was tempting. Instead, Joleigh headed over to visit the Hoovers to pay them for caring for the animals and for Mr. H picking her up at the bus depot.

Mrs. Hoover met her at their back door. "Good morning, Joleigh. Come on in." She led the way into their kitchen and set out a plate with slices of coffee cake in the center of the table. Mr. H came in from the garage.

Over iced tea and coffee cake, Joleigh asked their opinion on the many decisions that would shape her future, doing her best to keep as close to the truth as she could. "I need your wisdom on a few things, and I hate to bother you with it, but I don't know who else to ask."

Their daughter Paula's upbringing had been golden, with older brothers and parents to spoil her, but they had also raised Paula with enough guidance to keep her grounded. Mrs. Hoover reached across the kitchen table, and her calloused hand patted Joleigh's. "We're here to help."

"Thank you. I'm having problems deciding what I should do. I like the job where I'm working, and I've met some friendly people in my cousin's town." Joleigh felt like a traitor for voicing these thoughts. "With Unity gone and now Mack, it feels different at the house. It was awful after Unity passed away, and with Mack dying there..." She couldn't finish the sentence, a ball of tears lodged in her throat.

"We understand," Mrs. Hoover said, sliding the plate of coffee cake closer to Joleigh as if another slice would fix her problems. "Poor girl, you've been through so much."

"I can't say as I blame you, Joleigh," Mr. H said. "You're young, and living out in the middle of nowhere alone may be fine for us old folks, but you? You should be out enjoying life, exploring the world." He nodded. "I spent time in Germany, France, and Italy before coming back to the States and getting married. We lived in the Northeast then Colorado before moving here. You've been in this area your whole life. This may be the perfect opportunity to spread your wings."

Joleigh knew they had moved from Colorado but hadn't realized Mr. H had done all that traveling years ago. Grandfield wasn't like traveling overseas, but it was a start.

"If I stay longer, I'm going to need my own place, and I'll need to decide what to do with my animals." Joleigh would have loved to take Joplin and Groovy with her, but she had no place to keep them.

"As you mentioned in one of our phone conversations, the hens are ready to be butchered. We can keep your goats for as long as you'd like. We've got an extra pasture I can set up here so they're more accessible in the winter." Mr. H folded his weathered hands on the table. "I'm going to give you the same advice I'd give Paula if she was in your shoes. If you find yourself in need of money to rent or purchase a place, you've got quality land you can sell. I know you're leasing forty acres to Elmer down the road. You've got another forty you could sell separately from your home."

Joleigh leaned forward, listening closely to Mr. Hoover's input.

He continued. "Our sons out in Colorado have been looking for hunting land around here. If you're ever interested in selling anything, I believe they'd be interested in your back forty. Now, I'm telling you this because you asked for our advice. My advice to you is to go experience life and try something new—and know that if you need funds, you've got it here in your property."

Joleigh's father, Liam of the "Irish lace" descendants, with his dark, wavy hair and scruffy beard, had been the talker between her two parents. She sensed her dad's advice would have been similar to Mr. H's, which also mirrored what Unity had asked of Joleigh over the years.

By the time Joleigh walked up her driveway, she'd finalized a plan with the Hoovers. It was time to let go, at least partially. Joleigh spent the rest of the morning packing. She started with items from the shed—her chainsaw, shovel, axe, saw, and toolbox, all things she would need if she stayed in Grandfield and had to live off the land.

From inside, she packed her sewing machine, knitting needles, and yarn and most of her clothing and winter gear, along with favorite books and personal items like photos of Unity.

She emptied the cupboards, boxing up extra canned goods to bring to the Hoovers as a thank-you. She still had plenty to carry her over for the coming months until she could plant a garden next summer... wherever she ended up living.

Joleigh boxed up pots, pans, dishes, silverware, and towels. She would keep those items packed until she had a place of her own. She boxed up bathroom items like the lavender soap she'd made with Unity every year, looking forward to taking a lavender sponge bath when she got back to the hunting cabin. The back of her pickup was full by midday when she locked the front door.

You'll come back. Joleigh promised herself, even though she, of all people, knew life was a path of broken promises. From the moment her parents had died and with them their promises of a permanent home for the three of them, to her years in foster homes, Joleigh could write a novel about crushed hope.

When Unity appeared in her life, the promise of a better life took shape. Unity, a guest speaker at their school, had spoken to the students about the advantages of growing a garden and about the medicinal benefits from area plants. She'd taken notice of the over-weight child who sat at the end of a row, an invisible shell around her, shutting her away from others. And she'd taken that child in, fulfilling every promise Joleigh could ever want or need.

But not all promises lasted forever. Unity and Joleigh had lived as mother and child, teacher and student, until their roles reversed as Unity's memory failed.

After Unity's death, Joleigh had felt like a sailboat on a windy lake, unguided and untethered. Her plan to attend Moberly Junior College in Hannibal that fall had been her half-hearted attempt to do something with her life again. Classes would start in six weeks. She should finish college. Keep her house closed up, collect what she'd accrued back in Grandfield, rent an apartment in Hannibal, and go to school. The start of the semester would cut things close with her commitment to Ruby to work through Labor Day, but it could work.

Yet the idea of choosing classes and moving to a town full of strangers—again—felt like trying to swim upstream. And Hannibal was too close for comfort until they caught Mack's killers.

With the truck loaded, her snacks for the drive back to Grand-field on the front seat and a box filled with canned goods for the Hoovers in the back, she drove to their home after a tearful goodbye to Groovy and Joplin.

Mr. H was working in the yard and met her in the driveway. "We'll keep in touch. If you decide to stay in your cousin's town and sell some of your acreage here, please let me know before you call a realtor."

"I'll do that. I've got canned goods for you." She slid the box from the back seat and handed it to Mr. Hoover.

"Guess what? I keep forgetting to mention this when we talk on the phone," Mr. H said. "I stopped at a small town south of the Twin Cities back in May to eat lunch at a downtown café. After lunch, I drove down the street, and I'll be darn tootin' if I didn't spot a woman who looked like you walking into the Ben Franklin store. You must have a twin out there."

Joleigh gripped the open truck door for support in case her knees buckled. She forced out a chuckle. "Well, that would be nice, wouldn't it? You know, I always wished I had a sibling. And re-member, I've been living hundreds of miles *south* of Woodland, not *north*."

"That's what I told the young man who came by your place re-cently. Said he and his buddy were Mack's friends from the service and came to pay their respects. I was feeding your goats, and he asked where you were, said they'd stopped before and nobody was home. I joked that I'd have sworn I'd seen you in a small town south of Min-neapolis, but that you've been with your cousin in Arkansas."

Joleigh's stomach ached as if he'd punched her in the solar plexus. "How many men? What did they look like?"

Mr. Hoover's brow furrowed. "Two young men, but the driver stayed in the truck. Mack's friend that I spoke with had a long scar on his cheek. Oh, and he stuttered. Do you know him? He asked me the name of the town where I thought I'd seen your twin, but I'll be danged if I can remember."

In the years Joleigh had been with Mack, he had never men-tioned friends from the service coming to visit him. She had no clue if one of the men that night had a scar on his cheek, but every in-stinct told her that was the one she'd heard stutter. Those men hadn't come to her house to offer condolences. They wanted their drug money—and her, a witness to murder.

"You didn't get a good look at the driver? The man with the scar doesn't sound familiar. Do you suppose they had something to do with Mack's death? He never had friends from the service come to visit at my house before." Joleigh scanned the woods around them, as if the men would magically appear.

"You think so?" Mr. H's eyes widened. "Boy howdy, I sure wish I'd have gotten a good look at the driver! He wore a huge cowboy hat and sunglasses." He folded his arms over his chest and shook his head. "Dang it! You think that might have been that Darrell man the law is looking for?"

Joleigh opened the door to her truck, more eager than ever to get away. "Could be. I've got to go, but I'll contact Sergeant Williams and have him call you for more details." She *should* stop to meet with Sergeant Williams in person, but if she did, he would ask too many questions. Panic—and gut instinct—told her to get as far away from Woodland as she could.

They spoke for a few more minutes before Joleigh thanked Mr. H again and slid into the driver's seat. She waved goodbye and drove slowly down the driveway until she hit the main road. Then she floored it, putting miles between her and Mack's killers.

As Joleigh drove north, she couldn't decide if she was driving away *from* or driving *to* home. One thing was certain—those men were still looking for her and the money. The farther away she stayed from Woodland, the better.

Chapter Fourteen

By the time Joleigh arrived at the hunting cabin, the sun had set. She left most of the items in the flatbed of her truck, too exhausted from the day. She could unload them in the morning. Her relief at having her truck again—in case she needed to live in it—had been wiped away by the knowledge Mack's killers hadn't given up on finding her or the money.

The following morning, Joleigh unpacked what she could use in the cabin, careful to keep her things separate in case she needed to pack fast and leave. Having her personal items there made the cabin feel more like home, albeit a temporary one.

It was mid-morning by the time Joleigh drove to the motel and placed a call to Sergeant Williams. He was away from his desk, so she left a message with one of his coworkers, giving him Mr. Hoover's name and phone number. Law enforcement needed a detailed description of the stutterer from Mr. H. The sooner they put that man on their radar with Darrell, the better.

After she arrived back at the cabin, Joleigh repaired the flashing around the wood stove's pipe on the roof and secured several loose shingles.

The following day, Joleigh was back to work at Ruby's. While she'd been in Woodland, she had missed helping the Nielsons clean the motel on Monday and meeting Bits at the beach on Tuesday, both things she looked forward to on her days off.

There had been no more run-ins with Howie. But on the Thursday after Joleigh returned from Missouri, she and Bits ate after her shift, and Joleigh brought up something that would bring her face-to-face with Bits's father once again.

"Since I have my truck here now, I could pick you up on Tuesdays. That way, you don't have to bike into town." Joleigh was hesitant to create a long-term relationship with Bits. If she moved away, she would be one more adult who let Bits down. But at least for the summer, she would do her best to be there for the girl. The thought of Bits biking alone angered Joleigh, and it ticked her off that Howie wasn't concerned about Bits's safety. "Since you don't have a telephone, I can speak with your dad about it if you don't want to ask him." She didn't want him taking any anger out on Bits.

"I'll ask Papa. He doesn't like charity, but if we just go to the beach or something and I make sure he knows you didn't buy me anything, it might be okay."

"You know my work schedule," Joleigh said as she pushed her empty plate to the side. "If you're in town this weekend, stop in and let me know what he says. If I don't hear from you, I'll meet you at the beach at our usual time next Tuesday."

Joleigh wanted to ask where her dad thought Bits went every Tuesday. Maybe he knew and considered her a free babysitter. He was home every day, since Bits said he didn't have a job "due to him being sick a lot."

BITS STOPPED IN RUBY'S late Sunday morning. Joleigh met her between taking orders. "Papa said you can pick me up, but you have to stay in your truck." Bits's look was solemn, and Joleigh wondered if she would make her pinkie promise.

"I promise. I'll pick you up at nine Tuesday morning." Joleigh ruffled Bits's hair and its several layers of grime. Bits nodded before skipping out of the restaurant.

Over the next few weeks, Joleigh embraced the freedom her truck brought her. She ran errands for the Nielsons after helping with the motel on Mondays, she used it on Tuesdays to pick up and drop off Bits on their days together, and every Wednesday night, Joleigh and Bernadette went either to a movie, a restaurant other than Ruby's, or other small towns in the area.

Joleigh no longer had to bike home in the dark. She kept the windows and door locked at the cabin when she was gone and drew the curtains when she turned on any light at night. She'd spoken to Sergeant Williams after he called Mr. H, and although the case had no new information, he reiterated that it was in Joleigh's best interest if she stayed away and stayed alert, no matter where she was.

Still, Joleigh refused to live in constant fear. And as the weeks went on, she found periods of time when she forgot about the men and almost forgot Grandfield was a temporary home.

By early August, Joleigh's growing friendships with the Nielsons, Ruby, Bernadette, Moe, and Bits only reinforced that feeling, making her question whether she could leave Grandfield come September.

ON THE FIRST SUNDAY in August, Ruby asked to speak with Joleigh in her office after her shift ended.

"I know I asked you to commit to working through Labor Day weekend, but I could sure use you after that." Ruby leaned back in her desk chair. "Leo will be back to cook part-time for his last year of college, so Madge will replace him in the kitchen. And I lose two girls who will head back to college then."

Joleigh took a seat across from Ruby. "Initially, I thought of going back to college in Missouri..." Her voice faded as she looked down at her hands on her lap. "The thing is, I haven't registered for classes yet. I've been struggling a bit, trying to figure out what I want to do." She drummed her fingers on her knee. "Now that I have my truck here, along with some things from my home, I could stay longer. I'm thinking of looking for property around here. If I end up staying, I'll want a hobby farm similar to what I have in Missouri."

It surprised Joleigh that the thought surfaced, since she'd been doing her best to tamp it down, avoiding any permanent decision. "I'll have to move out of the cabin sometime this fall, since it's not winterized." It was a better excuse than the truth of the Grady family showing up to hunt. "If I stay in Grandfield, I'll need to sell some acreage back home and find a place here for the winter. Even if I find land to buy, I won't have time to build anything this fall."

One decision affected another decision, like a row of dominos falling so fast Joleigh couldn't stop them.

Ruby twirled a pencil, deep in thought. "If you're serious about buying land, let me know. My husband and I bought several parcels outside of town." Joleigh knew little about Ruby's personal life except that her husband had died of cancer in his forties. "We never had children, so we invested our extra money in property here and around Mille Lacs, where I grew up. I'm toying with retiring in the near future, and I plan to sell one or two parcels each year."

Joleigh's heart lifted. "You'd sell me some acreage?"

"Yes, if you're serious about staying around here. We can take a drive to check out the land if you'd like. I have a few ten-acre parcels close to where your cabin is, down Lonesome Road, if you like that area. But is ten acres enough for you?"

"I'm not sure. Ten acres might be better, though, so that I can save money to build a place." But before she decided anything, Joleigh needed job stability. "You said something about retiring. What would you do with Ruby's?"

"I'll sell Ruby's. I won't let it close. And I'll keep my house in town. My sister who lives by the Mille Lacs Lake area is a few years younger than me. She's been bugging me to sell so we can travel together. Our grandfather is from Puget Sound, where many Native American tribes lived. That's one of the first places we want to visit."

Ruby's plans reminded Joleigh of Mr. Hoover's travels before he married and of Unity's before she settled in Missouri. Until recently, Joleigh had never left her comfort zone in Missouri.

But when she walked down Lonesome Road later that night, she realized that wasn't true. She'd created a new comfort zone in Grandfield.

JOLEIGH STOPPED AT the motel office Monday morning to call the Hoovers before eight o'clock. She had no clue what her forty acres back in Woodland were worth.

"I have an idea of the value, but to be fair, you should get the property appraised," Mr. H said after Joleigh explained her situation. "I can look up appraisers in the phone directory for you if you'd like."

"Yes, please."

He was back in a minute with a few phone numbers for Joleigh to call. "Thank you. I'll call them and see if one of them can do an appraisal soon."

Her next call was to a real estate company in Macon, a decent-sized town near Woodland. Their office didn't open until eight, so she left the motel office's phone number for them to call back.

After she hung up, Joleigh asked Mr. Nielson if she could talk with him and Mrs. Nielson.

"Of course," he said. "We can sit on the patio outside and keep the door to our kitchen open in case someone comes into the office."

Joleigh had learned that Mrs. Nielson was like a sunflower, craving warmth and sunshine but dwindling in the cold winter months, which made her arthritis worse and seemed to bring a sort of depression to her spirit.

The three of them sat at the patio table, an umbrella shading them from direct sunlight, with iced tea Mrs. Nielson poured for them. Her flower garden blossomed with a dozen colors against the impeccable green lawn.

Joleigh explained the message she'd left for the realtor in Missouri and her idea to possibly sell some of her land. "I'll write down the address, et cetera about the property for the realtor if he doesn't call before I leave." Joleigh folded her hands on the table. "I have another favor to run by you, but this one also benefits you." She smiled at the couple, who reminded her so much of the Hoovers, only a decade or so older. "You've talked about how you used to drive to Arizona to stay with your brother for a month or more every winter and how you haven't done it for years now because the roads are too dangerous for you to tackle in the winter."

Mr. Nielson nodded, and Joleigh continued. "What if I moved into one of the motel rooms for the winter and ran the place for you? That way you could leave here while the weather is decent and stay there for months instead of weeks. You've said yourself that business is slow after deer-hunting season."

Joleigh took a drink from her iced tea. "It would give me a place to live this winter, and this way I could stay in town. If my acreage back home sells, I hope to buy ten acres from Ruby. I could build on it next spring if I end up staying here." Joleigh caught the look that passed between the Nielsons. "It could be a win-win. What do you think?"

Mrs. Nielson bounced in her seat and clapped. "I'd love it! My joints ache here in the winter. We've missed the friends we've made in Arizona over the years."

Joleigh turned to Mr. Nielson. "How do you feel about it? I promise I'll take good care of the motel."

"That's the last thing I'd be concerned about," Mr. Nielson said. "And I'd sure enjoy spending more time with my brother. I can check if he could tolerate us for a few months, maybe leave here by the end of November or early December. It would give us time to train you in before we go." He patted Joleigh's hand. "And as far as you staying here this winter, I think that's a splendid idea. We've missed having you around every day."

Joleigh smiled. Having a plan and a purpose helped put her future in focus, at least for the next several months.

The office phone rang minutes later, and Mr. Nielson answered it. "It's for you, Joleigh," he said through the open kitchen window.

She hurried into the office and took the receiver from Mr. Nielson's outstretched hand.

"Hello, Ms. Moore. My name is Wes, and I'm returning your call. I looked up the parcel you mentioned in our plat book, and if you'd like, I can send an appraiser over this week. Do you have the legal description?"

"Yes, I have the warranty deed with the legal description. I can mail you a copy."

"That would be good. Once we receive it, the appraiser should have something for me the following week. Is the number I called the best way to get ahold of you?"

"Yes. Thank you. It's not my phone number, but they'll take a message for me, and I can call you back. Or if I know when you're going to call, I can try to be here, as long as it doesn't interfere with my work schedule."

After discussing a few more details, they hung up, and Joleigh relayed the news to the Nielsons.

As she was leaving, Mr. Nielson walked with her to the motel parking lot.

"Let me know what your brother says about you visiting them this winter," Joleigh said.

"I will. We appreciate your offer. It would sure be a morale boost for the missus."

Joleigh drove to the bank and collected the legal documents she kept in the safe-deposit box then drove to the hardware store. She made a few copies of the deed, in case she needed extras, and mailed one copy with a note inside to Wes at the real estate office.

THE FOLLOWING WEEK, Wes scheduled a call with Joleigh and gave her an appraised value of the forty acres. "Thanks. I'll call my neighbor and let him know the quote so he can call his sons." She had already spoken with Wes about listing it if the Hoovers' sons chose not to purchase the property.

She called Mr. H and gave him the appraisal price.

"That sounds reasonable to me," he said.

"It does? I didn't know what to expect." Wes had pointed out the acreage was high ground, perfect hunting land surrounded by farmland, and the trees alone would bring in a decent price if the owners logged the property.

"I'll call our sons tonight. Can I call you around seven tomorrow morning?"

"Yes, that works for me." She loved that she still had a connection with Mr. H, yet understood their weekly calls would probably change if she sold the acreage. And she still needed to finalize plans for her animals.

On Tuesday morning, Joleigh arrived at the motel office before seven to wait for Mr. Hoover's call. The phone rang minutes later.

"It's a yes!" he told her. "Our sons didn't quibble on the price, and I gave them Wes's contact information, as you suggested. Sounds like he'll take care of everything from here."

Joleigh gave a silent cheer. One more hurdle down. The money she would receive from the sale would more than pay for ten acres and a small basement—something she could live in until she could afford to build the rest of her home... if that was what she ended up doing.

The idea of starting fresh without endless repairs or haunting memories became more appealing every day. But the thought of losing her animals felt like the last piece of her heart being ripped to shreds.

"We need to discuss the animals, Mr. Hoover. If you'll take Joplin and Groovy, I'll take care of calling someone to butcher the chickens." Sadly, it was part of the circle of life, one that Joleigh found she'd already experienced too often with those she loved.

It's like every other butchering season, Joleigh. It's okay.

But it wasn't. This time, she didn't have baby chicks to replace the hens. She paced, limited by the six-foot phone cord. "I can't expect you to keep taking care of my goats on my land. I want you to have Joplin and Groovy. Who knows when, or if, I'll be able to take them back. You've done so much for me. It's the least I can do."

Mr. Hoover gasped into the phone. "Let's not worry about that right now," he said. "We'll care for them at our place. But if you find yourself back here, or any other place that you can care for them, they're still yours, and you'll be welcome to take them."

The words reassured her that her animals were one less thing to think about. "Thank you. For everything," Joleigh said before hanging up with a long sigh of relief.

JOLEIGH WALKED INTO Ruby's early one Wednesday morning and felt something was off. The few employees already there huddled together, everyone speaking at once, hands flying in dramatic gestures. Two of the women dabbed at their eyes.

"What's wrong? What happened?" Joleigh loved the quiet at the hunting cabin, but with no TV or telephone, any major catastrophe could occur, and she would be the last to know. She often listened to her radio at the cabin but lately had been working in the yard in her spare time, and she didn't dare take the radio outside, where the sound might carry.

Madge turned to Joleigh, her eyes watery. "It's Elvis. Didn't you hear?"

"Elvis... Presley?" He was the only Elvis Joleigh knew of.

Leo, a few years younger than Joleigh, held up his hands. "Who else?"

Joleigh made her way toward the group as she tied an apron over her uniform. "Does he have a new song out or something?"

"He died yesterday!" the group bellowed in unison, some of them eyeing Joleigh as if she was an alien who hadn't kept up with life on Earth.

Throughout Joleigh's shift, the tabletop jukeboxes in the booths cranked out Elvis songs while many patrons sat with a look of disbelief.

Not Joleigh. No death blindsided her now.

THE FOLLOWING WEEK, Joleigh received the proceeds of the land sale, the money wired to her bank account. Afterward, Ruby accompanied Joleigh to the bank, where a closing company handled her purchase of ten acres from Ruby.

To celebrate her twenty-eighth birthday, plus her land purchase and sale, Joleigh and Bernadette made a nearly two-hour round-trip drive to dine at the Lowell Inn Restaurant in Stillwater. Joleigh had never splurged like that before, but she'd learned long ago that life was too short. *I deserve to live it up a little.*

In her spare time over the next few days, she explored her new property. She collected chicken-of-the-woods mushrooms off dying oak trees, ones she would cut down for firewood over the winter. She located golden chanterelle mushrooms living under a cluster of white oaks, and with all the fresh mushrooms, she cooked up a pot of homemade mushroom soup.

The property was less than a mile from the hunting cabin, less than a mile from Lonesome Lake, and only a hundred feet from Lonesome Creek. She'd picked out a building site that was close enough to hear the trickling of the creek but far enough back from the road for privacy. She could have a new place instead of one in constant need of repairs. The Lonesome Road property was closer to town and had enough land for goats, chickens, and maybe even sheep or a cow.

Unity's last cow, Bertha, had died of old age over two years before. A young Joleigh had become so attached to Bertha that Unity hadn't had the heart to have Bertha "sent away" after she stopped producing milk. Right until her last day on earth, Unity believed Bertha was still alive. Joleigh had never spoken of Bertha's demise or the barn cats' disappearance. It was easier to let Unity believe nothing had changed.

Every night after sunset, Joleigh worked on a house plan. With a tentative goal of building on the property next year, she would have to line up someone to dig a well and a contractor to dig the basement.

The Nielsons had taken her up on the offer to stay at the motel for the winter and run it for them. They had deer hunters booked in several rooms until mid-November and were full every weekend until November first.

Joleigh would be out of the cabin before then, early October at the latest. By then, she would have everything ready to live on her property until she could move into the motel in November. She'd purchased a sturdy tent for sleeping, planning to use the one she'd nabbed at a garage sale to hold extra household items.

And every time she panicked at all the decisions she had made, she reminded herself that nothing was set in stone.

WHEN JOLEIGH DRESSED for work on the first Friday of September, she couldn't believe it was the weekend that had seemed so far off in the distance last May when Ruby had asked Joleigh to commit to work through Labor Day.

And during those months, Sergeant Williams had yet to find Darrell or his sidekick with the scar on his face, even with the information Mr. Hoover had provided him about the men. What she and—ideally—Mr. H hadn't told the sergeant was Mr. H's thought that he had seen Joleigh's "twin" in Minnesota. The sergeant still thought she was in Arkansas. Joleigh wondered if the case would go cold and forgotten—at least by law enforcement.

Her Friday shift was busy, similar to the Memorial Day and Fourth of July weekends. It was everyone's last hurrah at the lake before the children went back to school. In the late afternoon, a thunderstorm moved in. Joleigh's windshield wipers worked double-time on her way back to the cabin.

Joleigh ran from the truck's parking spot behind the woodshed, dodging several puddles until she reached the cabin, and hurried inside. After toeing off her wet tennis shoes, Joleigh set them on an old towel of hers next to the front door so she wouldn't get mud on the braided rug. Although the temperature still hovered around seventy, the rain had chilled her. She took a warm sponge bath in the bathroom then dressed in comfortable shorts and a T-shirt.

As Joleigh leaned over the kitchen table to study the house blueprints, her hair, damp from the rain, gave off the aroma of her homemade lemongrass shampoo. Rain pelted the roof, competing with the transistor radio blaring out "No Matter What" by Badfinger. Another Friday night alone. Joleigh was well aware she was in the prime of her life and should have been out having fun with friends. Or dating. Or married. She might as well throw fictitious children on that list too.

As if her thoughts on love and family had crawled into the radio, it began playing "Witch Doctor," a song that triggered memories of Joleigh and Unity dancing and singing along with the silly song. Joleigh jumped up from the chair, belting out words she hadn't heard in years about how to win someone's heart. She danced around the small kitchen, feeling as if Unity were alongside her, singing and kicking up her heels.

And because of all the noise, it was as if a bolt of lightning hit Joleigh when the door burst open and a young man stepped inside, dripping wet on the braided rug, his eyes as wide as hers.

Chapter Fifteen

Joleigh stopped mid-word, mid-movement, mid-heartbeat, then screamed. She backed up and grabbed the cast-iron frying pan drying on the kitchen counter, ready to wield it.

"Who are you?" the man asked, shaking his wet arms and legs like a dog fresh out of the lake. He was tall and younger-looking than her, and he didn't give off the vibe of a killer.

She leaned over and turned down the radio. The man seemed less shocked to see Joleigh than she was to see him. "Um, I was going to ask you the same thing." She tried for a haughty air as if she was the one who belonged there.

"I'm David Grady. Are you a long-lost cousin of mine or something?" He scrunched his eyes and tilted his head, probably searching through his memory banks for an Asian relative.

Is he a grandson of the infamous Shady Grady who died last year?

"I'm Joleigh." She was too busy fighting off a panic attack to offer her last name. "What are you doing here? There's no hunting now, is there?" *What would they hunt in early September?*

David set a duffel bag down on the rug, closed the door behind him, and tugged off tennis shoes that squeaked with moisture. "Nope, but nobody has used the cabin for almost two years. We've been planning a trip here to make sure everything was okay before deer hunting but couldn't make it up until this weekend."

"We?" Joleigh said weakly, bracing herself for an onslaught of men parading through the door. Her eyes widened as she thought about him being a hunter. He might have a rifle with him, but his friendly attitude told her he didn't seem like the type who would shoot her.

"Probably just my brother, Franklin, but maybe our dad too. Do you know Franklin or my dad?" He swiped back his dark, wavy hair, wiping raindrops from his face.

"Um, no." Joleigh silently berated herself for thinking nobody would show up to check on the place. She'd become complacent.

"Edward's my dad. How are we related?"

Joleigh didn't answer. The game was over. She was so tired of lying and of juggling the lies. She closed her eyes and took a deep breath. He appeared harmless... unless he turned her in to the police. "Can we sit and I'll explain?"

"Do you mind if I change out of my wet clothes first?" He pointed toward the bedroom.

Joleigh winced. She'd taken over the bedroom as if she owned the place. "No, go ahead."

DAVID PICKED UP HIS duffel bag, walked into the bedroom, and closed the door. While he changed his clothes, Joleigh gathered her personal items from the kitchen, canned goods, her dish towels from home, her favorite can opener...

Everything sat on the kitchen counter by the time he'd entered.

"How did you get here?" David asked as he towel dried his hair. "I didn't see a vehicle in the driveway."

Joleigh sat at the kitchen table, and when David took a seat across from her, she blinked back tears. *Good God, don't cry in front of him!*

"What's wrong?" David groaned and leaned back in his chair. "Ugh, please don't cry. I have seven sisters—you may have met some of them—and I'll just say I'm sorry right now if you're going to cry because of me." He winced.

Joleigh's shoulders relaxed. "You did nothing wrong." She gave him a half smile. "Your sisters have you trained well to apologize ahead of time."

David grinned. "You've clearly not met them or you'd know how assertive they can be." He leaned his elbows on the table, his face close enough for her to spot some peach fuzz on his chin. She guessed him to be in his late teens.

"In answer to one of your questions, my truck is in the back, behind the shed." Joleigh cleared her throat. No need to tell him she parked there to hide it. "In answer to your other question, I can explain, but I have a question of my own first."

He nodded for her to go ahead.

"Do you have a gun in your vehicle?"

David's eyes widened. "No, why do you ask?"

Joleigh stood, walked to the cupboard for a glass, and filled it with water from the sink. "Want one?" She held it up before taking a long drink.

"I guess. Got any beer?"

Joleigh eyed him. "Are you old enough?" Then she berated herself. *Who am I to question* him *about breaking the law?*

"Um, I missed the cutoff by two months when Minnesota raised the drinking age from eighteen to nineteen last year." David shrugged. "But hey, I just started college. Doesn't that count for something?" He batted his eyes, and any fear Joleigh had of him hurting her evaporated.

Joleigh filled another glass and took a seat at the table again. "Sorry, I don't have any beer." She set the water in front of him. "Okay. I'm going to tell you everything, so please don't interrupt, or yell, or hit me, until I'm done." She let out a ragged breath. "Well, I hope you don't do any of that even after I'm done."

Slowly, Joleigh relayed how she'd stowed away in the back of her neighbor's station wagon, sneaking out when he stopped to eat at

Ruby's. She explained how she'd overheard Ken talking about the cabin's vacancy for almost two years and gestured to the calendar on the wall, still turned to November 1975.

"I biked out here and found the hidden key. I didn't have my pickup with me then, and I had planned to camp out somewhere until I decided if I was going to stay in the area or not."

David folded his arms over his chest, his eyes squinting in what she hoped was curiosity, not indecision about whether or not to turn her in.

"When Ruby offered me a job, I promised her I'd work at least through the summer, and I didn't want to tent it for three months." Joleigh took a breath and raised a finger as she listed each accomplishment. "I fixed the screen on the door and two of the windows, put new flashing around the stovepipe on the roof, and reattached loose shingles. I mailed a money order to the electric company and paid ahead on the bill, and I filled the propane tank outside for the stove. Oh, and I've been cutting firewood."

Joleigh slowed her words, realizing she sounded like a used-car salesman. "I know it's wrong, but the motels and resorts were booked for the summer." She picked at a cuticle. "I swear I've never done anything like this before."

David sat slack-jawed and silent.

"Please, say something," she said. "I'm so sorry for breaking in and squatting here."

"You asked me not to talk," David reminded her. "And I'm not sure what you want me to say. Am I supposed to yell at you?" Confusion creased his forehead.

"Please don't." She held up a hand. "I can't believe you did as I asked."

He chuckled. "Remember, I've got seven sisters, so I know I better listen or else."

Joleigh leaned back in her chair. "I've got a motel room lined up for the winter, but I can't check in until the first of November." That was two months away. "I bought property down Lonesome Road. I'll pack up right now, and I can stay there in my tent."

David shook his head. "You can't do that, especially tonight! You'll get soaked." He looked around the cabin as if he could hide her somewhere. "Could you sleep in your pickup for the weekend? We'll be leaving here on Monday, and you could move right back in."

Joleigh's hopes rose until David palmed his forehead.

"Oh shit! I forgot—some of the family is coming up to bowhunt in October. We'll be here for rifle season in November, but you said you'd be living in the motel by then." He rubbed his temples. "Ugh, and Franklin and Dad won't be happy about this." He stood and began pacing.

"Will they turn me in?" Joleigh looked at her watch. "How soon do you think they'll be here?" She rose and made her way to the bedroom, where she pulled several empty boxes from under the bed and filled them with clothing.

"Probably within an hour." David stood in the doorway of the bedroom, cracking his knuckles while Joleigh tossed everything from the dresser drawers into the boxes.

"How can I help? I feel like a heel, kicking a woman out into the rain. Maybe I can reason with my brother—and Dad, if he shows up..."

It was obvious to Joleigh by the pained look on David's face that he didn't believe for a minute he could reason with them.

"It's okay. I've lived in the woods before. I knew this day was coming." She handed David a box. "You can help by boxing up the things on the kitchen counter."

As David packed up her kitchen items, he said, in a loud enough voice that Joleigh could hear him over the downpour, "Franklin's a nice guy. It's just that sometimes he doesn't go with the flow. Vietnam did a number on him years ago."

Joleigh eyed his expression as she packed a box of clothing. "It's okay. You don't need to explain anything." She surveyed the room, relieved that everything of hers had been boxed up in a matter of a few minutes. "Do you want me to strip the bed?" she asked as she stepped inside the bathroom and scooped her few personal items into a bag.

"Nope, you can leave it. If Dad comes, he'll sleep in there, or Franklin. I'll sleep on one of the sleeper sofas. They live in Mason City, about two hours from here, and I just started college in Mankato. That's why I got here before them. Franklin planned to leave around seven." David didn't have to say anything else. Joleigh understood she needed to leave right away.

"I'm really sorry. Are you sure you're gonna be okay in your tent?" David grabbed his jacket, and Joleigh held out a hand to stop him.

"Don't apologize for kicking me out of a place I never should've been in. I'm the one who is sorry, and I am grateful you aren't turning me in." Joleigh slipped on her still-damp tennis shoes, wishing she had brought in her waders from the truck and that she hadn't parked her truck so far away. "You stay here. No need to get wet again. And don't worry about me in the tent. I'll sleep in the back seat of my truck tonight and set up the tent tomorrow."

"You said your property is down Lonesome Road? If I find anything of yours, I can sneak out of here tomorrow and drop it off."

"Thank you. I work at Ruby's at noon, so if you don't see my truck, I'm between the creek and the lake on the right-hand side, less than a mile off County Road Twelve." Joleigh had three boxes stacked next to the door, along with her backpack and canvas bag. "My splitting maul is out by the wood pile. I'll get that and my bike. I think that's it."

After slipping into her rain poncho, Joleigh made three trips to her truck and shoved boxes aside in the back to make room for her bike. Her few items from the fridge went in the cooler.

David stood in the open doorway and waved as Joleigh honked the horn before pulling out of the driveway. She prayed she wouldn't meet a vehicle on their long driveway, and when she made it to Lonesome Road, her shoulders relaxed as she took a left and drove away.

Chapter Sixteen

Franklin pulled into the pot-holed driveway of the cabin, his windshield wipers keeping a frantic pace. Light shone through the downpour, and he'd barely put the truck in park before David jogged down the steps, crouched under his hooded jacket.

David helped Franklin unload his overnight bag, a few tools, an instantly soaked brown paper bag with a few groceries, and a case of beer. They'd just stepped into the cabin when David popped open a beer.

"Thirsty?" Franklin grinned at his little brother.

David appeared jumpy and wouldn't look him in the eye. "A bit." He shrugged out of his jacket, pulled off his wet tennis shoes, and headed to the fridge to put the beer away, during which time he kept one out.

Franklin accepted the can from David, cracked it open, and studied the interior of the cabin. It didn't smell musty and appeared cleaner than he ever remembered seeing it. "Wow, you must've got here early. You already cleaned out all the mouse turds?"

"Yup. It wasn't bad. I think one of our relatives has been here. The place was clean, and someone fixed the screen door." David's knee bounced as he sat on one of the sleeper sofas and took a long drink from his beer.

"Huh." The news surprised Franklin, since he'd checked with the two uncles who lived in Minnesota. Neither had mentioned any family members opening up the cabin.

He unpacked before plopping down on the other sleeper sofa across from David, their long legs resting on the empty cardboard beer case between them. They stayed up late, catching up on life since David had left for college two weeks ago, and although his brother seemed preoccupied, Franklin let it be.

Probably college or girl problems. A good night's sleep and plenty of fresh air in the coming days would fix whatever was eating at David.

FRANKLIN WOKE BEFORE David, thanks to the sunshine filtering through the bedroom window. He made coffee and was on his second cup before David woke up.

"It's about time, lazy ass," he said when David poked his head out of his sleeping bag on the sleeper sofa. "We've got wood to cut, and Dad reminded me the flashing around the stovepipe was loose two years ago, although I didn't hear it flapping last night. The rain probably drowned out the sound."

David sat up and shot a wide-eyed look at Franklin.

"What? Are you afraid of going up on the roof? I can do it if you want..." They both knew that was an idle threat. With Franklin's ankle finally healing, the last place he wanted to be was on a ladder. But he enjoyed picking on his younger brother, happy to have a brother at all. After seven sisters, he had thought for sure he would be the only guy in their family besides their dad. And Dad wasn't exactly a barrel of fun.

David cleared his throat. "Um, I think someone might've already done some of the work around here."

"You think so? Guess we'll find out when I boost you up on the roof, right?" Franklin grinned. "I'll whip us up a big breakfast if you tackle the roof while I check the woodpile."

"Sure. Maybe whoever was here also cut firewood."

Franklin stepped outside while David got dressed, the air thick with humidity from the previous night's rain. He forgot how loud the birds sounded when there were no other competing noises. David joined him a minute later. They walked to the woodshed and found it filled with split wood. More was neatly stacked behind the shed.

"Guess you were right." Franklin nodded at the piles. "I wonder who was here." The cousins he thought may have done the work were not ones he would consider neat and tidy.

"Want to give me a boost so I can check the flashing?" David asked. "I don't trust the railing anymore." The railing on the front steps used to be sturdy enough to stand on, so a person could hoist themselves from it up onto the roof, but David was fifty pounds heavier since the last time he stood on the railing.

But before Franklin could answer, something caught his eye, and he let out a laugh.

"What's wrong?" David walked over to Franklin to see what he was looking at.

David's sharp intake of air at seeing the bra, panties, jean shorts, and tank top hanging from the makeshift clothesline told Franklin all he needed to know.

Especially when David muttered, "Oh shit."

Franklin slapped David on the shoulder. "Are those yours?"

David opened and closed his mouth like a fish out of water. "Um, maybe they're one of our cousins' girlfriends'?"

Franklin cast David a sideways glance. In 'Nam, they trusted fellow soldiers because their lives depended on them, but nobody else could be trusted in war. And while he was fighting for his country, Franklin's fiancée had deserted him for a schmuck she met at college, adding to his mistrust. He was even second-guessing his brother now.

"Well, that should make for interesting conversation when everyone's here to hunt this fall. We'll leave them there." Franklin elbowed him. "Let's get you on the roof."

David strapped Franklin's tool belt around his waist. With one foot on Franklin's locked hands and the other on the railing, David hoisted himself onto the roof and checked it out. "Someone repaired the flashing. Looks like they nailed down the loose shingles too," he yelled down to Franklin.

"Wow. I guess we can always cut more firewood, right?" Franklin helped David down.

"Sure." When they drove by the side of the shed to head into the woods, Franklin spotted an axe leaning against the shed. "Looks like our cousins left their axe behind."

David grunted a response, something about a hard-working cousin. Franklin struggled to think of who it might be, but with three generations using the cabin over the decades, it was a waste of his brain power. He would rather concentrate on enjoying a weekend outside doing manual labor, bonding with his brother, and not having to worry about his damn ankle anymore.

They drove into the woods behind the cabin and parked the truck, then they worked for two hours, cutting, splitting, and loading firewood into the back of David's truck.

When they were done, David wiped his forehead with the bottom of his T-shirt. "I'm ready for that breakfast you promised."

"Me too. Even though you didn't end up repairing anything on the roof, I'll feed you anyway, only because you're too skinny." Franklin poked at David's torso. He'd grown five inches during his senior year of high school, but his weight hadn't caught up yet.

David parked the truck next to the shed so they could unload the firewood after breakfast. When he hopped out of the truck, he muttered, "Son of a bitch!"

Franklin hurried around the truck to David's side. "What's wrong?"

David winced. "Nothing. Nothing's wrong."

As much as Franklin hated to ask what was eating at David—a question he avoided asking his sisters too—he had to find out what was bothering him.

But David wasn't paying attention to him. Instead, he was staring at the shed.

Something was off. "Hey, where's the axe?" Franklin circled the shed as if the axe had legs and could move on its own.

David rubbed the back of his neck and let out a drawn-out groan.

Franklin went to stand in front of him. "Care to tell me what's going on here?" He put his hand on David's shoulder.

"Um, it's hard to explain."

"Try me."

David acted like a dog that had peed on the carpet, looking everywhere but toward the master who was giving him the stink-eye. He kicked at the ground as his words stumbled over each other, and Franklin listened, his body stiffening with every sentence.

"Where is this woman now?" he asked.

"Joleigh bought property down Lonesome Road from Ruby at Ruby's Restaurant. Honest, she was going to move out soon, but she can't get a motel room until November. She's going to stay at the motel this winter and then build on her lot next summer."

Franklin surprised himself by letting out a guffaw.

"What?" David eyed him warily, as if Franklin had come unhinged.

"Did you two have coffee together? You sure know a lot about her, this lumberjack girl. Hell, you even remember her name." He winked. "How old is she? Do you have a crush on her? Although if she is strong enough to cut and split wood, she probably looks like

Paul Bunyan." Franklin chuckled at his own joke and led the way inside the cabin. "You can tell me more about her while I cook breakfast. And we can decide what to do about her breaking and entering."

As the eldest child, Franklin was used to calling the shots. And he couldn't do that on an empty stomach.

Chapter Seventeen

After a restless night in the back seat of her pickup, Joleigh crawled out as the sun rose on the horizon, illuminating fog hovering above the dewy grass after last night's rain. She inhaled the earthy aroma of damp leaves as she stretched out kinks, feeling like she was eighty years old instead of twenty-eight.

Joleigh started a fire with her fire stick and moss, adding pine sap to get it going, since the rain had drenched everything. She pulled out the five-gallon bucket containing some of her tools from the truck bed then looked for her axe to make wood shavings to build the fire up.

It wasn't there. She'd taken her splitting maul but forgotten the axe by the woodpile at the cabin. If David didn't get a chance to drop it off, she could stop there after they left on Monday. She'd left clothes on the line at the cabin, too, she realized.

Joleigh was raking a level, open space to set up the two tents when a chainsaw revved in the woods behind the hunting cabin. It had to be David and his brother and father, away from the cabin—and she needed her axe. While the men cut wood, Joleigh biked to the edge of the Grady property.

Between the noise of the chainsaw, she heard men talking in the woods and hoped the coast was clear. She made a beeline for the axe before heading to the clothesline. Joleigh blushed as she yanked her bra and panties from the line, hoping they hadn't noticed them from the other side of the cabin. She crammed everything into the bike basket and pedaled back to her property.

Joleigh used the axe for wood shavings to add to the fire, finished putting up her tent, and set up a tripod of symmetrical branches tied together at the top with parachute rope over the fire. She gathered water from Lonesome Creek and hung a pot from the tripod to use for boiling water. She'd kept two glass jars from the orange juice she'd bought and would use them to hold her drinking water.

Joleigh was busy cutting white pine branches to use for bedding under her sleeping bag when a man's voice broke her concentration.

"Hey!"

She whipped around, almost dropping her hacksaw. A tall, bald man stomped through the woods toward her, his long legs stepping over fallen logs and brush. It was broad daylight, and she had a hacksaw in her hand. Joleigh braced herself for a potential attack. For a second, she questioned if she'd settled on the wrong property.

"Are you Joleigh?" he barked as he came nearer.

"Yes." Her shoulders relaxed. If he planned to attack her, he wouldn't care who she was.

"You broke into my family's cabin?" The man was baiting her with a question he obviously knew the answer to. He wore jeans and an oversized, grease-stained plaid shirt that matched the smear of grease on one of his cheeks.

He must be David's father. "Mr. Grady?" she asked.

"You got that right." He stood several yards away, his arms folded over his chest. "You want to explain why the hell you thought you had the right to help yourself to our cabin?"

Apologize, Joleigh, just apologize a hundred times. "I'm so sorry, Mr. Grady! I apologized to your son, too, and explained how I ended up there. Not that it helps. Did you talk to your son?" Maybe David hadn't explained the work she'd done on the cabin.

"My son? What the hell are you talking about?" He wrinkled his nose as if she'd asked if he'd talked to a chipmunk.

David walked toward them from the road, and Joleigh sighed in relief. He would help smooth things over.

"David, thank goodness you're here. I was just explaining to your father about how I ended up staying in your—"

David's loud guffaw cut off her words. He bent over and clutched his stomach. His body shook with gut-busting laughter. "Oh, Joleigh, you made my day." He gasped, trying to catch his breath.

"I did?" She was certain she hadn't made his dad's day.

"Yep." It took a few more seconds before David composed himself. Meanwhile, Mr. Grady stood between them.

David's grin was so wide, Joleigh thought his cheeks would split. "Joleigh? I'd like you to meet my *brother*, Franklin."

Joleigh watched David's brother look down and inspect his dirty clothes, including the wood chips hanging from his baggy jeans. He took the tail of his shirt to wipe his face and bald head as if he'd just realized he might look a mess.

"I'm glad you think it's funny," Franklin huffed to David, who was still wiping tears with one hand and hugging his torso with the other.

"And for your information..." Franklin puffed out his chest and glared at Joleigh. "I'm only thirty." He took a step closer to her, his gray eyes pale against his tanned—and dirty—skin. "Yes, David told me how you ended up in the cabin. Doesn't make it okay."

"You're right, but I tried to compensate for it. I cut and split wood, filled the propane tanks, and paid ahead on the electric bill. I'm so sorry."

Franklin squinted, and he gave a slight nod. "You fixed the flashing on the roof?"

"Yes. I heard the flashing rattling and figured it was loose. I fixed some shingles too."

"How did you get up there?"

"I made a ladder from tree limbs. It's leaning behind the big oak tree by the cabin."

"You made a ladder?" He sounded like a parrot repeating her words.

"It's not that hard. My pet frog could make one." She rolled her eyes.

"You have a pet frog?" Franklin and David said together.

"No, but if I did, it could have figured out how to make a ladder. Geez."

Franklin pointed at the tools she had near her on the ground. "These are yours?"

"Yes. I brought my own tools from Missouri, things I can use here for clearing out the lot in case I build next spring."

"You're going to build your own house?" His voice raised an octave as if the idea was too ridiculous for him to believe. "Where did you live before this, in the jungle with Tarzan?"

"Yes. Call me Jane." Joleigh glared at him. "So, are you turning me in or not? Because if you're not, I've got work to do here."

Franklin turned to David, who'd been mysteriously quiet since his laughing jag. *Would he stand up for me if Franklin presses charges? And what would the cops do?* Joleigh hadn't vandalized the place. Still, she had knowingly broken the law.

Joleigh read the seesaw of emotions on Franklin's face as if there were a devil on one shoulder and an angel on the other. But when she removed her work gloves and put her hands on her hips, she watched his shoulders drop, his demeanor softening.

"Well?" She didn't have all day for him to decide.

He blew out a long breath and ran a hand over his shiny head. "Only a real piece of shit would turn in a woman who still wears a POW bracelet four years after they released them from 'Nam. But stay off our property from now on." His chin jutted out as he eyed

Joleigh. "Anything else you think you've left there? I see you collected your lingerie from the clothesline." He smirked.

So much for them not spotting her underthings on the line. "Nope."

"Good." He stood there a few seconds more before he turned and stomped back to the road, likely assuming David would follow.

Instead, David stayed. "I'm sorry he's being such a horse's ass." He kicked at the ground with his work boot. "Franklin's not always this grumpy." He tilted his head as he went on to explain a few things about his brother. "On the upside, he won't call the cops." He pointed at Joleigh's wrist. "He's got a soft spot for anyone who gave a shit about Vietnam."

Joleigh mouthed a thank-you to David before he turned and followed Franklin off her property. She gently rubbed the nickel-plated POW bracelet on her wrist and imagined the prisoner of war's family and of all they'd lost.

AN HOUR LATER, AS JOLEIGH drove to town to buy camping supplies before her noon shift at Ruby's, she thought about what David had said after Franklin stomped away. *Franklin's a good guy behind his gruffness. Vietnam did a number on him.* She knew what the war had done to Mack, and her animosity toward Franklin lessened.

At the hardware store, she purchased a large cooler, a five-gallon plastic collapsible water container, a cheap shower curtain, more rope, and a tarp. She would have to buy ice every couple of days and minimize grocery purchases that needed to be kept cold. A free hot meal at Ruby's every day she worked would help. She was tempted to ask Ruby if she could take ice from the restaurant, but then she would also have to explain why she needed it.

By the time she finished work at seven, Joleigh had about an hour of daylight to unload her purchases back at the property. She unfolded the large tarp and tied it to stakes she'd made from cutting tree limbs. It draped over a taller stake in the middle to help the rain drain to the sides instead of pooling and was enough to cover her tent and the surrounding area. Before Joleigh had left for work, she'd dug a trench around the area to reroute any rain falling from the canopy tarp over the tent.

Emotionally drained after her long day of conflict with Franklin, followed by a busy holiday weekend at Ruby's, she unloaded her new cooler and set it on a sled of blocks she'd made to keep it off the ground. She'd made two narrow skis for the bottom and looped the rope through the end so she could pull it.

Joleigh took out the collapsible water container and grabbed her towel, soap, and shampoo before making her way to Lonesome Creek for a quick sponge bath. In the morning, she would set up the shower curtain between two limbs to create a circle of privacy.

By the time Joleigh settled into the tent for the night, her chest burst with a pride she hadn't experienced in ages. Everything Unity had taught her over the years was coming back into play. The Grass Roots song "Walking Through the Country," a song from the year she graduated, played in her mind as she listened to the night sounds harmonize outside the tent and felt at ease, just as the song lyrics said. She fell asleep with a smile.

OVER THE COMING WEEKS, Joleigh embraced the beauty of early fall surrounding her, the simplicity of living with the land. Several maple trees burst with color around her campsite. The summer mosquitos dwindled with the cooler days and nights, and Joleigh relished walking the property, making discoveries, and watching deer, turkeys, and other wildlife. So far, she'd seen no sign of a bear, but she was careful to keep minimal food nearby. She missed her chickens and goats and Mr. and Mrs. Hoover. But they were all she missed from Woodland.

Joleigh found rose hips and wintergreen berries to make tea, along with more vibrant orange chicken-of-the-woods mushrooms and clumps of honey mushrooms for soup. She would love to bring Bits out here but wasn't ready yet to show Bits where she lived, since everyone still believed she was living at the Grady family cabin.

With Bits back in school, Joleigh picked her up for breakfast at Ruby's every Saturday. Afterward, they walked to the park or along the beach before Joleigh brought Bits home by eleven so she could get ready to work at Ruby's at noon.

There had been no activity at the Grady cabin since David and Franklin left on Labor Day. In the few weeks of living on her property, Joleigh had enough wood cut, split, and stacked to last her several months. She'd cleared a driveway that extended past her campsite, back to where she envisioned a small home. But as much as she enjoyed the land, something niggled at her. Something too familiar.

It was *too* quiet. She had too much alone time. *I'm right back to living like I was in Woodland*, she thought. *Minus my animals, minus Unity, minus Mack.*

Although Woodland had lost its luster for Joleigh, she realized that if not for her work at Ruby's, she would still be alone, still craving something more. She enjoyed her time with Bits, Bernadette, and the people she'd come to know through work, but everything felt so temporary. *Make a decision, Joleigh, and stick to it!*

Joplin and Groovy had settled in at the Hoovers, her poor past-their-prime chickens had been butchered last month, and every step severed more of her ties to Woodland.

But people she loved were buried in Woodland: Joleigh's parents, Unity, and Mack. No matter where she lived, she would always visit their graves. She spoke with Ruby about it one day after work. "Was it difficult for you to leave your family and home?"

"My body left Mille Lacs, not my heart. It's only a few hours away, and that knowledge comforts me," Ruby had said. She'd met her husband, who was from Grandfield, one summer on the shores of Mille Lacs Lake. "I didn't want to move here, but once the restaurant came up for sale, I changed my mind. My parents had owned a café in our hometown. After I opened Ruby's, this became my home away from home."

She understood Ruby's meaning. Woodland held Joleigh's roots, but with each passing month in Grandfield, layers of familiarity molded it to feel more like home.

As Joleigh punched out for her shift, Ruby said, "I keep forgetting to ask you how Teri Grady is doing. Last time Shady was in here, which was at least a couple of years ago, he'd said Teri wasn't doing well."

Joleigh nervously licked her lips. "Um, I think he's doing okay." She assumed he was a son of Shady Grady's.

Ruby raised an eyebrow. "Is that so?"

"Yes, that's what I heard, anyway. I'm pretty sure he's better now." *Dear God, will this lying never end?*

She had five weeks before she could move into the motel. Then she could stop pretending she was still living at the Grady cabin. She flashed Ruby a smile before walking down the hall and out the door, away from Ruby's stare penetrating her back.

IT WASN'T UNTIL JUST before the restaurant closed the following day that Ruby pulled Joleigh aside. "Can you stay after for a few minutes? I need to talk to you about something."

Joleigh's heart skipped a beat. "Sure. In your office?"

"Yes, please."

Once Joleigh's last customer left, she entered Ruby's office.

"Shut the door, please," Ruby said.

Joleigh closed the door and then took a seat opposite Ruby.

Ruby took off her glasses then set them on the desk in front of her and rested her elbows on the desk. "First, I want to let you know how happy I've been with your work over these past months. I try to keep my business and personal life separate, and I don't blame my employees for doing the same. However, there's something I need to address with you."

Joleigh sat in silence, bracing for the unknown.

Ruby leaned forward. "Yesterday, I asked you how Teri Grady was feeling." She nailed Joleigh with a don't-jerk-me-around look. "And I believe you've been lying to me."

Joleigh gulped, needles of remorse pricking her.

"I asked you about Teri, who is a woman, not a man. They diagnosed her with breast cancer a few years ago. She's married to one of Shady's sons. You, however, thought I was talking about a man, which makes me wonder if you're really related to the Gradys." Ruby's dark eyes locked with Joleigh's as if peering into her soul. "What's going on?"

Joleigh was so tired of lying. The question hooked the truth that had been swimming inside Joleigh and yanked it out. Ruby patted Joleigh's hand across the desk, and as Joleigh spilled the facts, they tasted like sweet surrender.

Chapter Eighteen

As Joleigh talked, Ruby crouched in front of Joleigh, listening to her account of the difficult decisions she had made from the moment she'd witnessed Mack's murder.

When Joleigh paused and took a ragged breath, Ruby pulled her in for a hug. "It's okay. It's okay."

After a moment, Ruby leaned back. "When David and Franklin busted you, did you tell them how you ended up in Grandfield?"

Joleigh dabbed her eyes. "I didn't think they'd believe me, and the fewer people who know the truth, the better. Sergeant Williams hasn't caught the men who killed Mack."

Ruby took Joleigh's calloused hand. "Listen, I think you need to tell him about the drug money. It may help with their investigation. You could wire the money to them so you don't have to keep worrying about it." Ruby's mouth pursed as she thought for a moment. "You not spending the money should prove to them you didn't purposely take it. For heaven's sake, you're living in a tent. Who would do that with seven grand tucked away?"

Joleigh nodded. "You're right. I'll call Sergeant Williams tomorrow."

"Where have you been making your calls from?"

"I use the office phone at the motel and pay the Nielsons. I make most of my calls before eight when the rate is cheapest."

"Silly girl. You can do the same here. When I get the phone bill, I'll charge you for the calls you make. And you should call law enforcement *now.*" Ruby reached for the phone on her desk. "I assume you know the number by heart?"

"Yes." Joleigh recited the number. "I'm so glad you're here for moral support."

"It's the least I can do, since I forced you into telling me all this," Ruby said. "Why don't you stay at my house until you can rent the motel room? I've got a small office that has a futon. I can clean it up and make room for you. That way, you aren't in your tent for five more weeks. The weather can dip near freezing at night."

"Thanks for the offer, but I've got a decent setup there. I enjoy working on the property when I have time. If we get a snowstorm before November first, I'll take you up on your offer."

Ruby dialed the phone and handed it to Joleigh. After several rings, the sergeant picked up.

"Williams here." His deep voice sounded like he'd smoked a thousand cigars.

"It's Joleigh Moore, Sergeant. Do you have a minute? I've got more information about the men who murdered Mack." Joleigh took a drink of water from the glass Ruby handed her before going into detail about where she was living and the drug money Mack had stashed in her plant journal.

"So let me get this straight. You've got seven grand with you?" Joleigh heard a muffled "dammit" through the phone.

"Yes. Well, it's in the bank. I put it in a safety-deposit box. I haven't spent any of it, I swear. They're all one-hundred-dollar bills." It was a currency denomination Joleigh had never seen before.

"And when you heard the men talking to Mack, they asked him for the money?"

"I don't remember them specifically saying the word 'money.' They kept asking if he had 'it' and where 'it' was. When I heard him lie about me visiting a sick cousin in Arkansas, I decided that was what I should do—leave town. Since he told them I'd gone south, I figured I should head north. I remembered our neighbor, Mr. Hoover, was driving to pick up his grandson in Minnesota that Saturday."

By the time Joleigh finished unloading every detail, Williams had Joleigh's contact telephone number at Ruby's. She promised to do a money transfer through Western Union in the morning.

"This information helps a lot, Joleigh. Now we have motive and evidence," he said. There was a lot of paper shuffling on the other end of the line then a long pause. "If you have any other information, I *need* it. Every detail counts. I can't stress that enough." The sergeant emphasized each word.

The urgency in his voice put Joleigh on high alert. His reaction was too intense for it to just be because she'd kept the money details from him. She swallowed the bile working up her throat. "What's going on there?" Ruby pulled her chair closer and patted Joleigh's arm.

Williams cleared his throat. "Mack's parents left town last weekend and came home to their house trashed. Doors were still locked, but someone had busted their kitchen window." Joleigh heard the drumming of a pen or pencil on his desk. "We've got no proof it was Mack's killers, but they're like bears, circling back to an area where they're sure someone will feed them. It makes sense they wanted to check his parents' home for the money."

Joleigh's gut churned, her heart breaking for Mack's poor parents. *As if they haven't been through enough.*

"The only decent thing the thugs did was wait until his parents had left town instead of attacking them too," Williams said.

They spoke a few more minutes before hanging up, with a promise from Joleigh that she would let him know if she heard or saw anything on her end—as long as he promised to do the same.

And instead of feeling like she'd purged a toxic secret, Joleigh was now worried they'd never find Mack's killers.

GRANDFIELD HELD ITS annual Oktoberfest celebration the following weekend. Between duck hunting and the town celebration, Ruby's was at full capacity.

Joleigh didn't plan to attend all the festivities, since she worked her regular weekend schedule beginning at noon. The kiddie parade began at ten on Saturday morning, and she picked up Bits early for breakfast so they could watch the parade afterward.

When Bits hopped inside Joleigh's truck, the girl announced, "Papa threw up all night long. His skin is looking mighty yellow," as casually as if she'd told Joleigh she wanted pancakes for breakfast.

Joleigh hadn't seen Howie in two months. She kept the truck in park with the engine running. "Should I go in and check on him?" Their house and yard were off-limits to Joleigh, per his strict instructions.

Bits had pulled her long hair back in a ponytail, and it swished back and forth when she shook her head. "I cleaned up the mess and gave him 7 Up to go with his medicine."

Joleigh had a pretty good idea of what his "medicine" was and why his skin was the color of mustard. She often discussed Bits with Ruby and the network of people who helped the girl and other children in need through the school system. Bits's dad was drinking himself to death. She cringed at what might happen to Bits afterward. Foster care, no doubt—a roller-coaster ride Joleigh was too familiar with.

It grated on Joleigh that there was a line she couldn't cross to help Bits. The best she could do was make every Saturday fun for the girl. Before the Oktoberfest parade, they ordered milk, bacon, and waffles topped with strawberries and whipped cream. After breakfast, they joined the crowd forming on Main Street to watch the kiddie parade.

The rest of the morning flew by. Joleigh dropped Bits off at home before heading to Ruby's for her work shift. Bernadette's ex-husband had their children overnight, and after their shift, Joleigh and Bernadette planned to attend the street dance.

It was after seven thirty when the last customer left Ruby's. Joleigh cleaned up and changed in the restaurant's bathroom before walking to meet Bernadette at the street dance entrance. A band playing songs from the last few decades plus current hits pulsed in the two blocks roped off on Main Street for the dance.

The weather cooperated in that it didn't rain, but the night had cooled enough so that everyone wore a sweatshirt or light jacket. Joleigh, comfortable in jeans and a kelly-green sweatshirt, let Bernadette lead the way through the crowd permeated with the scent of yeasty beer and happiness. She recognized a handful of regulars from Ruby's—including Leo, one of Ruby's cooks—with Peter from the bait shop, both dancing with other teens.

Even Moe was there with a group. "Hi there, ladies." He waved Joleigh and Bernadette over. A woman with long auburn hair and vivid green eyes held Moe's hand. "Bernadette, you know Diane. Joleigh, this is the woman who has put up with me for five years."

Joleigh shook Diane's hand and caught a hint of her Charlie perfume and her wistful look when Moe mentioned five years.

"Nice to meet you. I bet Moe keeps you laughing," Joleigh said.

The woman's smile returned. "He sure does." Diane slid her hand into Moe's again.

"Where do you live?"

"In Minneapolis. Moe and I mostly only see each other on weekends," Diane said.

As they visited, the band got the crowd going with "Twist and Shout."

"Let's dance." Moe wheeled into the dance area with Diane by his side. Bernadette and Joleigh followed the people gravitating toward the band, hands up in the air, hips swiveling. A young man Joleigh didn't recognize tapped Bernadette on the shoulder and asked her to dance.

"Will you hold my beer?" Bernadette handed her cup to Joleigh, making her look like a two-fisted drinker. Still, Joleigh was glad Bernadette was having fun. She tapped her foot to the music and almost tripped when someone came up behind her and pulled her into a side hug.

"Joleigh!" It was David Grady. Some of her beer sloshed on him as he hugged her. "What're you doing here?"

She chuckled at his extra-wide smile, feeling fairly sure he'd spent a few hours at the beer garden.

"I'm here with a friend. She's out dancing, which is how I ended up with two beers." She peered at the beer spilled on his jeans and tennis shoes. "Well, one and a half beers now."

They shouted out a conversation above the noise, and from the few words she understood, it sounded like some of the Gradys were at the cabin for duck hunting.

When the band finished the song, they transitioned right into "Brown-Eyed Girl." And in the middle of Joleigh telling David to stop by her property, someone tugged on Joleigh's elbow, careful not to spill her beer.

"Let's dance, Miss Brown Eyes," Leo said, interrupting Joleigh.

"I'd offer to hold your beer, but it may be gone when you come back," David said.

Joleigh looked around and spotted Bernadette heading her way. "Here comes my friend." She passed off the beer to Bernadette as Leo led the way into the crowd of dancers. Mack had loved to dance, a favorite date-night activity of theirs. She was no dancing queen but good enough not to embarrass herself or her partner.

Leo, a senior in college, had become a good friend. They danced a few songs before he led her back to Bernadette, who was talking to

David. And beside David stood Franklin, wearing a light-gray baseball cap and sweatshirt that highlighted his gray eyes. He gave Joleigh a silent nod before walking away to talk with another group of men.

It was midnight when Joleigh pulled into her driveway. She'd quit drinking beer a few hours earlier, topping the night off with Draft 1919 root beer. When she drove past the Grady cabin, there were several vehicles in the driveway, and the lights were on.

Joleigh pushed the Grady men from her thoughts. After getting ready for bed with the aid of her lantern and flashlight, she snuggled inside her sleeping bag, exhausted but content.

She'd had fun like a normal woman her age. And *normal* felt amazing.

JOLEIGH HAD GONE TRICK-or-treating three times as a child, and the last time was less than two weeks before her parents had died.

The following two Halloweens, Joleigh lived in foster homes. The first year, the foster dad was at work, and they left Joleigh home to care for a two-year-old foster child while the mother took two other children out to trick-or-treat. When she was eleven, she was living in the foster home she'd hoped would become her permanent home. The parents were nice, and they'd cared for Joleigh and spoken of possibly adopting her.

Then the mother's dad moved in with them because of poor health, and the couple found out they were expecting their third child. Joleigh became one more thing for them to deal with. She was expendable. The baby and grandpa were not.

By the time Joleigh had moved in with Unity, she was too old to trick-or-treat, and besides, they lived in the country.

On this Halloween, however, Joleigh dressed in costume for the first time in almost twenty years for her shift at Ruby's. Ruby had encouraged her employees to get in the spirit at work. To prepare her costume, Joleigh had bought two cinnamon rolls from Ruby's a few days earlier to let them dry out. She wrapped them in cellophane, glued them to a headband, and tucked her pigtails underneath the cinnamon rolls. She'd cut up a white sheet and hand-sewn a long-sleeved dress. Joleigh wasn't a dress type of girl, but it was fun to pretend to be Princess Leia from *Star Wars*.

If only she could find her own Han Solo. *Or is it Luke Skywalker?* She could never remember, since she hadn't seen the film. All she knew was that her biological clock was ticking like Big Ben in her head. Whatever had kept her parents from having more children was likely the reason she'd never gotten pregnant with Mack. Not that she planned to have a child before marriage, but even if Mack had lived, she wasn't sure they would ever have married.

They cared about and respected each other. It wasn't enough, yet deep down, Joleigh knew she would have settled for it—exactly what Unity told her *not* to do with her life. Settle.

Joleigh typically had Mondays off but had switched with a waitress who offered to take her Wednesday shift. After work, she would move into the motel room for the winter. It would feel like heaven to wash her hair in a proper shower again.

PRINCESS LEIA STOPPED in the motel office to check in with Mr. Nielson.

"Well, well, I didn't expect to check in a celebrity today." He winked at Joleigh.

Joleigh smiled. "I thought you'd get a kick out of my costume." She took her checkbook out of her canvas shoulder bag. "I'll pay November through March, okay?"

Mr. Nielson shook his head. "You aren't paying to stay here when you're doing us a favor and taking care of the motel." He wagged his finger at her as if she had spit at him.

"At least let me pay for November." The Nielsons weren't leaving until the end of the month, giving them plenty of time to train Joleigh.

"No, ma'am. You'll be doing on-the-job training this month."

Joleigh shook her head. "This was my idea. You're saving me from getting snowed in at my campsite." After Joleigh had told Ruby and Sergeant Williams the truth, she'd come clean with Mr. and Mrs. Nielson. They were as understanding as she had hoped they would be.

They would never have asked the details of what brought her to Grandfield, but not having to hide the truth from them eased the constriction in her chest. She reached into her canvas bag and slid a Zagnut bar over the office counter as Mr. Nielson slid the key for room seven to Joleigh.

"A two-bed room this time. We figured you could use the space, since you'll be here several months."

Joleigh thanked him and took the key. She opened the door to her room and then backed up the truck to unload everything. Items like her chainsaw and garden tools would stay in the truck bed. Her topper had a lock for it, and she would park the truck right outside her room.

On her next day off, she would take down the tent, tarp, and anything else that couldn't withstand snow. Joleigh would miss the peacefulness, but she could drive out and visit the property. The motel business was slow in the winter, since most reservations were made ahead of time. It would help fill her free time as she adjusted to her first winter without Unity or Mack.

Chapter Nineteen

Rifle season for deer hunting opened the first Saturday of November, bringing a sea of men dressed in red or blaze orange to Ruby's Restaurant. Joleigh wove her way through a chorus of exaggerated hunting stories to punch in for her shift at noon.

She'd shown up at Bits's house at nine to pick her up for breakfast, like any other Saturday morning, but Bits never came out of the house. Joleigh had braved a few honks with the truck horn, willing to suffer the wrath of Howie. Neither appeared, and Joleigh hadn't had the courage to leave the truck since Howie had forbidden it.

Her worries about Bits weighed on her mind as she waited on customers.

After the lunch rush, Bits burst through Ruby's door and made a beeline to Joleigh, who was taking an order. Relieved to see that Bits was okay, Joleigh held up a finger to Bits to wait until she finished with the customers.

After Joleigh brought the order back to the kitchen, she walked back to speak with Bits. "Everything okay? Where were you this morning?"

"I can't stay in town, or Papa will get angry," Bits whispered. They stood off to the side of the cashier counter for privacy. "He's hurting bad and told me I couldn't leave him this morning. He ran out of medicine, though, so that's why I biked to town."

"Your dad is still sick from a couple of weeks ago?" Joleigh tried to keep the frustration out of her words. His poor health decisions meant his young daughter had to bike to town in the biting weather.

"Yep. And it's cold in our house. The water froze in my cup last night."

Joleigh wanted to pull more information from Bits, but she had customers to wait on. "Tell you what. You go do your shopping and then come back here, okay?"

Bits agreed and ran out the door, leaving Joleigh's thoughts scrambling for ways she could help Bits. She didn't know if they used electricity, propane, or a wood-burning stove to heat their mobile home. She would talk to Ruby about it after she got more information from the girl.

By the time Bits came back to the restaurant carrying a ragged backpack, Joleigh had a break before the supper rush hit. "Did you get everything you needed for your dad?" Joleigh nodded to the backpack.

"Yes, most everything until I ran out of money."

"Can I look?" Joleigh was curious about what "medicine" he required.

"Sure."

Bits slid the backpack over. Joleigh unzipped it. The girl needed a new backpack, something Joleigh wished she had looked for at the garage sales that summer. Inside were two bottles of cough medicine with enough alcohol to put anyone to sleep for two days, a bottle of sleeping pills, some quaaludes, a Hershey's candy bar, and Ritz crackers.

Joleigh took Bits's grimy hand, noting that the girl's fingernails were in need of a trim. "Bits, have you told your teacher about your dad being sick and that your heat isn't working?"

Bits shook her head. "Papa says if I tell the teachers, he'll whup me. But he never said I couldn't tell *you*." She gave Joleigh a sly smile. "That's why I came to see you. It's getting cold out, and we've got no more wood. You said before that you cut firewood."

"That's what you heat with? You have a wood stove in your house?"

"Yes, but there's no more wood for me to put in the stove."

Joleigh eyed her tables to make sure they didn't need anything. She wished she knew more about Bits's family so she could let them know Bits needed help. "Do you have any grandparents?" She knew of Bits's mother's death but nothing about the rest of her family.

"Papa says his parents went to heaven. He's got a brother, but Papa said he lives clear across the United States in a place called California, crowded with too many people. Papa doesn't like people."

"Okay." Joleigh let out a long sigh. "I've got to get back to work, but I'll see what I can do. Do you have enough blankets?"

"We've got a couple. And Papa and I wore our winter coats to bed last night."

Joleigh cringed at the image, wishing she could leave work right then to deliver wood. "I'm off work at seven tonight. Tell your dad I'll be there later tonight with wood, and I don't want him yelling at me when I get out of the truck. I'll unload enough wood to get you by for a couple of days until I can talk to other people who will help." She squeezed Bits's hand. "You remember I'm staying at the motel now, right? I'm in room seven."

Bits nodded, and Joleigh hugged her before heading back to wait on customers.

Joleigh was cleaning off a table for eight when a man tapped her shoulder and asked if they could sit there.

She looked up at the man who'd spoken. "Sure. How many in your group?" Several others stood behind him, wearing hunting coats.

"Seven." He pointed at the group. "I'll try to keep them in line." His smile looked familiar.

Joleigh chuckled. "I'll hold you to that." She wiped the last of the crumbs into her palm with a wet rag. "Have a seat, and I'll bring your menus and water."

Several of the men were busy talking to one another, not giving her any more attention than she gave them—until she walked past the group to get their menus and recognized two of the men at the table. Franklin and David.

David waved. "Hey there, Joleigh!"

She watched him elbow Franklin, who was talking to another man. Joleigh waved to David before setting the group's menus on the table, her heart tripling its speed as she headed to the water station for a tray and seven water glasses.

Joleigh didn't mind waiting on David. Franklin was another story.

The group, which must have consisted of members of the Grady family, appeared to be in a good mood. Maybe their hunting party had started out the season by bagging a few nice bucks.

She walked around the table with their water glasses. "Hello, I'm Joleigh, and today's specials are chicken pot pie or our seven-layer lasagna served with a breadstick and salad. I'll give you a few minutes to look over the menu."

As she walked away to take orders at another table, she said a silent prayer that neither Franklin nor David would bring up how she'd helped herself to their family cabin.

Joleigh braced herself for a possible verbal attack as she walked back to the Grady table. The man who appeared to be the oldest gave her a squinty glare, a look she'd seen many times over the years, a look that said, *I'm not sure I trust you.*

He appeared around the age her dad would have been. He might have also served in the Korean War and may have felt the same about Koreans as Peter's mom.

The talkative man who had spoken to her when they arrived appeared to be close to her age. She stood next to his chair, across from Franklin's, ready to take their orders, and asked, "Any questions about the menu?"

Mr. Chatty nudged the baby-faced young man on his other side. "He does. He wants to know what your phone number is." A few of the men chuckled. The guy who was being teased turned beet red, and Joleigh's cheeks grew warm.

Flirtation, like prejudice, was best ignored.

Franklin stared down the man across from him. "Not funny."

"I wasn't trying to be funny, Franklin." The talker grimaced. He turned to Joleigh, looking up from his chair. "I'm sorry. I embarrassed you when I was only trying to embarrass my little brother here." His smile was genuine, and it softened Joleigh. "You're pretty and nice, and although my cousin Franklin is a grumpkin, I was simply trying to compliment you."

Joleigh couldn't remember the last time a man told her she was pretty. Mack used to make comments about her flawless skin, her thick and shiny hair, her muscles—but she didn't remember him calling her pretty.

She focused on taking their orders instead of the man's compliment. They all ordered one of the specials, making it easy. She began to relax. If Franklin or David had said anything about Joleigh living in the cabin, surely someone would have commented.

When it was time to deliver their food, the Grady men were all so busy talking about who shot the biggest buck, who shot "like a girl," and who would sit in which stand for the afternoon hunt that nobody paid her any attention.

So it caught her off guard when she brought them their bill and David spoke up. "Hey, everyone, remember when I told you last night about the local woman we let stay at the cabin for a few weeks until she could rent a room?" His raised voice got the men's attention, including Franklin's. His gaze drifted to Joleigh.

Joleigh's backbone straightened. *Here it comes*, she thought.

"Yep, why?" one of them asked.

"This is her. Joleigh's the one who made the nice rug next to the front door, fixed the screen door and the flashing on the roof, and cut and split all that firewood." David beamed as if he was a proud parent.

Joleigh was impressed with how he had twisted the situation so that it appeared they'd made the arrangement ahead of time.

"Holy hell, you cut and split that wood? I'm impressed," Mr. Chatty said. "Remind me not to mess with you."

"Will you please leave her alone?" Franklin clenched his jaw.

"Hey, what did I say? I'm impressed, that's all." Mr. Chatty held up his hands as if to fight off an invisible punch. "What the hell crawled up your butt?" He muttered it as if to himself, but Joleigh was pretty sure the question was for Franklin, who, she agreed, was acting like a jerk.

"Thank you. I take that as a compliment." She smiled at Mr. Chatty. "I grew up in Missouri and learned to live off the land. My adopted mother taught me how to cut and split wood, said it was purposeful exercise."

Joleigh handed him the bill, thanked them all, and collected several empty plates. "So, who is in charge of the cabin here? David was nice enough to work with me on staying at the cabin for a few weeks, but I have a favor to ask the decision-maker here." She would have batted her eyes if it had been her style.

All the men turned to the gruff-looking elder who'd given her the steely glare earlier. *Oh great.* Joleigh had hoped it would be Mr. Chatty, who seemed to like her. It was time to roll out a sales pitch, another trait she'd learned from Unity over the years.

The older man, who was seated at the other end of the table, took a long sip from the coffee she'd refreshed for him and raised his eyebrows as if to say, *Go ahead.*

"First, I appreciate the generosity of the Grady family for letting me stay at your cabin," she began. "I can only imagine the fun memories made there over the decades. It reminded me a little of the home I grew up in after my parents died when I was young. The woman who took me in is the person who taught me to do for myself. And to do for others."

Joleigh graced him with the most genuine smile she could muster. "Since you were so generous in letting me stay at the cabin, would you be willing to donate a little of the wood I cut? It's for a good cause. There's a young girl who lives with her ailing dad outside of town, just past your place. Ruby can attest they're a family in need. They ran out of wood the other day. I'm dropping off some of my own after work tonight, but I would like to round up more for them."

The man took another long drink of coffee, meeting her eyes. Nobody said a word, waiting for his decision, and Joleigh held her breath.

"You're donating your wood or ours?" He leaned his elbows on the table. "I don't give a rat's ass if you cut it. It's still our wood."

Franklin flinched. "Dad! Joleigh has property of her own now down Lonesome Road. She's cut wood on her acreage. *That's* the wood she's donating." His look all but added, *You pompous ass.*

It wasn't lost on Joleigh that Franklin, the man who had nailed her to the wall two months ago, was dressing down his father for questioning Joleigh.

Franklin turned to her. "Is this the young girl with long blond hair who bikes down County Road Twelve?"

She nodded, surprised he'd noticed Bits. They must have passed her on their way in or out of town.

"Yes, you can give them whatever wood you cut at our place," Franklin said. "We'll be up one more weekend to hunt, and then we're done for the winter. We've got plenty."

"I agree," David said, and another man chimed in. About the only one who didn't nod along was Franklin and David's father.

"Thank you," Joleigh said and left to wait on another table. She didn't have time to wonder about what had changed Franklin's animosity into kindness. She had no time to think about Franklin at all.

It was near closing time when Joleigh's last customers left. She stopped in Ruby's office. "Do you have a few minutes? I need to talk to you about Bits and her dad." Joleigh repeated what Bits had said about Howie's illness and their lack of firewood.

"It's likely Howie's liver. I think he has cirrhosis. He's stubborn and won't go to a doctor." Ruby sighed. "Can't help much there, but yes, I can contact the other businesses about delivering wood to them. You sure he won't chase you off the property tonight?"

"I told Bits to warn him and also that we'll try to organize another delivery later this week. I'll drop off enough tonight to last them a few days. The Gradys said I could take some of their wood, too, since I cut so much while I stayed at the cabin."

Ruby nodded. "I know a few people with a snowmobile trailer we can use. We can meet at my house, and whoever can donate wood can bring it there," she said. "I'll make some calls tomorrow."

"Thank you. I'll see you tomorrow." Joleigh left the restaurant then stopped in her room to change into wood-hauling clothes and drove out to her property, her work gloves and splitting maul already in the truck. With Bits having to carry the wood, Joleigh wanted to make sure the pieces were light enough.

Once she arrived, she stood for a moment outside the truck. She'd missed her land, even after only being gone for five days. She missed the peacefulness, the hoarfrost covering the branches and ground in the early mornings, and the physical labor of working the land.

But she didn't miss being alone. Ruby's gave her the people fix she needed as much as fresh air, and soon the motel would too.

Joleigh shone the truck headlights on the woodpile, loaded the smallest pieces she could find, and split a few larger ones, which she loaded as well. It would be enough to get them by for a while.

She pulled into their rutted dirt driveway, and Bits appeared at the door, waving. "Your dad is okay with me unloading this wood by your steps?" Joleigh hollered out the window before setting foot on the ground.

"Yep. He promised he won't shoot. He's cold." Bits stood with her winter jacket and boots on, a ratty blanket tied around her.

"Can he start the fire or do you want me to help?" Joleigh wasn't keen on stepping inside their home, but firewood would do them no good if Bits had to start from scratch to get it going.

"We have matches and newspaper."

Joleigh unloaded the wood as close as possible to the rotted, dank steps, where she insisted Bits stay. She didn't need the girl to help unload the wood. It was bad enough that Bits would have to carry it inside. The last trip Joleigh made was with a cardboard box with a few leftover newspapers from Ruby's.

"Here's more kindling and wood shavings. Those will help get the fire going." She handed the box to Bits. "I talked to Ruby about us bringing you more wood. Several people in town have extra firewood. Your job is to make sure your dad lets us on your property, okay?" Joleigh waited until Bits agreed. "We will be back sometime next week. Please make sure he knows that. You'll need a lot of wood for the winter."

Bits's nose was red from the cold. Joleigh reined in her anger toward Howie. He must think wood magically fell from the sky. She guessed the community had stepped up to help out in previous winters.

"I'll stop by here tomorrow morning before I go to work and make sure all is fine," she added. "I'll bring extra blankets for you."

When Joleigh arrived at the motel room, she gathered several blankets she'd stored in the closet. They needed them more than her. She was past caring about stepping on Howie's pride.

ALL WAS WELL WITH BITS when Joleigh stopped by the next morning before heading to work. As Joleigh took off her coat, Ruby told her, "We're all meeting at my house tomorrow night. We've got two trailers lined up for hauling."

"I assume this is how Howie got their firewood in the past?" Joleigh asked.

"Yes, they did, along with several other area families. We do what we can, but it's never enough." Ruby pressed her lips together in frustration.

"Should I bring the firewood from the Grady place?"

"Not yet," Ruby said. "We'll save it for later in the winter, when we usually run short."

The following night, Joleigh parked in front of Ruby's home alongside several other pickups. The outdoor lights illuminated volunteers loading wood on the trailers.

Joleigh slipped on leather work gloves to help carry and stack the wood on the trailers. Ruby introduced her to everyone, including the owner of the lumberyard and the high school principal.

"Who is making the delivery?" Joleigh asked Ruby.

"John and Bob will haul the trailers with their trucks." Ruby pointed at two men, probably in their thirties, one of them a teacher at Bits's grade school.

After they filled the trailers, they secured ratchet straps to hold down the rows of split wood. Then everyone gathered in Ruby's driveway, chilled in the cold air after working up a sweat hauling wood.

"I've got a pot of coffee on and water heated for hot chocolate, plus peppermint schnapps, if you're so inclined," Ruby announced to the dozen workers. Most everyone followed Ruby inside, including Joleigh. And by the time she got home and crawled into bed two hours later, she'd made several new friends.

Chapter Twenty

November turned biting cold, and business slowed at Ruby's, giving Joleigh a chance to visit more with the regulars, especially her friend Moe.

On a quiet, bone-chilling Wednesday, Joleigh took advantage of the rare occurrence of Moe dining alone to visit with him. "Have you always lived in Grandfield?" she asked after taking his order.

"Yes, although my parents moved to North Dakota after I graduated from high school. I stayed and have lived here ever since, other than my time in Vietnam."

"Is that how you got injured?"

"Sure is. I was one of the lucky ones, though." He took a drink from his water glass.

"How was that lucky?" She'd never heard anyone refer to being paralyzed as lucky.

"I took a bullet near my spinal cord three months into my tour of duty. It was better than getting killed—or captured." He pointed at her POW bracelet.

"Oh my gosh, Moe. That's awful!"

He handed her his menu. "Listen, I know I like to joke about things, but not this. It was hell over there, and when you get a ticket out of hell, even if the ticket has left you disabled, you take it, because the longer you stay in hell, the more likely you're going to die. Or wish you had." His brown eyes held none of their familiar sparkle. "As CCR put it, I'm a 'Fortunate Son.' Not because I was raised in a privileged family and was able to dodge the draft like in the song but because I was one of the fortunate who made it home."

Joleigh took a quick look around the café. No new customers had come in. "So, tell me, what's the best thing and worst thing about life after you got out?"

"That's easy. The best thing is I get to butt in line for most things. Special front-row seating at concerts, handicap parking, things like that." Moe's mouth twitched below his mustache. "The worst thing is being stuck in a third-floor apartment until one opens up on the first floor. If there's a fire and it shuts the elevator down, I'll have to jump off the balcony. At least I won't feel any injury from my waist down." He winked.

She tapped his shoulder with the menu. "You make me laugh even while I feel sorry for you. It's too bad they can't switch your apartment with someone on the main floor." Joleigh was well aware of the affordable-housing shortage in Grandfield.

"There's four on each floor, and the bottom ones are all rented by geriatric people. I don't blame them for not wanting to move upstairs." Moe studied Joleigh. "Okay, my turn now. What's the best thing and worst thing for you about being Asian?"

Joleigh didn't flinch at his question, just as Moe hadn't with hers. Nobody, including Unity, had ever asked her what it felt like to look different from most people. "I'd have to say it's the shifty looks I get. As if I've got a third eye or something."

He nodded at her answer.

"And the best thing? I have a built-in tan every summer. I remember my mother, who was full-blooded Korean, telling me our skin was 'kissed by the sun,' and that made me feel special when I was little." She hadn't thought of that memory in years.

Hours later, when Joleigh brushed her hair after showering, she stood in front of the bathroom mirror, remembering the nightly ritual of her mother slowly brushing her own hair in one hundred strokes and often doing the same for Joleigh as she nestled on her mother's lap.

Joleigh hummed the melody of "Arirang," a Korean folk song her mother had always sung in her native language. She had asked her mom what the words meant in English, and although Joleigh had long ago forgotten most of the lyrics, two verses played in her memory, words Joleigh's mother had said to keep in her heart. Lyrics that spoke of the many stars in the sky, much like the dreams in people's hearts.

The memory resurrected the haunting loss of her parents, both dying too young. *I'm only two years younger than Mom was when she died.* The realization reminded Joleigh to follow her dreams. She just needed to figure out what they were.

EVERY THANKSGIVING, Ruby closed the restaurant to the public and instead opened from noon to three o'clock to serve a Thanksgiving buffet to those in need or who would be alone for the holiday. Joleigh volunteered to help serve the meal and had asked Ruby if Bits could help too.

"You said Howie has never set foot in here, so I doubt she can convince him to come here for the meal," Joleigh said. "I'll pay for the food if you don't mind me sending home two meals with Bits."

"Of course I don't mind," Ruby said. "You are donating your time, so don't feel you need to pay for their meals. Those who can make a cash donation do so, since half the people who attend are here because they don't want to make a holiday meal at home for just themselves. Plus, we'll put Bits to work filling water glasses and setting tables."

The Saturday before Thanksgiving, Joleigh brought up the subject with Bits over their weekly breakfast at Ruby's. "Do you think your dad would come in for a meal?"

"Um, I don't think so." Bits looked past Joleigh as if she would find Howie's excuse written on the wall. "He still doesn't feel good."

Joleigh held back a grumble. "I thought that might be the case. I'd like to have you help me serve the meals. Can you ask your dad? When we're done helping here, we will send two meals home for you and your dad so you can have a Thanksgiving dinner together."

Joleigh had learned Howie accepted help as long as he didn't have to see the person helping. They received food stamps, and although the food-stamp program had improved over the past year, it was a supplement, not a solution.

"Ruby's opens at noon on Thanksgiving. I'll pick you up at eleven thirty and bring you home after we close at three. Please tell your dad that you'll bring home a Thanksgiving meal."

Joleigh planned to buy a special treat for Bits for helping. Ruby warned her to not give Bits cash, since Howie would spend it on booze.

After she dropped Bits off at her house, Joleigh got ready for work and walked to town early. She stopped at Ben Franklin, where she bought three pairs of thick patterned socks for Bits, some fancy barrettes, and a Ring Pop—new last year—in every color, along with colored pencils and a coloring book.

When Unity adopted her, Joleigh had wondered why an elderly woman would take on the responsibilities and expenses of caring for a child who wasn't hers. Joleigh's time with Bits had already taught her how easy it was to open your heart to a child. Caring about someone else was a gift to yourself. Unity had said so for years.

On Thanksgiving, Joleigh pulled into Bits's driveway, no longer worried she would find a shotgun pointed her way. Bits burst out their door and down the rickety steps, running through the deep snow and hopping in the truck.

Joleigh had splurged on new tires for her truck after selling the hunting land in Missouri, and they dug into the slippery driveway as she backed out. Over a foot of snow had fallen in the past week, and Joleigh imagined Bits trudging through the deep drifts to catch the school bus.

Ruby greeted them at the restaurant's back door, hours after she and two other cooks had begun the food preparations. Two more workers arrived behind Joleigh and Bits. Joleigh kept Bits's gift in the back seat of the truck but brought another one in with her for Ruby.

When Joleigh had told Ruby about Mack's murder, Ruby had shared stories of her family's past. She'd spoken of her grandfather, a man she held in high regard. Ruby had showed Joleigh photos of him, including one of him and his family in their homeland on Puget Sound.

That day, Ruby stepped out of her office for a minute, and Joleigh had taken the opportunity to slip the photo into her canvas bag. The following day, she stopped at the Fotomat hut by the beach and had the photo enlarged, then she had it framed at Ben Franklin. After Joleigh and Bits hung up their winter coats, she handed the wrapped present to Ruby.

Ruby accepted the flat package. "What's this?"

"Happy Thanksgiving." Joleigh leaned in and hugged Ruby, thankful for having the woman in her life.

Ruby's eyes widened when she opened the gift. "You're so thoughtful. Thank you!"

Joleigh smiled. "Sorry, I stole the photo for a couple of days."

"I know just where to hang it." Ruby led the way out into the restaurant and held it up on the wall facing Main Street, at the end of the checkout counter.

"Looks perfect there," Joleigh said.

Ruby retrieved a hammer and nails from her office.

"You keep a hammer and nails here?"

"I keep necessities in the cleaning closet. I got sick of running home to fetch something needed here. Plus, I can use this hammer on any customers who don't pay." Ruby wiggled her eyebrows at Bits and got to work hanging the picture.

"Okay, let's get this party started!" Ruby clapped her hands and put Bits to work arranging place settings at every table and booth. Joleigh hustled back and forth between the kitchen and buffet, setting out turkey, dressing, mashed potatoes, green-bean casserole, and candied yams in the warming dishes.

Ruby unlocked the front door at noon, and patrons soon filled the restaurant. Over the next few hours, Ruby's pulsated with the energy of people laughing and making new friends over shared meals. Joleigh was surprised at the number of attendees she'd never seen before. Many of the people were dressed in well-worn clothes and thin winter coats. Joleigh's youth hadn't been easy, but at least she'd never had to worry about her next meal.

When Joleigh drove Bits home after the restaurant closed, a bag containing two packaged meals sat on Bits's lap as they parked in the driveway.

"I got you something for your help today." Joleigh reached in the backseat and handed Bits the wrapped gift of striped socks, barrettes, and coloring items.

Bits tore into the wrapping. "Thank you!" Bits's thin arms wrapped around Joleigh's shoulders when she leaned over the seat for a hug. "The socks are cool. Most of mine got holes in them."

Joleigh swallowed her concern in an attempt at a cheery send-off. "Don't forget that this Saturday, we will go to my motel room after breakfast. I'll teach you how to knit so you can get started on a scarf for your dad for Christmas."

"I'm excited to make Papa a gift." Bits carefully stepped out of the truck with her bag of food and goodies then turned when she reached the top step and waved goodbye to Joleigh.

JOLEIGH HAD SPENT EVERY Monday and Tuesday in November going over the motel business with the Nielsons. The weekend following Thanksgiving was the first weekend Joleigh had free from work since starting at Ruby's. She'd switched schedules for the winter with a waitress who was saving for her summer wedding. The arrangement gave the waitress a chance of better tips by working the busier weekends, and it gave Joleigh weekends off to manage the motel.

She stopped in the office Saturday morning before driving to pick up Bits.

"Good morning," Mr. Nielson waved Joleigh back to the kitchen table, where he and Mrs. Nielson were sharing a pot of tea. "I spoke to a technician at the telephone company yesterday. They'll be here Tuesday to wire a phone jack in your room. They'll transfer our motel number to your room when we leave Thursday morning."

He slid a key ring in front of her. "There's your copy of the office key, our house key, and the key to the maintenance room. I added your name on our business checking account at the bank." They spent the next hour going over several last-minute things.

Mrs. Nielson's smile reflected pure bliss at the promise of a few months of sunshine in her future.

Joleigh smiled. "I'm so excited for you two."

"Not as excited as the missus." Mr. Nielson looked fondly at his wife.

Joleigh stood to leave. "I need to pick up Bits now. Let me know if you think of anything else I need to know." They'd written the phone number for Mr. Nielson's brother on several slips of paper in case Joleigh misplaced it.

As she left the motel and headed down County Road Twelve, she thought of her first week at the motel back in May. What a difference six months made. Back then, she wasn't sure she would stay the week. Now she would stay through the winter—and run the place.

After breakfast with Bits, Joleigh drove them both to the motel. When she unlocked her room door, Bits stopped in the doorway, her mouth gaping.

"Wow, Joleigh, you sure have a nice house!"

Joleigh stood behind Bits and took in the one-room view. It was clean and had everything she needed for the next few months other than a kitchen. "Yes, it is nice, isn't it?" Joleigh could only imagine what the inside of Bits's home looked like. "This isn't my home, though. I'm staying here through the winter and will take care of the place while the owners leave for a few months."

She explained that, normally, people rented a motel room just for a night or weekend when they were traveling and didn't stay for months like Joleigh would.

"Okay, let's get to work on our knitting projects." Joleigh gestured to the bag of knitting needles and yarn on the dresser. "I'll take your coat."

Bits took off her stained winter jacket, and Joleigh hung it up in the closet next to hers, wishing she could wash it. She wondered if they had a washer and dryer in their home or if they went to the local laundromat.

Joleigh took a seat next to Bits. "Unity, the woman who adopted me, taught me how to knit. Unity knit everything from sweaters to mittens. I never mastered sleeves, so I just knit hats, mittens, and scarves."

Joleigh opened the knitting bag she'd brought from Woodland. "I'll teach you how to knit a scarf. It's one of the easiest things to make, and I'll make the hat." She pulled out the special curved needles used for hats.

Bits bounced in her chair. "Papa's going to love his Christmas gift."

"What color does your dad like?" Joleigh pulled out several full skeins of yarn. She'd hidden the soft lilac skeins she would use to make a hat, mittens, and a scarf for Bits for Christmas.

"The blue, please." Bits pointed at two navy skeins.

Over the next two hours, Bits patiently learned to knit and didn't pout when Joleigh would rip out a row because it was too tight. Eventually, Bits's grip relaxed, and a scarf knit by love formed. Joleigh worked on a navy-blue hat for Howie, and they listened to the radio as they worked.

Joleigh had purchased a slow cooker and a toaster oven in early November and last week had borrowed the two-wheeled cart from the hardware store to bring the single-door Coca-Cola glass cooler to her room, as per Mr. Nielson's suggestion. They didn't use it in the office during the winter months, since business was too slow to bother with a few bottles of soft drinks, so it was Joleigh's refrigerator of sorts.

"I've got tomato soup warming in the Crock-Pot, and we can make grilled cheese sandwiches in the toaster oven for lunch," Joleigh said. "Ready for a break?"

"Yes. My fingers hurt a little." Bits flexed her thin fingers.

While they buttered bread for their sandwiches, "On Top of Spaghetti" came on the radio.

"This song reminds me of when I moved in with Unity," Joleigh said. "We listened to the radio a lot, and any time a silly song like this played, Unity would stop what she was doing and hop up and dance." Joleigh chuckled at the memory. "Unity was a large woman, taller and broader than me. And old. But she had a young spirit."

Bits stopped buttering the bread to listen to the lyrics and held a hand over her stomach in a fit of giggles. "Would you eat that meatball after it rolled out the door?" She smiled up at Joleigh.

Joleigh shrugged. "Depends on how hungry I am."

After lunch, Joleigh suggested a walk. The sun was out, and the snow had turned to trickles of water in the motel parking lot. They dressed in their boots and winter coats and headed toward the woods near the motel. They talked about nature, how their ancestors lived off the land decades ago, and Unity's hobby farm in Missouri.

"I wish I had a Unity," Bits said wistfully.

Joleigh's eyes watered, and not because of the cold air. "I'd love to be your Unity."

"But I live with Dad, not you."

"Yes." Joleigh swallowed her emotions. "But you can spend time with me whenever you want. Okay?"

Bits nodded a solemn response. They continued down the trail through the woods, squirrels skittering up tree trunks making the only noise as Joleigh wrestled with her feelings for Bits.

Howie didn't have a phone. *What do they do if there's an emergency?* No neighbors, no phone...

Joleigh shook her head. No sense in stressing about something she had no control over. Yet she couldn't help it. She cared about Bits—possibly too much.

Chapter Twenty-One

The Nielsons eagerly packed their belongings the week before they pulled out of the snowy motel parking lot on December first.

"Remember, call us with any problems," Mr. Nielson said as Joleigh walked them to their vehicle. "My brother has one of those fancy answering machines. We will check it every day."

"Don't worry about the motel. Enjoy your winter." With no hobby farm or animals to care for, Joleigh was thankful to have the motel's weekend business to offset her shifts at Ruby's. They had a few rooms booked for upcoming weekends but nothing like their summer business. Joleigh understood why the motel was a hard sell with an upcoming five-month stretch of slow business.

The weekend after the Nielsons left, the motel had reservations for three rooms. With check-in time after three in the afternoon, Joleigh had time to shower after her Friday shift ended at Ruby's. She took her meal of meatballs, mashed potatoes, gravy, and corn in a to-go container instead of eating with her coworkers.

Joleigh dodged slippery spots on the sidewalk and ducked her head to avoid the frigid wind as she walked to the motel. After showering, she looked over the reservation calendar while she ate. Mr. Nielson said during the slow winter months, he put guests in the rooms nearest the office so he didn't have to have the side parking lot plowed.

One reservation was for two adults and two children, one for two adults and one child, and one reservation for... *Franklin Grady?* Joleigh nearly choked on the meatball in her mouth.

Why is he renting a room? The weather forecast projected more snow for the weekend along with gusty winds. Not exactly perfect getaway weather. There were no notes of any plans to check in late, which meant all the guests should arrive by six o'clock. Along with having the office phone ring in her room, Mr. Nielson also had an electrician wire the office doorbell to ring in Joleigh's room for any late arrival or unregistered overnight guest.

She finished her meal, the meatballs performing a tango with the mashed potatoes in her stomach while she played a guessing game of why Franklin would have a room reserved. Joleigh double-checked her red cowl-neck sweater to make sure she hadn't spilled food and then applied tinted lip gloss, feeling as if she no longer had control of her actions.

Joleigh stepped into her winter boots and grabbed the Nielsons' shovel she kept by the door. She shoveled the walkway in front of the office before collecting the bag containing her macramé and knitting so she would have something to work on while she waited for check-ins.

The two families arrived first. The wives were sisters whose parents lived in Grandfield. "It's easier for us to stay here. More room and less disruption when we put our little ones to bed," the women explained while they checked in.

Dusk had arrived by the time truck headlights shone into the office. Joleigh sat up straight in the chair behind the counter, stashed away her knitting, and braced herself for Franklin, rehearsing a nonchalant attitude.

The outdoor office light illuminated his tall silhouette. Franklin opened the office door and pulled off his stocking cap. "Hello, Joleigh," he said, as breezily as if they lived next door to each other.

"Aren't you surprised to see me here?" She'd gone off script already.

He jammed his hands in his jean pockets. "Not really. I knew you moved here at the end of October for the winter."

"Yes, but I'm checking you in." *And checking you out,* she thought, taking in his charcoal-gray sweater. It was as if he intentionally wore that color to bring out the piercing gray of his eyes. *Stop looking at his eyes. Stop looking at him, period.* "The Nielsons left yesterday for the winter. Did he mention that when you made reservations?"

"Yep, but he didn't say who was running the place."

"Have you stayed here before? I thought you would stay at your cabin." *Don't interrogate the guests, Joleigh.*

"Not this time of year. Yes, it has the woodstove, but it's colder than the Arctic in there now. We closed it up after they finished hunting."

"They? Don't you hunt?"

"Nope, I'm the camp cook."

"Really?" That news surprised her. Most men she knew weren't interested in cooking.

"Being the oldest of nine, I could either help Mom in the kitchen or change poopy diapers. It was an easy choice."

She pulled a key off the wall hook. "You're in room number three. Checkout is by ten on Sunday, and if you have questions, I'm in room seven. If you need anything, they forwarded the office phone number to my room."

He pocketed the key and gave her a nod before walking out to his truck.

Joleigh walked out of the office after him and locked the door. Back in her room, she stewed, unsure what was eating at her.

Oh, Joleigh, you know. You wanted Franklin to stay and visit with you.

She wanted his approval—it was something she craved from everyone, which she knew was an unrealistic expectation. She stood in front of the bathroom mirror and studied herself. People often commented on her smooth skin, the way her dark lashes appeared as if she wore eyeliner, her friendly smile. But what Joleigh saw was a woman who stood out in a crowd and the chubby little girl inside her who was once labeled "Much Moore."

She spent the rest of the night working on mittens for Bits, the scratch of the knitting needles against each other like an incessant tune that sang, *This is your life, knitting on a Friday night instead of going out on a date. Next, you'll live in a house full of cats.*

To be fair, Bernadette, Leo, and a few others from Ruby's had asked Joleigh to join them after work. They were heading to listen to a band play in a Minneapolis nightclub. Joleigh would've gone if it weren't her first weekend with guests at the motel. There would be other weekends to live like a twenty-eight-year-old instead of a seventy-eight-year-old.

FRANKLIN'S TRUCK WAS gone when Joleigh left the next morning to pick up Bits for breakfast. Ever since the Nielsons left and she worked in the motel instead of Ruby's on the weekends, Howie had approved of Bits's spending most of the day with Joleigh. And although she'd felt sorry for herself for missing a night out with friends, Joleigh sympathized more with Bits.

Do her classmates ever invite Bits to their birthday parties? Bits likely never invited friends to her home. Joleigh had never had friends over at her parents' apartment and certainly never when she was in foster care. But after Unity adopted her, she'd made sure Joleigh had friends at their home as often as she wanted.

Joleigh didn't ask Bits about any playdates, not wanting to make her feel bad. After breakfast, they walked back to the motel. While

Bits made progress on her dad's scarf, Joleigh worked on Howie's hat. The Nielsons had encouraged Joleigh to use their kitchen while they were gone, and earlier, she'd fried up a pound of hamburger for the cheeseburger soup simmering in the Crock-Pot in her room.

"Ready for a break?" Joleigh stood and looked out her room window. "The snow has quit, and the wind has died down. Looks like it will be nice for sledding this afternoon."

"I told my friends at school that we might go sledding on the hills by the park." Bits's eyes twinkled. "Maybe they'll be there."

Joleigh hoped so. After bowls of cheeseburger soup, they dressed in their outdoor gear and drove to the hills near the park with the plastic-disc sleds Joleigh had purchased.

For the next few hours, they trudged up and slid down three hills so full of other people on sleds that it was hard to tell if Bits's friends from school were there. Hats, scarves, and zipped-up jackets did their job in staving off the snow blowing in people's faces while those people slid down the hill, making it difficult to recognize anyone.

When Joleigh pulled back into Bits's driveway at sunset, Bits, who had been chattering non-stop on the way home, suddenly went quiet, and her shoulders slumped.

"What's wrong?" Joleigh put the truck in park.

Bits picked at her coat, which was wet from snow. "I had fun today, but..." Her chin quivered.

"Oh, sweetie, you can tell me." Joleigh reached for Bits's hand. "You had fun, but what?"

"I think I'm sad there's no more fun today?" Bits's tone phrased it as a question.

Joleigh took a deep breath. "That makes sense. But if we did this every day, it wouldn't feel special. Like if we ate ice cream every day for lunch, it would just become 'lunch' instead of something special." She forced a smile.

"I'd love ice cream every day!" Bits said, leaning into Joleigh's hug before she slowly exited the truck.

As Joleigh drove back to the motel, she thought about one of her fondest memories of her father. It was a day he'd packed them a picnic lunch and taken her to a playground. The playground was like a hundred others, and her peanut butter-and-jelly sandwich was like a hundred others she'd eaten. But on that special day with her dad, the slide seemed extra-fast, his underdog pushes on the swing sent her extra-high, and her sandwich tasted like the best one she'd ever had.

It had been a special day with his undivided attention, coating everything in glitter and sunshine. They'd flown a kite in the park, and when it got caught in a tree, he hoisted her onto his broad shoulders for her to retrieve it. That was one of her best memories of her dad.

JOLEIGH WAS SNACKING on cottage cheese and peaches when someone knocked on her motel-room door.

She looked through the peephole and about choked. *Franklin? What does he want?* Joleigh ran to the bathroom, splashed water on her face, and brushed her teeth, all the while reminding herself to calm down. *He's just another guest at the motel.* There was no reason to double-check her face, hair, and clothes before opening the door.

But reason didn't keep her heart from doing an Irish jig.

Chapter Twenty-Two

"Hi, Franklin. Do you need something?" Joleigh said after she opened her door.

Franklin had asked himself a hundred times on the way to Joleigh's room why in the hell he was stopping. He dodged her question. "Hello to you too." He dragged his eyes from her deep-brown ones to focus on a bowl and spoon on the table. "Sorry, I didn't know you were eating." It was after seven o'clock.

Joleigh turned toward the table. "I had company earlier, so I had a late supper. Is there something wrong with your room?"

Franklin shook his head. "Nothing's wrong. I walked by and noticed your light on." *Liar, liar. You've been thinking about stopping by since she told you her room number last night.*

Joleigh furrowed her brow. "Oh. Did you want to come in?"

"Sure." Franklin jammed his hands in his jeans pockets to keep from reaching out to smooth the crease between her furrowed eyebrows. Any excuse to touch her. "I thought I'd go for a walk, saw your light on, and wondered if you'd like to come with." He nodded to the walls. "Maybe take a break from here."

Joleigh blinked several times. "You want me to go for a walk with you?"

He laughed. "Is that such a shock? Unless you're tired from work."

Joleigh shut the door behind him. Franklin inhaled a yummy aroma. She put her bowl of whatever she'd been eating in a small

Coca-Cola glass cooler and took her spoon to the bathroom sink to wash.

"I don't work at Ruby's on weekends now so that I can be here for guests," Joleigh said over her shoulder. He itched to study her from the back, but with Joleigh facing the bathroom mirror, she could see his gaze reflected there. "Sure, I'd like to go for a walk." Joleigh dried her hands and walked back to where he stood.

Franklin breathed deep again. "Some sort of cheese soup?"

"I made cheeseburger soup in the Crock-Pot." She gathered her coat, hat, and mittens.

"Have you ever tried Gruyère cheese? I use it in several soups."

"You cook that much? I've never heard of that type of cheese."

Franklin nodded. "It's a hard yellow Swiss cheese that also tastes great in fondue. And I don't cook that much now, since I live alone, but I end up hosting most of our family holidays plus serving as cook at deer camp."

Joleigh wrapped a scarf around her neck, zipped up her ski jacket, and pulled on boots before adding warm mittens. There was no wind, but the temperature had dropped into the low teens.

"I just came back from downtown and planned to walk the trail through the woods. Is that okay with you?" Franklin nodded at the woods on the far side of the motel.

"Sure." Joleigh followed him out the door, walking alongside him toward the woods. "I was just on this trail."

"With your, um... guest?" *Does she have a boyfriend? Of course she does, you idiot.*

"Yes." She cast him a sideways glance. "Bits, the young girl who lives past your cabin, whose family needed firewood."

"Oh." The tightness in his chest relaxed. "Did they get enough wood? I drove out to the cabin this morning, and it looks like you didn't take any from there."

"We had enough from other donations, but I'll stop at your property soon to get some of that wood to drop off at Howie's. I checked their woodpile today, and it looks like it's about half-gone." She paused in her stride to look at him. "That is, if it's still okay to take some."

"Of course. You did the work."

"It was payment for copping a squat at your place." She smiled. "I hope your dad isn't still angry with me."

"His bark is worse than his bite. I used to be scared as hell of him. Now, I know better. He never once laid a hand on any of us kids, and we gave him plenty of reason to."

They walked in silence for a few minutes. A three-quarter moon lit the sky, and streetlamps illuminated the trail.

"That day in Ruby's when you told your dad I was talking about my wood for Bits," she said. "How did you know I had my own wood cut?"

"I walked down to your land while the rest of them hunted that morning, figuring you wouldn't be there, since you said you were moving to the motel. I spotted your woodpile and assumed that's the wood you were referring to." He'd been impressed by the improvements Joleigh had made to the cabin. And even more impressed when he checked out her property. "You've done a lot of work on your land already. It looks nice."

"Thanks. So, what brings you to Grandfield this time of year?"

Joleigh's face looked so smooth and radiant in the moonlight, begging Franklin's lips to explore her cheek, her neck, her mouth. He shook his head to break free of that thought.

"Downhill skiing. I get together with some guys I met in the service that live around the Twin Cities. There's a ski hill, Buck Hill, about fifteen miles from here. I sometimes stay with them or get a hotel in the area, but I thought I'd stay here and have dinner with Moe."

Joleigh stopped walking. "Moe? You mean Moe from the insurance agency? Did you serve in Vietnam together?"

"Yep, that Moe, but no, we didn't meet in 'Nam."

"I didn't realize you knew him."

"We met at Ruby's several years ago and got to talking. The Friday after Veteran's Day when I was in Grandfield with family for deer hunting, Moe had a red poppy tucked in his shirt pocket." Franklin glanced down at Joleigh, thinking of how her lips reminded him of the color of poppies. *Stop thinking like a sappy teen!* "I stopped to talk to him that day. It was a year after he'd come back from 'Nam. We've been friends ever since."

"I like Moe. He's funny."

"Yes, he is. Informative too," Franklin said.

"What do you mean?" Joleigh cocked her head.

"He told me you were going to be running the motel this winter."

"I thought you said you didn't know I was running it." Joleigh put her hands on her hips. "What else did he tell you?"

Franklin chuckled. "I said *Mr. Nielson* didn't tell me you were running the place. I never said my informant didn't snitch on you."

"Hmm... I didn't realize you had an informant in town." She elbowed him.

As they continued deeper into the woods, they talked about his family, her decision whether to stay in Minnesota, and downhill skiing. "You should try it," he said. "It's a freeing feeling when you fly down the hill."

"I'm terrified of heights, and those chairlifts look unsafe."

"*You're* afraid of something? That surprises me." In the short time he'd known her, Joleigh seemed invincible.

"Why? Aren't you afraid of anything?"

"Sure. Heights aren't one of them, though." Franklin could list several things that petrified him, but Joleigh would probably run the other way. "Hey, the smaller hills have a T-bar. You could try those."

He explained how they worked. "Your skis are on the ground the whole time."

They had rounded the trail loop and were on their way back when Joleigh said, "It does sound fun. Maybe Bernadette—one of the other waitresses at Ruby's—would go with me."

Franklin kicked himself for not being more direct. "I'll come up next month and take you, if you'd like. We can start on the bunny hill."

"Gee, thanks. I've seen pictures of bunny hills, and they're filled with kids."

"They aren't just for children. That's where most of us have learned to ski. I'll stay with you on the bunny hill until you feel ready to hit the next hill." He paused. "What do you think? Is there a weekend in January that doesn't have reservations at the motel?"

Do I sound too eager? Damn, it's been a while since I've asked someone out on a date.

"I'll look when we get back. Sometimes people don't make reservations until that week."

"Buck Hill is nearby, so if we skied a few hours, you wouldn't be away too long."

Joleigh clapped her mittened hands together as they reached the clearing to the motel parking lot. "I'd like that. The Nielsons said it's okay to leave during the day. I could put a note on the door saying when I'll be back if anyone is here that weekend."

Franklin looked at his watch. "It's only eight thirty. Do you want to walk to the bar?" The idea of sitting in his room alone, knowing Joleigh was a few doors away in her room, held zero appeal for him.

Joleigh's smile and the twinkle in her eyes made him wonder how this beautiful woman with snowflakes in her hair could be the same one who could out-work most men he knew—including himself, if he was honest.

"I'm a one-drink drinker," she said, "but yes, that sounds good."

Franklin suggested a bar two blocks down Main Street. They found an empty booth and slipped off their coats and hats.

"What would you like?" he asked.

"A beer?"

"Too boring. How about something like a Tom & Jerry?"

"What's that?"

"It's a hot eggnog drink with either brandy or rum. It'll warm you right up. I'll have one too."

"Okay." Joleigh sat in the booth while he ordered their drinks at the bar.

Most of the crowd appeared to be people around their age. "Do you know any of these people?" Franklin asked when he rejoined her a few minutes later.

"Me?" Joleigh glanced around. "I don't see anyone I know. A few people look familiar, probably have been in Ruby's, but honestly, I don't go out a lot." She shrugged. "I enjoy people, but I'm not a fan of crowds." She chuckled as she pressed two fingers to her forehead. "Wow, I sound like a ball of fire, don't I?"

The quiet, reserved Joleigh vanished after her first Tom & Jerry, replaced by an outgoing, animated Joleigh as she worked on her second. The warmth of Joleigh's outlook on the pleasure of embracing nature, the sparkle in her eyes as she spoke of the young girl Bits, the laughter as she talked of funny songs she would sing with Unity, a woman she described to Franklin as a "grandmother type who chose me to be her daughter"—all of it warmed Franklin and made him doubly glad he took the chance and knocked on her door.

And when Joleigh asked Franklin about Vietnam, he chose to focus on the bland food. "Most of us carried around a bottle of hot sauce to spice up the C-rations." He shuddered at the memory of some of the food—like the pork and beans. Things he would never eat again. "It helped fuel my love for cooking when I came back to the States."

It was after ten, and once her second drink was gone, Franklin remembered what Joleigh said about being a "one-drink" person and suggested, "Let's get you back to your room, since you have to be up early for checkout."

He stood, held out her ski jacket, and helped Joleigh put it on and zip it up. As they stepped out onto the sidewalk, cold air jolted him out of the warm cocoon of her company. Franklin offered his elbow for Joleigh to loop her arm through, even though the snow was sticky instead of slippery—perfect for making a snowman.

As they crossed the motel parking lot, Joleigh stopped. "Go ahead. I'll be right with you." She wore a devilish grin.

He raised an eyebrow, curious, but turned around. He'd barely gone twenty feet when a hard thump punched his back. He whipped around in time to take another snowball to the chest, and his surprise gave way to the challenge.

"You sure you want to do this, Joleigh?" he said with a playful edge to his voice.

"Yes! Come on, you grumpy old man," Joleigh taunted him. "What did your cousin call you... grumpkin?"

"I'm not old." He huffed. "Or grumpy."

"Well, you act like it sometimes." She stood with her feet planted in the snowy parking lot, her chin jutted out as if to taunt him.

Without another word, Franklin walked to Joleigh, his eyes meeting hers. As they stood in silence, the sound of cars on the freeway humming in the distance, the sparkle of snow illuminated by the streetlights, he stepped close enough to catch the scent of cold cream on her face. He watched her eyes widen and her smile fade.

"You already know how old I am, but you haven't told me how old you are." Franklin's gaze fell to Joleigh's mouth.

"Twenty-eight," Joleigh whispered.

Franklin wouldn't have cared if she said forty. "Works for me." And then he did what he'd been thinking about all night. He pulled her in for a kiss.

Chapter Twenty-Three

During the night, the growl of Joleigh's stomach woke her, followed by a fierce thirst. Her head pulsated and her stomach roiled. She stumbled out of bed, chugged a full glass of water, and followed it with a few saltine crackers.

Joleigh sat on the edge of the bed as it all came back to her. Well, not *all,* but enough to make her cringe. She hung her head in her open palms, looking down to see the jeans she'd worn the night before. Yet she also wore the oversized T-shirt she used as pajamas.

Did I half dress myself? Please tell me Franklin didn't help me, Joleigh begged the quiet room.

It was three o'clock, which meant Joleigh had four more hours before she had to get up. She set the alarm for seven, just in case, and fell back into a fitful sleep. When the alarm went off, playing "Tonight's the Night," she groaned. Rod Stewart's lyrics dragged thoughts of the previous night front and center in her mind.

Joleigh flipped off the music and took her time under a hot shower, feeling almost human again. She rummaged in her packets for some ginger to brew tea. She dressed in jeans and a ribbed powder-blue turtleneck, slipped on boots, grabbed her canvas bag filled with things to keep her occupied while she waited for people to check out, and made her way to the office with a mug of hot ginger tea.

The two families arrived in the office soon after she opened the door at eight, surprising Joleigh. She commented on their early-morning departure.

"Thanks to our kids," one of the men said. "Our two-year-old is up before the sun every day, even when there's no sun." He pointed out the window at the cloudy sky.

Joleigh took their checks and thanked them for their stay, proud that her first weekend had gone off without a hitch. Unless making out with a customer in the parking lot was a problem. She remembered that much about last night.

Joleigh had never been one of those girls in school who craved a boy's attention. Yet she understood what had driven her to throw snowballs at Franklin. It was her way of saying *look at me* without uttering a word.

The taste of last night's kisses had been like silky chocolate, enticing her to want more. The memory of Franklin cradling the back of her head when he pulled her to him, and the way every cell of her body zapped to life when her hands wrapped around his neck, mortified her. *Did I beg him to never stop kissing me or was that a dream? Did he help me change into the T-shirt?*

Only one person knew those answers. *There is no way I'm asking him.*

Joleigh was so immersed in the book she'd brought along that when Franklin walked into the office an hour later, she jumped and dropped the book. Maybe he would toss his key and payment on the counter and walk out, and she would never see him again.

She stood. "Um, good morning."

He smiled at her from across the counter with a look of mischief. "So, feel like a snowball fight this morning?"

"I'm sorry about last night." She rubbed her still-throbbing head.

Franklin leaned on the counter. "Sorry for what, exactly?" His eyes penetrated hers.

She didn't enjoy being pinned down for a specific apology. "I think I'm sorry I didn't eat more before drinking last night. It might have helped soak up the booze."

He laughed and pushed away from the counter. "Yes, that may have helped. And I'm sorry for interrupting your dinner, so it was my fault."

Joleigh rolled her eyes. "I don't believe for a second you're sorry." Her brain cells regrouped. "I mean about me drinking too much, not about the kiss." She cringed, regretting bringing it up. "I didn't eat enough, drank too much, and then acted like a grade-school bully itching to pick a fight. I'm adult enough to take responsibility for my actions."

Franklin's eyes traveled to her mouth. "Then I'll take responsibility for the kiss."

She let out a sigh of relief. *Thank goodness he kissed me first!* Her memory had been vague about that part. "And I'm pretty sure I begged you to keep doing it. I swear, I'm never drinking again." She covered her face with her hands.

He pulled them back. "Begged? Okay, we'll call it that."

She studied him, a baseball cap covering his bald head, one she vaguely remembered running her hands over last night. Franklin had gorgeous eyes and a devilish smile, and against her better judgment, she suspected she was falling for him. "Can I ask you something?"

Franklin rocked back on his heels, his mouth twitching. "Sure."

"Are you interested in me? I know that sounds awful direct, but I'm wondering why you would be." She had a long list of reasons why a relationship between them wouldn't work.

Franklin arched back, laughing. "I'm not sure a woman has ever asked me that before." He leaned over the counter, his laughter fading. "And yes, I am interested in you. Quite different from the day I met you, when I only felt pissed off."

He grew serious. "I was engaged after high school before I went into the service. I thought it was the thing to do, even though we weren't right for each other. She pushed, and I let her. And when she broke it off while I was in 'Nam, it crushed me." He pressed his lips together. "When I got out, I remember having a rare heart-to-heart with my dad about women. He told me, 'You can't chase a mare if she's running toward you.' What he meant was that a lot of women chase men for many reasons, and often the woman worth pursuing is not the one running toward you."

Joleigh's breathing slowed. When he bridged the space between them and placed a soft kiss on her lips, she stopped thinking.

Franklin pulled back. "You, Joleigh, aren't a chaser. You're independent and don't need me or anyone else. It's admirable." He stepped away from the counter and studied the office floor. "The thing is, I have a hard time trusting people now."

Joleigh thought back to David's words about how Franklin changed after Vietnam.

"You're easy to talk to." Franklin looked up and grinned. "And you're easy on the eyes."

Warmth flowed through her, as if someone had filled her body with warm syrup.

Franklin set his room key on the counter, pulled out his checkbook, and tore out the check he'd written. "Are you still interested in downhill skiing next month?"

"You really want to do that?"

"Yes, don't you?" He raised an eyebrow. "I thought I'd made it pretty obvious I want to spend time with you."

Joleigh relaxed. "Okay, then. Yes, I'd love to go." She pulled out the calendar for January. "So far, nobody has booked the second weekend in January. If someone does, I can let them know ahead of time that I'll be gone for most of Saturday."

He looked at the calendar. "New Year's Eve is on Saturday. Do you have plans for that weekend? We could ski and then maybe do something with Moe and Diane."

She flipped the calendar back to the last weekend in December. "There are a few rooms rented that weekend, but I should be able to leave for the day on Saturday. Everyone will have checked in on Friday for the weekend." Her heart soared at the thought of having plans for New Year's Eve. Last year, she'd spent that night sitting next to Unity's bed, knowing it would be their last together. Even if the motel had been booked full, she would have found a way to leave for the day. "And no, I don't have plans for that weekend."

"Okay, let's shoot for that day. Please put me down for a room on Friday and Saturday night that weekend." He took a slip of paper and pen from the counter and wrote his name and phone number on it. "There. Now you have my number."

Joleigh tucked the paper into the outside pocket of her bag before walking with him out to his truck. And when he kissed her and pulled her in for a full-body embrace, it felt like sizzling sunshine on that cloudy winter day.

JOLEIGH'S DECEMBER flew by, her time balanced between work at Ruby's and weekends at the motel. Even with only a few rooms booked each weekend, Nielson's Nest kept her busy.

It was the week of Christmas, and nobody had booked a motel room for the coming weekend. Not that it would have made much of a difference for Joleigh. She would still be alone at Christmas, and she wondered if next year would be the same.

Joleigh tried picturing her next Christmas—back in Woodland, alone in the house, or in a new home down Lonesome Road, alone there too. It wasn't a matter of *where* she would be as much as who she would have in her life. No Unity, no Mack. Like Paula, the few close friends she'd had in high school had moved away, married, had families. They'd moved on, while she'd lived in limbo for the past several years, treasuring her time with Unity yet missing out on life.

Her promise to Unity that she would live her own life, along with the knowledge that she would have to decide come spring if she was moving out of the motel to her property on Lonesome Road or moving back to Woodland, weighed on her. The knowledge that Mack's killers were still on the loose factored into her decision, but so did finances. If she wanted to build on her property in the spring, she would need to sell the house in Missouri.

Joleigh picked up Bits after her shift at Ruby's on Friday, since school was on Christmas break. She had put in an order for spaghetti and meatballs and had it in a to-go container for her to share with Bits before they worked on their knitting projects. They had two days for Bits to finish Howie's scarf—and Howie, Bits said, was still sick.

They pulled into the motel parking lot, and Joleigh shut off the truck. She turned to Bits on the seat next to her. "Has he gone to the doctor? It sounds like he should get checked out." She didn't want to worry Bits, but the man needed help.

"Papa doesn't believe in doctors. Says they're quacks that want to take our hard-earned money." Bits spoke in earnest as if every word her dad said was gospel.

Joleigh stifled a scoff at the idea of Howie having "hard-earned money." She let the subject drop. Joleigh picked up the to-go container of their meal from the back seat. "Okay, let's get to work. We've got spaghetti to eat and a scarf to finish today." She had finished Howie's hat last week.

While they ate, Joleigh watched Bits mow her way through two plates of spaghetti. "Is spaghetti one of your favorite meals?" she asked.

"Yep. Even Papa eats the SpaghettiOs I make."

Joleigh grimaced at the mention of the canned substitute. "Would you like spaghetti for your Christmas meal?" The next day was Christmas Eve. Ruby's was open until noon, and since the motel had no reservations for the weekend, Joleigh had taken Bernadette's morning shift so she could spend the day with her children.

Bits nodded, and since Ruby's was only serving breakfast on Christmas Eve, Joleigh called and placed an order for them to set aside two servings of today's spaghetti to pick up when she worked the next morning. It wasn't a traditional Christmas dinner, but it was something Bits could reheat on the stove.

Joleigh dropped Bits off at her house a few hours later. "I'll be here at one tomorrow. Tell your dad it should only take an hour or two, and I'll have you back home before dark so you can celebrate Christmas Eve with him."

"Okay. He's going to be so excited about his present." Bits clapped her hands together, full of happiness stemming from the joy of giving.

ON SATURDAY MORNING, Moe stopped in at Ruby's with his girlfriend Diane.

"I'm not used to seeing you here on a weekend," Joleigh said.

"Diane and I are heading out to ice fish this morning, and she refused to go unless I fed her first."

"You're dang right. I need sustenance to pull in the fish." Diane grinned.

Joleigh missed fishing. "What's a good ice fishing lake nearby?"

"Lonesome Lake is decent if you fish along the drop-off areas. Just be careful if you drive out on the ice. There are springs to the left of the lake access. Plenty of vehicles have sunk there over the years," Moe warned Joleigh. "They put markers out, but they're often blown over in the wind. It's not over your head, but you don't want an ice bath. Neither does your vehicle."

"I'll walk out. I don't use an auger, so I can carry everything. Is the ice safe for driving out now?"

"It's safe in most areas. When you walk out, stay clear of that area," Moe said.

"We drive out for obvious reasons." He gestured to his wheelchair.

"That's if I can squeeze into his car, between his eight-track player and tapes and his CB radio." Diane playfully nudged Moe.

Joleigh visited with them a few more minutes before she left to place their order. And while she worked the rest of her morning, she thought about Moe and Diane's plans for the day. Joleigh decided that tomorrow, Christmas Day, she would go ice fishing.

After her shift, Joleigh picked up Bits, who bounced her way into the truck, excitement illuminating her face. Her positive outlook always amazed Joleigh, who still felt frustration about Bits's home environment.

But Bits was happy, and that was all that mattered. "Excited for Christmas?" Joleigh asked.

"Yes! Papa is going to love his present. And guess what? Someone dropped off our groceries, and there was a can of Spam inside the box." She clapped. "I'm going to make Papa and me Spam and eggs for our Christmas breakfast."

They arrived at the motel, and by three o'clock Bits had completed most of Howie's scarf. Joleigh finished it by casting off the end. Bits wrapped the scarf around her neck and pulled the matching navy hat over her blond hair, prancing around the motel room like a runway model.

Joleigh whistled. "Look at that gorgeous model." Bits did indeed resemble a younger version of Twiggy—model-thin, which was not healthy for a growing child.

Joleigh opened the closet door and took out a wrapped gift for Bits. "Merry Christmas to you. Do you want to open it now, or do you want to save it for tomorrow? It's up to you."

Bits's eyes widened. "Thank you, Joleigh!" Her mouth hung open at her unexpected gift. "I should open it now, so you can see how happy the gift makes me."

Joleigh chuckled. "How do you know the gift will make you happy? What if it's a dead mouse? Or toilet paper?"

"Because you love me, and you only do nice things for me."

A lump formed in Joleigh's throat. Bits felt Joleigh's love. It was the best Christmas gift Joleigh could ask for.

They sat on the edge of the bed, and Bits unwrapped the box containing two Nancy Drew books and her lavender-colored knit hat, scarf, and mittens. Joleigh wasn't sure how much time Bits had to read, but Nancy Drew had helped a young Joleigh through some tough times, enabling her to escape into the pages. Perhaps the books would do the same for Bits.

For once, Bits was speechless, her eyes moving in rapid time to blink back tears. Without saying a word, she leaned over and hugged Joleigh with such force that they almost toppled onto the floor together. Joleigh clung to the child she had come to love.

Several minutes later, Joleigh announced the inevitable. "I better get you home so you can spend Christmas Eve with your dad. I've got spaghetti for you in the cooler."

Bits fished something out of her ski jacket pocket. "I made you an ornament to hang up." She pulled out a piece of paper and handed it to Joleigh.

It was a tiny sketch of Bits and Joleigh holding hands, standing at the beach. Bits had glued it to cardboard shaped like a Christmas bulb with a hole punched in the top and a red ribbon tied through it.

"It's beautiful, Bits! You are a talented artist." In the three-inch circle, Bits had captured their looks so well—Joleigh's long, wavy black hair, her almond-shaped eyes, her muscular frame, and Bits herself, thin and pale, with light-blond hair. "Did you make this in school?"

"Yes, it's for your Christmas tree, but you don't have one." Bits looked around as if a tree would magically appear.

"I'll have a tree next year in my house. For now, I'll hang it on the wall. I can get a push pin from the office and hang it from that. I don't think Mr. Nielson will mind a tiny pinhole."

Joleigh retrieved the two generous servings of spaghetti packed in a container with garlic bread wrapped in tinfoil on the lid. A gallon-sized plastic baggie held a lettuce salad with a handful of various packaged salad dressings. She packed everything in a paper bag.

When she pulled into Bits's driveway, Bits and Joleigh leaned into the middle of the truck and hugged. Joleigh never wanted to let her go.

"Merry Christmas, Bits." Joleigh forced herself back to meet Bits's eyes. She touched the girl's cold cheek. "Getting to know you has been the best gift for me."

Bits's chin quivered. "Me too," she whispered. She turned and opened the truck door and stepped out before Joleigh handed her the bag of food and Howie's wrapped gift. After Bits entered her house, Joleigh took a minute to dab away tears so she could see to drive.

In the span of half a year, Bits had moved her way up to become the number-one reason Joleigh could no longer imagine moving away from Grandfield.

Chapter Twenty-Four

Joleigh opened her eyes on Christmas morning, her first without Unity and Mack and nearly two decades after her last with her parents.

After showering, Joleigh turned on the radio to catch the local weather while she ate two bowls of Cheerios. Grandfield could expect a high of thirty-five degrees with little breeze and partly sunny skies, perfect ice fishing weather.

She headed outside, opened the back of her pickup, and crawled into the truck bed to retrieve the five-gallon bucket containing her fishing jigs and ice dipper. Her steel chisel lay along the edge of the truck bed. The bait shop was closed for Christmas, but Joleigh had a pack of grub worms she'd purchased two days ago when Peter was working. She knew his schedule, so she could avoid any interaction with his mother.

As Joleigh drove toward Lonesome Lake, she passed her property. She imagined a quaint home, animals, a garden, and a family. She could control everything but the family part. If she built there, she would need to line up a contractor soon to dig the basement in the spring when the ground thawed. The only way to pay for it would be to sell her home in Woodland. Unity's home.

The thought of cutting that tie to her past ate at her like a tapeworm. Even if Darrell and the others were captured, Joleigh understood that she couldn't go back to her old life now. It was no longer *her* life. It was a subject Joleigh ran past Franklin when they'd spoken on the phone the other night. He'd called three times since his stay at the motel two weeks before, and every time she heard his voice, knowing he was over two hours away, it made her feel like a teenager again, waiting to be picked up by her date.

It had helped to share the weight of such a major decision. Not that Franklin knew Joleigh well enough yet, but as someone who moved back to his hometown after coming back from Vietnam, he understood the pull of being "home."

As Joleigh parked at the lake access, she reflected on one of the many wise things Unity had said. *"Home isn't a place. It's a feeling. One that wraps around us like a warm cocoon, making us feel safe. Wherever your heart is, that's home."* Over the past months, Grandfield—and the townspeople—had seeped into Joleigh's heart.

Fish houses dotted the ice, none near the lake access where Joleigh walked. She kept to the right side as she'd been warned, away from the open springs, as she carried the bucket of equipment and a chisel.

Joleigh cleaned out previously used holes with her chisel, rigged two fishing poles, and sat on the overturned five-gallon bucket. Sunshine reflected off the snow, warming her enough that she took off Unity's fox hat, made years ago from the pelt of a fox Unity caught in the chicken coop.

By noon, Joleigh had a small walleye and two decent-sized crappies lying on the ice. She packed up her fishing gear, tossed the fish in the bucket, and carried it to her truck before driving back to her property.

After clearing the snow around the firepit, Joleigh built a fire from rolled-up newspapers left in the motel office, placing them under a tepee of twigs combined with feathering she'd made by angling her knife on branches to produce wood shavings. Unity had taught her how to use a bow drill to start a fire, but she wanted something quick and easy to cook her Christmas meal.

In the back of her truck, she pulled out a cast-iron pan from a box and hung it from the tripod above the campfire. She used the tailgate from the truck as a table to fillet the fish then dug out the oil and spices she kept in a box of staples she'd taken from her kitchen in Missouri.

Joleigh cooked and ate her fill of fish and went back to the motel with enough for another meal. She spent the afternoon catching up on her laundry and the motel's, using the four washers and dryers located off the vending-machine area.

The phone rang soon after she arrived in her room. "Merry Christmas," Franklin said. "I tried calling you earlier. Please tell me you weren't out celebrating Christmas with another man, even if you have to lie." Joleigh laughed. She heard the smile in his voice.

Joleigh had been counting the days until New Year's Eve weekend. "I went fishing on Lonesome Lake and caught enough for two meals. How was your Christmas? Are you sick of cooking?" Franklin's family had gathered at his parents' house, where he and his mother made the meal.

"I ate enough for a week, and although we fed over forty people, we sent leftovers home with everyone. Want me to run you up some ham and mashed potatoes?"

Joleigh plopped in the chair next to the phone. "I'd like to have you here, food or no food." She tried to keep her voice light, void of need or want.

"I wish you'd have been here with me and my noisy family." He had invited her. But with spending Christmas Eve day with Bits and working the morning shift at Ruby's, it would have been a lot of driving for Joleigh on Christmas Day. "Maybe you should move here. You'd be close to Grandfield and closer to Woodland."

"Ha! It should be obvious I'm no city girl." Joleigh didn't need to add Iowa to the list of places she could live. And they hadn't known each other long enough for her to upend her life—again.

After they hung up, Joleigh got out her box of yarn and chose a skein of pearl gray she'd bought last year. Originally, she'd planned to knit a hat for Unity out of the soft yarn, but within a week of her purchase, Unity had taken a turn for the worse, and the hat was forgotten—until Franklin showed up at the motel two weeks ago. His eyes reminded her of that beautiful skein of yarn. And she knew exactly what she would do with it.

After changing into her pajamas, she flipped on the television and watched *White Christmas* while she went to work with her circular knitting needles to create a hat for the man who'd been taking up a lot of space in her mind lately.

When Joleigh still couldn't sleep several hours later, her brain creating an endless slideshow of pros and cons, she made a mental list. In the plus column for Missouri: familiarity, Unity's house, the goats, the Hoovers. In the Minnesota plus column: Bits, the Nielsons, Ruby's, her property, and her new friends. She didn't want to jinx things by adding Franklin to the list.

One name on the list for Minnesota offset everything in Missouri. Bits was the deciding factor and the reason Joleigh vowed to call Wes, the realtor in Missouri, after the holidays.

The idea that had been slowly seeping into her thoughts recently would depend on the sale of her home.

WHEN FRANKLIN ARRIVED at Joleigh's motel room to pick her up for skiing the following weekend, she welcomed him into the room and handed him a small wrapped package. "Belated Christmas gift." She waved her hand at the look of panic in his eyes. "It's nothing." The last thing she wanted was to have Franklin think *she* thought they were in the gift-giving phase of a relationship.

His shoulders relaxed. They stood mere inches apart, close enough that when Franklin unwrapped the gray stocking hat made from merino-wool yarn, she heard his soft gasp.

"Wow, Joleigh, this is beautiful! And so soft." Franklin rubbed his thumb back and forth over the hat then leaned in and kissed her. "Thank you," he whispered before pulling away. "I'll wear it today." He tugged it on over his head, the gray instantly bringing out his eyes.

"Okay, let's get going. Those mountains are waiting for us." Franklin smirked when Joleigh flashed him a look of horror at the word "mountains."

An hour later, they stood at the base of the ski hills.

"You call that *mountain* a bunny hill?" Joleigh pointed at the steep slope in front of them, dotted with people. Her rental skis and boots weighed down her legs, feeling like cinder blocks that would never allow her to soar down any hill. Or turn. Or stop.

"You've spent too many years on flatland. Time to elevate you." Franklin nudged her with the handle of his ski pole.

"I don't know. These skis seem mighty long to be swishing back and forth." Franklin had already gone over the basics of how to snow-plow to stop. "They're a lot longer than the other people's skis." She pointed at the figures skiing down the hill in front of them.

"That's because they are kids." He grinned at Joleigh's scowl. "The length of the skis goes by your height. And you, young lady, are tall. Come on, follow me."

He led the way to the towrope that climbed up to the top of the bunny hill. "Make sure there's no ice on your ski mittens, or they'll slip on the rope."

Joleigh checked her mittens.

"Line your body up with the rope so it doesn't jerk your arms out of their sockets when you grip it." He demonstrated as they moved up to the front of the line.

Joleigh followed his instructions and grinned as she made it to the top of the hill and skied out of the way as Franklin instructed. Her grin faded, though, when they crested the top of the hill.

"Yikes! That's too steep." She looked at her skis, ready to take them off and walk down.

Franklin read her thoughts. "Oh no, you don't. You won't get hurt, and once you get the hang of it, I think you'll enjoy yourself."

He reiterated a few tips he'd mentioned earlier for when—not if—she fell. "Remember, tuck and roll, and avoid landing on your hands or back. I'll be with you to help you back up."

Joleigh slowly pushed off, her sunglasses reflecting sunshine onto her cheeks.

An hour of skiing on the bunny hill boosted Joleigh's confidence. She'd fallen more times than she could count but eventually mastered four trips down the hill without falling once. "Okay, I'm ready for the next hill."

Franklin patted her on the back. "See? I knew you could do it. Should we try the hill with the T-bar? Your skis will still be on the ground."

"I like my skis on the ground. Thank you." When they arrived at the top, what she didn't like was the view—it seemed twice the height of the bunny hill. "Are you sure this isn't a black-diamond hill?" Franklin had explained the different slope ranks to Joleigh earlier.

Franklin laughed. "No. If it was, you'd see moguls on the slope. And it would be a lot steeper." He stood next to Joleigh. "I'll be right behind you. Take your time, and remember what you learned on the bunny hill. With the wider terrain, there's more room here for you to slow yourself down. I'll meet you at the bottom." He signaled for Joleigh to go ahead.

She fell twice on her first run, finding it more difficult to navigate the steeper slope. After her third time down the hill, she relaxed.

By the time they stopped for lunch, Joleigh's cheeks hurt from smiling so much.

Over cheeseburgers, fries, and hot cocoa in the lodge, Franklin apologized. "I'm sorry you aren't having any fun." He sat across from her, a mock frown on his face.

"Okay, do I have to say it?" Joleigh breathed in the lodge's scent of wet wool, hot chocolate, and popcorn. "You were right."

"Ah, I never get sick of hearing those words."

"Yeah, well, you won't hear them too often from me." She took another bite of her cheeseburger to hide her smile.

"You up for the chairlift? The next hill is a little longer, about the same slope as what we just skied, but the only way up is on a chairlift."

Joleigh struggled to swallow a bite as the slow burn of fear crept up her neck. "Unity said fear can never take the place of common sense. And common sense tells me I probably won't fall out of one of those chairlifts, right?"

"That would never happen." Franklin nodded, contradicting his words.

"You aren't making any points, buster." She pointed a French fry at him.

They finished eating, and he led the way to their next hill. "The chairlift has a bar we can lower over our laps if that will make you feel safer."

"I don't just want to *feel* safe. I want to be safe." She eyed the people in front of them who were sliding their pole straps onto one wrist. When it came time for Joleigh and Franklin to board, their butts had barely hit the bench when she lowered the metal bar over their laps.

"There, feel better?" He met her eyes.

She nodded.

"Don't look straight down. Look out at the view. It's beautiful."

"I'm not looking anywhere but at you." She had a death grip on the bar over her lap. "Take my mind off the height. Tell me what you're afraid of. You must fear *something*."

Franklin sighed. "Fireworks. I'm not a fan of fireworks or any loud noise."

Of course. Any loud *bang* would resurrect memories of Vietnam. "I should've known. My old friend Mack served in Vietnam. He flinched every time he heard a car backfire."

She'd mentioned Mack a few times to Franklin but glossed over their relationship—and why he was no longer in the picture. "One of my neighbors back in Missouri had a truck that backfired a lot." Her mind drifted to the night that backfire likely saved her life. It took her mind off the chairlift.

They neared the top of the hill.

"Watch the people in front of us as they slide off the chairlift," Franklin said. "I'm going to lift the bar now so we're ready, okay?"

Joleigh peered down. They were still thirty feet in the air. "I shimmy to the edge of the seat, right?"

"Yes, and make sure your skis are straight. Be ready with your poles so we can ski out of the way for the next people to get off."

When her skis hit the snow, Joleigh glided to the side to avoid getting hit by the chairlift and other skiers. Franklin high-fived her before she took off ahead of him down the hill, adrenaline encouraging her along. Joleigh kept her pace slow, controlling it with several turns along the way. She took a few more tumbles, one time landing face-first in the powdery snow, but she kept at it.

After several rides on the chairlift, she braved a look out at the skyline. The high of the day hovered several degrees below freezing, but the sunshine and lack of wind offset the temperature. Crystal Lake sparkled in the distance with a large ice-skating rink cleared.

By mid-afternoon, Joleigh's feet were dragging, weighted down with fatigue.

"Had enough?" Franklin said.

"Yes. You can keep skiing, though. I'll hang out in the ski lodge and watch." The lodge's floor-to-ceiling windows gave its guests a perfect view of the slopes. "I'm going to be sore tomorrow." She was glad she had the day off.

"I'm fine with quitting for the day. This was more about getting you comfortable on the slopes. And you're right. You are going to feel every muscle in your body tomorrow. But it was worth it, right?" He gestured with his arm to the lodge.

Joleigh sat on the bench next to him and removed her ski boots. She rubbed her shins. "It feels like I'm still wearing the boots."

"It will for a while."

They gathered their belongings, returned Joleigh's rental equipment, and walked to his vehicle.

"Thanks so much for taking me. This was fun," Joleigh said when they reached the truck. "I can't say I'm a fan of the chairlifts, but they were worth riding to hit the bigger hills."

"You're a natural," Franklin said as he pulled out of the crowded parking lot. "I'm not surprised, though. You look like you play a lot of sports."

"I played basketball and softball in junior and senior high. My mom was your typical petite Korean, and I used to hate that I took after Dad's brawny Irish side of the family." She gazed out the passenger-side window. "I was chubby after my parents died, during my years in foster care." Her words came out like a timid confession.

"I can't imagine what you went through." Franklin reached for her hand as he steered with the other. "My dad can be a hardnose sometimes, but I've been lucky to have my parents and all my annoying siblings."

"Unity saved me. I went from an overweight foster child who other people teased to a child who felt loved and secure. She gave me a permanent home, taught me the value of hard work, and helped me shed the grief and weight I'd cushioned myself in. She gave me the confidence to be proud of my heritage."

They talked all the way back to the motel, Franklin briefly mentioning his time in the army and his hard work at the bank to make his way up the ladder.

"I'm going to shower and will be back here before six. Moe made six-o'clock dinner reservations for the four of us," Franklin said as he pulled into the motel parking lot.

While Franklin showered in his motel room, Joleigh did the same, wondering at what point he might share her room. In high school, she'd never done more than kiss a boy. Her relationship with Mack was different than this. They had been friends first. Joleigh didn't remember how they ended up in bed that first time, other than it had been late at night, well after she'd made sure Unity was asleep.

How will things play out with Franklin?

You are twenty-eight, Joleigh. Figure it out.

Chapter Twenty-Five

Joleigh hadn't eaten at a fancy supper club in years. Mack had taken her out one time for an elegant meal on her birthday a few years ago. It wasn't a setting Joleigh wanted in her daily life, but it felt good to dress up and dig into a scrumptious meal of prime rib.

The supper club had an attached bar with a dance floor. The bar was hosting a New Year's Eve celebration Joleigh hoped she would be able to stay awake to enjoy.

"Smokescreen plays a decent blend of rock and roll from the late sixties to new music," Moe said, nodding toward the band. "Creedence, The Doors, Rolling Stones, Bob Seger—maybe even some of that bubblegum music you like, Franklin." He reached up and slugged Franklin's arm in jest.

"We've listened to Smokescreen before," Diane explained. "I went to high school with the drummer. They formed the band after we graduated and have played together for about ten years now."

Moe led the way from the restaurant to the attached bar, stopping often to visit with other patrons. Franklin stayed with Moe as Joleigh and Diane nabbed a booth in the bar.

"How did you and Moe meet?" Joleigh asked as she slid in across from Diane.

"We met at an insurance convention through our jobs. He's not too keen on coming to visit me in Minneapolis, and my apartment isn't any more handicap-friendly than his." Diane sighed. "We need to get him out of his apartment. I hate that he's stuck on the third floor."

Franklin and Moe joined them a few minutes later, and soon, the bar was filled with others eager to ring in 1978. Franklin and Joleigh squeezed in on the crowded dance floor, the band playing a variety of songs from "Ramblin' Gamblin' Man" by Bob Seger, one of Moe's favorites, to "We're All Alone" by Boz Scaggs, one of Joleigh's new favorites. Moe and Diane joined them on the dance floor, Diane sometimes sitting on Moe's lap as he spun his wheelchair around. Anyone watching them could see their love for each other, and as Joleigh's body melted against Franklin during a slow song, she wondered why Moe and Diane hadn't married.

But the thought that kept her awake after Franklin walked Joleigh to her door in the early hours of the new year was what the future—if they had one—held for her and Franklin.

FRANKLIN HAD A BIRTHDAY party for one of his sisters the following weekend, so they planned a ski trip for the Saturday after that. Joleigh would miss him, but she had plenty to do.

On the second of January, she placed a call to Wes, the realtor who had helped with the land sale to Mr. Hoover's sons. "I'm thinking of selling my home and the forty acres it sits on," she said. "My neighbors, the Hoovers, have a key. If you let me know when you think you'll be there to look the house and property over, I will let them know."

"It's a slow time of year," Wes said. "I can get out there tomorrow—say, around one o'clock? It's a good time to get your house on the market. Buyer interest picks up in February when the weather warms up."

Joleigh gave him the motel's phone number. "Please don't give it out to anyone," she said. Mack's killers might see the For Sale sign near her driveway and call the realtor for information.

"I won't. I'll call you once I come up with an appraised listing estimate."

Afterward, Joleigh touched base with the Hoovers, and they agreed to meet Wes at her house on Tuesday. The Hoovers told her that Joplin and Groovy were thriving, and they had added two goats of their own.

Wes called her Wednesday night with a suggested listing price. "That's 'as is.' If you want to make suggested improvements, we could raise the list price. It's up to you."

The listing price Wes quoted was higher than she'd expected, thanks to the acreage and outbuildings. It was a good starter home, a good hobby farm. "If I lived there, I'd do it, but it's not worth my time." Joleigh verbally agreed to the listing price.

"I'll find out tomorrow morning if we can get it in the paper for next week, and I'll mail the listing agreement. We want it in the newspaper ASAP," Wes said.

"I work tomorrow morning. Can you call me there?" She recited the phone number for Ruby's.

"Sure. I'll call you tomorrow."

When they hung up, Joleigh's neck grew warm as her heart raced. She was excited and scared. But every time she felt as if she was betraying Unity by selling her home, Joleigh remembered how often in those last years Unity had made Joleigh promise to live *her* life.

"I'm trying, Unity," Joleigh said to the empty motel room.

JOLEIGH HAD MISSED Saturday with Bits since she'd picked up a shift at Ruby's, so they spent Sunday together, building a snow fort on Joleigh's land and roasting marshmallows over a campfire. They sat alongside each other on a log, their faces warm from the fire.

"I can't wait for you to move here. We'll almost be neighbors," Bits said.

Joleigh wiped a smidge of melted marshmallow from Bits's mouth. "Remember, it's only if I sell my home in Missouri. But yes, if nothing else, I hope to camp here next summer. Did I ever tell you about the two weeks Unity and I spent in the woods?"

Bits shook her head.

"It was the first summer after she adopted me. Unity wanted me to learn about the land, and we had an adventure of sorts in the woods. We weren't too far from the house, so we could take care of the animals, but otherwise, we spent all the time in the woods."

Joleigh remembered the warm August days, the cool nights. The singing around the campfire, the stories Unity told of her youth. Joleigh's young brain had been a sponge for it all. "We made a shelter with brush and tree limbs, dug a hole to protect our food, and filtered our drinking water from the nearby swamp through sand and gravel before boiling it. I learned how to start a fire with flint and also with a bow drill. But you know what the coolest thing was that I learned during our adventure?"

She smiled at Bits. "It was the end of August, before school began, and Unity taught me how to gauge what the temperature was by listening to the crickets." Joleigh explained how the frequency of a cricket's chirp reflected the temperature. "You count the number of chirps in fifteen seconds and then add thirty-seven. The total number will give you the approximate temperature."

"Wow!" Bits's eyes darted around their snow-covered surroundings. "I sure wish the crickets were out now so we could test it."

Joleigh patted Bits's knee. "We can try it next summer."

She continued with stories of adventures with Unity until it was time to pack up. She'd promised Bits they could watch *The Wonderful World of Disney* in her motel room—a treat for Bits, since Howie didn't own a TV.

When Joleigh dropped Bits off that night, she reminded her about the following weekend. "Remember, I have plans next Saturday, so I'll pick you up Sunday instead, okay? I'll be here by one o'clock." It would give her time to take care of guest checkouts and laundry from the motel rooms—and spend time with Franklin before he headed back to Iowa.

Bits nodded before getting out of the truck. "I'll let Papa know. Bye."

Joleigh watched Bits trudge through the snow into her dimly lit home, wondering if Howie was awake to greet his daughter or if Bits would spend the rest of the night alone.

IN THE TWO WEEKS SINCE Franklin had been in Grandfield, time had flown by for Joleigh, but he was never out of her thoughts, no matter how busy she was.

Franklin arrived after the sun set on Friday night. "That's the one thing I don't like about winter." He stomped the snow from his shoes in the motel office's doorway. "I left work early and still ended up driving in the dark most of the way here."

Joleigh felt the same. "Luckily, it's not too cold out." She registered Franklin, one of five guests at the motel for the weekend. With twenty-four motel rooms, it amazed Joleigh that the Nielsons could keep up in the busy summer months. "Will it be too warm for skiing tomorrow?"

"The snow conditions should be fine, but dress for cold weather. It's supposed to be windy." He leaned in and gave Joleigh a quick kiss as a vehicle pulled up in the parking lot, its headlights shining into the office.

Franklin and Moe were meeting some other guys for dinner and drinks, so Joleigh wouldn't see him until Saturday morning.

After she checked the guests in, she spent the rest of the evening going over her finances and doing her best to ignore an idea that kept resurfacing. An idea she couldn't afford to think about. Yet.

The following day, Franklin and Joleigh were on the slopes by ten. She had notified the motel guests when they checked in the night before that she would be gone most of the day. So it surprised Joleigh to spot a sheet of paper taped to her room door when they pulled into the motel parking lot late in the afternoon, exhausted from several hours on the slopes.

"Uh-oh, it looks like a motel customer left me a note." Joleigh leapt from the truck, regretting having left the motel unattended for the day, certain a catastrophe had occurred.

But it was a note from Ruby. *Where the hell are you? CALL ME ASAP! Two men stopped in the café looking for you. A tall guy and a guy with a scar on his cheek! - Ruby*

The blood drained from Joleigh's face. She had described the men to Ruby, the men Mr. Hoover had met at her Missouri house, Mack's killers. She opened her room door, and her hand shook as she dialed Ruby's number, avoiding the what-the-hell look on Franklin's face.

Ruby answered on the first ring.

"I was skiing with Franklin. Just got back and read your note. When did they come in?" Joleigh's teeth chattered between the words. She peered out the window in case the men showed up, feeling Franklin behind her, his body tense with unasked questions.

"A couple of hours ago. I've been sitting at the phone since then, waiting for your call."

Joleigh felt awful for getting Ruby involved.

"You're lucky I was at the cash register when they walked in," Ruby continued. "If they'd spoken with another employee first, they'd have blabbed where you live." Joleigh could hear the frustration in Ruby's voice. "The man with the cheek scar was a dead giveaway. It took me a second to think of who I'd heard had a scar like that. When they asked for you, I knew."

"I'm so sorry you're being put in the middle of this. What did you tell them?"

"I said I knew who they were and what they did to your boyfriend. Then I picked up the phone and called the Grandfield police department. As soon as the dispatcher answered, I told her I had two killers standing in front of me and to send law enforcement to Ruby's. They ran out the door before I finished talking." Ruby blew out a sigh. "I'm pissed at myself for not blocking the doorway or checking to see what their vehicle looked like."

Joleigh swallowed. "That's okay. I'm glad you recognized them. I'll call the police to see what I need to do."

"Yes. When the cop arrived, he asked for you to stop by the police department. I spoke with every employee here and told them to not give anyone information about you, especially about where you're staying."

"Thank you. I appreciate what you did, Ruby. I'll call the Grandfield police." They hung up, and Joleigh turned to address Franklin, who looked like he was ready to burst.

"Care to tell me what in the hell is going on?" he asked.

Joleigh struggled for air as anxiety percolated inside her. She took a seat at the small round table and gestured for Franklin to do the same.

He folded his arms over his chest, and his chin jutted out as if he was deciding whether to sit or leave. Finally, he pulled out the other chair, sat, and waited.

Joleigh took a long, ragged breath. "I've told you a little about Mack, but I couldn't tell you the reason I left Missouri. The only people in town I've told were Ruby—because she busted me in a lie when she realized I wasn't related to any of you Gradys—and the Nielsons."

Joleigh's heart raced as if she were finally coming face-to-face with the monster she'd had nightmares about for months. "I've led you and everyone else to believe I left Missouri because I wanted to. I didn't. It was because I witnessed men murder Mack at my house—men who knew I was there, hiding, and who have now tracked me down."

With each new confession, Franklin clenched and unclenched his fists.

By the time she finished, Franklin was out of his chair. He pulled Joleigh up and into his embrace, and her shoulders sagged in relief. He wasn't angry with her for withholding the truth.

She clung to him. "I figured the fewer people who knew, the better. Even my old neighbors, the Hoovers, don't know. I was afraid the men would threaten them to find out where I am." Joleigh's tears dampened the front of Franklin's shirt as she clung to him. "I'm sorry I didn't tell you." She pulled her head back from his shoulder to look at him. "But honestly, I didn't expect us to have any sort of relationship where you'd have cared about my past."

Franklin blew out a long breath. "Oh, I care, Joleigh." He rested his forehead against hers. "I care much more than I expected." He kissed her cheeks, which were damp with tears. "If you don't mind, I'd like to go with you to the police department."

Joleigh nodded. Franklin shrugged back into his ski jacket and held hers open.

"I'm not leaving you alone," Franklin added. "I'm staying here tonight. I'll sleep on the extra bed." He crossed his arms. "And yes, I know you can take care of yourself, but please let me pretend you need me, at least for this weekend, okay?"

Stress from the last several months pushed at Joleigh like a tidal wave, ready to knock her legs out from underneath her. Leaning on someone else would be a welcome relief. "Okay, my knight in shining armor, you can stay."

Joleigh looped her arm through Franklin's, and she double-checked that she'd locked her motel-room door before they drove to the police department.

She was back on high-alert status again.

Chapter Twenty-Six

As Franklin drove, his mind attempted to organize the information Joleigh had just purged. "I wonder how they found out you live in Grandfield. They must not know you don't have their money anymore."

"Probably not. If Missouri law enforcement had contact with them, they'd have arrested them by now." Joleigh fidgeted with the mittens on her lap. "I'm afraid they're here to silence me."

Franklin drummed his frustration out on the steering wheel, his nerves jittery. *How did you not question Joleigh's sudden appearance in Grandfield, Columbo?*

A few minutes later, they pulled into the police department's parking lot, which was near-empty on a Saturday. Franklin held Joleigh's hand as they entered the building, the halls smelling of burned coffee and bleach. The clerk called one of the officers to the front desk, and Joleigh gave him detailed information about Mack's killers. Since the Grandfield department was small, the young-looking officer told her they would work with the local sheriff's department, who would keep in contact with Sergeant Williams.

The Grandfield cop placed a call to Sergeant Williams, who agreed to send wanted posters with the two men's information to the Grandfield police department to distribute.

The sergeant asked to speak to Joleigh, and the young cop handed her the phone. Franklin stood next to her to hear the conversation.

"I'll make a few more phone calls around here," Williams assured Joleigh. "We'll put the word out that we've got their drug money and that we're trailing them from Minnesota. I'll get back to you later this week."

Joleigh thanked the Grandfield police officer, who promised to keep in touch.

Franklin put his hand on the small of Joleigh's back as they walked out to his truck. He tried to reel in his agitation. *Joleigh has been carrying this burden, this worry, alone, while you've been thinking of joining her in her motel room. Well, you got your wish, but only to protect her, not bed her, you horny bastard!* They rode back to the motel in silence.

"All I want to do is shower then crawl into bed," Joleigh groaned. They were supposed to have had dinner at Moe's an hour ago. Moe and Diane had spent the day in Minneapolis and picked up Chinese takeout for the four of them on their way home.

Franklin had called Moe from the pay phone at the police station to let him know they'd be late. He put his hands on Joleigh's shoulders. "I'm with you on that, but we need to eat, and it will be good to get out and take your mind off of things."

"You're right. If I sit here, I'll think about where they are, if they left town, and if they know where I live."

As much as Franklin itched to pulverize the murderers, he also didn't want them anywhere near Joleigh. "I'm guessing they've left Grandfield," Franklin said. "Ruby likely scared the shit out of them. Nobody messes with Ruby." He rubbed Joleigh's shoulders. "I'm still going to stay here tonight, just in case. I want reassurance that those thugs are long gone."

"And I want world peace." Joleigh forced a smile. "I shouldn't joke. I appreciate you staying here. I'll move my things off the extra bed. Also, I was thinking I should park my truck in the Nielsons' garage before we go to Moe's. They'd said I could park in there. If those men are still in town or come back to Grandfield, I don't want them spotting my Missouri license plates."

"Good idea. I can do that if you give me your keys."

"Thanks." Joleigh fished in her coat pocket for the keys. "I'll change while you do that."

After parking Joleigh's truck in the garage, Franklin stopped at his motel room to change clothes and gather his things. By the time he arrived back in Joleigh's room, she had changed into dark-brown suede bell-bottoms and a gold cowl-neck sweater.

Franklin set his overnight bag on the extra bed that Joleigh had cleared off. His stomach growled, and it lightened their mood. "I hope they bought enough food, or those two may go hungry." He patted his stomach. "Ready?"

Joleigh walked to Franklin and wrapped her arms around his waist. "Thank you for being here for me." She stood on her tiptoes and kissed him. "Let's go. Even though my stomach is doing flips, I'm starving."

They arrived at Moe's apartment with beer and wine they had picked up at the liquor store. "Come on in." Moe met them at the door and led the way into the kitchen, where six white takeout bags stood on the counter.

"I think there's enough food," Joleigh said as Diane took their coats.

Moe gestured toward the kitchen table. "I bet you both are beat after the day you've had." Franklin had given him minimal details over the phone. Hell, that was all he knew so far. It ate at him that Joleigh hadn't trusted him enough. *You're one to point fingers, you secret-keeper.*

Over dinner, Joleigh filled Moe and Diane in about Mack and his killers and how she ended up in Grandfield. Now that the men had traced her there, it no longer mattered who knew the truth. *They* knew where she was.

"How do you think they found you here? Other than law enforcement in Woodland, have you had contact with anyone else there since you moved to Grandfield?" Diane asked.

"Yes. A local realtor and my old neighbor, both involved with the property I sold to my neighbor's sons. In fact, I just listed my house and forty acres with the same realtor."

Franklin wasn't keen on Joleigh building a home in Grandfield and hoped he could convince her to move to Mason City before she started construction.

"Are you going to check with the realtor and neighbor to see if they gave out your phone number?" Moe asked.

Joleigh shrugged. "My neighbor thinks I'm in Arkansas, and I never told the realtor where I am, but I gave him strict instructions not to give my number to anyone. I'll call them both tomorrow."

After dinner, they moved to the living room, where Franklin and Joleigh settled in on the couch. As the four visited, Joleigh rested her head on his shoulder, and he imagined the day of fresh air, skiing, and stress had wiped her out.

He looked at Moe. "We should go before Joleigh falls asleep on your couch."

"I'm glad you're staying with her tonight. And I hope they arrest those bastards soon."

Moe and Diane followed them to the apartment door. They made Joleigh promise to call Moe if anything strange happened after Franklin left the following afternoon. "I may be in a wheelchair, but it doesn't mean I can't still kick ass." Moe twirled the bottom of his trimmed mustache like a villain.

Back at the motel, Joleigh and Franklin took turns in the bathroom, getting ready for bed. Joleigh showered first, and he tried to occupy his mind by watching TV instead of thinking about her naked in the shower. *Remember, you're a monk tonight, Franklin.*

Once Joleigh stepped out, dressed in gray sweatpants and a gray smiley-face T-shirt, Franklin took his turn. When he emerged from the shower, dressed in navy-blue gym shorts and a white T-shirt, she was sitting on top of her made bed, leaning against the headboard, the radio playing low on the nightstand.

The steam from the shower fogged up the mirror as he brushed his teeth, his nerves rattling around inside him. *No need to be nervous! You promised to sleep on the other bed.* But damn, even from several feet away, he could smell her fruity shampoo, could almost feel her soft skin beneath him.

He closed his eyes a second to regroup his thoughts before he turned to face her. "With all the vehicles out front, if the men find out you're staying here, they'll see you aren't alone."

Joleigh nodded. "I'm going to ask if any of my coworkers at Ruby's have an extra car. If I get a few parked out front, it would look like people are here this week. I'll leave lights on in some of the motel rooms. I've got a few rooms rented next weekend, and I can't imagine they'd stick around town longer than that."

"Let's call Moe in the morning. I bet he knows several people with an extra car who'd be willing to park it out front for a few days."

"I like that idea." She bit her lower lip as he came to stand by her bed. "You know what I keep thinking about? That I traveled all this way, changed everything in my life, and yet they found me. I could've just stayed in Woodland."

Franklin sat on the foot of her bed. "They'd have found you right away there. At least here, you've been able to start a new life away from them, away from the memories of what happened." His eyes met hers. "And we'd never have met."

The room was quiet, other than the soft din of Bob Welch singing "Sentimental Lady." And all Franklin could think about was the lyrics, how he could blink one day and Joleigh would be gone from his life. *I can't let that happen.* Without a word, he went to kneel on the floor beside where Joleigh sat.

"I was an ass to you in the beginning, and I hope by now you see that isn't who I am. I care about you a lot." Her lips were mere inches away, but he focused on her eyes. "I'm worried about your safety, although I know I don't need to be. I'm pretty sure you could kick my ass with one hand and take out those guys with the other."

Franklin barely got the words out before Joleigh bridged the distance between their mouths and whispered, "Shhh. Suddenly, the last thing I want to do is sleep." She pulled his body toward hers, and every promise he'd made to himself got kicked to the curb.

Chapter Twenty-Seven

Joleigh opened one eye and peered at the clock radio. *Eight minutes after seven?* For a second, she freaked out, thinking she was late for work. It was Sunday. *No work at Ruby's today.* And in that same second, the chain of events from the previous day played back in her mind—skiing, Mack's killers tracking her to Grandfield, telling Moe and Diane her story... and making love with Franklin.

Joleigh turned her head on the pillow and spotted Franklin sleeping in the extra bed. When had he left her bed, and why? His smooth head faced her, and her fingers itched to sneak over and touch his skin. Still, she was glad he wasn't awake. She needed time to reflect on how it happened.

It was easy. Joleigh had made the first move, and he didn't turn her down. She hadn't been drinking, so she couldn't blame any fuzzy judgment. She'd been fully aware when she pulled Franklin on top of her, aware of running her hands under his T-shirt, aware of his skin sizzling against her palms as "Falling" by LeBlanc and Carr played on the radio.

And she'd been aware of Franklin bracing himself on his elbows above her, asking her if she was sure, if they needed protection, giving her an out. One she didn't want or need. What she wanted was to experience life, something she'd pushed aside for far too long.

While Franklin slept, Joleigh showered. When Joleigh stepped out of the bathroom with a white towel wrapped around her, Franklin was brushing his teeth at the sink.

"Good morning." His smile reached his eyes.

"Hiya." She grinned back. "Do I have to apologize for last night?"

"You'd offend me if you did." Franklin dried his face. "That would mean you thought it was a poor decision." He stepped toward Joleigh. "I'm glad you made the first move. Because it was front and center in my head, but I'd promised to sleep on the extra bed, remember?" He put his hands on her hips. "I didn't want to be the asshole who went back on his word."

She stepped back to look at him. "But you ended up sleeping on the other bed. Why? Was I snoring?" Joleigh didn't think she snored. "Did I hog the bed?"

"Nope and nope. Are you hungry? I am. I can whip us up breakfast in the Nielsons' kitchen, or we can go to Ruby's. Your choice." Franklin turned away, walked to his overnight bag, and packed his things.

So he didn't want to talk about why he'd moved to the other bed.

"Thanks for staying last night," she said. "I slept great knowing you were here. I've got bread and eggs if you'd like French toast, and I have sausage in the Nielsons' freezer."

"Perfect. I'll make breakfast. If you don't mind, I want to follow up with Moe this morning, and I'd like to hear what your realtor says when you call him today."

"We can call Moe after breakfast. I'll call Wes after that. I have his home phone number, and he said to call him anytime."

While they ate, Franklin asked for more details of Mack's murder, and it felt good to finally share it all with him.

After breakfast and a reassurance from Moe that he would organize cars for the motel parking lot, Joleigh called Wes. "I'm sorry to bother you on a Sunday, but I need to know if two men have been asking about me in your office. One has a scar on his cheek, and the other is very tall."

"Hmmm. They sound like two men I saw through my office window the other day. I had customers with me. The men spoke to our receptionist for a couple of minutes and then left. One had a scar on his face. I'll call the receptionist and get back to you."

Wes called Joleigh back within minutes. "Yes, she said the men fit your description. They introduced themselves as relatives of yours. They said they had some personal things of yours, and when they stopped at your house, they noticed our For Sale sign in the yard. The receptionist found the phone number for your work on a notepad from when I called you last Saturday. She gave them the phone number." He paused. "I'm so sorry, Joleigh. I have a feeling they weren't your relatives."

"No, they're men wanted by law enforcement. Hasn't your secretary seen the wanted posters around town?" His office was in Macon, though. Joleigh wondered if law enforcement hadn't placed posters there.

"Aw, hell, that's why those guys looked familiar! I've seen their posters in Woodland," Wes said. "They don't have them up around here."

"I'll tell the sergeant working the case. I can't go into details, but they're after me, Wes, and I need to make sure nobody gives any information about me to anyone unless it's Sergeant Williams."

Wes promised he would speak with his staff on Monday morning.

Franklin rubbed the knot between Joleigh's shoulders while she called and updated Sergeant Williams.

"I'll send a deputy to the real estate office tomorrow to get details from the receptionist. We'll put up wanted posters around Macon," Williams said.

After they hung up, Joleigh reached for Franklin's hand, wishing he didn't have to leave. Wishing she wouldn't have to be alone. Again.

Bundled in her ski jacket and knit hat, she followed Franklin outside. He started his truck to let it warm up then threw his overnight bag in the back seat before he leaned against the truck and pulled Joleigh to him. "I wish we lived closer to each other." He wrapped his arms around her waist. "I'll be up next weekend."

She rubbed her fingertips over his head. "I'm looking forward to it. Did I tell you that you look darn handsome as a bald man?"

Franklin snorted. "I began losing my hair after I enlisted in the service. If you come to Mason City, I'll dig out photos of me from high school." He smiled. "Can you leave this place for a weekend? I'd like to show you around my hometown."

"The Nielsons said I can close for a weekend if I need to go anywhere. I can turn off the vacancy sign. I'll look ahead on the schedule and pick a weekend. There hasn't been a last-minute booking yet, and Mr. Nielson said most people traveling north on I-35 continue to the Twin Cities to get a hotel room for the night." She stood on her tiptoes and kissed him goodbye. "And yes, I'd like to see where you live."

Minutes later, after he drove away, Joleigh stood in the too-quiet parking lot, missing his smile, his support, his... everything. *Why did I have to fall for a man who lived so far away?* As hard as she'd tried to steer her future, that was one thing she had no control over.

Moe called soon after Franklin left. "I'm going to stay in a room there this week. Four of my buddies should be at the motel by tonight to park extra vehicles there for the week," he said. "They said you can keep them around all winter if needed."

"You don't have to stay here. You've got your own place."

Moe laughed. "I know that. But it's a plus for me, a room where I don't have the hassle of an elevator. Who knows? You may have to kick me out after a week."

"I think you'll feel cramped after a while. Your apartment is more spacious. But I won't turn down your offer. It takes a lot to scare me."

She stopped and swallowed her emotions. "But when I have flash-backs of what those men did to Mack? It reminds me they're cold-blooded killers who want their drug money and want me silenced."

"I don't blame you, Joleigh. But we've got your back, and you are one tough-as-nails woman. I'll be over later with my things. When my friends get there, they'll move furniture if needed in the motel room. If it's laid out like yours, I should be fine with my wheelchair."

"I'll put you in a room with two beds, like mine."

The motel had been built with plenty of room to move around and wide doorways to the shower and toilet, which had been one of the attractions for the Nielsons when they'd purchased it. "We had planned to stay here until we were old and gray," Mr. Nielson told Joleigh months ago. "I guess our plans worked out. I wanted to make sure that if I or the missus ended up in a wheelchair, we could still access every room, every bathroom. Back then, I was foolish enough to think we'd have the energy to run this place in our old age."

He'd chuckled, but Joleigh detected a hint of sadness in it. They'd put their heart into the motel, a business they struggled to sell with-out losing everything. A business she'd spent a lot of time thinking about lately.

JOLEIGH USED THE NIELSONS' kitchen to make meatloaf and baked potatoes for her and Moe for dinner. It was the least she could do for him, and she enjoyed his company. After he'd unpacked in his room, Moe wheeled over to Joleigh's.

"I brought my appetite—and dessert," Moe said, nodding to the frozen boxed Sara Lee chocolate layer cake on his lap.

"I've never tried her desserts, but I've drooled over the box-cover photos in the grocery store," Joleigh said.

"As you can see, I slaved like a son of a bitch over this," he joked.

While they ate, they talked about the motel. "The rooms are nice. I can't believe I've lived in this town almost thirty years and never been inside Nielson's Nest," Moe said.

Joleigh filled him in on the Nielsons' desire to sell for the past several years. "They don't put a sign out front because they don't want customers to think there's something wrong with the place. They've listed it with a realtor off and on, but the business is too seasonal, so most of these rooms sit empty for several months."

After dinner, she showed Moe the rough draft of her house plans. "First, I need to sell my house and acreage back in Missouri before I can build here. I just can't decide if that's what I want to do. I love living in the country, but I love being around people too."

"Good thing you've got your job at Ruby's. Plenty of people time there, right? And as far as money for building, many people around here finish their basement and live in it until they can afford to build the rest of the house."

"I thought about that." She couldn't tell Moe that she could be out of a job, since Ruby's would be up for sale soon. "Is that your plan, to build eventually?"

"Yes. I'm just not sure where. If you hadn't noticed, I sort of like Diane." He grinned. "But she's got her life in Minneapolis, and I sure as hell don't want to live there. So, for now, I'm renting until I can figure things out."

"Do you think you'll get married?" Joleigh assumed that was in the picture if he was weighing where they would live.

He played with his napkin. "I don't know. I love her, which is why I haven't asked."

"What do you mean?" When a person loved someone, didn't they want to get married and spend the rest of their lives together?

"I don't want to burden Diane with a lifetime of challenges."

Joleigh reached for his hand. "You don't mean that. Diane loves you. Anyone who sees you two together can tell. If you're talking about you being in a wheelchair, that could happen to any of us. Do you think people who love each other quit if one person gets injured in a car accident or something?"

He rubbed his jaw. "It would chain her to a life of adjustments because of me. I can't ask her to do that. It's easier to just keep dating so she can leave whenever she wants."

Joleigh shook her head. "If she wanted to leave, don't you think she would have by now? And you delaying buying or building a home tells me you have hope for a future together."

Moe folded his arms over his chest. "Wounded people like Franklin and me keep people at bay so that if the person leaves, the rejection doesn't hurt so bad. It's a defense mechanism."

"Franklin? He's wounded?" Joleigh'd had a decent view of his body over the weekend, and she'd not seen a single mark other than a couple of small scars.

"Not all wounds are visible," Moe said softly. "Between what he went through in the jungles of 'Nam, and his fiancée leaving him for another guy—well, he's a little standoffish if you get too close."

"Thanks for telling me." The chocolate cake on her plate lost its appeal, so Joleigh set it aside. "Mack, my old boyfriend, refused to talk about Vietnam, but I'm sure what happened over there fueled his drug dependency. I didn't think about Franklin—or you—feeling like you're not worthy of love. You've got a lot going for you, and any woman with a brain would know that." Joleigh forced a smile. "I'm pretty sure Diane has a brain."

"Eh, I guess she's kind of smart," Moe deadpanned. He took a deep breath. "Here's the thing. I don't know if I can father a child. I don't want to rob her of that chance."

Joleigh leaned toward him. "I don't think I can have children, either, Moe. Nobody has that guarantee. Would you love Diane less if you were able-bodied and she couldn't have kids?"

Moe furrowed his brow. "Hell no."

"I figured as much. And I bet Diane feels the same." Joleigh hoped whoever she ended up with would give her that same unconditional love. Franklin came from a large family, and she wondered if he would be disappointed if he couldn't have the same.

After they packed up the leftovers, Moe left for his room, with a reminder to call him if she had any concerns. "Although you can take care of yourself, there's safety in numbers." He bid her goodnight, and Joleigh locked the door behind him.

When she slid into bed that night, she thought of Franklin and his past, wondering if he would ever feel comfortable enough to share it with her.

Chapter Twenty-Eight

By the time Franklin arrived the following Friday night, Joleigh had spoken with Sergeant Williams, who had followed through with widening the area of the wanted posters and interviewing Wes's receptionist.

"She remembered their old truck because it looked like one people would use for hunting, and she thought they might be interested in the property. It was dark-green with rust and a broken front grill," Williams informed Joleigh. "We have entered the information in the nationwide database, so your local sheriff's office will be on the lookout for the truck. At least you know what to look for now."

Moe moved back to his apartment Friday morning, but three other rooms had occupants for the weekend, and nobody had spotted the men in town over the past week. Still, Joleigh didn't believe for a second that the men wouldn't be back.

Franklin arrived Friday night, and on Saturday morning, he and Joleigh picked up Bits to take her ice fishing. They'd had several above-freezing days, and the snow had turned to slush in some areas. As the three of them walked out, staying to the right of the access, Franklin threw down a challenge.

"First fish caught gets a dollar. Biggest fish caught gets a dollar. What do you say, Bits?" He walked slowly so Bits could keep up with his long stride.

"But I don't have a dollar. I have to pay you?" She squinted up at him.

"Nope. This is a challenge where Joleigh and I have to pay *you*. If we win, you have to help fry the fish, okay?"

She shook his hand. "I like that deal."

They each carried a five-gallon bucket with supplies and over-turned their buckets to use as chairs once they cleared the fishing holes of ice. After baiting their hooks with shiner minnows, they all reeled them down into the icy water.

Over the next few hours, Franklin changed the rules so Bits won. The "biggest fish caught" changed to the "biggest crappie caught," which excluded Joleigh's two-pound walleye. By the time they drove to Joleigh's property to have a fish fry, Bits was two dollars richer.

While they enjoyed a meal of fresh fish sandwiches, Franklin told stories about living with his large, boisterous family, and Joleigh told stories of her upbringing and learning to live off the land.

"If I live here next summer, we can walk to Lonesome Lake and fish on the shore," she told Bits.

"I can ride my bike here," Bits said.

"And my family's cabin is just down the road." Franklin pointed in the direction of the cabin. "I'll be up here a lot once the weather turns nice. I expect you to visit so I can try to out-fish you this summer."

"That's a deal." Bits patted the money zipped inside her coat pocket.

When they dropped Bits off late that afternoon with a Wonder Bread bag filled with extra fish fillets they'd fried up for her and Howie, Joleigh noticed their dwindling woodpile. "Did you move some of your wood from the pile by the steps, Bits?" She would have to talk to Ruby about getting the wood crew together again, but she and Franklin could drop off the wood from the cabin that she'd cut and split.

"Nope, that's it. I haven't put much in the woodstove because it's been warm out, even though Papa always says he's chilled," Bits said.

"Thanks for taking me fishing. Can we do it again sometime? Papa doesn't eat fish, but I will."

"Yes, we'll go again. And we will deliver more firewood tomorrow. Please let your dad know we'll be there." Joleigh let Bits out of the truck and hugged her before she ran inside.

As they pulled into the motel parking lot, Franklin said, "You up for going somewhere tonight?"

Joleigh avoided his eyes. "I don't know. I've got to stop and check something in the office. Want to come with?"

"Sure." Franklin turned off the truck and followed Joleigh to the office. When she unlocked the door and they stepped inside, a heady aroma of roast beef enveloped them.

He shot her a quizzical look, and she gave him an impish grin. "Happy early birthday!" Joleigh took him by the hand and led him through the door to the Nielsons' kitchen, where a Crock-Pot sat on the counter, the cause of the mouth-watering aroma.

"How did you know?"

"Know what? Your birthday? While you were showering in my room last time, I sneaked a peek at your driver's license. I remember you saying you'd turn thirty-one in January." Joleigh lifted the lid off the slow cooker and poked the meat, potatoes, and carrots with a fork. "And as far as this being your favorite meal, I remembered when your hunting crew was at Ruby's for lunch, David said something about roast beef being your favorite meal."

Franklin rubbed his hands together. "This is great. Yum! Are we eating here or back at your room?"

"Here," she said. "I've got a cheesecake in the fridge I baked yesterday." She nodded to the cupboards. "You want to set the table?" She'd already triple-checked with the Nielsons that they were okay with her making herself at home there.

"After this, I'm leaving it up to you on how you want to celebrate your last day of being thirty." In the morning, she would give him the hardcover book she purchased last week, *The Shining*, a novel Joleigh had heard enough about to make her glad the motel didn't have hallways like a hotel.

"When do you turn twenty-nine, Miss Getting-Old-Too?" Franklin laughed when Joleigh scowled.

"Not until the end of August. A looong time from now." She didn't want to think about twenty-nine. It was too close to thirty. But if someone had asked Joleigh how old she felt over the past five years, she would have said much older than her age. Growing up too fast had pushed her into maturity earlier than others. She'd never felt young and carefree.

After their meal, topped off by strawberry cheesecake, Franklin chose roller-skating.

"You're joking, right?" Joleigh raised an eyebrow. "Won't we be about twenty years older than everyone else?" She had never gone roller-skating at all, other than a birthday party when she was twelve.

He grinned. "Not on a Saturday night. Most kids go during the day. I haven't roller-skated for years, and it's as close to hockey as I can get right now."

"Will your ankle be okay?"

"Yep, it's fully healed. I went skiing without any problem, remember?" They stood next to each other at the kitchen sink, washing and drying the dishes, and he nudged her with his shoulder. "Something tells me this won't be your strong suit. Now I for sure want to go."

"Okay, fine. But you better hold on to me."

"Oh, I will. I promise." Franklin leaned over and kissed the tip of her nose.

An hour later, they arrived at Saints Roller Rink outside Minneapolis. Franklin was true to his word, holding hands with Joleigh and helping her up off the floor more than once.

And when the music that pumped through several speakers turned to an old Roger Miller song, "You Can't Roller Skate in a Buffalo Herd," Joleigh sang along with yet another quirky favorite of Unity's, her smile wide at the message of the lyrics.

Yes, she could be happy if she put her mind to it. She was making choices that brought her joy, and Franklin was one of them.

THREE NIGHTS AFTER Franklin went home to Mason City, Joleigh's phone rang around midnight, the shrill sound jarring her from a deep sleep.

"Hello?"

It was Ruby. "Bits's mobile home is on fire! The fire trucks went past my house, so I turned on my police scanner. I'm heading out there now."

Joleigh yanked on jeans and a flannel shirt before Ruby finished talking. "I'll meet you there."

She spotted the flames as soon as she hit a flat stretch on County Road Twelve. She'd just passed Lonesome Road when flashing lights appeared in the distance, and the acrid scent of smoke filtered inside the truck.

Three fire trucks lined the road, their hoses shooting water at the flames, illuminated by the rotating beacons of light from two police cars. Joleigh flung the truck door open and ran toward the commotion, picking Ruby out of the handful of gawkers alongside the road.

"Where is Bits?" Joleigh asked.

"They're both in one of the cop cars. They're okay." Ruby pointed down the road, away from the blaze.

Joleigh jogged down the slushy road, thankful they weren't loading Bits into an ambulance.

Inside the cop car, Bits wore the knit hat and scarf Joleigh had made her for Christmas, looking like a shell-shocked soldier from the trenches. Howie wore a similar look, propped up next to Bits and looking like a jaundiced skeleton wrapped in a blanket.

A police officer sat in the vehicle's front seat, writing notes about the disaster. Joleigh checked Bits over to reassure herself that Bits was indeed okay, at least outwardly.

"Were you able to salvage anything?" Joleigh asked her.

The cop answered for them. "Two of the early firefighters on the scene pulled a few things out." He added a mumbled, "Not much worth saving."

Bits, her mouth trembling, held up her school bag, sitting on the floor of the back seat. "I shoved Papa's pills in here. And some clothes." She held a tattered gray stuffed bunny. Probably her only stuffed animal.

"Quick thinking, Bits. Good job. I'll be back in a minute. I need to speak to a firefighter." Joleigh would have addressed her question to the police officer sitting in the front seat, but she didn't want to ask in front of Bits and Howie.

Joleigh found a firefighter working the water-pump truck. "Excuse me, can you tell me where people stay when their house burns down? Is there a shelter in town?"

"Usually the local churches step in," he said.

She thought of Howie and Bits sleeping in a church basement or somewhere like that for the rest of the night. No, it made more sense for them to stay at the motel. Nobody argued with her suggestion—one she would clear with the Nielsons in the morning.

It was after two a.m. by the time she settled Bits and Howie in a two-bed motel room. Joleigh cranked up the heat and brought them fresh towels, and they showered before crawling into clean sheets.

Back in her room, Joleigh drifted in and out of sleep before it was time to get ready for her shift at Ruby's. *Will Bits make it to school?*

At the restaurant, Ruby informed Joleigh that the school and local churches would step in to provide clothing. As Joleigh had learned from Moe over the past few months, lodging was in short supply in their area, so she hoped to keep them at the motel. Bits's teacher would make sure the bus company added Bits to the in-town bus route.

"I'll call the Nielsons when I'm done with my shift," Joleigh assured her. It had been too early to call them before her morning shift. "I'll pay for their motel rent, assuming the Nielsons are okay with it. Hopefully, they'll let them stay until motel reservations fill up in May." It would buy Bits and Howie a few months.

"I'm so angry with Howie." Ruby shook her head. "It's not my business, but they shouldn't have had a wood-burning stove in a mobile home, much less a stove that Bits had to fill."

"The firefighter said creosote built up in the stovepipe from the warmer-than-normal temperatures." Joleigh said. "I doubt Bits kept the fire hot enough, causing the buildup."

Ruby put her arm around Joleigh as they stood in the hall outside her office. "All we can do is help Bits and try to help Howie."

"At least she'll be where I can help every day now." The money she'd saved to pay for her motel rent over the winter would come in handy.

Joleigh took her hot ham sandwich to-go after her shift ended and paid for an extra one for Bits. If Howie was hungry, he could share theirs.

Before she stopped at their motel room, Joleigh called Mr. Nielson from hers. She relayed the tragedy of Bits and Howie losing their home.

"Oh dear! I know you've become fond of Bits. What will happen to them?" Mr. Nielson asked.

"That's why I called. I put them in a room early this morning. Can they stay here for a couple of months? I'll pay for their room if you come up with an amount for their rent."

"Don't be silly, Joleigh. You don't need to pay anything for those poor people. The motel doesn't hit 'no vacancy' until early May. That gives them a few months, no charge. It's not costing us anything other than a bit of heat and water. You're doing all the work."

"Thank you so much, Mr. Nielson. You are so sweet."

"You are the sweet one, Joleigh. Caring about others is a gift. It's a good thing you work at Ruby's so you can be around people. Sort of balances things out if you build on your Lonesome Road property in the spring."

"Thank you, Mr. Nielson. And I'm still not sure if that's what I'll do." Joleigh had reworked her floor plans so many times over the past several months, asking herself, *If this is what you want to do, why aren't you finalizing things?* "Anyway, I'll keep you updated on what the status is for Bits and Howie staying here. Again, I appreciate your generosity."

"Well, I was going to ask a favor of you, but I think we're going to wait. The realtor mailed us a listing agreement again, since we list the motel every spring. We haven't signed the listing yet. I don't want you bothered with people coming to check out the motel." Mr. Nielson chuckled. "Listen to me. I'm acting like we will have a gaggle of people interested."

"I don't mind, Mr. Nielson. I'll make sure everything is clean if you have the realtor let me know ahead of time before a showing."

The news was like a match to gasoline for Joleigh. She could no longer avoid the idea that had settled in her heart over the past several weeks. The house fire felt like another sign to follow her instincts.

If Ruby's sold, she may be out of a job, and a life of solitude was never in her plans. *People* were what she wanted. And control of her future. The motel and her plans for it could give her both. Her house on Lonesome Road would happen, Joleigh promised herself. *But first, I need financial security.*

"I think we will wait," Mr. Nielson said. "We'll be back in March and can sign the listing at that point. You've done enough for us already and don't need this additional burden."

"Can you send me the information on the motel? The listing price, the square footage of the rooms, things like that?"

"Why in tarnation would you want that? Don't feel you need to take on helping us sell the place," Mr. Nielson said.

"I'm not trying to help you sell it." Joleigh closed her eyes, rubbing her forehead as if it were a magic lamp and a genie would appear to tell her whether her idea was silly. "I'm trying to determine if I should buy it."

Mr. Nielson gasped into the phone. "Why?"

A calmness overtook Joleigh as she explained, "Because it could be the best way for me to help people I care about, including myself."

Chapter Twenty-Nine

Within a week after the house fire, Bits and Joleigh had a routine, with little help from Howie. After the school bus dropped Bits off at the motel, she did her homework in Joleigh's room. Bits helped make dinner in the Nielsons' kitchen before eating with Howie in their room. Some nights Joleigh and Bits worked on knitting projects, and on others, Joleigh taught her how to macramé belts and hanging-plant holders.

Franklin's mother had surgery the end of January, so he spent the following two weekends in Mason City helping care for her, which meant Joleigh could focus her free time on Bits when she wasn't poring over the motel information Mr. Nielson sent. So much still depended on whether her Missouri home sold and for what price.

And while Joleigh thought about several different options for her future, she told no one.

Bits helped with the laundry, stripping their sheets to wash every week with Joleigh's and washing their towels and clothing twice a week. Joleigh ventured into their room only once, when Bits needed help to pick Howie up off the floor. He'd fallen on his way out of the bathroom. Although he was nothing but skin and bones, he was too heavy for Bits.

Joleigh brought her worries to Ruby. Between the breakfast and lunch crowd, she pulled Ruby aside in the hall between the kitchen and her office, asking Ruby for insight on what to do about Howie.

"He looks horrible, and I'm afraid he's going to die in that room. I want to step in and intervene, but I know it's not my place."

"Good luck with that," Ruby said. "I've known of the man for years. He's stubborn and sick, both physically and mentally, and I'm afraid you may have a problem getting him to leave that motel room."

Joleigh thought the same thing. "I don't know what drugs he's taking or what he's drinking—or how he's getting it, since Bits can't buy it all for him. He needs help."

Leo stepped into the hallway from the kitchen. "Sorry, I heard your conversation, and I know who you're talking about," he said. "Can I give you my two cents?"

Joleigh respected Leo. He was a level-headed college kid who seemed years older than his age. She nodded.

"My mom had a drinking problem. Actually, 'problem' is sugar-coating it. She drank from the time her feet hit the floor until she passed out at night." Leo's voice was void of emotion, but his eyes reflected the pain.

"What happened to her?" Joleigh braced herself for Leo's answer.

"My parents divorced. Dad couldn't take it anymore. Took us kids and moved out. Mom wasn't ready for his help." Leo blinked several times. "It wasn't until Mom ended up in the hospital that she found the strength to get help. She ended up at the Hazelden Treatment Center."

"Did it help?" Ruby asked.

"Yes. We had three good years with Mom before she passed away when I was twelve. She'd done too much damage to her body." He sighed. "My point is, you can't help Bits's dad unless he is ready to help himself."

Joleigh thanked Leo for his input. As she returned to work, she questioned what would drive Howie to seek help. Bits seemed the obvious incentive, but it hadn't worked yet.

FOR THEIR WEDNESDAY-night outing, Joleigh and Bernadette walked to the local movie theater to watch *Saturday Night Fever*. It had been out for a couple of months and had finally hit Grandfield.

Bernadette slipped on an icy patch on the sidewalk, and Joleigh caught her arm before she fell. She pointed at Bernadette's goofy-looking shoes.

"Why're you wearing those shoes with wavy soles in the winter?" Joleigh never understood fashion. She understood comfort.

Bernadette grinned and held on to Joleigh's arm as she carefully lifted one foot. "Haven't you seen Famolare shoes before? They've got good traction on the bottom."

"Yes, about every other inch." Joleigh held out her arm to Bernadette. "Hang on. I don't want to have to pull your sorry butt up off the sidewalk."

They walked the rest of the way to the movie theater arm in arm, talking about the challenges of parenting.

"Take my situation," Bernadette said. "I'd have an easier time finding a place to rent and a better job in the Twin Cities, plus I'd be closer to the college for night classes." She hit an icy spot on the sidewalk and tightened her grip on Joleigh. "But it would make things worse for my children. My ex and I need to live in the same town so the kids can spend time with both of us."

"Your ex-husband won't agree to move from here? He could commute."

"He could, but he's so involved at the high school. Besides teaching, he coaches football and basketball. Plus, our daughter is in junior high. I don't want to make her change schools."

"What's your plan once you're done with night classes?" Joleigh asked.

"I'll have a nursing degree. If I can't get a job at the clinic here, I should be able to find one south of the cities. We'll continue to live here, and I'll commute. That's why I need to find something around here to rent. It will take a few years for me to afford to buy a place."

Bernadette's situation felt like another sign for Joleigh—another person who needed a place to rent in Grandfield.

Franklin called the following afternoon to cement their plans for the coming weekend, the one before Valentine's Day. Wes had called Joleigh a few days earlier with news of two potentially interested buyers, but she didn't want to jinx anything by telling Franklin—or anyone else—of her motel idea. She would keep quiet until she received a firm offer for the Missouri house.

Several rooms were booked for the weekend. "I'll be free by noon if you want to do something," Joleigh told Franklin when he called. "Moe said Diane's out of town until late Saturday night, but Sunday lunch will work for them."

"Yep, I heard from Moe yesterday. We have reservations Sunday at one o'clock at Lakeville's on Main," Franklin said.

Joleigh smiled. That was a great steakhouse between Grandfield and Minneapolis.

"How about fishing?" he asked.

"Sounds good to me. The weather looks decent. If we catch anything, we could have a fish fry at my lot." Joleigh hadn't been to her property for two weeks, and although she likely wouldn't be building there in the spring if all went as planned, she considered it a good getaway retreat.

"Did you want to ask Bits to go with us again? By the way, how're things going with Bits and Howie?"

"No. I've spent every day with Bits since they moved into the motel, making it too easy for Howie to do nothing but lay in bed and watch TV." Joleigh would gladly spend every day with her, but she walked a fine line between knowing what was best for Bits, Howie, and even herself. "Bits and I have been using the Nielsons' kitchen every night, making dinner for them and me. Well, Howie eats nothing, but at least Bits and I are enjoying the meals. I'm guessing she's eating better than she ever did at home." Bits looked less pale, her hair shiny and clean every day, hair that Joleigh had trimmed four inches from.

"Plus, it's our early Valentine's Day weekend together." Joleigh smiled into the receiver. "How is your mom feeling?" Franklin had been cooking for his parents and helping care for his mother after her hysterectomy. His dad did what he could, which apparently did not include cooking or cleaning.

"She's doing well. One of my sisters is staying at Mom and Dad's this weekend." Franklin's voice dropped an octave. "I can't wait to see you. I've missed you."

The want in his voice echoed the desire that had pulsated through Joleigh over the past several weeks.

On her next weekly Wednesday-night outing with Bernadette, they went shopping, and Joleigh splurged on a lacy bra and panties, confessing that she'd never purchased anything like that before.

"Are you serious?" Bernadette's jaw dropped. "And you're how old?"

"Twenty-eight. But remember, I was a hermit for about six years." Bernadette had heard enough about Joleigh's precious time with Unity in her final years to know how true that statement was.

Franklin entered the motel office Friday night, carrying a vase of red roses for Joleigh, who was helping Bits with her homework.

"Hi, Mr. Grady." Bits stood and smiled. "Wow, those are pretty!"

"Hello, Bits. Remember, you can call me Franklin. You make me feel old when you call me Mr. Grady. Joleigh already does a good job of making me feel old. Please don't make it worse." He winked at Bits. "And yes, these are for Joleigh. It's Valentine's Day in a few days."

Bits's mouth formed an O as she turned wide-eyed to Joleigh. "Does that mean you're his girlfriend?"

"I hope she is," Franklin said before leaning over the counter to kiss Joleigh.

"Thank you. They're beautiful." Joleigh inhaled the scent, so closely associated with romance.

"I'll be back in a minute." After Franklin dropped off his bag in Joleigh's room, the three of them played several games of Go Fish and Crazy Eights in the office while Joleigh waited to check in the rest of the weekend guests. Afterward, they walked Bits to her hotel room, opening the door to Howie's snores. It pained Joleigh to know that Bits would get ready for bed alone, tuck herself in, and have nobody to talk to before she fell asleep.

As Joleigh snuggled next to Franklin in bed later that night, the heady scent of roses permeating the air, she thought about what a great father he would make. As the eldest child in a large family, he related to children. Although Joleigh didn't foresee that she would ever be able to have children of her own, she imagined a family of sorts, hoping to adopt someday. Family wasn't just biological. Unity had taught her that.

JOLEIGH AND FRANKLIN'S snow pants and ski jackets crackled in the late-morning cold as they walked out on Lonesome Lake with their ice fishing gear on Saturday.

Within minutes of setting the hook, Franklin hooked an eight-pound northern, one Joleigh would have kept to pickle if she had a kitchen of her own.

After drilling a few more holes in a different location, they caught several crappies, enough for a meal, by late afternoon. The sun was setting by the time they walked off the lake, loaded their gear into Franklin's pickup, and drove to Joleigh's land. Franklin filleted the fish on a board laid across the truck's open tailgate while Joleigh built a campfire and brushed the recent snow from the logs they used for sitting around the fire.

The warmth of the sun dissipated as it set, and they warmed their hands and feet near the fire after feasting on grilled fish.

"Ready for s'mores over the campfire?" Joleigh asked. She stood and headed to the truck to remove a box from the backseat.

"Yum," Franklin said. "I haven't had those in years."

Joleigh unpacked marshmallows, Hershey's bars, and graham crackers, then found two long sticks for roasting the marshmallows. Franklin had brought a transistor radio and music played in the background. When "You and Me" by Alice Cooper came on, he pulled Joleigh up from her chair and into his arms.

"I like this song," he said against her ear as they slow-danced in the glow from the campfire. "Not your typical Alice Cooper song."

Joleigh pulled back to look at him. "And here Moe gives you a hard time for liking bubblegum music." She grinned, feeling as if she could spend the rest of her life right there in his embrace.

Joleigh listened to the song lyrics about leading a simple life together as they danced next to the campfire on her bare land. She had no idea what Franklin's life was like back in Mason City, and she worried their lives would never blend together, that things would never be simple.

When the song ended, Joleigh threw more logs on the campfire while Franklin unzipped a sleeping bag he'd thrown in the truck and spread it out on the pickup bed. They hoisted themselves up on the open tailgate then lay back on the sleeping bag, staring up into the midnight sky dotted with stars.

"I love the scent of pine trees," Joleigh whispered.

"Me too. Our hunting shack gives us a chance to get back to nature. The past couple of years were tough with Grandpa Shady dying. Nobody dared venture far from home, certain the family patriarch wouldn't make it another day." Franklin chuckled. "We should've known the tough old bird would outlast any timeline doctors gave him."

"Well, I'm glad you came to the cabin when you did, or we wouldn't have met."

"Yep. If I'd have seen you in Ruby's, I wouldn't have known what a badass you are."

Joleigh elbowed him. "You silver-tongued playboy."

He rolled on top of her with a devilish grin. "Normally, I'd make a move now, but I'm getting cold. What do you say to a hot shower?"

"I'd say this badass girl's hair smells like campfire. Let's go."

They packed up, put out the campfire with snow, and drove back to the motel.

"Might as well shower together. You know, conserve water," Franklin said as Joleigh unlocked the door to her room. Once she closed it behind them, he backed her up against it, leaning his forehead on hers. "I've missed you. It's been a hell of a long time since I've missed anyone." His confession was followed by a heated kiss.

After their shower, as they sat side by side propped against the headboard, Franklin told Joleigh how the service had always stressed not making friends, not getting too attached to fellow soldiers, just in case. "They didn't want us to develop those relationships and then struggle if our friends died. But those men had my back. We all relied on each other, understood each other. Since then, it's been hard to let anyone in, to care about someone so much."

Joleigh reached for his hand and held it to her heart. He'd allowed Joleigh through that protective layer, and she understood how difficult it must have been for him.

FRANKLIN LEFT EARLY Monday morning when Joleigh woke for her shift at Ruby's. They'd spent Sunday with Moe and Diane, and as Joleigh worked through her morning shift, her butt dragged, and self-doubt pecked at her thoughts.

All three nights, Franklin had left her bed at some point to sleep in the extra bed. When she'd asked him why, again, he mumbled something about sleeping better alone. She wanted to believe him but sensed there was more to it. Although she felt their relationship was getting serious, there was still so much they didn't know about each other.

Business was slow at Ruby's, the temperature outside cold enough to freeze exposed skin in a matter of minutes. Before the lunch crowd trickled in, Ruby called a short employee meeting in the hall outside her office.

"I'll get right to the point. You've all heard me talk about my sister and me retiring so we can travel together. Businesses can take a long time to sell, since it's often difficult to find the right person. This is your official notice that I'm putting the place up for sale this week."

Joleigh's roiling stomach shifted focus from her relationship with Franklin to her future at Ruby's.

Ruby's gaze worked its way around the circle of employees. "I assume you are curious about how this will affect your job. It shouldn't, but that depends on who buys it and what their plans are for the restaurant. As I said, it could take months or years to sell Ruby's." Her dark eyebrows furrowed. "I believe Grandfield needs a restaurant like this, but who knows what the new owner will have in mind? If I get a reasonable offer, I'll be honest with you and let you know as soon as possible. Any questions?"

"If someone asks us about Ruby's being for sale, we can tell them, right?" Leo asked.

"Yes, this will be public knowledge. I don't believe it will affect our business. It's not like I'm selling because people aren't coming in or I can't find decent employees." Ruby gave them an affirmative nod. "Okay, back to work."

After her shift, Joleigh hunched down in her ski jacket on her way to the motel, her knit hat pulled low over her head and her hands warm inside thick mittens, as she mulled over Ruby's news. She showered, changed into a sweatshirt and jeans, and sat at her room's table, spreading out notes with financial figures.

Ruby's announcement had kicked Joleigh in the butt. It was time to call Wes. It had been a week since he'd mentioned two interested parties in her Missouri property. *Maybe I should drop the price on the home and acreage.* She placed the call.

"Hi, Wes. This is Joleigh Moore. Do you have a few minutes to talk?"

"I sure do. In fact, I planned to call you later today. I think we have an offer for your place. The potential buyer is calling me when they get home from work," he said. "Can I call you after five? I should know more by then."

"Yes, that works. Thanks." Joleigh hung up, relieved.

When Wes called her a few hours later with an offer of two thousand less than the listing price, she jumped on it. "How soon can we close?"

"They're paying cash, so it should be within a few weeks after a title and lien search. It's two families buying it for a hunting cabin and land and for their newly married children to live in until they can afford their own home."

Joleigh flopped down into a chair in her room and leaned her head back with her eyes closed. Finally, she had a dollar amount to work with so she could get her financial affairs figured out. "Thanks for your work on this, Wes. I'll rent a U-Haul and clean out the rest of my things in the next week or two." She'd gone through most of Unity's things after she'd passed. Unity had been of the "keep only what you need" attitude.

"I'll let you know once we have a firm date. Since it's a cash deal, it could be as early as mid-March," he said.

"That works for me. I can get away during the week if I need to." Joleigh felt certain Ruby would give her a couple of days off, since it was a slow time of year.

After they hung up, Joleigh reworked her numbers. She excluded the forty acres being leased by a farmer, since the annual payment was a good financial boost.

She dialed Mr. Nielson's phone number.

"This is a pleasant surprise," Mr. Nielson said after his sister-in-law handed him the phone. "How are you? Everything okay at the motel?"

"I'm fine, and all is well here. We had several guests last weekend celebrating an early Valentine's Day, and two rooms are booked for this weekend." Joleigh tapped a pencil on the table, drumming out her nerves. "The reason I called is about the motel. I would like to talk to you about buying the place. You said before that you might do a contract for deed. Is that what you want, though?" She wondered how many good years they had left to enjoy the money.

"Yes, we would do that," he said. "We added the contract for deed option in hopes it would entice young buyers."

"I have a cash offer on my place in Missouri and should receive the money in a few weeks. I would need to finance half the purchase price so I can use the rest of the money for remodeling." She'd recently confessed her apartment idea to him.

"I believe you will bring fresh life into the place," Mr. Nielson said with pride. "Yes, save some of your money for construction, Joleigh. I think your idea is necessary for the community. Let me speak with the missus about this and I'll call you tomorrow, okay?"

"Okay. That will give me time to run my idea by someone else," Joleigh said, wishing that someone could be Franklin. But when she told him the news, it would need to be in person, not over the phone.

Instead, the someone was Moe.

Chapter Thirty

"Your idea to turn some of the motel rooms into apartments is just what this town needs," Moe said.

Joleigh had stopped at his office after her shift at Ruby's the following day. She hadn't wanted to speak with him about it in front of his coworkers when they came in for lunch.

Moe added, "I can put you in touch with a couple of local contractors to give you an estimate. And please put me on your list of future renters."

"Well, first things first," Joleigh said. "Contractor bids, selling my home in Missouri, a purchase agreement with the Nielsons, and then there's that super-fun time of construction."

As she mentioned each step, her heart skipped beats. She couldn't finance the motel, remodeling, and also build her house. But Unity had taught her about wants versus needs. For now, control of her livelihood would help ensure her future home on Lonesome Road.

"Please don't say anything about this to anyone, including Franklin," she said. "I need to make a trip to Missouri to pack up the last of my things, and I'll spend a couple of days with him in Iowa. I want to tell him in person."

"Yeah, he won't be thrilled about the motel eating into your weekends together."

"I hope it's temporary. If I can turn the motel rooms that face the woods into apartments, that will take care of half of the room reservations. The rest of the rooms, I want to rent week by week, at least during the summer. I'll have to play it by ear this first year." Joleigh stood. "I'll let you get back to work. I appreciate you listening."

"Nonsense, Joleigh. That's what friends do. And then they step in when another friend gets his underwear in a knot when things don't go his way." He grinned, and Joleigh forced a smile with a sinking feeling in her gut.

Surely, Franklin's offhand remarks about how I should move to Mason City were just that. Offhanded. They hadn't dated very long.

For the first time in her life, Joleigh's instincts told her she was making the right decision for her future. Unity would be proud.

The following day, when Moe and his coworkers came into Ruby's for lunch, he handed Joleigh a paper with two contractors' names and their phone numbers. "My first choice would be Ron. He's reasonable with his prices and does excellent work."

"Thanks, Moe. I owe you."

Franklin called Joleigh later that night. "Since you're coming to Iowa next week, I'll stay here this weekend. Some of Mom and Dad's outlets need replacing, so it will give me a chance to get those rewired."

"Sounds good. I've got three rooms rented this weekend, and Bits got invited to her first sleepover. I'm going ice fishing before the lake gets too slushy to walk on." Fish houses had to be off the lakes by the end of February. The ice was still solid in most places, but with the days warming, the iffy spots would only get worse.

PETER WAS AT THE BAIT shop most weekends and was working when Joleigh stopped in for bait Saturday morning.

"I've got a late morning room check-in, so I'll miss the best fishing by the time I get out there after lunch," Joleigh said. "I always walk out on Lonesome Lake, and with this warm weather, I may need my waders today."

Peter chuckled. "Be careful out there, and good luck." He rang up Joleigh's minnows.

"I'll be wearing my lucky plaid fishing coat." Joleigh waved goodbye and walked the few blocks back to the motel. She stashed the minnow bucket in the glass cooler until she could get to the lake.

She was in the office around eleven, waiting for her late check-in, when the door opened. It was Peter. "Did I forget something at the bait shop?"

Peter looked over his shoulder like someone might have followed him. "No. I snuck out, told Mom I had to run an errand. I'm here to warn you that two men just came into the bait shop, asking about you. They said they're friends of yours from Missouri. They said since you love to fish, they thought I might know you and know where you live—or if you're fishing this weekend."

Fear seized Joleigh's throat. "What did they look like?"

"One was tall, and the other had a long scar across his cheek. They didn't even pretend to be friendly." Peter kicked at the floor. "I'm probably not supposed to know this, but Leo told me about the two men looking for you at Ruby's a few weeks ago, that they killed your boyfriend in Missouri. I figured these might be the guys." His eyes widened. "Did that really happen?"

Joleigh nodded, unable to speak, her chest tight.

"Holy shit! Please don't get mad at Leo." Peter fidgeted. "I told him I feel bad that my mom is so mean to you. And then he told me about those men and how Ruby called the cops to report them." His words picked up speed. "Before I could get rid of those men and lie about knowing you, Mom came out of her office and told them you'd be fishing on Lonesome Lake after lunch today. She gave them directions to the lake and told them you'd be wearing a plaid fishing coat." Peter gritted his teeth. "I'm so pissed off at her!"

"She overheard me this morning?" Joleigh's mind whirled like a tornado. "I can't thank you enough for warning me. And I'm grateful your mom didn't point them to the motel."

"Mom doesn't know what room you're in and probably figures there'd be people at the motel this weekend."

An idea began to take shape. "Did you see what they were driving?"

"Yes. A rusted dark-green pickup. Anyway, I better get back before she tracks me down." He dug his hands into his coat pockets. "Should you call the cops? I thought about it, but I didn't know if that's what you would want."

"Yes, I probably will. Thank you for warning me." After Peter left, Joleigh picked up the phone and dialed Moe's number with a shaking hand. She had a plan, but she needed his help.

When Moe answered, Joleigh filled him in on the men's likely plan to find her on the lake. "If you aren't busy, I need your help. I want to call the cops, but I'm afraid they'd park a car at the lake access and scare the men off. I don't know what to do."

"Of course. I'll help you."

Joleigh told Moe her plan, and he spent the next half hour on the phone, calling his friends.

While she waited, she took deep breaths to calm her nerves. *You're in control, Joleigh. For the first time since Mack's death, you're in control.*

"We'll be out there by twelve thirty," Moe said when he called her back. That gave them almost an hour. "One of my buddies is a cop. He's got today off and will help us. He'll be ready to call in for backup."

"Thank you. It makes me feel better that law enforcement will be on alert. I'll wait for you." A vehicle pulled into the parking lot. "I think my late arrival is here. After I've checked them in, I'll pack my fishing gear, including my binoculars, and head out to Lonesome Lake."

"I'll drop off a CB radio for you. You're walking out on the ice?"

"Yes. I'll wait in my truck at the access until you get there. See you soon."

After she checked in the couple, she forced herself to eat something. It could be hours before she was back from the lake.

Joleigh's knees knocked like cymbals on the drive to Lonesome Lake. Peter's mother told the men she wouldn't be out fishing until the afternoon, so she needed to get there ahead of time to set things up. When she pulled into the lake access, several vehicles were parked in the lot, none of them a dark-green pickup.

Anglers dotted the lake like marbles.

Joleigh stayed in her truck until Moe pulled up, the sounds of "Carry On Wayward Son" by Kansas vibrating through his car even with the windows rolled up. Two pickups pulled in behind him, neither of them green. Joleigh watched as two men hopped out of the first pickup, three out of the second truck. They all looked familiar.

Moe rolled down his car window. "You know these dudes, right?" He thumbed toward the men unloading fishing gear. "They'll walk out. I'm driving out and will hang to the right where the drop-off is. Here's your CB radio." He went over a few instructions with Joleigh. "You doing okay?"

She felt like she'd drunk a river of coffee. "Yes, I just want to get this done. What if they don't show up?"

"Oh, they'll show up. Nobody drives this far just to change their mind. This is good, though. You're in control, not them." He looked back at the men. "They have CB radios too. We will spread out. Two will go out farther behind you."

He squeezed Joleigh's gloved hand. "You've got an off-duty cop, two big, strapping farmers, and another Vietnam vet on your side, and I've got ropes and equipment in the back seat we can use to rescue the monsters."

"I can't thank you enough, Moe." Joleigh leaned into his car window and kissed his cheek. "See you out on the ice."

She headed out to the drop-off before veering left beyond the open springs. Once in place, she chiseled two holes, baited her lines, turned over the five-gallon bucket, and sat on it, facing the shore. Facing her fate while her nerves jumped like high-voltage wires.

Moe drove out on the ice, revving his engine to keep from getting stuck in the slush forming on the lake. His friends walked out, carrying their fishing equipment under the pretense of fishing. They split into three groups—one guy setting up with Moe, two behind Joleigh to the left of the lake access, and two men on the other side. They all formed a half circle around Joleigh.

When a fish pulled her bobber into the water, Joleigh reeled in a small walleye. She didn't want to catch anything, since it would detract from her monitoring the lake access, but it helped to pass the time. A fish on the ice was a good prop. She tossed it down next to her and picked up the CB radio. "Catch anything yet?"

"I'm waiting to catch two slimy fish any minute here," Moe said. "We're foaming at the mouth, waiting for those fish to show up."

Joleigh itched to catch Mack's killers, too, even though the anxiety made her want to lie on the ice so she wouldn't faint. The sun warmed her back, tempting her to take off the plaid fishing coat since she had dressed in layers. But the men would be looking for someone on the ice wearing a plaid coat, so she kept it on. She didn't rebait her hook after catching the walleye, just kept a sinker on her line so she could focus on the lake access.

She'd been on the ice an hour when a green pickup came barreling into the parking lot. *Bingo.* She broke out in a cold sweat. *It's real. It's happening. Focus, Joleigh, focus.*

Joleigh looked around at the men there to back her up, keeping her binoculars in her coat pocket so it wouldn't appear she was looking for anyone. The two men got out of the pickup and stood in front of it, perusing the people on the frozen lake. The tall one, likely Darrell, held binoculars up to his eyes.

Joleigh lowered her head, pretending to focus on her two fishing lines. Perspiration trickled down the center of her back.

Two doors slammed, breaking the relative quiet. There was a possibility they would walk out to Joleigh instead of driving, but she didn't think so. They would need a quick escape. Just then, they jumped back in the truck. The truck revved at the access.

In the seconds that followed, Joleigh felt as if they were all in a movie playing in slow motion. The ice shifted and heaved under her as the truck made a beeline in her direction. She stood, ready to move either way, her body reverberating as the ice boomed like an explosion under her feet.

Joleigh clutched her bucket to use as a flotation device if the ice collapsed under her, just as the truck speeding toward her plummeted, the ice breaking around it like a rock to a windshield. The frozen lake erupted like a volcano around the sinking truck.

Shock immobilized Joleigh as chaos played out in front of her.

Moe had reassured her that the water was only six to eight feet deep there until the drop-off where Joleigh had been fishing. His voice crackled over the CB radio. "We're on our way. The cop is on his radio now with the police department."

As much as Joleigh wanted to be the first on the scene so she could confront them, she knew it was wiser to wait until backup arrived. There was movement on the passenger side of the truck. The window rolled down as the driver's side sank. Two of Moe's friends arrived at the truck seconds before Joleigh, and the rest arrived with ropes and chisels to break the window if needed.

Moe's cop had brought handcuffs. Scarface was the first out of the truck, drenched, shivering, and wide-eyed from shock—or possibly from spotting Joleigh watching as the men pulled him to safety. Darrell crawled out next, spitting, sputtering, and swearing up a storm as if it was someone else's fault that they'd driven out over the snow-covered springs.

The cop shook his head. "Yeah, yeah, save it for law enforcement, buddy. They should be here any minute."

Joleigh cut in. "You murderers! Mack didn't deserve that. What a horrible, senseless death!" Joleigh didn't realize she was crying until hot tears seared her cold cheeks. Her hands clenched at her sides as she fought to keep from pushing the men back into the icy water. "You're evil!"

One of the farmers tugged on Joleigh's jacket, making her aware of how close she'd stepped to the cracks in the ice that led to open water. "C'mon, let's get off this ice before we all go swimming," the farmer said.

Moe's friends held the two wet men down on the safe ice away from the truck, and the cop slapped handcuffs on them before joining Joleigh and the farmer.

"The sheriff's department will take over and work with the sergeant you've been talking to in Missouri. Our police department is too small to have our own investigator," the cop explained to Joleigh as her mind whirled like a fan on high speed, trying to take it all in. "They'll need you at the police station to answer questions. Okay?"

Joleigh agreed and followed him back to the rest of the group. Moe had driven to the lake access to wait for the police. They wrapped the blankets he had in his car around the two men.

His cheek still down against the snow, Darrell glared at Joleigh where she was crouched several feet away. "Where's our money, you bitch?" Spit flew from his mouth, and she hoped it would freeze his lips to the ice.

"Hey, don't talk to our friend like that." The cop's voice was as void of emotion as if he'd said, "Please pass the butter," but he yanked Darrell's arms farther behind his back, causing more cursing from the murderer.

Joleigh leaned forward and jeered at Darrell. "It will *never* be your money, and even if it was, it wasn't worth killing for!" She took a ragged breath, hoping to calm the anger boiling over inside her like a poisonous witch's brew.

It had been over nine months since they had murdered Mack. And, almost like a pregnancy, Joleigh had finally received the reward she'd labored over for months. Mack's killers would be behind bars soon. She concentrated on the closure she hoped it would bring to Mack's family. And she could get on with her life without feeling a sword hanging over her head.

Moe and his cop friend followed behind Joleigh as they each trailed the police car, with Darrell and his co-conspirator in the backseat. At the police station, while Joleigh waited to be questioned, she sipped on a hot chocolate from the vending machine. In the meantime, Moe went to call Franklin from a pay phone down the hall, telling her, "He can freak out on me instead of you."

Moe knew his friend. Franklin would get wound up at what *could* have happened. She'd thought of calling him after Peter left the office but decided against it. He would have driven like a maniac and possibly crashed trying to get to Grandfield in time to save the day.

As Joleigh waited, she thought of her upcoming trip to Woodland via a stop at Franklin's in Iowa, the sale of Unity's home, the motel purchase and remodel—and realized that with Darrell and Scarface arrested, she *could* go back to Missouri and likely be safe, as long as the killers coughed up information on the other two who had been there the night of Mack's murder.

But even if all four men ended up behind bars, Joleigh's heart had moved from Woodland to Grandfield. There was no going home when it no longer felt like home.

A police officer met with Joleigh, going over the process of what would happen next. The investigators, county attorneys, and sheriff's department in Dakota County would work with those in Macon County, where Mack's murder had taken place. They would coordinate Darrell and Scarface's extradition.

"It's noted here that Darrell is the one who beat Mack with the baseball bat, correct?" The police officer pointed at the paperwork.

"Yes." Joleigh wanted Darrell punished more than the others. "He's also the one who insisted they drag Mack's body onto the campfire." She closed her eyes, reliving that horrific night.

They went over other details as Joleigh tried to focus, her body and mind numb from the events of the day. Afterward, the officer walked her back to the reception area, where Moe waited for her. "We will keep in touch, and I'm sure you'll hear from Sergeant Williams soon."

Stars shimmered in the dark sky by the time they left the police department. Joleigh had offered to buy breakfast for Moe and his friends at Ruby's the next day after the motel guests left, but it wasn't enough for everything they had done.

"You sure I can't buy you dinner?" Joleigh asked him. "I owe you so much." She dabbed at her eyes.

"Thanks, but Diane and I are having a late dinner with my parents tonight. I'll see you tomorrow morning at Ruby's for a late breakfast."

He wheeled to his car and turned to Joleigh, who stood next to him. "Here's the thing, Joleigh. You don't owe me anything. You're a good-hearted woman who has already made an impact in our community and will continue to do so with the motel."

Moe reached for her hand. "I'm glad you're staying here with us instead of going back to Missouri. And don't let that bullheaded Franklin try to talk you into moving to Iowa. You belong here." He leaned down and planted a kiss on her hand, his mustache tickling her skin.

"You flatterer." Joleigh smiled. He was like the brother she never had, part of her makeshift family. "Franklin's expecting my call, right?"

"Yep, and he swore a blue streak when I told him what went down while he was stuck over two hours away." Moe chuckled.

"I'll smooth things over when I call him, and I'll see him in person next week."

They parted ways, and although Joleigh dreaded calling Franklin, she also wished he could have been by her side. She needed his comfort, but she'd also needed to take care of things her way and not let him—or anyone else—make decisions for her.

Chapter Thirty-One

F ranklin was certain he would combust when Moe called to tell him about the danger Joleigh had placed herself in. *Talk about feeling helpless two hours away!*

When Joleigh called him a couple of hours later, some of the hot steam pumping through him had cooled, and he could focus on the fact she was safe. She was a tough, independent woman and didn't need him—no matter how much he wanted to ride in on a white horse and "save" her.

"I'm taking next Thursday and Friday off from Ruby's so I can make a trip to Missouri to collect the rest of my things," Joleigh said. He heard the exhaustion pulling at her words. "Closing should be within a couple of weeks."

"I'd like to go with you to Woodland to help you move. That way, you can show me around your old place."

"I would love your help, and I'd like for you to see my home before it sells," she said. "The purchase agreement includes the kitchen table and living room furniture, so it's mostly my bedroom things and tools from the shed. I'm borrowing a snowmobile trailer. Between that and my pickup, I should have plenty of room for the things I have left there."

It sounded like Joleigh had it all figured out. He would wait until she was with him next week to work on convincing her she should move her household items to Mason City, not Minnesota.

JOLEIGH ARRIVED AT Franklin's house the following Thursday morning, in time for the jalapeno-and-bacon egg bake he made for their late breakfast.

When Franklin opened his front door to see Joleigh standing there and wearing a deep-red sweatshirt matching the mouth he'd missed kissing the past two weeks, he pulled her in for a tight hug and kiss, yearning to do so much more.

"It's so good to see for myself that you're okay. Things could have gone so wrong with your plan." He leaned back to study her face as if she might be hiding a bruise or two.

"I know, but I had backup dudes," she mumbled between kisses.

They'd dissected her actions a hundred times over the phone in the past few days. What Joleigh didn't know, what Franklin couldn't dissect himself, was his fierce desire to be with her every day.

There was no doubt he'd fallen in love. *But what is love? Is it the craving to share your life with someone? The thrill of seeing them, touching them? Desiring them?* Hell yes. But Franklin knew love and desire were two separate things.

He also knew he would have to come clean to Joleigh about a few issues he had, thanks to Vietnam. Lay his heart wide open for her to decide if she could handle his emotional scars. He hoped to God she could, because living two-plus hours away from Joleigh wasn't how he wanted to spend the rest of his life. He needed to convince her to move to Mason City before she built on her land in Grandfield.

So, he was blindsided when, over breakfast, Joleigh confessed her intention to purchase the Nielsons' motel.

Son of a bitch!

That was not in his plan.

FRANKLIN SAT THERE, stunned, waiting for a punchline that didn't come. "You're going to buy the motel and renovate it?" He gave up digesting his breakfast. It was all he could do to digest Joleigh's idea.

"Maybe?" She blew out a breath. "It would mean putting my plans aside of building on my lot, and I'm waiting to get the contract for deed terms worked out with the Nielsons..."

He sat back in his chair and crossed his arms. "Wow. So I have to compete with either you building a home or running a seven-day-a-week business?"

Joleigh's eyebrows rose. "You feel you're competing? I'm trying to plan a future for myself. Everything I thought would be my future was taken away from me or ruined by awful memories. You've got your home here and your family. I'd like to have the same." She shook her head. "You're being selfish." She muttered the last sentence.

But Franklin heard the words. *Selfish?* Perhaps. But he missed her. A lot. *Doesn't she miss me every day?*

Before he spoke, he unclenched his jaw so that his words wouldn't come out cutting like jagged glass. "I'm sorry. I guess I hoped that once you sold your home in Missouri, you'd be willing to move here. You haven't lived in Grandfield that long."

Joleigh pushed her plate aside. "Moe suggested I talk to you about this last week, but I wanted to tell you in person. I'm sorry I blindsided you."

"Moe already knows about this? What the hell?"

"Yes. I wanted his input on what contractors to ask for construction bids and also what he thought of my draft of an apartment layout. I wanted to make sure it would be enough room and would be easy for him to maneuver around. He's interested in being one of my first tenants."

Franklin closed his eyes for a second, but it only made the information in his head spin faster, nauseating him. He tried to see it from Joleigh's point of view. "If you renovate the motel rooms into apartments, it'll free up the need to be there all the time. I guess that's a good thing." It would cement her in Grandfield, though.

"Yes. And if they work, I might do the same to the rest of the motel rooms. At least for this summer, I hope to rent the motel rooms out by the week or month, like resorts do with cabins."

Joleigh sat back in her chair, and it was then that Franklin noticed how relaxed she was. There were no murderers looking for her and no drug money to worry about, and clearly, she'd found a business idea that made her happy.

I need to be happy for her. Happy with her. "I'm still going to do my best to sell you on Mason City these next couple of days," he said with a wink. "You can't blame a guy for trying to change the mind of the woman he loves so he can spend more time with her."

Joleigh choked on a drink of water. "Huh?"

Franklin stood and rounded the table to her side, crouching beside her. "I know it's happened fast, but I'm pretty damn sure I've fallen in love with you. All I want is for us to be together." He held her hand. "Yes, we both have our own lives, but I'd hate for things to become so hectic that we see less of each other instead of more. To paraphrase the band Chicago, say you'll stay with me. Make me happy."

"It's 'Make Me Smile,' not make me happy." Joleigh grinned.

"Whatever." He brought her hand to his lips and kissed it.

She sighed, and he sensed it was more her frustration at their situation than it was his proclamation of love. Her words confirmed that. "Ever since Unity's memory began failing, I stopped thinking about what I wanted to do with my future," she said. "I wanted to spend my years with her. I pushed any other plans aside, especially the last few years, when she needed round-the-clock care. Unity was my focus. My heart."

Joleigh wrapped her arm around his neck. "Now that I've had time to think about my dreams for what I want, I've realized I want time with people I care about and control of my career. I think my plans for the motel and apartments will eventually give me that freedom, along with the ability to rely on myself and not Ruby or anyone else."

She looked into his eyes. "Yes, I'll be tied down to the motel and apartments these next several months, but I hope that it's temporary and that I can eventually build on my property."

"I thought *I* would be what you wanted." Franklin inwardly grimaced. He reminded himself of a spoiled toddler.

Joleigh reached out and put her hands on his cheeks. "You *are* what I want! You're a choice for me, Franklin, not a convenience. Definitely not a convenience." She chuckled. "But I need to make my own future, not move again and start over again when we've only dated a few months."

Franklin placed his hands over hers. "Okay, I'll stop my whining." He refrained from saying that the past few months with her were like nothing he'd ever experienced before. *No need to scare her off, Franklin.* "But I'm still going to do my best at selling you on Iowa before you sign that contract for deed."

She grinned. "Well, then, let's get going. Show me what you've got."

AFTER THEY CLEANED up the kitchen, Franklin gave Joleigh a tour of Mason City, including a drive down Federal Avenue. "This is where we used to cruise when I was a teenager. We'd 'scoop the loop,' which meant driving between the drive-ins on the north and south ends of Federal Avenue. Unfortunately, it's a dying tradition."

They ended the drive at an outdoor ice-skating rink at the edge of a park. He'd asked Joleigh if she owned ice skates when they spoke on the phone.

"I brought my skates to Minnesota but haven't been on them for about ten years."

Franklin had experienced firsthand how wobbly Joleigh was when they went roller-skating and hoped she would at least need him for support, if nothing else. "It's like riding a bike. You'll be fine. They still fit?"

"Yes. I spend more time on my butt than on my skates. The pond by our house froze over every year, and Unity and I would shovel off an area and skate. She was good. Me? Not so much."

"Good. Bring your skates, along with a pillow for your butt," he had teased.

That day, as they sat side-by-side on the bench, lacing their skates, sunshine took the bite out of the winter wind. "Okay, Dorothy Hamill, show me your moves," he said, standing.

Joleigh pulled a knit hat over her hair. "I should wear a helmet."

Franklin held out his hand. "I'll keep you upright." It was the best part of Joleigh's lack of skating ability. She needed him for something.

They had the rink to themselves. As they skated, Joleigh clutching Franklin's arm, the breeze carried the delicious aroma of yeast and spices from nearby Pappy's Pizza Parlor.

After an hour, Joleigh said, "I've got to give my feet a break, or I won't be able to walk." They skated to the bench, where they'd left their shoes. Joleigh unlaced her skates, took them off, and rubbed one foot.

"Give me your other foot. I'll massage it."

Joleigh raised an eyebrow. "You sure?"

"Yep." He patted his lap, and she rested her ankles over his thighs, stifling a moan as he massaged the bottom of her feet.

"Ah, I think this is how we should spend the rest of the afternoon." She closed her eyes.

"You're so needy," Franklin teased, thinking of the need that pulled at him whenever he was with her. "I thought we'd go to Birdsall's Ice Cream for an early supper if you're hungry."

"We're having ice cream for supper?" Joleigh opened one eye.

"You can have whatever you want for supper. For dessert, I suggest either their hot fudge sundae or hot fudge marshmallow malt—they're famous for both." He slipped her tennis shoes on her feet before changing out of his ice skates. "Come on, I'm starving."

They beat the supper crowd, feasting on piled-high Maid-Rite sandwiches and hot fudge marshmallow malts.

"Don't come near me with a sharp object—I may burst," Joleigh groaned afterward.

"It was worth it, though, right? Are you up for bowling? If you can bend over, that is."

"Did you research sports I stink at? I've bowled like three times in my life, and my ball rolled in the gutter far more than in the lane."

"Anything to build up my self-esteem." Franklin grinned. "Notice how I'm steering clear of shooting baskets at the indoor gym? I'm not as dumb as I look." He stole a kiss as they walked through the café's parking lot.

"Fine. Bowling it is. But you're not helping sell your city by making me feel like a failure." Joleigh nudged him in the side.

"I sense it's a losing battle, so I may as well have fun losing." He winked.

In the third game, Joleigh rolled her first strike. She fist-pumped the air in celebration.

He clapped. "Okay, we can quit after this game, or before I know it, you'll beat me." He glanced at his watch. "Besides, I told Mom we'd stop by tonight."

He'd asked Joleigh on the phone if she would mind meeting his mom, assuring her his mother was much sweeter than his dad.

"You sure know how to show a girl a good time, don't you?" They changed out of their ugly bowling shoes back into street shoes. "First, you torment my feet with ice skating, then you whip me in bowling, and now you're feeding me to the wolves?"

"I'm doing you a favor. Dad won't be home."

Franklin adored his mother. She'd saved his sanity during the war, insisting each of his siblings write a separate letter to him, rotating their turns, so almost every day, he had a letter from home to share with his troop. Everyone was so hungry for an escape that they shared letters to give themselves a break from their nightmare reality.

When he opened the front door to his parents' home and called out, "We're here, Mom!" his mother, a petite woman with faded red curls, came bustling from the kitchen, wiping her hands on her paisley-print apron with a smile from ear to ear. Franklin made introductions.

"Come and sit down." His mother beamed at Joleigh. "I baked Franklin's favorite cake. Would you like coffee?" She led the way through their living room into the seafoam-green kitchen decorated with flowered wallpaper that hadn't changed since Franklin was young.

Joleigh shook her head. "No coffee for me, thank you."

"I'll make the coffee, Mom. You sit down and visit with Joleigh. I'm sure your questions are strangling you." He leaned over and kissed his mom's cheek. "It's okay. I warned Joleigh."

Joleigh took a seat across from his mother. A two-layer cake with cream cheese frosting sat on a lazy Susan between them along with small plates and forks.

"Would you like a slice of carrot cake?" His mom cut into the dessert and lifted out a hefty piece for Franklin's plate.

"Yes, thank you. So, this is his favorite? I've never made carrot cake before."

"It is. I think he chooses it because it is time-consuming—right, Franklin?" The look she gave him melted any bite in her words. "The grating of the carrots is the worst," she informed Joleigh. "But enough about cake. Let's talk about you." Franklin stifled a laugh. His mom had likely been writing down questions for days.

She leaned forward as if she might miss a word Joleigh said, her slice of cake untouched. "Your upbringing of working on a hobby farm and learning about living off the land intrigues me. Tell me more about it."

Joleigh spoke of learning about nature's bounty from Unity. Franklin watched his mom's eyes widen as Joleigh explained how to trap leeches.

His mother turned to him. "How did you get this amazing woman to date you?"

He shrugged. "Eh, she lives in a small town. Slim pickings for her there."

His mom shared a few stories of her own. One was about Franklin decorating his bedroom wall with "treasures" from his diaper as a toddler. Another was of the time he came home crying from school because another boy had beaten up his friend. Then she told Joleigh about the time he broke her heart—when he told her he was enlisting in the army.

"I'd seen what war did to my father and my husband. I dreaded what it would do to Franklin." She reached for his hand across the table.

"Way to wreck the mood, Mom." He grimaced and turned to Joleigh. "And just so you know, I no longer decorate my bedroom walls with poop." He wished he could confess other issues he had.

An hour passed before he announced they should get going. "I haven't given Joleigh a chance to relax since she arrived."

His mom walked them to the front door and took Joleigh's hand. "I'm so happy to meet you. This is the first time Franklin's brought a girl here. Well, his girlfriend from high school was here a few times, but that doesn't count. I already knew her from school events."

"Geez, Mom, don't give away all my secrets." He pulled his mom in for a long hug, and Joleigh thanked her several times for her hospitality before they left.

His house was ten minutes from his parents. On the drive, Helen Reddy belted out "I Am Woman" on the car radio.

"When this song came out in '72, Unity's memory was already failing," Joleigh told him. "Not with music, though. This was one of her favorite songs to sing. It got to where she could no longer speak much that last year or so, but she could sing along with most songs."

"It sounds like Unity was the tough type of woman Helen sang about," he said. "Same with you."

Joleigh was quiet until he pulled into the garage and shut off the car. "The line where she sings about how wisdom can come out of pain is true. I think of the painful times in my life and how they've shaped me, helped me to focus on what's important in my life." She turned to him. "I'm guessing you feel that way about the war."

He took her hand, too choked with wartime memories to say a word. She was right, though. The things he thought were important before he entered the army—his sports car, his fiancée, partying with his friends—changed. After suffering exhaustion, pain, and fear during the war and watching his comrades die... people, not things, became all that mattered.

The war changed him from a teen to a man in a matter of days. A man who still had nightmares, who kept people from seeing the wounded side of him. Maybe Joleigh was right, and they were better off living in separate states. But that wasn't the answer, and he knew it.

That night, after Joleigh fell asleep in his arms, Franklin slipped out of bed to lie down on his living room couch. Unable to sleep, he paced the floor during the night. Their relationship couldn't move forward until he came clean with Joleigh.

Chapter Thirty-Two

The aroma of coffee greeted Joleigh as she stretched in the otherwise empty bed. During the night, she'd woken up to find Franklin no longer by her side.

She pulled on sweatpants and a sweatshirt and met him in the kitchen. "Good morning."

"Good morning. How about omelets for breakfast?" Franklin pulled out a dozen eggs and a pound of bacon from the fridge.

It appealed to Joleigh's stomach, but she couldn't eat until they had a conversation about the elephant in the room. She helped herself to coffee and stood beside him. "Omelets sound good, but I think we need to talk first."

Franklin groaned. "Aw, no man ever wants to hear those words."

Joleigh took a seat at the table. "Why don't you sleep with me? Please tell me what's going on."

Franklin stood, studying his coffee cup for so long she wondered if he was wishing it were whiskey for liquid courage. Slowly, he took a seat across the table. "I was going to talk to you about it this morning." He cleared his throat. "It's 'Nam. I have had trouble sleeping ever since I came home." Franklin's eyes met hers, pleading for understanding. "I'd like to say it's just that I wander around the house sometimes at night, as if I'm still on high alert, but it's more than that." He paused. "Didn't Mack have problems sleeping?"

"Not that I know of. But honestly, Mack was often drunk—or possibly high on whatever his drug of choice was—and maybe that's what helped him sleep." Joleigh remembered one of their few conversations about the war. "I remember him telling me he had it easy compared to others in Vietnam."

That comment seemed to open the door for Franklin. As their coffee cooled, he let the words flow, ones she sensed he'd kept buried for too long.

"In the army—on the ground, in foxholes, in the jungle—I had a front-row seat to the atrocities of war."

She reached for his hand and held it, encouraging Franklin to continue. He spoke of nightmares in which he woke up in a sweat, screaming. Of staring out the windows in the middle of the night, sure someone was out there. Of the few times he'd slept with someone and woke up ready to fight if their bodies touched. And of punching one of his sisters when she touched his arm to wake him up the first summer he came home from war.

"I clocked her so hard she had a bruise on her cheek for weeks." Franklin winced. "I felt like a piece of shit. Mom came to my defense, reminding my siblings that if they had to wake me up, they needed to do it from the doorway and with words, not touch."

Joleigh reminded him of her insecurities from her childhood. "Sounds like we've got more in common than we thought." She squeezed his hand. "Thank you for telling me."

Franklin's voice was soft. "There's a lot I'll probably never tell you—or anyone—but at least you know now that my not sleeping with you has nothing to do with *you*."

Joleigh closed her eyes for a few seconds, a wave of relief washing over her at his reassurance. But mixed with that relief was a deep empathy for what Franklin had battled with for years. Those must have been some of the invisible wounds Moe had spoken of and likely what David had referred to when they first met.

The difference in Joleigh's and Franklin's upbringings blurred a little for her. They weren't so different after all. They carried wounds from the past that shaped how they viewed others—and life.

AFTER THEY SHOWERED, Franklin and Joleigh headed south on I-35. Franklin offered to drive, and Joleigh spent most of the five-hour trip staring out the window, grateful she didn't have to concentrate on the road.

"I can see why you love it here," Franklin said as they drove down the long gravel road to her old home. Sunshine was melting the remaining snow, sending a constant stream of water along the ditches. Open fields mixed with thick woods around the hobby farm, where all was quiet.

They stepped out of the truck onto spongy ground. Joleigh looked around. "Let's get our rubber boots on." She unhitched the snowmobile trailer from the back of her pickup so she could open the tailgate and the topper to get their boots. "I want to make sure everything's good in the house, and then we'll walk the property."

She unlocked the front door and pulled it open to take a final walk through the house. It still held the familiar blended aromas of lavender, hay, and various dried herbs that had seeped into the walls and floorboards over the years. For a second, Joleigh almost expected Unity to walk out of her bedroom or in from the chicken coop.

"The place looks good." Franklin walked over to stand next to Joleigh in the kitchen.

"The Hoovers have been checking on the place. We'll go see them after we're finished here." She led the way down the short hall. "I'm taking my bedroom furniture, and that's about it, other than books and knickknacks. I gave Unity's bedroom furniture to the Salvation Army store in town after she passed." She nodded to the empty bedroom.

"Let's load the things from the shed before we do the household items, okay?" Joleigh suggested.

As they headed to the shed, walking past the stacked rocks of the firepit was difficult. Images of Mack's body being dragged into the flames flashed in her mind.

Franklin pointed ahead into the woods, where the ground sloped into the swamp. "Is that where you were?"

Joleigh's throat thickened with the memory. "Yes."

"This has to be hard for you, being here again." Franklin hugged her from behind, resting his chin on her head. "I was going to have you show me around the property, but maybe you want to pack up and head out." They had agreed ahead of time to drive back to Franklin's and spend the night there. Joleigh didn't want to mess up the house before it sold, didn't want to sleep in a house where the walls wept with memories.

"No, I want to walk the property one last time. Let's do that first, before we load up the shed items." There was no way Joleigh could leave the land without saying goodbye to it. "We'll skip the back forty that I sold to Mr. Hoover's sons. Beyond that is the forty-acre plot I lease to a farmer. I'll show you the swamps where I trapped leeches."

Joleigh stepped out of his embrace, and they walked hand in hand toward the swamp and surrounding acreage. Slush covered much of the wooded ground hidden from sunlight. They walked the well-traveled trails made by wildlife.

When they came to the swamp, Joleigh showed him where she was the night of Mack's murder. "It feels like it happened a lifetime ago until I'm here, then it all comes rushing back as if I'm living it again." She blinked away tears and whispered, "I can't shake the guilt."

"If you'd have charged in, they'd have killed you too." Franklin reached for her hand. "The guilt of living when others die never goes away. But what they drummed into us in the service is that my death wouldn't have saved the other men." He turned Joleigh's face to his.

"Mack wouldn't have wanted you to die with him. He lied to those men to save you. Remember that."

Joleigh's chin quivered. "That's not all of it." She let go of Franklin's hand so she could dab at her wet cheeks. "I'd have settled for Mack. I'd have married him if he asked because I wanted a home and family so bad. And it would've been unfair to him. I didn't love him. Not enough." She fished a tissue from her coat pocket and blew her nose. "You must think I'm a horrible person."

Franklin scoffed. "You wouldn't have been the first person to settle in marriage. My high school girlfriend, who became my fiancée, did the right thing by breaking off our engagement. I'd asked her to marry me because it was what I thought should happen next, what I assumed was the right thing to do before I went into the service. And I wanted someone to be waiting for me when I came home."

As they loaded the garden tiller and other tools from Joleigh's shed, she reflected on their conversation. One good thing would come out of Mack's death—she would never *settle* for something she didn't care enough about ever again.

"Unity used to say if we don't chase our dreams, nobody else is going to run them down for us." Joleigh rubbed the dull pain in her temples. "Letting go here is a necessary step for me. Another Unity wisdom was that memories travel with us, no matter where we are."

"She's right." Franklin squeezed Joleigh's shoulders. "That's the best thing about good memories. They travel well and are easy to carry."

When they loaded the last of the household items into her truck bed, Franklin unpacked the lunch he'd made for them. They sat on the tailgate then and ate pastrami sandwiches on a hoagie bun, potato salad, and peanut butter cookies.

"You make these?" Joleigh waved a cookie.

"Sure did. The potato salad too," Franklin said.

"Yum. Your expertise in the kitchen is tempting me to rethink moving to Iowa."

"Hah!" Franklin wiped a crumb off Joleigh's cheek. "If I truly believed that, I'd gladly spend the rest of my life in the kitchen." He turned away, his focus on the nearby woods. "One of my favorite dishes to make is a coveted spicy gumbo soup recipe I received from our *mama-san* when I was in Vietnam." He spoke softly and slowly, as if he'd stepped back into the memory.

She put her head on his shoulder, trying to imagine their mamacita. "I'd love it if you made that for me sometime."

Franklin kissed the top of her head. "She's one of the few things I miss from there. She was a spunky, petite Vietnamese woman who got after us if our bunker got too messy. One American dollar could feed her family for months."

He cleared his throat. "Sometimes I forget how damn lucky we are."

Joleigh peered up at him. "I'm lucky to have you." And she meant it with every fiber of her being.

Chapter Thirty-Three

Joleigh's chest constricted as she drove away from her old home and up the Hoovers' gravel driveway. When she neared their house, she slammed on the brake and threw the truck in Park so fast that Franklin threw out an arm to avoid hitting the dashboard.

She jumped out, screaming in joy as she ran to the fence, where her goats grazed along with their two new goat friends.

Franklin walked up beside her. "I believe you've just morphed into farm-girl mode," he said, grinning.

Soon, Mr. Hoover, dressed in jeans and a jean jacket, joined them. His weathered face creased in a wide smile as he welcomed Joleigh, gathering her in his arms. "Ah, Joleigh, what are we going to do without you next door?"

"You'll survive, just as you have these past ten months." Joleigh's eyes watered. She turned to Franklin and held his hand. "Mr. Hoover, this is Franklin Grady."

Mr. H shook Franklin's outstretched hand. "Good to meet you, Franklin. Come on. My wife has coffee cake, hot out of the oven." He put an arm around Joleigh's shoulders. "We'll head out to the pasture later so you can have a proper visit with Joplin and Groovy. That's if Joplin doesn't give you the cold shoulder."

"Still sassy? How is she doing with your new goats? Trying to be the boss?"

"You know it. They ignore her, just as Groovy does." He held open the porch door and gestured for them to walk through.

After introductions, the four of them took a seat at the kitchen table, Mrs. Hoover making a thumbs-up sign to Joleigh before she cut the caramel-nut coffee cake. Mr. H filled their coffee cups. "Now, tell us how you're enjoying Minnesota."

"What?" He caught Joleigh off guard. "How did you know?"

Mr. H chuckled. "It took me a while to figure it out." He took a sip of coffee. "And for the record, I'd have gladly given you a ride last May. But I sense you were protecting me. If we knew where you were, we would be vulnerable. Do I have it right?" His pale eyes searched Joleigh's dark ones for understanding.

Joleigh looked back and forth between him and Mrs. Hoover. "Yes, that's why I couldn't tell anyone. And I didn't know if people would believe me. What if people thought I'd killed Mack?"

"Ah, Joleigh, we'd never have thought that. It took me a while to put the pieces together. When those men stopped by your place, asking for you, and I told them you were in Arkansas but that I could've sworn I saw your twin in Minnesota, that's when the light-bulb switched on."

Franklin reached for Joleigh's hand under the table.

"When they asked the name of the town, I lied and told them I couldn't remember." Mr. H leaned toward Joleigh and winked. "But I did. Grandfield. I ate a delicious meal at Ruby's Restaurant."

Relief welled in her chest. "I'm so glad I don't have to lie any-more. And guess what? I've been working at Ruby's ever since that weekend."

"Well, then, when I drive to pick up our grandson in May at his college, I'll stop in."

"You better." She hoped that would be possible, considering that even if Ruby's sold soon, the sale transfer would take time.

After an emotional goodbye to the Hoovers, Joplin, and Groovy—and with an invitation from the Hoovers that they were always welcome—they left an hour later for Franklin's house. There was no reason to go to the Woodland sheriff's department—Joleigh had told Sergeant Williams on the phone last week about her upcoming visit and had offered to stop in, but he was on vacation. The Hoovers had been her last stop.

Joleigh didn't bother hiding her tears as Franklin drove them back to Iowa.

JOLEIGH STAYED AT FRANKLIN'S house until Sunday morning, enjoying a rare weekend away from the motel and work. On Saturday, Franklin gave her a tour of the bank and his cushy office as vice president. But a few days spent in Mason City reaffirmed something she already knew about herself—she would never be a city girl.

As Joleigh drove home from Franklin's, she thought about their situation. She wouldn't make it in Mason City, and he had no plans to leave. Franklin had moved up the ladder at the bank, and his family and job tied him to Mason City. Meanwhile, her heart had planted itself in Grandfield.

She took comfort knowing Franklin had ties to Grandfield long before she arrived. He would continue to visit, she hoped, and Joleigh had faith that, over time, they'd figure out a solution together. For now, they would continue with a long-distance relationship. They wouldn't be the first people to make it work. War separated couples for much longer than weeks at a time.

Joleigh foresaw busy months ahead for her with the motel along with continuing to make improvements on her property so she could live there one day. And Bits—spending time with her was a priority. One that might change in May when the motel filled.

Joleigh's vision for the future—owning her own business, being self-reliant, and eventually living on her Lonesome Road property—would all begin once she closed on her property in Missouri.

When she arrived back in Grandfield on Sunday, Leo and Peter met her at the storage unit she'd rented to help unload and store her things from Missouri.

"Leo said you're going to turn some of the motel rooms into apartment rentals. That's a good idea," Peter said. After Ruby's announcement of listing the restaurant, Joleigh and some of the other workers had talked about their future plans. "I'm interested in renting. I'm more than ready to move out of the house."

Joleigh didn't blame him. It was time to spread the word on her apartment plans. "Yes, I'm remodeling twelve motel rooms to make six small apartments. I'm hoping they'll be ready by summer."

The Nielsons and Joleigh had discussed purchase options over the previous two weeks and had agreed on contract for deed terms two days after Mack's killers were captured. Twenty percent down and a three-year balloon payment with a closing date in March, as soon as the funds cleared on the sale of Unity's home. If Joleigh sold her forty acres in three years to the farmer who'd been leasing it, it would cover half of the balloon payment, but she hoped it wouldn't come to that.

"I might rent with Peter," Leo said. "Will you have two-bedroom ones?"

"They'll all be two bedrooms and two bathrooms, with an open kitchen, dining, and living room area. I meet with the contractor this week. He hopes to have three of the apartments ready by May." She rubbed her hands to warm them. "Moe is renting the first one that's ready, and Bernadette and her son and daughter are moving in when the second apartment is done."

Leo nodded. "Can you put us on your list, please?"

"I will. Once I get the final blueprints and pricing, I'll let you know," Joleigh said. "Thanks again for helping me unload my things."

After locking the storage unit, Joleigh drove to the motel, eager to check on Bits. She'd felt awful leaving them for four days but had reminded herself that Bits had taken care of herself and her father long before Joleigh met her. She had stocked a cooler for them with food for the weekend and made sure Bits had money in case she needed to walk to the grocery store.

At least they were close to town, no longer living seven miles away. If something happened, Bits could always run to one of the nearby businesses.

Joleigh unpacked and showered before checking on them. When Bits opened their door, an overwhelming stench assaulted Joleigh's nose, and she took a step back. Bits's hair was uncombed, her T-shirt stained, and her eyes ringed in purple circles.

"Oh my gosh, Bits, are you okay? Is your dad okay?"

Howie's rules were Joleigh had to stay out of the room after the one time she'd brought him hot herbal tea and he'd taken the ceramic mug and thrown it against the wall. She had hoped to help him but had only upset Bits and made a mess for her to clean up.

Bits's slumped shoulders answered for her. Guilt at leaving them alone for four days stabbed at Joleigh. *They're not your responsibility, Joleigh. She's not your child.* The reminder did nothing to lessen her feelings for Bits.

"I'm coming in." Joleigh left the motel door open to let in the cold fresh air before she stepped inside. Howie had soiled the bed, so Bits had pulled the sheets and covers off and was soaking them in the bathtub. She'd made a bed for herself on the floor so her dad could sleep in her bed. The air reeked of sickness and despair.

Howie slept, his jaundiced body covered in blankets even though the room was stuffy and warm. His concave chest below a thin, stained white T-shirt barely moved up and down. But it moved.

Joleigh felt his forehead, and it was hot to the touch. "How long has he been sleeping, Bits?"

"He was up during the night. I helped him go to the bathroom, and he drank some water."

It was almost noon, which meant he hadn't moved for several hours. Joleigh ran to her room to get a clean towel. She dampened it and came back to wipe the perspiration from Howie's face. As much as he would want privacy, she couldn't ignore his need for medical attention. She pulled back the sheet and blankets to see legs so swollen that they didn't appear to belong to the rest of his skeletal body.

As calmly as she could, Joleigh said, "I'm going to call the hospital. Your dad needs help."

Bits's exhausted eyes widened at the news. "Is Papa going to be okay?"

Joleigh squeezed her shoulders. "I hope so."

She called the hospital and cleaned up Howie before the paramedics arrived. In a matter of minutes, the ambulance siren cut into the quiet Sunday, dimming any remaining sunshine in Bits's world.

As the paramedics loaded Howie into the back of the ambulance, Joleigh gave them a quick history of his health, as much as she knew. "We'll meet you at the hospital," she told them before pulling Bits in for a comforting hug.

Bits ran the end of a sleeve under her eyes. "What if I get scared here at night now?"

Joleigh crouched down to the girl's eye level. "Oh, honey, you won't stay here alone. You will stay with me until your dad is well enough to come back here."

Bits's thin chest rose on an inhale. "I can stay with you?"

"Of course. I wouldn't leave you here alone. And I'm looking forward to the company." Joleigh studied the motel room. "After we check your dad in at the hospital, we'll come back here, clean up your room, and pack up your things to bring to mine, okay?" Joleigh would need to clean off her own extra bed and box up items to store in the motel's laundry room.

Hope crept into Bits's damp eyes. "Okay."

When they arrived at the hospital, Joleigh gave what information she could about Howie, along with her motel-room telephone number and Ruby's restaurant's number.

Howie was found to have bacterial peritonitis, and the doctor diagnosed him with end-stage cirrhosis. He spent three days in the hospital before they transferred him to a nursing home. His coming "home" to the motel didn't sound promising.

DURING THAT FIRST WEEK back from Missouri, Joleigh spent hours after her shift at Ruby's going over floor plans and construction options with Ron, the contractor, and Moe. Bits did homework or worked on puzzles while Joleigh went over the blueprints.

On the day they transferred Howie, the Nielsons arrived back in Grandfield. Mr. Nielson joined the brainstorming that evening, giving his input and knowledge of the motel construction.

After everyone left on Thursday night, Joleigh and Bits joined the Nielsons for ice cream in their dining room. After their few months in Arizona, Mrs. Nielson appeared ten years younger. It was clear she needed to live in a warmer climate.

"It feels good to be home," she said. "Although the Arizona dry heat was wonderful."

"Did you look at places around your brother's house?" Joleigh asked. The Nielsons had talked of renting or buying a place in that area.

"We did," Mr. Nielson said. "We found a cabin to rent in Grandfield starting in April so you can move in here. We will head back to Arizona in September. It's a rental place there. We want to make sure that's what we want before buying anything."

Joleigh was excited for them. "Wes, my realtor, called two days ago. He mailed the closing papers to me. I should get them tomorrow and will have my funds early next week. Once they clear the bank, we can close on the contract for deed."

Over the past week, exhaustion and a queasy tummy had haunted Joleigh. There was too much going on in her life, and she felt like a railroad engineer unable to stop the train.

"This is so exciting." Mr. Nielson rubbed his hands together like a young child anticipating a surprise. "I'm looking forward to seeing the apartments." He took a bite of ice cream before pointing his spoon at Joleigh. "You have good business insight."

"Thank you. I'm glad this is Ron's slow season. His goal is to have three apartments ready by May first." That gave him almost two months if they closed on the property next week.

She reached for Mr. and Mrs. Nielson's hands across the table. "I'll miss you."

"We will miss you, too, but we will be back every summer. This motel has been like a child to us, and we are appreciative that you're giving our child new life." Mr. Nielson smiled.

The following week, Joleigh and the Nielsons met at the realtor's office to sign the contract for deed. Funds from the sale of her home had cleared the bank, and a portion of those funds were used as her down payment for the motel.

Ron and his crew had three days of work under their belt before Franklin came to visit the following weekend. With Bits staying in Joleigh's room, Franklin stayed at Moe's on Friday night. On Saturday, Bits was at a friend's house for the day and the Nielsons were visiting friends, allowing Joleigh and Franklin the morning to themselves.

It was much needed after two weeks of chaos on Joleigh's end.

"The Nielsons said I could show you their house, since they're gone for the day," she told Franklin. "Why don't we do that first before we check out the apartment construction?"

"I'd like that," Franklin said. The weather had warmed enough that they could walk outside between motel rooms without a jacket. Joleigh led the way to the office, unlocking the door to the Nielsons' house.

The entryway led into the kitchen and dining room. "Your basic kitchen." Joleigh spread her arm like Carol Merrill on *Let's Make a Deal*, revealing what was behind door number three. She led the way down the dark-wood-paneled hall. "Three small bedrooms, one with a half bath, and the full bathroom here."

Joleigh flipped on the lights. "Nothing fancy, but it will be plenty for me. When I build on my property, I'll rent this out." She'd crunched the numbers several times.

Franklin's pinched expression resembled that of someone trying to figure out where a vicious stench came from.

She met his gaze. "You'll come and see me on the weekends, right?"

He shoved his hands into his pockets. "Yep, that's my plan. I hope to drag you away from here as often as I can."

Joleigh could almost taste the tension radiating from Franklin and understood the cause of it. "I know you hoped I'd move to Mason City, but you know me well enough to see I'd never make it in a city. I wouldn't be happy, and I deserve to be." She leaned against the wall of the hall. "If someone would have asked me a year ago if I was happy, I'd have said yes, but I wasn't. I was content, bordering on restless."

She pushed away from the wall and led Franklin back out to the office. "I needed people in my life, and I didn't have that. What I've realized is that if I build a home on my property, I'll be living alone out in the country, just like in Woodland. But I want *people* in my life. I want *control* of my life. The motel and apartments give me both." Joleigh closed the office door behind them as they walked alongside the motel.

Franklin walked in silence next to her as they headed to the end of the motel to the rooms facing the woods. Joleigh unlocked the door to the end room, a one-bed motel room that adjoined a two-bed motel room.

Joleigh flipped the lights on before unlocking the adjoining door. "This is the apartment Moe wants. It will be the quietest and has the best view of the backyard and woods. As you can see, Ron and his crew are making headway." The rooms were empty of furniture, bathroom doors and cupboards removed, and the wall between the rooms taken out.

Franklin studied the room, his jaw jutted out.

"Ron determined the walls between the rooms aren't load-bearing, so we won't need support beams." Joleigh swallowed back nervousness that tangled with excitement. "The bedroom doors will be handicapped accessible, just as the existing bathroom doors are. It's cheaper per room if Ron orders the materials for all six apartments at once. After the initial three, he'll work in the other three around his schedule, since he had other jobs lined up for summer and fall."

With the room opened and empty, it was easy to envision the apartment. "I've compared the square footage to apartment layouts. These are seven hundred square feet, larger than Moe's apartment, although his is one bedroom and bath, and these are two bedrooms, two bathrooms."

"The Nielsons have kept everything in good condition," Franklin said. He inspected the windows, woodwork, and plumbing in the bathrooms as Joleigh walked alongside him.

"Yes, they have. The one-bed motel room will be made into a small kitchen, dining, and living room area, keeping the bathroom where it is. The motel room with two beds will contain two bedrooms, and one of them will include the bathroom." She picked up the floor plans Ron had left laid over plywood between sawhorses to show him.

"I like it," Franklin said. But his crossed arms and the strain pulling at his face told Joleigh a different story.

Chapter Thirty-Four

A few minutes later, they walked back to Joleigh's room. "You said you've got your first three renters lined up?" Franklin asked.

"Yes. Moe gets the first apartment, and Bernadette and her children will move into the second."

Joleigh brewed coffee and set out caramel rolls she'd bought from Ruby's earlier, and they sat at the table. "Leo, a cook at Ruby's, and Peter from the bait shop are friends, and they'll move into the third apartment when it's ready."

Franklin took a drink of coffee, silently studying Joleigh over the cup.

"The town needs these apartments," she added. "The rentals near the park were renovated last year into expensive apartments. With their location, people from the Twin Cities rent them as lakefront getaways. They're too pricey for most locals. They remodeled another apartment complex into a nursing home. And there are only twelve apartments in Moe's complex."

Franklin nodded. "Speaking of Moe, I told him we'd meet him and Diane at the park at one for the snow-golf and snow-bowling tournaments."

Ruby had told Joleigh of the annual town event, which featured several food booths set up inside the indoor park pavilion along with many end-of-winter events in the park.

"Moe plans to take home the ugly trophy in bowling today," Franklin said. It was the first time Joleigh had seen him smile that morning.

"I'm looking forward to a fun afternoon at the park," she said. "And cheese curds."

"Me too." He pushed aside the paper plate. "Listen, I want us to have fun today, and I know I'm being a jerk about the apartments and motel. I'm happy for you." Franklin reached for her hand. "I'm not thrilled about the time it will take away from us being together. But I'll do my best to be here as much as possible this summer, even if it's during the week. Whatever works best for you."

Joleigh leaned forward in her chair. "I appreciate that. This first summer will be the hardest. Who knows? If someone buys Ruby's and they remodel, I may be out of a job there. There's been talk of the owner of a fancy restaurant with a few locations in Minneapolis coming to check out Ruby's."

Thinking of it made Joleigh's stomach turn. "We've got the tiny Grand Diner, but that holds six tables and closes at one every day. Our town needs Ruby's, not some fancy restaurant." Joleigh couldn't imagine herself waiting tables where she had to recommend a wine to pair with a meal.

She sighed. "Anyway, let's not think about that today. Bits said she'll be at the park with her friend, and I don't pick her up until later tonight." Joleigh stood and went to sit on Franklin's lap. "Hmm... what could we do until we meet Moe and Diane at one?"

A mischievous grin crept across Franklin's face. "I can't imagine. Why don't you show me?"

Joleigh sighed as he laid her on the bed, laugh lines crinkling around his eyes as she gazed up at him. *This. This is what I want. For both of us to be happy.*

After an afternoon at the park, taking part in snow-golf and snow-bowling, it was all Joleigh could do to stay awake on the drive back to the motel after picking up Bits at her friend's house. She had asked Franklin to drop them off early, queasy from too much greasy food and too little sleep.

Bits had eaten supper at her friend's house, Franklin was at Moe's, and Joleigh couldn't wait to crawl into bed.

"I'm glad you had fun today," she said to Bits as they settled in the motel room. "I'm going to shower and go to bed, and if you want to watch TV, that's fine."

Bits stayed up and watched *The Bob Newhart Show,* seeming too wired to sleep.

Before Joleigh drifted off, she remembered that the next day, they would visit Howie in the nursing home—one more situation that emotionally exhausted Joleigh.

ON THEIR TRIPS TO VISIT Howie, every Wednesday after school and every Sunday, Joleigh observed equal parts excitement and trepidation in Bits. Joleigh remembered what it was like when she was Bits's age, her future so uncertain. Bits likely felt the same, as if her life was an out-of-control carnival ride.

Joleigh and Bits often had to wake Howie when they arrived. He spoke little, and his health showed no signs of improving. After he had been in the nursing home several weeks, Joleigh felt she needed to talk to Howie about his plans for Bits. The nursing home was located twenty miles away, making it difficult for Joleigh to drive there for a visit after work and make it back to the motel before Bits arrived home from school, so she enlisted the Nielsons for help.

"I need to speak to your dad in private, Bits. I'm visiting him after work today," Joleigh said as they drove to Ruby's Wednesday morning. Joleigh needed to be at work before seven every weekday, so Bits came with her and caught the school bus from Ruby's at seven thirty. "When you get off the bus this afternoon, go to the motel office. The

Nielsons are expecting you. You can hang out with them until I get home."

Bits frowned. "What do you need to ask Papa?"

"I need to talk to him about adult decisions, mostly concerning you." Joleigh gave Bits a reassuring smile as they entered Ruby's. "I promise I'll tell you what we discussed when I get back, okay?" She led Bits to the chair the girl occupied every morning in the corner of Ruby's, facing the window to watch for the bus.

Throughout her shift that day, Joleigh practiced what she would say to Howie.

As usual, he was resting when she arrived at the nursing home. "You can wake him up if you'd like," the nurse said as she led Joleigh to his room. "He's slept a lot the last few days."

Howie's sleep seemed more peaceful than usual. At least he was clean and well cared for.

After watching him for a minute, Joleigh gently shook his shoulder before pulling up a chair next to his bed. "Howie? It's Joleigh. I need to talk to you about Bits."

A slow groan escaped his lips as his eyelids fluttered.

"Howie? Can you hear me?" Over the months since she'd first met him, his gruff attitude toward her seemed to have dissipated into one of acceptance. Joleigh's time with Bits had made his life easier, as long as she didn't tell him how to run it.

Howie opened one watery, yellowed eye. "What?" His voice cracked.

How does one address the fact that someone's dying without sounding crass?

"Howie, you know you'll probably be here in the nursing home for a long time, right?"

He squinted as if she were speaking another language.

"As you know, Bits has been staying with me. Have you thought about what you want for her future? Who you want to care for her if you're unable?" Joleigh refrained from saying that *she* could provide Bits a decent home, afraid Howie would take it the wrong way.

Even so, Howie's reaction was instant. His mouth snarled. "She's *my* daughter!"

Joleigh leaned forward. "Howie, Bits staying with me is only a temporary solution, since I'm not her legal guardian." Her knees bounced with agitation. She'd thought of applying for foster care, but that was temporary. She wanted to offer Bits permanence, if it came to that, just as Unity had done for her.

He grumbled and opened his other eye, staring hard at Joleigh. "My brother."

"You want Bits to move to California? When?" Heart sinking, Joleigh regretted bringing it up. "We're moving into the Nielsons' house next week. Can't Bits stay with me for now? She could stay in the same school, stay where everything is familiar. Please."

"No! My brother's married. They got no kids of their own. Bits can live with them. They're her family—you aren't. She can go once school's out. Now let me sleep." Howie closed his eyes in dismissal.

As if Joleigh needed reminding that Bits wasn't her biological family. She ran from the room so Howie wouldn't see her tears.

Difficult as it was to digest Howie's plans, it pained Joleigh more to have to convey them to Bits. She waited until they'd finished with supper that night. "I'd love to have you live with me, Bits, if your dad ends up staying in the nursing home, but there are legal procedures, and I'm not family. Your dad wants you to live with family—his brother in California." The words stuck like tar to her tongue.

Bits scrunched her face. "But I don't know them." They sat along-side each other on Joleigh's bed, their backs resting against the head-board. "When is Papa coming home? Can't I stay with him?"

Joleigh clutched Bits's hand, her heart aching at the questions. No matter what kind of father Howie had been to Bits, he *was* her father, the only person Bits ever really had in her brief life. *And "home"? Does Bits mean here at the motel?*

Unity had always been direct with Joleigh. She would say, "Better to address the situation instead of dancing around it." Now Joleigh would have to do the same.

"Bits, I don't think your dad will be well enough to leave the nursing home. He's so sick. That's why I wanted to talk to him about his plans for you, while I still could."

Bits stuck out her chin, her thin mouth in a full-blown pout. "I want to live with you. I don't want to live in California. My teacher said it's hot there all the time."

Joleigh pulled Bits in for a hug, hoping to convey the depth of her love. "Hey. Let's talk about our big move next week instead. And then soon, Uncle Moe will live in his new apartment here. Won't that be fun?"

Like the flip of a switch, Bits's face lit up. "I get a room of my own!"

The Nielsons were leaving most of their furniture in the home, much as Joleigh had done with Unity's house. They would rent in Grandfield and Arizona for a while, so they wouldn't need their furniture. In ten days, Joleigh and Bits would move into a furnished home.

Construction on Moe's apartment was on schedule, and Bernadette's apartment would be ready by early May. Franklin had stayed in Iowa last weekend, and although Joleigh missed him and wanted him by her side, she understood he couldn't—or wouldn't—make the trip to Grandfield every weekend.

BY THE END OF MARCH, the Nielsons' items were out of their house and garage. The next Saturday, in his first trip to Grandfield in three weeks, Franklin helped Joleigh and Bits move Joleigh's items out of the storage unit and into the motel garage. Her bed would go in the third bedroom of the house.

While Franklin and Joleigh did the heavy work, Bits organized and put away the smaller items in the home. In Moe's apartment, Moe and Diane stained the kitchen and bathroom cabinets, and after everyone finished their work for the day, they met with the Nielsons for a pizza party in their former home, now Joleigh's.

"I'm going to miss this place," Mr. Nielson said, looking at everyone gathered around the table. "You will all come and visit us at our rental cabin in the summer, right?"

"I'd never turn down an invitation to a lake cabin from you two," Joleigh said.

Pepperoni pizza swirled inside her stomach like an eggbeater combining the food with stress, exhaustion, and uncertainty. Joleigh hated to wish the upcoming months away, but she wanted Bits's future and stability settled for the girl's sake. She wanted her apartments done and rented, her garden planted, and the motel rooms booked for the summer.

I want. I want. She reminded herself of a demanding child. Or someone ready to jump off the deep end.

As if Unity were sitting beside her, Joleigh sensed her presence, heard Unity whisper the words to a favorite song of theirs, one popular when Joleigh was in high school—"They're Coming to Take Me Away, Ha-Haaa!" by Napoleon XIV. Every time she and Unity heard the song, they'd burst out into giggles.

Something similar brewed in Joleigh just then. The more she imagined men in their white lab coats coming to haul her away to the funny farm, the harder it was to stifle it. Full-blown laughter erupted from her, surprising everyone at the table, including herself.

Wow, what a stress reliever!

Everyone quit eating and stared at Joleigh as if she'd grown another limb, but she just smiled and gave a silent thanks to Unity for pulling her back from the edge... again.

ON SATURDAY AFTER DINNER, Bits hung out with Moe and Diane, so Joleigh and Franklin had taken a walk to give them some time alone. Franklin had spent Saturday night at Moe's and, on Sunday morning, stopped at the motel to help Moe and Diane stain more cabinets at the new apartment before heading back to Iowa.

Joleigh and Bits were unpacking items from Missouri and would visit Howie in the afternoon. Joleigh also needed to meet with Ron in the apartments to go over work plans for April.

Joleigh and Bits joined Ron and the others in Moe's in-progress apartment at ten o'clock. Bits swept up sawdust, keeping it far enough away from the cabinet staining to avoid creating a mess for Franklin, Moe, and Diane. Joleigh and Ron headed to the next apartment—Bernadette's—and went over plans for the estimated finished date.

"If you can get someone to stain the cabinets for this apartment and the next one, it will free up my crew a bit," Ron said.

Joleigh wanted to kick herself for adding to her workload, but she said, "I can stain them after I'm done at Ruby's during the week."

"We'll keep them all in the fourth apartment so they're out of the way of construction."

As they headed back to Moe's apartment, Joleigh's legs felt like they were dragging heavy chains. *When will I have time to plant vegetable seeds indoors with Bits? Ride bikes with her? Show her how to trap leeches? Go mushroom hunting with her?*

Howie planned to have his brother come to get Bits when school ended in early June. That meant Joleigh had two months left with Bits, and she would spend most of that time working.

Joleigh needed a pause button for everything so she could spend time with Bits before she moved. *I'm going to miss her.* It caused an intense ache in her heart, a heart that would soon be ripped apart. And she didn't want to think about what would happen if Howie died before then. The doctor had said Howie could last a week or months—it was hard to tell.

When Joleigh and Bits left Moe's apartment to prepare for the trip to the nursing home, Franklin walked out with them. Bits went back to the house while Franklin and Joleigh spoke outside the office. "I'll head home before you get back." He pulled her body to his. "But I'll be up next weekend."

"Okay, but I'm going to be swamped." Joleigh flinched at her cutting words. "Oh, I sound like a bitch. I didn't mean I don't want to see you. I do. I'm just feeling overwhelmed."

She leaned her forehead against his shoulder, closing her eyes as a headache brewed, one fueled by a hundred things. "I wish that the apartments were finished and I didn't have motel bookings for April. But I need the income. And I want to spend time with Bits while I can." She'd told Franklin of Howie's plans for Bits.

Franklin pulled back from Joleigh and rested his hands on her shoulders. "You can't love her like she's your own child, Joleigh." His voice was tender, but the truth was harsh. "She has a parent, has an aunt and uncle... You have to let Bits go."

"Well, it's too late." Joleigh choked on the words. "I love her already. And speaking from experience, a child can never have too many people who love them."

Unity had shown her that. Theirs was a relationship she hoped to experience again one day with her own child, whether blood-related or not.

Franklin thumbed a tear from Joleigh's cheek. "I know that. I just hate to see you getting hurt. And, if I'm being honest, I hate losing even the little bit of time we have together." His lips brushed hers before he turned and headed back to Moe's apartment, his long strides creating an even bigger wedge between them.

As nauseated as she'd been last night after the pizza, it was nothing compared to the queasiness she experienced watching Franklin walk away without a goodbye.

Chapter Thirty-Five

Motel reservations began pouring in the first week of April. Joleigh soon had three motel rooms rented for the full summer and several one-month motel-room rentals. She'd removed the Vacancy/No Vacancy sign below the motel name near I-35, which would take care of overnight guests. After the Minnesota fishing opener hit in mid-May, all reservations would need to be for at least one week.

The first thing Joleigh did every day when she arrived home from her shift at Ruby's was to check the answering machine.

Joleigh sat at the kitchen table with the bookings calendar, her head in her hands. She felt like a wimp. *What happened to the endless energy I used to have? Stress, that's what, Joleigh.* And there would be a lot more stress on her plate for the next several months.

When the phone on the kitchen table rang, Joleigh jumped. "Hello?" She picked up her pencil, ready to take a motel reservation.

Instead, the voice on the other end blindsided her.

Joleigh swallowed. "Excuse me, what did you say your name is?"

"I'm Bits's aunt, Sharleen. I'm flying to Minnesota tomorrow to visit Howie. His nurse gave me your phone number. We need to discuss when Bits will move in with us. I understand she finishes school in early June." Her voice was matter-of-fact, as if they were discussing a business proposal.

Bits would arrive home from school in half an hour. "We can discuss it when you visit Howie. I'll meet you there any day after three o'clock." She would have to find someone to stay with Bits that day.

"I want to meet with Bits too. We need to get to know each other again."

"Again? I didn't realize you've met before." Joleigh wondered how many years it had been and if they were aware of the dire situation Howie and Bits had been living in. "I'd like to meet with you first without Bits, unless you have time to talk now."

"My husband and I met Bits at her mother's funeral, when she was a toddler. I don't have time to talk now, but we can meet first before I meet with Bits. It might help smooth things over to find out more about their situation."

Joleigh couldn't imagine they knew how dismal things had become. "I think so too."

They agreed to meet in two days. After Joleigh hung up, she called Bits's friend's mother, asking if Bits could go there for a couple of hours after school on Thursday. The woman assured Joleigh that Bits was welcome there any time, and Joleigh hung up, ran to the kitchen sink, and splashed water on her face and neck, feeling as if she might be sick.

Instead, she burst into tears.

"REMEMBER WHEN I TALKED of planting a garden on my property this spring?" Joleigh asked Bits when she arrived home that afternoon.

"Yep. Are we going to plant one today?" Bits bounced on the heels of her new lime-green tennis shoes. The girl's face had filled out, and there was a healthy sparkle in her eyes.

"Not this year. With the apartment construction, there's too much going on here to run out to the property. But we can plant it in the backyard here when the weather warms up." She smiled. "Let's walk to the hardware store and pick up seeds after you have a snack. We'll plant them in the bay window here in the dining room. Once the ground is warm enough, we will transplant them in the back-yard."

Bits might not be around to help weed or harvest the garden, but Joleigh would make the most of their weeks together. She would do what she could to plant memories for Bits to take with her to California.

After a snack of graham crackers and peanut butter, they walked the few blocks to the hardware store. *Focus on the pebble in front of you today, not the boulder of tomorrow*, Joleigh reminded herself, appreciating the warm, sunny day.

She held hands with Bits as they entered the hardware store and headed for the seed display. "I know you like tomatoes and green beans. What else?"

"Strawberries and raspberries," Bits said.

"Me too, but those are things I want to plant on my lot, so we'll wait on those."

They ended up with two types of tomato seeds, peppers, and green beans—enough to give Bits a taste of gardening. One of the many things Joleigh yearned to teach her.

After purchasing the seeds, they walked home and made seed pots from old newspapers Joleigh had saved from Ruby's.

April had brought enough warmth and sunshine that most nights after supper, Joleigh and Bits rode their bikes out to the lot on Lonesome Road to clear fallen limbs and branches to make way for the future garden. Sometimes they took their rods and fished in Lonesome Creek.

Soon, Joleigh would set the leech traps in the same swamps she'd used the previous spring. On weekends, Bits could go with her to pick up the traps, and they'd sell the leeches. During the week, Joleigh would go when she could. The demand for leeches wouldn't hit hard until mid-May. Until then, Joleigh focused her spare time on staining cabinets for the apartments.

As an added perk of becoming friends with Peter, he finagled a deal with his mother for their bait shop to sell Joleigh's leeches. She wouldn't have time to sell them via the motel office or resorts like last year. Joleigh focused on simplifying her life as much as possible because she could no longer ignore one thought that had been niggling at her. One that said her life would soon become more hectic than she had bargained for.

JOLEIGH FLUBBED TWO orders at the restaurant the next day, something she'd never done before.

"You doing okay?" Ruby asked after Joleigh punched out at the end of her shift.

"Yes, just rattled. Remember I told you that Howie wants Bits to move to California and live with his younger brother and his wife when school ends? The sister-in-law, Sharleen, called me yesterday. She's flying in today to visit Howie and wanted to meet with Bits and me." Joleigh rubbed the back of her neck. "Bits hasn't seen them since she was a toddler—at her mother's funeral."

"So, you're meeting her today?" Ruby asked, her eyes downcast.

"Tomorrow, after work. Bits will go to her friend's house after school. I want to make sure the woman has an idea of what Bits has gone through these past years and what a drastic change it will be for her."

Ruby kept her gaze on the floor.

"Hey, are *you* okay? You've been quiet the last couple of days." Joleigh had been so focused on her problems that she had barely noticed Ruby's quiet demeanor until then.

"I'm okay." Ruby picked at the lint on her shirt. "I sold Ruby's."

A slow trickle of heat made its way down Joleigh's body as the news hit her. "To one of the people who toured the place?" There'd been a couple of interested buyers given tours during business hours, none of them appearing friendly. Joleigh would miss working with Ruby. "Will they change things?" Joleigh had enough change in the past year to last her a lifetime.

Ruby shook her head. "Neither couple that was here during working hours." She avoided Joleigh's eyes.

"Who is it? And when will they take over?" Joleigh paced the short hallway between the office and kitchen, her mind ticking like a bomb at the possibility of losing her job.

"I can't say. The new owner doesn't want it to be public information yet."

Joleigh grimaced. Certain food scents aggravated her stomach, pulling up the acidic swirl of nerves that took up residence in her. Today's special—rigatoni—was now adding to the mix.

"I don't want to think about working here without you." Joleigh gave Ruby a fierce hug.

"Remember, I'm not moving, just traveling. And I'll be here off and on through the summer, helping the new owner transition."

The following day, after a sleepless night thanks to Ruby's news and the upcoming meeting with Bits's aunt, Joleigh made a beeline home after work to shower and change before driving to the nursing home.

When she arrived in Howie's room, Joleigh was taken off guard. She'd imagined Bits's aunt Sharleen would be sporting a cocktail dress, heels, and pearls. Instead, she came face-to-face with a woman a decade older than Joleigh, dressed in beige linen slacks and a baby blue cowl-neck sweater, her light brown hair pulled back into a chignon.

After introductions, they visited in Howie's room while he slept instead of moving to a public area.

"Why isn't your husband here? Shouldn't he be the one visiting his brother?" Joleigh kept her voice polite, even though she seethed inside. *Doesn't he care enough to make the trip?*

"He's at work. My husband is a lawyer in the middle of an important case." Sharleen studied her jeweled fingers as if reminding herself of the money he made. "I'm here to assess Howie's health, meet with Bits, and determine a time when we can both fly to Minnesota and bring her with us to California. We're planning early June, unless Howie's health worsens."

"I imagine that will be an adjustment for both of you," Joleigh said. "Bits is such a sweet girl, so open and loving. But she's had to fend for herself from a young age." Joleigh told Sharleen of Bits biking to town to get food, caring for the wood stove, and dealing with a hundred other things a young child shouldn't have to worry about.

"Yes, we've got an idea of what things were like for them. And although we never had children of our own, we'll figure it out." Sharleen arched a groomed eyebrow. "We may not know Bits well, but that's through no fault of our own. Howie pulled away from his brother years ago when he chose booze over blood. He's been a mess since I met him twenty years ago."

Joleigh rubbed the back of her aching neck. "I'd hoped Howie would let Bits stay here with me. We've grown so close. I've taught her to fish, how to trap leeches, what mushrooms are edible and which aren't, how to build a fire without matches, and how to knit."

Joleigh choked on the words as if she were on a witness stand, defending someone she loved. "Bits has started a vegetable garden from seeds, learned the medicinal and health benefits of moss, dandelion greens, pine pitch. She enjoys learning, and there's so much I can teach her. She's smart, she's optimistic even though life has given her no reason to be... and I love her."

Joleigh fished in her canvas bag for a tissue. "I guess that's the most important thing of all. The rest is gravy."

They sat side by side in silence, their knees touching. Joleigh fought for composure as Sharleen twirled her diamond rings. "Well, given time, we can do the same for Bits," she said. "We're minutes from the ocean and less than an hour from Disneyland, and we have a swimming pool in our backyard." She articulated the advantages Bits would have living with them.

Joleigh couldn't compete with those materialistic gifts. Nor did she care to. *Is that what Howie wants for his daughter? A lifestyle he's been unable to provide her?*

"I'm flying home in three days," Sharleen added. "I need to meet with Bits before then."

Joleigh slumped in the molded chair. "I'll bring Bits here tomorrow after school. We can make it here by three thirty."

"That works for me." She stood as if to dismiss Joleigh.

Joleigh glanced at Howie's emaciated body. *Will he make it until June?*

Twice on her drive home, Joleigh had to pull over to the side of the road to dab at her eyes. *What is wrong with me?* She had experienced loss before, way too many times. She should be used to it.

JOLEIGH WAS STAINING cabinets that night with the apartment door open to let in the spring air when Diane stopped by. Joleigh greeted her. "I'm surprised to see you here on a Thursday night. Are you and Moe packing things up at his apartment?"

"Yes, we're bringing over boxes of things he won't need for the next couple of weeks. I took tomorrow off, so we should get a lot done this weekend," Diane said. "Is Franklin coming up for the weekend?"

"I honestly don't know." Joleigh pinched the bridge of her nose. "He hasn't returned any of my calls this week. I've left messages on his answering machine, and I'm too busy to keep bugging him." *Too busy, too tired, and too upset at the possibility of never fixing things with him. Of not having him in my life.*

Diane asked about Bits and the status of her future. Joleigh filled her in.

"You're right," Diane said. "Between Bits, the motel rooms, the apartments, and your job, you're juggling a lot."

"How're things with you and Moe?" Joleigh yearned to tell Diane of the other stressors in her life, but she couldn't yet.

Diane's eyes sparkled. "He asked me to move here. I've accused him of setting up roadblocks over the years to keep us from having a future together, and although he won't budge, I will. I'm not willing to give up on us."

"He's told me the same thing about himself," Joleigh said. "How after Vietnam, both he and Franklin—and too many others—put up armor around their heart, feeling like they were damaged goods with their internal and external wounds from war. He said they set themselves up to be rejected just to reaffirm their feelings about themselves." She paused. "In his case, I think him drawing the line about moving to Minneapolis with you was his way to test your love."

Diane grinned. "Well, I'm calling his bluff. They have offered me a job in the finance department at the Grandfield grade school."

Joleigh put her staining brush down and hugged Diane. "I'm thrilled for you and Moe!" At least one relationship was working out.

After Diane left, Joleigh's mind wandered back to a movie she and Bernadette had gone to back in December, the romantic comedy *The Goodbye Girl*. It featured a new hit song by David Gates from Bread. The lyrics made Joleigh think about the last time she'd seen Franklin.

He'd walked away without saying goodbye, and Joleigh couldn't bear for that to be the end for them. Because, as the song said, though she and Franklin lived far apart, he still had her heart. Their future held too much promise for them to give up on each other.

THE FOLLOWING AFTERNOON, Bits folded her spindly arms over her chest in a huff, staring out the passenger window of Joleigh's truck. "I'm not going to California."

Joleigh let Bits rant, hoping it would help her work through things before she met Sharleen.

Their conversation about California the night before hadn't gone well. Joleigh did her best to paint a pretty picture for Bits, throwing in the enticing information her aunt had recited earlier that day. Bits, normally agreeable and optimistic, hadn't bought the sales pitch.

"Don't you want me to stay with you?" Bits had asked, her chin quivering. "I thought you said we'd plant a garden at the lot next summer and that I could help with the animals when you have them on your property."

They had been sitting out in the backyard watching the sunset, the grass tickling their bare feet.

"Yes, I said that, and yes, I want you to live with me. I love you, Bits, as if you were my daughter. But your dad makes the decisions, and he wants you to be with family. Your aunt and uncle are excited to have you live with them."

Joleigh knew the underlying fuel for Bits's distress was knowing her dad was dying. She empathized with Bits, remembering those frayed emotions.

When they arrived in Howie's room, Sharleen was there, dressed in a yellow blouse and white slacks. Bits stayed a safe distance from her, offering a nod instead of a handshake.

"It's good to see you again, Bits. I don't know if you remember seeing me at your mother's funeral?" Sharleen clasped her hands. "You were only a few years old."

Bits stared at her aunt. "Just so you know, ma'am, I'm not going to California with you. I'm staying with Joleigh." Her words held an edge, determination puffing out her chest.

Howie, whom they thought was sleeping, growled from behind them. "Like hell you are." He spit out the words like coffin nails. "You're going to California to live with your aunt and uncle, and that's final." He wheezed out the last words.

Sharleen furrowed her brows as she studied Bits as if she was seeing her as a young girl for the first time instead of a duty.

"Why, Papa? I like it here. I want to live with Joleigh." Bits blinked back tears. She turned to her aunt. "I'm sorry, ma'am, but I don't even know you." Then a dam inside Bits broke loose, and she ran the few steps to Howie's bed, throwing herself to her knees beside it as agonized sobs erupted from her. "Please, please, Papa. Let me stay with Joleigh."

Howie shook his head, his gray face pasty, blending in with the pillowcase. "No! Now, go on, all of you. You give me a headache." He lifted his hand a few inches off the covers as if to push them out of his life.

Joleigh bit her tongue. Nothing she could say would change his mind.

The three of them walked in silence down the polished hallway and out into the sunshine. Joleigh's mood hoped for a downpour to commiserate with. "You have my phone number, Joleigh. I'll keep in touch," Sharleen said, then she turned to Bits. "I'm sorry you have to go through all of this. Your father is trying to do what's best for you."

Bits blinked in staccato mode before running to Joleigh's truck.

After the door slammed, Joleigh turned to Sharleen. "You mean what he *thinks* is best?" There was no malice in her voice. Joleigh was past the anger and deep in the pain of losing Bits.

Sharleen's rigid posture softened. "Yes, I guess so," she whispered. A moment later, she pulled out of the parking lot in her shiny blue rental car.

The finality of it all brought Joleigh's lunch of soup and crackers back up her throat. She held up a finger to Bits where she sat several feet away in the truck, as if to say *give me a minute*, then ran back inside the nursing home and down the hall to the restroom. There, she knelt before the toilet to empty her stomach, overloaded with loss.

When Howie's brother called Joleigh the following night, he asked to speak to Bits. Joleigh handed Bits the telephone, and the poor girl cringed as if she'd been handed a bloody knife. Joleigh left the kitchen to give Bits privacy, but when she heard Bits crying, Joleigh ran back down the hall to where Bits clutched the phone.

"We're doing you a favor, young lady," he was saying. "This is between me and my brother…"

Joleigh caught the edge in Bits's uncle's voice. She wanted to yank the receiver from Bits and tell him that having Bits would be a favor to *them*, not Bits. And that she would give anything to be in their place.

He spoke a few more minutes before Bits hung up the phone, looking pale and dejected. Joleigh pulled her in for an embrace. There were no words that could defuse the pain. All she could do was promise to save her money so she could visit Bits in California.

Chapter Thirty-Six

Franklin's phone rang like clockwork every night after eight o'clock, and it killed him not to answer. He wasn't ready to speak with Joleigh. There was too much to say, and it needed to be said in person. Instead, he lived vicariously through her messages, giving him pieces of her world: Bits, Ruby's, and the motel and apartments.

Each message ended with a plea for him to call her back.

When Joleigh left her final message the third week in April, it about tore him apart.

"I won't bother you again," the message said. "I'm sorry that you are feeling left out, but I'm doing the best I can. I don't want to live without you. I love you, Franklin Grady, but I also need to follow my dreams here. Please, please call me back."

Moe had told Franklin he would move into his new apartment the following weekend. Joleigh hadn't said anything in her messages, but he had kept in contact with Moe. He and Moe had plenty to hash out over the last month, and although Moe knew Franklin would be there to help them move, Franklin had also asked him to not tell Joleigh anything. They would speak soon enough.

All through March, Franklin had stewed, had thrown himself a good booze-induced pity party. Whined like a pouty child. He'd reeled in his grumpy mood long enough at the bank to stop his coworkers from making wide circles around him. But if they'd taken a vote in March for grumpiest employee, he would have received every vote.

His cousin would have relished pointing out what a grumpkin Franklin was—if Franklin socialized with anyone at all. But his coworkers were about all he could handle.

When Joleigh had spilled her news about buying the motel, he tried to be reasonable and supportive. And for a brief period, he had thought about moving to Grandfield. That lasted until he went back to work the following Monday. He had a good job that he enjoyed, true banker's hours with a nice salary and benefits. Franklin liked his coworkers and his house, and he enjoyed having his parents and many of his siblings nearby.

That was when the pendulum swung back to his pissy-mood side. *Why should I move?* It made more sense for Joleigh to come to him instead of buying a seven-day-a-week business in Grandfield. He had taken her decision to mean she didn't love him, didn't need him in her life.

And dammit, Franklin needed to be needed.

Well, he had no clue what he needed anymore. But the booze—again—had only made things worse, resurrecting nightmares while he was awake.

After a lot of self-pity and a visit from his mother instructing him to get over himself, Franklin revisited the idea that had taken root when he and Joleigh ate lunch on the tailgate of her truck back in Missouri.

When he made the trip to Grandfield to help Joleigh and Bits move into their home at the motel the first of April, he acted on the idea. He had made a special visit downtown before driving back to Iowa but made no definite commitment to change his life.

A few days later, while he'd been raking in his backyard, Franklin listened to the kitchen radio blaring through the open windows, tuned to a station that played songs from the last twenty years. Each song resurrected memories for him.

He realized his body was in Mason City, but his heart was in Minnesota. He was lonely, something he'd not experienced before falling in love with Joleigh. Lonesome Road—that was where he belonged, certain that living there with Joleigh would wipe out the lonesomeness that had been gutting him to the point that he had no appetite.

But she wouldn't be living on her property down Lonesome Road, at least not in the foreseeable future. He'd always focused on what he *should* do as the responsible eldest of a large family, the responsible man who'd survived 'Nam. He was thirty-one and stuck in what he thought he *should* do, what steps he'd imagined his life *should* follow.

When George Harrison's voice cut into Franklin's thoughts that day, he stopped raking to take in the words he knew by heart. He needed to be beside Joleigh, not one hundred thirty miles away.

Yes, he would have to open up to Joleigh, tell her of his breakdown the summer after he'd come home from 'Nam and had too much time on his hands, giving him time to think, to allow the memories to surface. He thought he had a solution for their sleeping together, at least until he adjusted to having someone next to him. The rest of his trauma he would play by ear.

Joleigh was nonjudgmental, and he trusted her. So, despite enjoying his job and his house, Franklin set the rake aside and headed into his home. On the second Saturday in April, he placed a call he'd been thinking about for too long.

Joleigh had been through enough changes in her life. It was time for Franklin to make one for her.

Chapter Thirty-Seven

J oleigh and Bits walked to Ruby's for a special supper on the last Tuesday in April. Weekends were busy at the motel, and Moe would move into the apartment the following weekend. Soon, business would blossom, much like the flowers and vegetables in their backyard gardens. Much like the leeches in the traps every weekend. Much like Joleigh's love for Bits.

Yet as much as everything felt like it was finally going right, the weight of her broken relationship with Franklin pressed on her heart and chipped away at her concentration.

Since it was their special dinner, Joleigh told Bits to order whatever she wanted from the menu. Bits was in a growth spurt, and she ordered spaghetti and a cheeseburger.

"It's been almost a year since I moved to Grandfield," Joleigh said.

Bits had heard the story before of Joleigh hiding in the back of the station wagon but hadn't been told why Joleigh had to leave. She filled Bits in without going into detail.

"Holy smokes, Joleigh. Those mean men could have killed you!" Bits's eyes widened above her sun-kissed cheeks. "Did you love Mack?"

Joleigh hesitated. *How to describe the levels of love to an almost-nine-year-old?* "I did but more like a friend. We'd been friends in high school. When he came home from Vietnam, our friendship turned into something more."

"But you didn't have hearts in your eyes like you do when you're with Franklin?" Bits studied Joleigh over her half-eaten cheeseburger.

Joleigh choked on the mashed potatoes in her mouth. "Is that what happens when I look at Franklin?" It had been almost a month since she'd seen him—one long, draining, roller-coaster month. They had so much to talk about, if he would only return her phone calls.

"Yes. Papa once told me my mama used to look at him that way. I don't know why the hearts in her eyes stopped." Bits picked at her napkin as if love was one of life's great mysteries. Joleigh guessed alcohol and drugs had a hand in wiping out that love between Bits's parents.

Joleigh finished her meal before Bits was halfway through her spaghetti. "I'll be right back. I need to check with Ruby and make sure she's okay with me taking this Friday off to help Moe and Diane move," Joleigh said, sliding out of the booth. As she walked down the hall to Ruby's office, she heard a familiar voice.

She rounded the corner. There stood Ruby, two of the cooks... and Franklin.

"What are *you* doing here?" *Am I so exhausted that my mind is playing tricks on me?*

"I could ask you the same thing," Franklin said. "Your shift ended two hours ago." He raised an eyebrow as if scolding Joleigh for being in Ruby's after work.

Ruby stepped in and separated them with outstretched arms. "Can you give us a minute?" She motioned to the cooks, who gave Joleigh a friendly nod before heading back to the kitchen.

Ruby shut the door behind them and turned to Joleigh. "You asked me last week who bought the restaurant." Ruby's mouth twitched. "Joleigh, meet Franklin, the new owner of Ruby's."

Joleigh was rarely speechless, but Ruby's announcement accomplished it.

Franklin put up his hands as if surrendering. "I was going to tell you this weekend when I came back to help Moe move."

She stepped forward, getting in his face. "And you couldn't tell me over the phone? You couldn't return my phone calls?" Joleigh's happiness at the news Franklin was moving to Grandfield became overshadowed by another thought. *Did he break things off between us and neglect to inform me?*

"I'm sure you both have a lot to talk about," Ruby said, fighting a smile. She looked at Joleigh. "Can you give us time to finish our meeting with the cooks first?"

"Can I stop over later?" Franklin asked Joleigh. "We'll finish here by eight."

Bedtime was eight o'clock for Bits on a school night. "Yes, that's fine." She would make sure Bits was in bed before Franklin arrived. Joleigh had enough unanswered questions in her life. She didn't need Bits's curiosity about their relationship added to the mix.

Joleigh's thoughts ping-ponged back and forth imagining what Franklin might say, still trying to catch up with the idea he'd bought Ruby's.

When they arrived back home, she put Bits to work watering the vegetable garden and flowers. Anything to give Joleigh time to get her thoughts organized. She had a lot to tell Franklin but would let him speak first.

No matter what he said, she promised herself not to cry—at least, not in front of him.

JOLEIGH WAS SITTING on a lawn chair outside the office, wearing comfortable gym shorts and a tank top, when Franklin pulled up.

She stood to greet him. "I don't want Bits to know you're here, or she'll want to stay up and visit. Let's walk around the side and sit in the backyard. Do you want something to drink?"

Franklin peered at the coffee mug she held. "What are you drinking?"

"Lavender tea."

He stood close enough that Joleigh noticed that he had bags under his eyes and needed a shave. "Got a beer?"

"Sorry, no. I've got a key to Moe's apartment, though. He's moved in some things, and I know he's got beer in his fridge. We could raid it."

"That's okay. Water is good." He did a panoramic scan of the yard, the sun setting over the vegetable and flower gardens Bits helped plant. "The place looks nice."

"Thank you. I'll be right back." Joleigh walked into the kitchen and came back with water for both of them and snickerdoodle cookies she and Bits had made.

They sat across from each other at the patio table.

"Okay, who gets to talk first?" Franklin asked.

"You. I've been waiting to hear from you for a month." Joleigh folded her arms across her chest as if it might shield her from a potential breakup announcement.

Franklin hung his head for a second. "That's the first thing I want to address. I'm sorry for not returning your phone calls." He reached for her hand and massaged her calluses with his thumb. "I was a grumpkin at first, thinking you should be the one to change your life—again. When I got past being a self-centered ass, I came up with a solution, but I didn't want to talk to you until I had all my ducks in a row."

Joleigh raised her eyebrows. "Ruby's?"

"Yes. I'd been so set on the idea of staying in Mason City, since I had a good job, a nice home, and most of my family nearby. I realized none of that was important to me anymore." He gestured to Joleigh. "Not as important as you."

He smiled. "I'm well-versed in cooking and have a business and finance degree, and when you'd complimented my cooking that day in Missouri, it sparked the idea of buying Ruby's place. I fought the notion at first." He took a long drink of water. "Finally, after hearing too many sad songs on the radio, I had an epiphany. I could either continue with my same life, or I could listen to the sappy lyrics of the love songs and follow my heart."

He leaned back in his chair. "I called Ruby, and two days later, I gave my notice at the bank."

"What about your house?"

"One of my sisters and her husband will buy it. They've been living in an apartment in downtown Mason City. I could have listed it with a realtor, but I don't have the time to wait, and they've been searching for a home to buy. They'll move in June first. I've got two weeks left at the bank, but I'm taking vacation days off and on to make trips here."

He'd yet to mention a future with her. Joleigh cleared her throat. "So there is still an 'us'?"

Franklin's head pulled back in surprise. "Of course there is. At least, I hope there is. Otherwise, I'm living in the hunting shack for no reason, ready to work a seven-day-a-week job for the next few months. I want a future with you, Joleigh. A permanent future together."

Joleigh closed her eyes for a moment, allowing his words to penetrate through the shield she had built around her heart when he didn't call.

In one of her messages, she'd told him of Howie's insistence that Bits move to California. "There's so much you don't know. Things have changed these past few weeks." He had no idea what happened since her last message.

"I've also got a few things to tell you about before asking you an important question," Franklin said, his eyes meeting hers. He spoke of his previous vow not to allow anyone to get too close, of the emotional roller coaster after his fiancée dumped him, of his hellish months back home after Vietnam. "If you'll forgive me for everything and take me—and my emotional scars—I have an idea that we could push two beds together. We'd be close but not touching. Just until I got used to it." He cleared the emotion from his throat.

Joleigh touched his cheek. The stubble underneath her palm was prickly yet comforting. Franklin was there, in person, wanting a future with her. "I appreciate you being honest with me." She hadn't flinched at his confession, guessing his trauma had an enormous effect on his relationships. "I assume you listened to my messages?"

"I did. Several times."

"I love you the way you are, Franklin, warts and all, just as I believe you love me, warts and all. Our lives are going to change, but I believe we're strong enough to weather it. Communication is the key."

Joleigh had thought of what news to tell him first. "I'd left you a message about my meetings with Howie and Bits's aunt. Well, I met with Howie and an attorney yesterday. I'm adopting Bits. Howie is signing the papers this week."

Howie had called a few days ago, with the aid of a nurse, admitting he'd thought over what Joleigh and Bits had said. That it was more important for Bits to be happy with Joleigh.

Joleigh didn't know what had changed his mind. Whether the nurses—who often overheard their conversations—helped Howie see what was best for Bits or Sharleen admitted California wasn't the place for Bits... or, more likely, Bits's plea penetrated Howie's heart, Joleigh didn't care. What she did know was that love trumped money. A blood relative wasn't always the answer.

"That's why Bits and I went out to eat at Ruby's tonight. To celebrate. Yes, Howie is dying, and Bits understands that, as much as she can, but knowing she can stay here will help lessen her grief when Howie passes away."

Franklin kissed her hand. "I'm so happy for you and Bits. I've been hoping Howie would come to his senses." He took a ragged breath before pushing back his chair and dropping to a knee. "I don't have a ring yet, and this isn't the romantic place I'd hoped for, but I'm asking you to marry me, Joleigh. It took hearing George Harrison's 'What Is Life' to knock sense into me. George is so right. Life means nothing without you by my side." His hand and voice shook as he gave her a half grin. "I would sing it, but I'm afraid it would lessen my chances of you saying yes."

Happiness bubbled inside Joleigh like someone had filled her with champagne. She'd braced herself for the worst, never daring to dream for the best. Yet here it was.

Here *he* was.

"I want us to be a family," Franklin continued, blinking several times. "It will take time for me to get things rolling at Ruby's, but I'd like to build a house—with your help—for the three of us next year, either on your land or somewhere else."

Joleigh leaned forward, holding his hands as he knelt in front of her, studying this bald man with deep dimples, a five-o'clock shadow, and love illuminating his beautiful eyes.

"Four," she whispered.

"For? What do you mean? For you, me, and Bits, silly." Franklin squinted at her.

Joleigh smiled and patted her stomach. "No, like the number four. We're pregnant. It's a good thing you don't deer hunt anymore, because I'm due mid-November."

Franklin stared at her, slack-jawed, before he jumped up, swooped Joleigh into his arms, and danced with her around the cement patio. "A baby? I thought you said we didn't need protection, so I assumed you were on the pill!" He let out a loud whoop.

The patio door behind him opened, and Bits came running out. "Hi, Franklin," she said, running to hug his waist. "My bedroom window is open. I heard you yell." She peered up at him with a smile. "Joleigh didn't tell me you were coming to visit us. I've missed you."

"She didn't know until tonight." Franklin let go of Joleigh and crouched in front of Bits. "I'm here to ask Joleigh to marry me, and I want to make sure it's okay with you, Bits. Your approval is important." He eyed Joleigh, unsure if Bits knew the baby news.

Bits jumped up and down. "I vote yes!" Bits reached for Joleigh's hand and took Franklin's hand to make a small circle as she danced around.

"And there's something else," Joleigh said, her heart about ready to burst. "We're going to have a baby in November." It wasn't the order she had envisioned things would play out in her life. She felt a tinge of guilt telling Bits that she was pregnant before she and Franklin married, but that was life. Things didn't always go as planned. Joleigh understood that far too well.

An hour later, after Franklin left for the hunting cabin, Joleigh took a shower and got ready for bed, humming a tune that would forever remind her of Unity. As she slipped into bed that night, the words to the song played on her lips, and Joleigh whispered them into the night air, much as Unity had done all those years ago when she had tried to convince Joleigh to stay in college instead of moving home to care for her.

As Simon and Garfunkel had promised in "Bridge Over Troubled Water," Joleigh's time had come to shine.

Around the lump in her throat, Joleigh whispered to Unity, who she swore was in the room with her, "You were right. All my dreams were on their way."

Epilogue ~ Unity
Two Years Later ~ Summer 1980

And there you have it—my daughter Joleigh's story of perseverance after I abandoned her for the afterlife. Yes, technically, my
adopted daughter. Not in my eyes, though. Joleigh was as much my
offspring as if I'd birthed her myself. No need to address how old I'd
have been when she was born, possibly setting a Guinness world
record. Keep that opinion to yourself, please.

Joleigh thrived on living off the land, embracing wildlife, nature,
and animals, much as Bits has done while living with Joleigh and
Franklin these past two years. There's nothing better for a child than
love, acceptance, and simple living.

Howie hung on until the week after Bits finished second grade,
long enough for Bits to show him her report card. Long enough for
him to tell her he loved her and was proud of her. Although he'd
been too weak to speak, Howie conveyed his love by allowing Joleigh
to adopt Bits.

In mid-June, Joleigh and Franklin married in the park, inviting
anyone who wanted to celebrate with them. After the brief ceremony, they gathered in the pavilion, where Ruby's catered sloppy joes,
coleslaw, fruit salad, and wedding cupcakes. Joleigh wore a simple,
knee-length powder-blue dress as she strolled down the flower-petal-
covered aisle on the grass, escorted by both Mr. Hoover and Mr.
Nielson.

Moe performed the ceremony. David was best man, and Bits was maid of honor. Ruby played her Native American flute, accompanying Bernadette as she sang "God Only Knows" by the Beach Boys.

In the wedding photos taken of the group, there's Ruby, who has designated herself as Bits's adoptive grandma. There's Moe, a brother of sorts to Joleigh, two elderly men who've taken Joleigh in as their own, and Franklin, Joleigh, and Bits, whose colorings couldn't be more different. None look like family. But they love like a family.

And when baby Eden was born in November with wisps of red hair in a similar hue to that of Franklin's mother and two of his sisters, she expanded the family color wheel.

I've enjoyed watching Joleigh persevere through the tragedies of her life, and if I coordinated her meeting Franklin, well, it was the least I could do. She did the rest. And what a job she's done.

Her pregnancy surprised me, though. Sometimes I don't know as much as I think I do.

It has pleased me to find out the wisdom I uttered over the years has played in Joleigh's mind. Honestly, I didn't think the girl was listening to this blithering old woman. It also pleased me when Bits took in the old stray dog that had been hanging around their home at the motel and named the mutt Unity. I'm not offended. I'm glad to still be part of the family.

Now, I'd have been miffed if they named their donkey after me. Instead, she's Joplin, after the sassy goat Joleigh had to give up in Missouri. Turns out chickens and goats weren't enough for Bits. She finagled her parents into buying the donkey and a cow. Now they're talking sheep. I think they may need to buy more land.

Ruby's is still Ruby's. Franklin didn't change the name or the cuisine. Smart man.

Joleigh purchased the shop next door to Ruby's last year and turned it into a local market of sorts, renting spaces out to locals to sell their wares. Joleigh and Bits have their own space there, selling everything from dandelion salve to lavender soap.

Within three months, tenants filled the six apartments at the motel. Last year, Joleigh had the remaining twelve motel rooms remodeled into six more apartments. Moe and Diane moved from their apartment into the motel house last summer, after the Gradys moved to their new home down Lonesome Road.

The family traveled back to Woodland for Darrell's trial last year. Joleigh received a bit of closure knowing he would spend years behind bars for manslaughter. The other three men got off with lighter sentences. It was not enough for Mack's life being cut short, not enough for his grieving parents, and in her heart, not enough for Joleigh. Still, it was something.

As we all know, some things will never be enough, and sometimes settling for less is okay. Joleigh is living the life I hoped for her—one she created. And she's far from lonesome. Along with her family at Ruby's and the tenants in the apartments, Joleigh's plenty busy with their family of animals and the Grady family she and Franklin have created.

Bits is the best big sister for Eden, who is a spunky, curious toddler now. Word in heaven here is Joleigh and Franklin will be blessed with another child in the future. A boy this time. A son not of their genes but of their hearts.

When Eden was born, Bits wanted to name her Ingalls, after the family on her favorite TV show, *Little House on the Prairie*, because she couldn't decide which of the daughters' names to choose. Franklin and Joleigh stepped in and gave Eden Belle her name, using the first half of Franklin's middle name, Edward, and the last half of Joleigh's middle name, Ellen. And Belle, my middle name.

Joleigh, my daughter from another mother. The heart of my soul, who is now the heart of the Grady family down Lonesome Road. A road Joleigh has renamed by adding "un" in front of the street sign.

As usual, she's right.

Acknowledgments

When I mentioned to my friend Liz Deshayes that I couldn't decide what to write next (after *A Life Unraveled*), she said, "Why don't you write about the people in our area who know how to live off the land?" Thank you, Liz, for planting this idea. It was fun giving Joleigh that environment to offset the chaos I created for her.

Thank you:

To Lynn McNamee, owner of Red Adept Publishing, for bringing this story to readers, and to content editor Rashida Breen and line editor Mary Morris for helping make Joleigh's story shine.

To Vietnam Veteran Ken Moe for sharing some of his story with me. Nobody likes to talk about the horrors of war, and I appreciate Ken speaking of his experiences in the army so I could portray some of the emotional effects of war after soldiers came home.

To my friend Diane Gooley, a woman who can outwork most people half her age, for sharing her knowledge of leech trapping back in the 1970s. To my friend Sandy Bodle for explaining to this city girl about raising chickens, and to my husband, Don, for sharing his living-off-the-land feedback. If there's ever an Armageddon, you'll want these people in your camp.

To retired Minneapolis Police Lieutenant Bill Whisney (who, sadly, passed away last year) for sharing his wisdom on how law enforcement worked in the 1970s. And thank you to Alan and Vicki Rathbun for connecting me with Lieutenant Whisney. Any research errors are mine.

People ask where I get my ideas for characters. Bits was originally in my second book, *Crazy Little Town Called Love*. Although I loved her character, she wasn't necessary in that story. But Joleigh needed Bits in this book. Bits is loosely based on a Kinship Partner I had years ago, a young girl who opened my eyes to a child's perseverance, no matter the enormous challenges they faced.

I'm also asked how I come up with characters' names. Joleigh's name is derived from my two daughters' middle names combined. Unity was my great-grandma's sister's name. Both were tough Irish farm girls with a sense of humor. When Joleigh appeared in my mind, I pictured an older version of one of my granddaughters, Eva, with her kissed-by-the-sun skin and dark, wavy long hair. Although Eva's and Joleigh's childhoods were very different, they share a zest for life, kindness to all, sense of humor, and spunky determination. But I can't quite picture Eva trapping leeches!

The title for this book came to me from a song on my Spotify playlist for this book: Grand Funk Railroad's "Closer to Home (I'm Your Captain)." Home is what Joleigh wants in this story, a place to feel safe and secure.

To the supportive people in Women's Fiction Writers Association. The WFWA zoom crew of "writing inmates" helped prod me along as Joleigh's story took shape.

To my husband, Don, for being my early reader and giving his feedback on "guy viewpoints" for this story. To the librarians, bookstore owners, book reviewers, ARC readers... every person who helps spread book love.

There were several drafts of this story written before it went to edits. During those drafts, the POW bracelet Joleigh wears was added to the story, thanks to me finding the POW bracelet my mom wore back in the 1970s as we all waited for them to arrive home from Vietnam. I discovered the Prisoner of War was still alive (at ninety-one) and from a nearby small town. I've met with him over the past two years, and Joleigh's POW bracelet will link this book to my next one, so stay tuned. (Sadly, he passed away in early 2024. I'm so thankful he shared some of his story with me.)

A final thanks to you, the reader, for spending your time with my stories. Reading, recommending, and reviewing books you enjoy help both the author and fellow book lovers.

About the Author

Jill writes about women determined to reclaim their lives. Stories of family, friendship, forgiveness, and fortitude.

She lives with her husband on a lake in central Minnesota where they enjoy visits from their adult children and their many grandchildren. When Jill isn't writing or reading, she enjoys the outdoors, curling, pickleball, and time with family and friends. She is an active member of her local Lions Club.

Read more at www.jillhannahanderson.com.

About the Publisher

Dear Reader,

We hope you enjoyed this book. Please consider leaving a review on your favorite book site.

Visit https://RedAdeptPublishing.com to see our entire catalogue.

Check out our app for short stories, articles, and interviews. You'll also be notified of future releases and special sales.